W9-CHB-780

# THE VETERAN IN A NEW FIELD

By,

W. H. Payne

AUTHOR'S NOTE:

This is a work of fiction. Names, characters, places, and incidents either are the products of the author's imagination or are used fictitiously, and any resemblance to actual persons, living or dead, events, or locales is entirely coincidental.



Library of Congress Registration No. **TX 6-842-562**

**ISBN 978-0-6151-9592-6**

Published in the United States of America

*For Anita,*

CONTENTS

# I

## An Arrival

'Seamus Delaney', he wrote in a respectable, but not too ornate hand.

The clerk, in his stiff white collar, craned his neck around to read the register as
Seamus signed in.

"See-Amos," the clerk mispronounced.

"Irish?" he said. Distaste was in his tone.

"No, 'SHAY-mus'," replied Seamus, "American."

He completed his signature; 'Lieut. Col., 69th Regt. N.Y. Vols.', and quickly spun the register book around on its rotating frame so that the clerk could crane less and read more easily.

When the clerk looked up from the page, he found a pair of curiously expressionless eyes fixed on his. From behind those eyes came a soft voice;

"They did not have the 'No Irish Need Apply' notice out at Gettysburg did they, sonny?"

"I do not know . . . ah . . . I was not there," the clerk fumbled, "I . . . ah, did not serve."

"Really?" said Seamus. The clerk had no response and so Seamus went on.

"You will have my trunk and bag taken up," he said, "and dinner is at . . .?"

"Yes, sir." The clerk looked down, avoiding the pale gray eyes. "Um, half-past eleven until one o'clock, sir, and supper from five until seven o'clock, front!" He struck a small bell on the desk and a porter in green and white livery appeared from the office behind the counter.

"My key." said Seamus.

"Yes, sir! Here you are, sir."

"Thank you," said Seamus. He leaned across the register book and spoke into the
clerk's face. "Times are changing. You should change with them."

"Yes, sir." said the clerk. To his relief, the agent of his discomfort faced left and strolled unhurriedly down the long central hall toward the piazza.

The clerk found it necessary to blot with his handkerchief the sweat beaded on his brow, although the heat of the day had not yet arrived here on the mountain top.

He began to fulminate in a low and testy voice to the young porter.

"One has to be so careful around these returning war veterans," he said.

He busied himself about his small empire in the little wainscot paneled corner with its numbered pigeon holes for mail and keys and the big steel safe on cast iron wheels.

"One hardly knows what to say to them, they are so . . . strange . . . so . . . dangerous . . . and now an Irishman, of all things, staying at the Cauterskill Mountain House, the premier resort in the nation." The clerk threw up his hands, and went on.

"Surely this is unprecedented . . . except for Mr. Tyrone Power's stay here and even that was some time ago, before my time to be sure, and Mr. Power was an actor of note and probably not a Catholic."

The clerk was interrupted in his sweaty grumblings by the approach of man clad in a suit of black broadcloth and wearing a tall silk hat. The man's gray hair was combed straight down, in the old style and partly covered his ears. His chin was wreathed by a nearly white beard, and the absence of a mustache gave him the appearance of an antique Quaker.

"I overheard your comment," he said, "on that guest's nationality and religion and I warn you that your bigotry and prejudice will bring ruination only to yourself. Times ARE changing, and this house will be open to all. Courtesy and welcome are our stock in trade and in this case Colonel Delaney is my special guest. You will accord to him all the service and cooperation which you would to me were I to be guest here. Is that understood?"

"Yes, sir." said the clerk.

For his part, Seamus had halted in his walk down the hallway, both to admire a plaster bust of Daniel Webster displayed upon a marbleized wooden pedestal, and, by force of habit, to eavesdrop on the clerk's protestations to the porter and the ensuing conversation with the man in the tall hat.

As he stood, Seamus looked at his dim reflection in the window of a door marked in burnished brass letters; 'Reading Room.' He smoothed his mustache with his fingers and performed the same function upon his unruly forelock, adjusting the hair to cover the scar on his right temple.

Seamus recognized the older man at the desk from an engraved portrait in the guidebook he had read on the night boat from New York City the previous evening.

Before the clerk stood Mr. Charles Beecher, the owner of all the stage coach lines on both sides of the Hudson River between New York and Albany, most of the presently expanding railroads in roughly the same geographic area, most of the steam-boats on the great river and, not incidentally, this vast hotel.

Mr. Beecher was the clerk's employer.

"Then, Mr. Twilling," said Mr. Beecher, "if we are of an understanding, we need speak of this no more."

"No, sir!" said the clerk.

His eavesdropping concluded, Seamus continued, hat in hand, toward the open double-door at the end of the hall.

The hall ran completely through the building from the rear entrance to the eastward facing front. The decoration was sumptuous; rich curtains in red velvet hung at the windows and doorways off either side of the central corridor, the floor was deeply carpeted.

He came to the end of the hall and there, to the left of the small front lobby, a beautifully executed double oval staircase spiraled up from this, the ground floor.

He paused for a moment to admire the delicate workmanship of the staircase; the banisters painted the color of cream, the turkey red carpet with fleur-de-lis pattern complimenting the red damask wall coverings of the curving stairwell. Shimmering roses stood out in shallow relief on the wall paper, creating depth and texture.

Even the air he breathed, it seemed to Seamus, held a certain richness. The freshness of the outdoors had been brought into the building by the clever agency of festooning garlands of evergreens along the corridors. The perfume of cedar and pine was everywhere.

Well, Seamus my boy, you have arrived, he thought.

He had been to Willard's Hotel in Washington City, which had been designed with considerable modern flash and snap, but which could not compare to the traditional taste and style of this venerable establishment.

Yes, he thought, I have arrived, through famine and pestilence, wars and wounding and murder, half-way 'round the world. And here I am and why?

There must be a reason why I have been spared, and not just to give the poor clerk such a difficult morning.

Seamus already regretted his rough response to so small a slight.

Yet, he thought, there should be just treatment for all, myself included; and I will not be pushed, not anymore.

More humility would also do you some good, the better side of his nature told him.

He went back to considering his reason for being where he was. The answer was simple enough. He was at this grand hotel because the Secretary had insisted, had virtually ordered him to take a rest. The Secretary had made reservations for Seamus via the telegraph and was financing an indefinite stay at this resort. Mustered-out volunteer Lieutenant Colonels could hardly afford this kind of luxury.

And that was another question, thought Seamus, am I indeed mustered-out or not? I still receive a salary through the regimental paymaster.

In any case, the Secretary still gave orders and Seamus still followed them, and the Secretary had told him that he had much to learn and that he particularly needed to learn how to be at peace.

Well, he thought, I have not made a very good start to that lesson, going to war with the clerk as soon as I arrive and calling him 'sonny'. Surely he is not much younger than I; about age twenty-seven. And then why was he not at Gettysburg with the rest of us?

So his thoughts went, battling back and forth until at last he commanded himself to leave off this useless thought and to step out into the cool air and bright sun beyond the wide door.

There he found himself on the lower level of a broad open porch or piazza. Stout square pillars, supported the upper story porch and marched away at intervals on each side. Guests sat in the shade on wicker arm chairs and straight-backed rockers gazing out at the far distant horizon to the east.

To his right front was the base and back wall of a wide staircase case which descended from above and also faced the east. He walked past the staircase, across a strip of grass and a flagstone footpath to the cliff edge, where he was presented with a magnificent view. The view which alone had caused the Mountain House to be constructed on this ledge overhanging the Hudson Valley.

Looking down, Seamus saw that the ledge itself had been carved and inscribed with the names, initials and dates of passage of many travelers over the years. Cryptic ciphers blended with heraldic crests, coats of arms, and the names of hometowns; a history written in stone.

He turned his attention again to the view. The sun burned in a bright blue sky. Across the Valley of the Hudson, not quite lost in the azure haze, were the mountains of far away . . . what? he wondered; . . . Massachusettes, . . . Vermont . . . ? Yes, both, he answered himself . . . and perhaps New Hampshire as well.

Beyond the foreground of regular, cultivated fields of green and amber coursed the deep blue Hudson River dotted with innumerable white sails. The progress of steam boats was marked by plumes of white or gray or black smoke. On the far shore , perhaps fifteen miles distant, a string of railway cars could be seen heading south behind a laboring, smoke-trailing locomotive. A column of smoke and steam rising straight up, also on the far shore, betrayed the presence of a train stopped at a station.

Individual farms and communities could be discerned amid the rolling fields and as yet uncut stands of timber

To the north appeared the spires of the state capital at Albany and to the south the hills of the Hudson Highlands, the home of the Military Academy at West Point and still further south the City of New York was evidenced by a brown cloud of soot.

Seamus could see, as did a bird, places which could take hours or days to reach on foot or on horseback, and all in an instant of time. He found that fact alone inspiring and even more so the notion that all before him lay in peace. Thousands of citizens were pursuing constructive enterprises across this countryside, going about their lives unseen and unheard and unmolested.

During the last several years, Seamus had viewed many such vistas; Chattanooga from Lookout Mountain, the Valley of the Antietam and the ridges of the Shenandoah came to mind, as did other scenes farther afield.

Each of those sites, as Seamus beheld them with memory's eye, was, however, filled with masses of marching men, racing squadrons of cavalry, clouds of gun smoke and shells bursting orange and black in the air. All accompanied by the deafening blast of artillery, the unending roar of musketry, the screams of horses and the simultaneous groans of thousands of souls.

Here all was at peace and overlaid with a comforting quiet which seemed to rise from the valley to the highest heavens. And, thought Seamus with some satisfaction, I had a part in securing that peace.

As the sun climbed toward the zenith, Seamus roused himself and thought to don the hat which he held in his hand. It was a wide-brimmed old cavalry article which he had inherited from a friend with whom he had served while detached to duty on Phil Sheridan's staff. Since the peace, he had removed the crossed saber insignia from the front, but had left the gold bullion cord around the crown. The impression of the insignia was still evident, however, against the dark felt material.

He looked down to the left from where he could hear the muted sounds of wagons and coaches on the steep winding road which climbed from the valley floor. He could just pick out the movement of the vehicles through the tops of the trees on the shoulder of the heavily wooded mountain. The road led from the Village of Catskill; about four hours away, on the west shore of the Hudson. It was from that road that Seamus had caught his first near glimpse of this great hotel that morning as his coach had rounded a bend.

The building had been visible as a small white square close to the summit of the mountain during the entire journey across the plain of the valley, and indeed from the deck of the night boat even before she had docked at Catskill to connect with the regularly scheduled coach. The white square and the mountain itself had grown in size and definition by the hour as the coach had approached this escarpment of the Catskill range known as the Wall of Manitou.

Seamus had seen the sparkling white facade from the last turn in the road, where it had appeared above and at an oblique angle. With the green timbered brow of the summit behind it, the building had looked to be jarringly out of place. The hotel, with its thirteen Corinthian columns across the front, could have been placed most comfortably in Washington City, alongside the Executive Mansion or the newly completed Capitol. Here, amid the wild pine forest, precipitous cliffs and gloomy chasms, the effect was startling.

He turned his back to the valley and surveyed the architectural apparition.

The columns spanned the central portion of the building. Each stood on one of the square pillars and rose two stories to support the roof of the upper porch. Above and behind the pediment of the porch roof was yet another story of rooms forming the fourth and topmost story of the central wing. On either side of the center section was a three story wing of rooms not fronted by the piazza, but presenting only row upon row of tall windows, each framed by open black shutters. The whole effect was again reminiscent of the President's House in Washington, but on a much larger scale.

Set as it was in the middle of a virtual wilderness, the building gave an even greater impression of luxury, elegance and power, than had it been situated in the more likely location of a city or even in a cultivated agrarian district.

Seamus had seen plantation houses in this Neo-classical style at the South during the war, but none so large as this. Few had been intact.

Yes, he thought, grand it is, but it could all be brought to nothing by one lucifer match, or time, or both. In Ireland he had been brought up among the gutted remains of castle and keep, built only God knew when, by the elegant and powerful and now they stood as ruined monuments to something no one living could remember. Drear roosts they were for carrion crows, their decaying walls grown over with ivy. All the things of this world pass, he thought, picturing in his mind the hollow castle of the Clanricardes on the River Shannon and the O'Connor keep at Roscommon holed by Cromwell's cannon.

But, for now, scores of visitors to this great wooden palace were enjoying their late morning stroll on the upper piazza. Ladies and gentlemen stepped along slowly or stood by the rail of the porch and studied the view.

Seamus could not get out of the habit of counting quantities of things he observed, estimating heights, distances, ranges and of timing movements, rates of transit. This habit had comprised an important part of his craft for many treacherous years, when a degree of elevation, or the width of a river, or the time it took to get from here to there, could mean the difference between life and death for hundreds or thousands of his comrades. He now estimated the piazza to cover about ten rods, or one hundred and fifty feet of the frontage of the Mountain House. He had cast his eye again to the left and right of the base of the stairs ascending to the upper piazza when he looked up and saw her.

She was standing by the column to the left of the top stair. Her gloved right hand rested on the banister as if she were about to descend. In her left hand she held a folded parasol. She wore a hoop skirt in light blue and gray plaid with a short jacket of the same material. On her head was a small round hat of yellow straw set off by a black velvet band. She was looking down at Seamus and he looked right back up into her blue eyes. Her eyes were so blue that the irises seemed to fill up the whites with blue. Her hair was chestnut and gathered in a net.

Seamus registered this all in a moment, and he continued to look into her eyes and she into his. When he thought to take off his hat, he felt compelled to speak, but hesitated to be so rude as to address a lady to whom he had not been introduced . . . never even seen before . . . and so he stood there with his hat in his hand.

And then, a look of recognition came into the young lady's eyes. Her face had remained expressionless, but now a look of knowing, a kind of familiarity dawned.

He could not bring himself to look away despite his fear of seeming impolite. He began to be aware, however, of a metallic tapping sound off to his left; *clink,* . . . *clink* . . . *clink,* . . . *clink, clink* . . . *clink*, regular and rhythmic. He realized that the sound had been there before, but only now had caught his attention. He glanced reluctantly away to see the source of the tantalizing sound.

A man in shirt sleeves, perhaps twenty paces away along the ledge, in front of the south corner of the building, was on his knees carving with a hammer and chisel on the rock cliff. He was surrounded by a small group of spectators. When Seamus looked back the lady was gone; vanished. She had stepped into the concourse of visitors on the piazza, or she had entered the building itself, but she was gone.

His first thought was to pursue her, but he immediately checked himself.

That would be fine, he thought, chasing some young lady you have never met through a first class hotel. The management would be justified in having you ejected. But still and all, he thought, who is she, how does she know me? Or am I just imagining that she does know me. Don't I wish that she DID; she is quite lovely.

The *clink, clink* . . . *clink* continued and Seamus turned and walked the few steps to investigate the activities of the man with the hammer and chisel.

He joined the circle of onlookers to observe the carver putting the final flourishes on the inscription:

SMITH'S CORONET BAND
1866

The carver's task complete, he rose, and handed his hammer and fine chisel to another young man who had been holding a white linen coat. Having exchanged tools for coat the erstwhile carver donned the garment, adjusted his pince-nez spectacles and addressed the group.

"Ladies and gentlemen," he said, "I have the honor to be at your service. I am Otis Simpson Smith, the leader of Smith's Coronet Band."

He again adjusted the spectacles upon his nose, which organ itself rested above a substantial mustache, the ends pointed upward in the French Imperial manner.

He continued, "Our band is composed entirely of veterans of the late War for the Union, and as such represents a collation of the finest field musicians of the leading regiments of the army.

"We will be playing tonight in the casino commencing at eight o'clock, and invite you to join us to listen to and to sing along with our renditions of the popular tunes of the day. We will also be providing sacred music for tomorrow's traditional Saturday Sunrise Service as well as for the Sabbath Service on Sunday morning.

"We invite one and all to join us tomorrow night in the Grand Ballroom for a hop starting at eight o'clock at which waltzes, polkas, gallops and reels of the very finest quality will be performed.

"Thank you for your kind attention, and we look forward to seeing you all this evening and at our subsequent performances at your pleasure."

Mr. Smith's speech completed, the small crowd of guests drifted back in the direction of the piazza as dinnertime approached.

Seamus lingered and engaged his fellow veteran in

conversation. He introduced himself, briefly noting his rank and regiment. In Seamus experience, veterans stood on little formality with one another. Having shared the experience of war, they hardly felt as strangers; much more as brothers.

"Professor," he addressed the bandleader as was customary, regardless of the actual academic achievement of the musical conductor, "who were you with?"

"Well, Colonel," Professor Smith replied, " while you and the Irish Brigade were at the Sunken Road at Antietam, I was field music and bugler with the 11th New York; the Fire Zouaves, as we strove to take the bridge across the creek. Later in the war, I served with Duryea's Zouaves."

Seamus imagined the professor in the exotic uniform of the Algerian Zouave, with scarlet fez and broad pantaloons. He took an instant liking to the man, who as their further conversation revealed, had survived some of the war's most brutal engagements.

The two, as it turned out had shared other battlefields besides Antietam. They remained on the ledge for a time reminiscing and examining the other inscriptions, some of which dated back to the 1820's.
Professor Smith then excused himself to an early lunch with his musicians and rehearsal for the remainder of the afternoon in the ballroom.

Seamus walked back along the ledge to the foot of the staircase and took his room key from his pocket. The numerals "135" were stamped on the brass tag attached to the key, his room was on the second floor.

He ascended the left side of the stairs to the upper piazza. At the top of the stairs his hand rested briefly on the banister where the unknown lady had rested hers. He paused and lifted his hand, turned to look up at the deep blue sky, and turned again and entered the hotel.

In this, the second floor lobby, the oval staircase stood to his right. Beyond the stairwell, were the open doors of the Grand Ballroom. Seamus put off the search for his room and entered the beckoning doorway.

The room was wide and long and empty of persons except for two black men dressed in hotel livery, who were setting up chairs and music stands before the French doors at the far end. The ceiling was high and domed above an ornate gilt molding; from it hung a row of crystal chandeliers. All was spacious, light and airy, the result of large floor to ceiling windows spaced about every ten feet along the side walls. Gold brocade sofas stood against the walls between the windows.

Seamus walked to the nearest south facing window and found that the sunlit effect was achieved, despite the fact that the room was situated in the very center of the hotel, through the use of interior courtyards about which the building had been constructed.

He looked out the window and down into a neatly designed patch of lawn where grew beds of flowers, shrubs and even a few small trees. The court was surrounded by clapboard walls and rows of windows reaching up to the fourth floor. Directly above, the sky and a billowing white cloud could be seen.

He continued along the south wall to the end of the room. Behind the assembled chairs and music stands, the French doors opened onto a balcony, the smaller cousin of the grand piazza, with four Corinthian columns supporting a little roof. From that vantage could be seen the broad lawns and circular drive behind the hotel. In the distance, dark green mountain ridges framed the intense blue of two pine fringed lakes. The view out the north facing windows was similar to that of the south courtyard revealing a miniature garden. It was, Seamus thought, very pleasing to the eye, but not to be compared to the natural magnificence to be seen from the windows on the outside perimeter, especially those which overlooked the valley.

He completed his circuit of the ballroom and considered that the rooms facing on the inner courtyards must be the least desirable and therefore the cheapest to rent. He hoped that the Secretary had not stinted on the price of his room. It would be pleasant to awake in the morning to the sun rising over the valley, framed in the window of one's room.

As if having read his thoughts, one of the porters approached and said, "If I may be of assistance, Colonel Delaney, your room is down the corridor to the right."

Seamus followed the stocky, powerfully built young man across the second floor lobby and through a hallway with room doors on the left and right. Those on the right Seamus now knew looked down into the south courtyard and those on the left looked to the east and the excellent view. He was delighted therefore when his guide stopped at the last door on the left and opened it with a pass key.

"Yes, Colonel," said the porter," this is one of our very best rooms."

He ushered Seamus into the room, opened one of the two windows and introduced himself.

"I am Sampson," he said, "and if I can be of further assistance, please call for me."

Sampson appeared to be a distinctly studious youth, an impression enhanced by the silver-framed spectacles which he wore. He politely declined the offer of a gratuity and left.

Seamus noted that his trunk and carpetbag had been brought up. The former stood at the foot of the brass and iron bed against the interior wall and the latter stood next to the simple pine washstand to the right of the bed. Next to the washstand was a chiffonier of blonde, buck-eye maple with a curved front. An armchair, a straight-backed chair, a hall tree in the corner by the door and a gilded mirror on the wall behind the washstand completed the furnishings. The walls were papered in vertical stripes of cream alternating lines of roses.

He hung his hat on the hall tree and stood before the mirror.

"Well my lad, you have truly and indeed arrived," he said aloud to his reflection.

The reflection presented a face of naturally fair complexion but now rather weathered and reddened, mostly from the sun. His hair was dark with some wave to it. The eyes were cold, but the rest of the face seemed to be perpetually on the verge of a smile. The nose was straight with a barely noticeable bump in the middle; the result of a lucky punch years ago on a different continent. The forehead was unlined, except for a crease running back from the corner of the right eye brow into the hairline at the right temple. Fortunately, fashion permitted him to wear his hair long enough in the front so that he could keep the scar pretty well covered.

"Don't be vain," he said to the face in the mirror, "as scars go you have been getting off easy."

That self-same vanity had dictated the retention of a luxuriant mustache, which also served the purpose of covering a laceration of the lip that predated the broken nose, and which had resulted from an even earlier lucky punch.

The chin was unremarkable and was no longer concealed by a beard.

Over the last years, Seamus had variously worn a full beard; *a la* General Grant, muttonchops, or Burnsides; *a la* that occasionally successful general, or a Van Dyck goatee; *a la* the typical rebel cavalry officer, like the one he had recently seen depicted in one of Mr. Homer's paintings at the National Academy of Design. His barbering had depended, in each instance, upon the vagaries of style or the imperatives of his assignment at the moment.

He returned to the eyes gazing back at him.

The eyes of a killer, he thought. Well, perhaps a killer but not a murderer, he answered himself.

In two wars, on two continents, while serving in two different armies, he had never intended to take the life of a man, except on one occasion. He had given orders, of course, which had resulted in the deaths of the enemy's troops and for that matter the deaths of his own men. He had lead troops into battle on many a field and had led some of them inevitably to their doom. In certain tight places, in the Wheatfield at Gettysburg, for example, he had fired his pistol more or less blindly into the mass of the enemy and had probably hit some poor soul, but only once had he taken careful aim at a particular individual and fired with deadly intention. Among a myriad of horrors, that one solitary moment had remained for him the focus of all horror. He thought back on that occasion, all the time holding his own eyes with steady gaze in the mirror.

It had been at the great battle at Antietam, on that bright clear September day, four years ago now, in front of the Sunken Road. The green fields rolled before him and the Irish Brigade was down. The rebels, well defended behind the parapet of the road, were delivering a galling fire.

Seamus, lying on his belly, looked over to his cousin Felim Duffy, recumbent beside him, pale face toward heaven, staring up through dead eyes.

Seamus himself barely able to move, a ball through his thigh, looked toward the rebel line to see another eruption of smoke and fire from the split-rail fence along the road. The bullets whistled overhead and the rolling report thundered in his ears.

"I have to do something to stop this," he said to himself or to the unheeding Felim.

He saw a rebel officer, just visible from the chest up, directing fire in the road.

If I stop him, thought Seamus, on the verge of insensibility, I will stop the battle.

He lifted his .44 caliber Remington Army Model revolver in his right hand, cocked it, and steadied his aim with his left hand. He planted his elbows in the Maryland soil. He carefully pictured his target, placed his point of aim below the officer's left eye and slowly squeezed the trigger as the rebel raised his arm, sword in hand. He saw the glitter of the gold trim on the officer's sleeve, the fair mustache and thin beard on the gaunt face.

The shot blasted from the pistol, a cloud of blue-white smoke issued forth and was blown away in the breeze.

The rebel's head snapped back, blood exploded from his face, his gold embroidered gray cap feel over his eyes. He pitched forward out of sight behind the fence.

"My Jesus mercy," Seamus had prayed and then himself slipped into unconsciousness.

And Seamus still knew that he had never deliberately killed another human being. In time, he had been able to determine that his target had almost certainly been Colonel John B. Gordon, who survived that awful wound to the face, as well as several others which he had received earlier in the day. Gordon had gone on to become a General, to serve for the rest of the war, notably at Gettysburg, and had been present on other fields were Seamus had also served, including Appomattox. General

Gordon was still living, presumably in some comfort, in his native Georgia. It was that happy end to the story that allowed Seamus to examine the episode at all. For months after Antietam, until he had chanced to learn of Gordon's survival, he had thought himself a murderer. The Sunken Road was eventually taken by Union forces and whether Seamus' accurate pistol work had contributed to the victory was debatable. In no case, however had the victory or his part in it given him any solace for what to him had continued to be an act of murder on his part. Now, when he awoke mornings from his nightly return to the Sunken Road, he did at least have the comfort of the fairly certain knowledge that his victim had not died.

"Well," he said to his reflection," let off the reminiscences or you will surely return to Antietam tonight."

He would probably return there in his dreams tonight, anyway, he knew. He busied himself unpacking his carpetbag until the sound of a gong floated up from below, signaling that the midday meal was served. He hastened to the washstand, bent and lifted the big porcelain pitcher from the bottom shelf. He poured cool water into the matching red, Chinese patterned bowl which rested on top of the stand and scrubbed his hands and face. Hunger spurred him on and he quickly combed his hair and smoothed his mustache.

He left the room after setting it in order, as was his routine. He locked the door behind him and noticed that an interior stairwell descended on the south-most wall of the building. The entrance to the stairs was at a right angle to his room door. He considered that if it had not been for the backstairs, his corner room would have also had a south facing window instead of a blank wall with the stairs behind it.

He had noticed that the dinning hall was on the ground floor, so he went back the way Sampson had lead him toward the oval staircase. Passing the open doors of the ballroom, he saw the Professor and his bandsmen milling about the music stands.

Seamus descended, and turning by the door to the piazza, gained the passageway to the main dinning hall. At the head of that corridor, on the right, was a door framed in red velvet draperies. A polished brass plaque on the door read; 'Private

Dinning Room'.  As Seamus passed, the door opened and an elderly black man, in a crisp apron, exited carrying an empty silver tray.  In the moment before the door swung shut, Seamus caught a glimpse of she whom he had seen earlier on the piazza. The lady sat alone in the room eating her solitary meal.

He continued toward the dinning hall, the question now incessant in is mind; Who is she? Who is she?

He entered the bright doorway in front of him and found the main dining salon to occupy an immense space, as befitted the scale of the hotel.  The hall took up the entire front half of the north wing. Tall windows in the east wall provided abundant light and a splendid vista of the valley to those who were seated along that side of the room.  The brightness was enhanced by the powder blue paint on the walls. The white enamel on the moldings, baseboards and trim work, put one mind of the antique pottery of the English Wedgwood factory.  This impression was heightened by the rows of white enameled cast iron columns; miniatures of those on the exterior porches, which supported the lofty ceiling. The decoration was complimented by several examples of the actual Wedgwood on the marble mantel and in niches in the corners. Several hundred of Seamus' fellow guests had already sat down to dinner at long tables spread across the gleaming hardwood floor. There was a pleasant clatter of dishes and a cheerful hum of conversation. He chose a small, lone table before a window, seated himself and looked down into the valley thinking still; Who is she?

Yes, indeed, who is she?  And how does she know me?  And how am I so well known when I have never been here before?

Seamus considered that if the war were still on, and if he were, as he often had been during that time, in enemy territory, plying his trade of scout . . . or *vidette* . . .  or well, yes . . . of spy, he would start planning a hasty retreat had he found himself to be so familiar to the local population.

No surprise, he thought, that once he had signed in, Sampson would know his name and rank.  Black people in America had, perforce, made it their business to know more about white people than the white folks knew about themselves. This was for the same reason that the Irish in Ireland made it their business to know all about the English in Ireland; intelligence may be the only weapon of the captive. That was why Seamus had included many Africans in his network at the South. They were absolutely fearless in the cause of freedom, and they made excellent scouts, *videttes*, spies, and partisans.

But Seamus wondered still; How did the lady on the piazza know me? How did Mr. Beecher know me, when we have never before met, and how is it that I am his special guest?

He pondered these questions until the waiter brought the bill of fare and then he set himself to briefly pondering it.

As it was Friday, he ordered the smoked mackerel.

# II

## An Afternoon's Diversion

After lunch, Seamus stepped out onto the lower piazza to enjoy one of the four slim cheroots he allowed himself each day. He took the thin cigar from the black Moroccan leather case he carried in his inside coat pocket and lit up.

He contemplated the view while standing close enough to the front door to observe any who might chance to exit the private dinning room. None did by the time he had finished his smoke, so he decided upon a ride around the countryside for the balance of the afternoon.

He briefly returned to his room, examined it, donned his knee high riding boots and army spurs, and returned to the ground floor walking back through the central corridor. He passed the front desk where the clerk was now engaged in browbeating a handsome black woman who was dressed in the uniform of a chambermaid.

A few steps further on, he passed, on his right, the entrance to the barroom. The door was open and within the dim interior all was sleek mahogany and burnished brass. A hefty, red-faced barman in white apron stood by the counter polishing a glass.

Seamus stepped out the back entrance and onto the crunching gravel of the circular drive. From above him came the strains of *Somebody's Darling*. The sweet, sad melody drifted down from the open French doors of the ballroom, where Professor Smith was rehearsing his musicians.

Seamus crossed the drive at the place where the coach had deposited him that morning. He walked down the flagstone walk toward the stables he had seen as the coach had turned into the drive. The walk divided the wide green lawns behind the hotel and threaded among tall, old oaks and maples. To the right, a line of low buildings lay nearly hidden in a grove of pines. Where the lawn and the flagstones ended began a shale-paved common from which branched a number of trails and roads.

He crossed the common and walked to his left to the largest of a cluster of barns and stables. The heat was oppressive in the early afternoon, and he was glad enough to reach the shade of the overhanging roof on the side of the barn.

He stood in the shadow and watched as a dozen guests boarded a big, red tally-ho coach. A tall, very serious looking black man supervised the activity and carefully arranged the passengers in and on the vehicle in the best interests of safety. When all met with his satisfaction, the man gave leave to the driver and the coach rolled down the trail to the left and rear of the hotel amid cheers, laughter and dust. A small, light buckboard, driven by its sole occupant, crossed the common behind the departing coach and disappeared into a tree shrouded lane around the corner of the stable.

Seamus stared at the spot where the buckboard had gone out of sight and it occurred to him that the lady driving it, had been she whom he had last seen in the private dinning room.

"Colonel," the tall man was addressing him, "Can I help you?"

Seamus looked up into the man's face. It was a face which seemed to be incapable of smiling. A face with high cheek bones, a prominent nose, high and arched, and fierce black eyes. The brows were knit in what appeared to be a state of permanent anger.

The man wore rough work boots, sailcloth trousers and a bright red checked shirt. On his head he wore a blue forage cap with the shining brass numerals '54' on the flat crown.

"The 54$^{th}$," said Seamus. The number spoke of the glorious 54th Colored Volunteer Infantry Regiment of Massachusetts.

"Yes, Colonel," said the man, "while you were at Gettysburg with the 69th, we were campaigning in South Carolina."

Again, thought Seamus, the African intelligence network knows all.

"And then," said Seamus, "Fort Wagner."

"And then, Fort Wagner," said the man. "I am Luther Van Bronc, ex-First Sergeant, and Mr. Beecher's general foreman. Did you wish to have a mount?" Luther apparently had no interest in small talk.

"Yes, if you please, I should like to have a ride. Can you tell me where that trail leads?" Seamus indicated the spot where he had last seen the buckboard.

"Yes, that is the road to the Kaaterskill Falls, a very pleasant ride mostly in the shade. Frederick!"

At the sound of the name, a lad about age twelve emerged from the barn. He was leading a tall bay horse.

"This is my son, Frederick Douglass Van Bronc." Luther introduced the young fellow, who greeted Seamus with a formal, "Good afternoon, sir."

"And this," said Luther, running his hand over the big horses flank, "is Sarge. He is like us, Colonel, a veteran."

Seamus noted immediately the brand; 'US', above the left foreleg. A line had been branded through it and the Mountain House brand; 'CMH', had been burned next to the old marking. A series of numbers was branded on the left side of Sarge's neck and a line run through that as well.

His eye followed Luther's forefinger to the clipped out section of the horse's right ear and the raised furrow angled across the rump behind the saddle; each scar the work of a bullet.

Seamus stroked the white blaze on Sarge's face.

"Mr. Beecher bought these horses from the army as surplus down at West Point." said Luther, "I was his agent and I picked the best they had. Sarge here is the best of the best."

"And a McClellan saddle," said Seamus.

"That's right, we bought the tack and other accouterments from the army too."

The same woman whom Seamus had seen by the front desk on his way out of the hotel now hurried up to them. She was tall, but not as tall as Luther. Her face was slim, and although she wore the white and pale blue garb of a chambermaid, her manner was more regal than servile. The queenly effect was enhanced rather than diminished by the turban-like headdress which she wore.

"Pardon me, Colonel Delaney, Luther we must speak. That Mr. Twilling . . .," she said all in a breath, her big brown eyes fairly burning.

Seamus tipped his hat, and Luther said, "Colonel, this is my wife Sarah."

"Ma'am." said Seamus.

"Colonel," said Sarah. She turned again to Luther, and Seamus mounted Sarge, while young Frederick held the bridle.

Seamus and Luther nodded a mutual farewell and Luther turned back to his wife.

"That Mr. Twilling," Sarah went on, "now he insists that I must act as lady's maid for that Southern woman because, he says, I am the only one with experience as a lady's maid. That is true enough, but, he expects me to do this in addition to overseeing the work of the kitchen help and the chambermaids and to be on call at all hours for the woman at no extra consideration in wages."

Seamus touched spurs to Sarge's flanks and withdrew to the trail entrance. As he entered the shade of the trees, he could yet hear Luther saying; "Very well, Sarah, I will speak to Mr. Twilling and if need be to Mr. Beecher, before I go down the mountain tonight."

Seamus was glad to be in the cool dim of the trail and cantering away from the domestic discussion. Raised mostly as an orphan, he felt out of place and uncomfortable around families and their interactions.

Sarge proved responsive, calm and steady. Seamus felt he had known the horse a lifetime in just a few minutes on the road. The thoroughfare was wide enough for two wagons to pass each other, and was well surfaced with flakes of red shale.

Once out of hearing of the voices and traffic around the hotel and stables, Seamus slowed Sarge to a walk.

The road formed a tunnel through a mixed forest of cedar, pine and hardwoods. The wilderness closed in quickly away from the hotel and its immediate grounds. The damp closeness of the day was increasing, but an occasional breeze provided relief and stirred the treetops, while keeping at bay the swarms of mosquitoes which danced in patches of sunlight on the forest floor.

Overhead the sun, shinning through the leaves and pine boughs, shifted shades of green and light in subtle movement. Few other travelers appeared on the trail, and Seamus noted that those who overtook him on horseback, or in dogcarts or buckboards, invariably took the fork ahead and to the right. He paused when he reached it. A rustic signboard, carved of cedar, pointed right to the 'Boat House', and left to 'Kaaterskill Falls'. The sounds of voices and laughter came from the boat house road.

Seamus considered a long moment whether the lady of the piazza and the private dinning room might be more likely to choose the conviviality of the boating set or the apparent solitude of the Falls.

"You are being ridiculous," he said to himself aloud but under his breathe as there were others in the intersection.

Sarge looked around to Seamus, as much as to say; "I beg your pardon."

"Right you are," said Seamus to the horse, and reigned him around to the left. He spurred gently and they cantered away down the Falls road.

Shortly, he slowed Sarge again to a walk. Through the trees on the right lay the shinning blue lake rimmed with towering pines. The trees closest to the lake shore were dead and their gray, gnarled and weathered branches gave a wild and ominous look to the scene. Afloat on the waters, were parties of young men and ladies in canoes and row boats. Gaily colored parasols and jaunty straw hats were the order of the day. A small steam launch with brass mounted engine, red and white striped canopy and happily tooting whistle, plied the lake.

The shore curved away as Seamus proceeded, and the shallow stream which drained the lake, ran parallel to the road for a time. Soon it too, wandered off into the woods and Seamus and Sarge were again in the cool dark tunnel of the forest.

No traffic had passed either coming or going since Seamus left the fork to the boat house, but now, around a bend in the trail, appeared a lone buckboard, about fifty yards distant. It was driven by the lady dressed in blue and gray plaid, wearing the small yellow straw hat.

Sarge quickened his pace without being asked. Even the horse can read my mind, thought Seamus.

Horse and rider reached the point of passing, following, or accompanying the buckboard and Seamus could not think of which of the three he should do.

The four wheels of the buckboard rolled along, the spokes flashing in the sunlight, the driver apparently unaware of Seamus and Sarge behind her.

A buzz at the side of the road, and the horse pulling the little vehicle reared in the traces and dashed down the trail at full gallop. In no time, buckboard, horse and driver were far down the road and nearly out of sight.

Now at the spot where the horse had bolted, Sarge calmly raised his right front hoof and stomped it down on the coiled body of the still buzzing rattlesnake. The next instant, Sarge was off after the runaway with Seamus hanging onto his mane.

Seamus looked back to see the snake writhing over and over in its splattering blood, now appearing mottled black, then yellow, then red. Someone was running away through the woods to the right. A blur of brown jacket and hat and gray trousers caught in Seamus'memory.

He turned his attention back to the matter at hand, and spurred Sarge needlessly, as the horse was already bounding at top speed after the buckboard. The woods flew by on either side and Sarge deftly sidestepped the lady's straw hat which lay upright in the road.

Horse and rider rounded a bend, and the buckboard, racing out of control, was again in sight. The driver had lost the reins, and as Seamus drew nearer he could see that she was making no effort to regain them. Instead, she remained stoically clutching the iron handles of the seat as the terrified horse dragged the little carriage from side to side along the road. Showers of flaked stones and clods of earth scattered left and right.

The shallow stream came closer to the road again, and ahead Seamus could see a sharp turn to the right and a crude bridge of logs across the stream.

He slowed Sarge for the turn and the runaway did not slow, but went straight through the curve at the near end of the bridge railing and disappeared down the embankment.

Never hesitating, Sarge followed, leaping and sliding into the rocky bed of the creek.

The buckboard swerved left and splashed and bumped down the stream with Sarge and Seamus in pursuit. The shallow water course, as had the road, threaded a dim, dapple-lighted tunnel through the woods, the treetops almost joining overhead. The driver still made no attempt to regain control, but sat abandoned to the will of the frightened horse. The poor beast, goaded to near madness by the spewing water, pressed on even faster. Seamus spurred Sarge to catch up and the veteran war horse narrowed the distance immediately.

Seamus looked up and ahead could see the trees on either side of the creek widening out to form an end to the tunnel. Closer and closer by the second the horses, buckboard and two souls came to the brightening clearing.

A splash from the rear wheels of the buckboard caught Seamus in the face and blinded him for an instant. He swiped his sleeve across his eyes, and looked to the front.

The cloudless blue sky filled his view ahead and two distant green clad mountains curved down to the center with the dark hump of an even more distant mountain rising in the notch.

Pretty as a picture, thought Seamus in the curious, detached, *ballet-adagio*, dream state of mind, which he remembered from each and every cavalry charge in which he had ever participated. From somewhere came the thought that between Seamus and that lovely view was nothing but air. They had nearly reached the Kaaterskill Falls.

All Seamus knew of the Falls was what he had read in his guide book and that knowledge informed him that the stream, and this racing party of horses, rider, buckboard and driver were now about to plunge over a narrow lip and down about one hundred-seventy feet into the gorge below.

"Up Sarge!" he shouted and sprinted around to the left of the runaway carriage. He passed the lady on the seat. She looked serenely up at him. Another bound and he seized the wild horse by the bridle. He guided Sarge to the right and slowed and pushed the runaway to the right in the very last pool at the very brink of the Falls.

The buckboard turned sidewise in the stream bed skidding on the moss-slick bedrock. Sarge skidded too. He lost his footing on all four hoofs and Seamus looked down and down into the gorge where the waterfall crashed on jagged, broken boulders.

Don't look down, he commanded himself. He let loose a savage scream from deep in his throat, and spurred Sarge, while he muscled, pushed and dragged the crazed runaway to the side of the stream. Straight up the washed-away, gravel and clay, root-thatched bank they went, never stopping until they had climbed to flat and dry ground.

A plain, three storied hotel stood there above the Falls and next to it, a gazebo was set on a promontory over the gorge.

Seamus led the horse and buckboard to the hitching rail before the little summer house and dismounted. He tied the horses close together and gentled the exhausted runaway. The creature calmed almost as quickly as she had stampeded.

He turned to the driver, who returned his gaze with a nearly vacant aspect. He helped her down from the seat, up the two steps into the gazebo and sat her in a white wicker chair at a table by the railing.

Their spectacular arrival had created considerable excitement among the knot of guests in front of the hotel. A red, white and blue sign on the porch roof read: 'The Laurels.' The building looked to be a smaller, more modest version of the Mountain House. The assembled adults and children now began to throng the gazebo, gawking at the daredevils who had arrived so suddenly in their midst.

Seamus assumed his drill field voice; "Right! That's all there is to see, folks, step back if you please and go on about your business. Kindly give the lady some air. There's nothing more to see. Step back please."

Another voice was added. "That's right ladies and gentlemen. Please make way. Leave these people alone. Make way please."

The speaker of these words; a rotund, bespectacled man in his fifties, clad in dark stripped trousers, vest and shirtsleeves, made his way hurriedly through the crowd. He balanced on a silver tray a pitcher of lemonade and two glasses. Perspiration stood out on his high pink forehead.

The curious began to take heed and started to straggle away to some distance where they could stand and stare.

"There, now," said the busy little man. He entered the gazebo and set his burden on the table.

"I am Peter Scott," he said, "the owner and proprietor of 'The Laurels', if you are in need of anything at all, please ring." He indicated a bell cord hanging in a corner nearest the big house. A square basket hung on a cable by the cord and the cable lead to a window on the side of the hotel. The wheeled basket could be sent up with an order and returned with the desired refreshment. A pencil and pad hung next to the basket for the writing of orders.

Brilliant, thought Seamus.

He thanked the man, assured him that he and the lady were as well as could be expected. Mr. Scott took his leave, reiterating his readiness to render assistance as needed.

Seamus picked up the pitcher and a glass and turned his back to the lady. He did not want her to see his hands shaking. He half-filled the glass, placed it before her, and again turned away to pour some for himself. This time his hands trembled so as to chatter glass and pitcher together loudly. He swore inwardly, and wished mightily to be able to take something stronger than lemonade. Indeed, such strong drink was readily at hand, though he dared not start so early in the day and not in the presence of this lady, who strangely seemed calmer than he himself felt.

Up close, he saw that her lips were full and shapely and though he judged her to be his junior by some years, the lines about her eyes made her appear older.

He very carefully placed the pitcher on the table and the effort and concentration on not shaking made him feel light-headed so that he as much as collapsed into the other chair at the table. He took off his hat and rubbed his forehead.

"I can see that you were a soldier," said the lady, her face still expressionless.

At last, thought Seamus, she speaks!

"Yes, ma'am," he said, ready with an introduction. "I am Seamus Delaney and…"

"My late husband was a soldier," she said, now smiling sweetly and staring at a point in space about halfway down into the gorge which the two of them had so nearly visited a few moments before.

"Often, after Manassas, he would shake the way you just did now, and at night he would call out in his sleep."

Oh God, thought Seamus, she has a Southern accent. A dark, familiar sensation of foreboding filled him.

"I did not want him to go back to the war for I knew that it would kill him, but I knew that go he must. And he did go and the war did kill him as I was sure that it would. Truly the good do die young. He was so good and so young. He will never get any older and now I am older than he was when he died."

She was silent for a moment. The Falls roared into the gorge. She went on.

"He was not a 'fire-eater'; he had no politics at all. Nor was he a slave owner. He did not even own any land, just his books. He was a teacher before the war, you see. My father did not want us to marry because Robbie, I called him Robbie, his name was Robert Bruce Coltrane, Lieutenant Robert Bruce Coltrane, CSA, because he was poor. But when Robbie was one of the first to volunteer for a commission in the regiment that father was raising, why, then father could hardly say no. And father did love Robbie too, especially after they had been in battle together. I am sure that they are in heaven together now.

"My Robbie was like a knight of old, he truly was, so kind and devout and chivalrous. Our life could have been so beautiful, but now Robbie is gone. He died at Sharpsburg, you know, at the Bloody Lane, but at least it was quick and he did not suffer. His comrades told me so when they brought his body home. It was a blessing that they could recover the body so that we could care for him after his death and bury him in Hollywood Cemetery in Richmond. I had stayed at Richmond to be near him when he was at the front. I could not have borne it to have never had at least that much of him back.

"He was quickly gone his comrades said, shot in his face below the left eye as he raised his sword to direct the fire of his troops. His men all loved him and many cried like babes at the funeral.

"He is gone and father to, killed at Gettysburg. We buried father at Hollywood as well, right next to Robbie. Now my life is a misery, and I keep coming closer to death or it closer to me all the time.

"After the war, I nearly died of some illness, strangely with no fever, just the gripe and growing weakness, until I was taken north to Georgetown, where my Aunt nursed me back to health. We came up here to the mountains to avoid the fevers of summer, but when we landed at Catskill, a drunken man fired a pistol in the air and a herd of cattle broke from their pen and rushed down the street at me. I would have been crushed under their hooves, but the coach driver for the Mountain House ran out waving his jacket and yelling so as to divert them. He risked his life as you did just now, and I thanked him as I do you, but now my life is a misery and might better be over, as anyone I ever loved or who ever loved me is in heaven now."

With these last words, she turned and looked into Seamus eyes.

Seamus could form no words of reply. He had wished to know more about this lady and now he knew more than he would ever have wished to know.

"You must not think that way ma'am. We are spared for a reason. You must keep living. We all must, until it is our time," he said at length but he had to look away from her eyes.

"Ma'am . . . ," he started again.

"Emily, my name is Emily," she said. "When I saw you earlier, on the piazza, I thought you looked familiar, but I am sure that we have never been acquainted with one another. And you must not think that you resemble my late husband and that I was therefore upset. You are quite different from the way he was, sir. He was very slender with a very thin face. As the war went on, he became positively gaunt. He had fair hair, a thin blond mustache and beard."

Of course, thought Seamus.

"I cannot say why I found you to be familiar," she said.

I can, thought Seamus. Sharpsburg; what the rebels called the Battle of Antietam. Bloody Lane; that part of the battlefield which was what the Sunken Road became; puddles of blood, bodies piled up, thirteen hundred dead in the road at the end.

He was back there again; the gaunt face, the fair beard, all the rebel officers wore so much gold braid. Could you tell the glittering sleeve of a lieutenant from that of a Colonel? Strange, he thought, the Union was richer than the Confederacy, yet Union officers wore little brocade, except of course Custer and he was . . . different. Seamus saw the upraised sleeve glinting gold, the face gaunt, exploding in gore.

I murdered her husband, he thought. I murdered her husband.

His mind raced. Did the spirit of her husband, he wondered, somehow unite with that of his murderer in the air above Anitetam? Did the shade of the dead man, commingled with some essence of his killer then pass by the lady on the way to the next world? Is that how she could recognize me whom she had never seen?

Madness, he told himself in silence.

"But you are shaking again," said Emily. "I have upset you."

Seamus was summoned back by her voice.

"Please forget the war," she said. "I am sorry if I have brought back some sad recollection."

No, I cannot, he thought, I cannot forget the war.

"No," he said. "You have not upset me. Allow me to accompany you back to the Mountain House."

As they rose, Mr. Scott, who had been hovering near by, approached and gave them directions to return to their hotel by the more conventional means of using the bridge across the stream.

Seamus offered to drive the buckboard and tie Sarge on behind, but Emily insisted that she was a capable driver and no weakling. Clearly, she was not to be argued with. So they proceeded along together on the trail up the north bank of the creek.

Shortly, they came to the bridge which they had bypassed earlier. They crossed and retraced the route toward the boat house and stables.

They traveled in silence, until Seamus saw ahead on the trail the round yellow straw hat, still resting where it had been left. He rode up, dismounted, picked up the hat and walked Sarge back to the buckboard. Emily stopped the vehicle and when Seamus dusted her hat with his sleeve and handed it to her, she burst into tears.

Her deep sobs echoed along the empty road and within the dark stillness of the pine forest. It sounded to Seamus as if the whole woods, the whole lonesome world itself, were crying; crying for all that had been lost.

Emily held the hat to her face and cried and cried.

Seamus did not know what to do and worse felt tears coming to is own eyes.

Her hand rested on the handle of the seat, and he took her hand in both of his. He looked down to hide his tears.

"Please don't cry . . . please don't . . ., " He lost his voice.

He let go of her hand and went up and took her horse and Sarge each by the bridle and lead them along the road.

He walked looking down; the dead body of the snake came into his view and Emily's horse shied again.

Seamus held her firmly and talked soothingly to her and gentled her until they reached a stout tree further up the trail where he tied the two horses.

Emily still held the hat to her face sobbing softly. A long shuddering sigh escaped her throat.

Seamus determined to dispose of the snake's carcass, least another runaway be caused by the creature even in death. He walked back and picked up a stick. He used the stick to push the bloody, limply flopping mess off the road. The flies which he displaced hummed in protest. He gouged out a shallow depression in the loamy leaf-litter of the forest floor, and stuffed all six feet of snake into it. He piled a few flat rocks on the serpent's grave, in hopes that the cairn he thus built would prevent disinterment by scavenging animals and possible postmortem return of the remains to the roadside.

When he had finished his task, he threw the stick farther into the woods, and beyond where it landed, he saw a light colored bundle. He walked up to the bundle and found it to be a plain, and empty, cotton sack, of the type used to hold salt or flour. He picked up the sack and into his mind came the picture of the brown and gray clad figure running away from the road along this very line.

Seamus saw that a game trail, the path of wandering deer, led straight in the direction the running person had traveled. He thought to follow the trail, but knew that the present needs of Emily must come first.

He returned, carrying the sack, to the place where he had tied the horses. Emily had stopped crying, and even presented a wane smile, which Seamus answered with a broad grin, to which Emily responded with a chuckle, and a cough, and renewed sobbing.

Lord, thought Seamus, I am certainly helpless with women.

With sack in hand, he reached to untie the horses and Emily's horse again shied most violently. He again tried to gentle her and she reared up in the traces.

The horse would not be calmed until it occurred to Seamus to ball up the sack in his fist and throw it as far as he could into the trees. That accomplished, the mare regained her normal composure.

A scent, he thought. Is there a scent on the sack which frightened the horse?

The scent of a snake, he answered himself in his mind. Had the snake been in the sack? Had it then been placed on the road deliberately and just as Emily was about to pass? Had the person in the brown and gray placed the snake in the road with the intention of causing the runaway and Emily's likely death? Why else would the person have been dashing through the woods away from the road at that instant?

Seamus moved now with a purpose. He retrieved the sack and tied it behind Sarge's saddle. Sarge was no more impressed by the aroma of the late snake than he had been by the actual living creature when he had so economically dispatched it earlier.

Seamus tied Sarge on behind the buckboard and untied Emily's horse from the tree. He climbed into the seat beside Emily, took the reins and drove back to the stables.

Sarah and Luther Van Bronc were standing under the shed roof. Sarah's eyes scanned Emily's wet and mud-stained clothing and her reddened and tear-stained face and flashed a look of accusation at Seamus. She fairly sprung to Emily's side and helped her from the buckboard.

"Come ma'am I will take you up to your room by the back stairs. You needn't go through the lobby," she said and with another dagger like glance at Seamus was off and hustling her charge toward the hotel.

I am just after saving the lady's life, Seamus thought to say to Sarah's rapidly departing back, but instead, he said nothing.

Young Frederick came and tended to the horses and Seamus unfastened the sack from the saddle and asked the senior Van Bronc for a few moments in private.

Luther led the way along the shed toward the back of the stable. As the two men passed, those horses with their heads hanging out over the half-doors, variously, and in succession, shied, whinnied or kicked at their stalls. Luther continued on the way, but glanced quizzically over his shoulder at Seamus, who was still carrying the cotton sack.

Luther turned into a doorway at the end of the shed and Seamus followed.

They had entered the domain of Luther Van Bronc. The room comprised an office partitioned from the rest of the stable. A battered old roll-top desk stood in the far corner with ledger books and yellow bills of lading neatly stacked. Above the desk hung engraved and individually framed portraits of John Brown, Frederick Douglass and Abraham Lincoln. Seamus had often seen that same pictorial trinity displayed in the homes of black families.

On the wall adjacent to the desk was a large color engraving, in an ornate gilt frame, listing the names of those who had served in the 54th Massachusetts. A small red cross was printed by the names of those who had died. There were a great many crosses.

An illustration of the assault on Fort Wagner was pictured at the bottom of the list, and portraits of Colonel Shaw and Sergeant Carney at the top.

Against the wall opposite the desk, stood a round iron stove upon which rested a large steaming coffee pot fashioned of blue enamelware.

Luther took two tin cups from a shelf behind the stove, filled each and handed one to Seamus. Seamus took a tentative sip of the strong dark brew and sat himself in a captain's chair by the desk.

He recounted the story of the snake in the road, the man in the woods and the runaway buckboard. He did not describe the details of Emily's unhappy discourse, holding that conversation in confidence.

When Seamus was done with his story Luther took the sack from him and turned it over in his big hands.

"There are," he said, "timber rattlers in these mountains, but I have never heard of any on our carriage trails. They usually stay around the higher ledges and, although a hiker may find one sunning itself on a cliff, rattlesnakes generally avoid people and we hardly ever get any reports of them even being seen. When they are seen they are usually killed, which may be the reason they are so shy of people and why there seem to be so few of them. They are more common around the bluestone quarries down in the valley.

"You are more likely," Luther went on, "to see the other poisonous snake, the copperhead, in the woods and even they are uncommon. If they are found at all, it is usually around abandoned cabins or in nests among rotting logs. They avoid people too, and you really have to go looking for them. I have never heard of a runaway being caused by a snake on any of the trails around here."

Luther was silent for a moment and then spoke again. "We have seen more of the other kind of Copperhead in recent years; the slave catcher, the rebel sympathizer and spy. We knew how to deal with them too." Luther's eyes were distant.

"Anyhow," he returned to the present, "this sack tells us nothing, and I do not care for the effect it has on our horses." He opened the door of the stove and tossed in the bag before Seamus could raise a protest.

Seamus asked for Sarge to be brought around again to the front of the stable. He determined that he would go back and search for the trail of the person he had seen running through the woods.

Luther led Seamus from the office through the interior door, and together they walked the length of the cool, dim, horse and leather smelling building toward the afternoon glare at the wide front door.

Sarge had been rubbed down and was waiting in the company of Frederick, who held the bridle while Seamus mounted.

He departed under the watchful gaze of Luther with whom he exchanged a parting nod for the second time this day.

He retraced his journey passing the turn to the boat house. As the afternoon progressed the revelry at the lake was drawing to a close and many were returning to the hotel in anticipation of supper. Beyond the fork, the road was deserted.

Seamus thought to check the time. He reined Sarge up, and hauled his gold cased watch from his waistcoat pocket. The timepiece had been a gift from the men of the Irish Brigade and chimed the first few notes of *The Garryowen* as the cover popped open at his touch. It was a quarter past four.

He admired the watch resting in the palm of his hand. It was the finest thing he had ever owned and gave both time and date. In the center of the circle of black Roman numerals surrounding the face was enameled a green sprig of shamrocks. Inside the lid was the inscription; 'To Lt. Col. Seamus Patrick Delaney', and under that the Gaelic war cry; *Faughaballagh!*

He closed the watch. On the lid was embossed the Harp and Sunburst from the regimental battle flag, and on the back of the case, the trefoil insignia of the second corps of the Army of the Potomac.

Seamus returned the watch to his pocket adjusting the fob to hang free from the heavy gold plated chain. Upon the fob was a representation of the 69th regiment coat of arms; two Irish wolfhounds rampant flanking a shield with stars and stripes, sunburst, harp and round tower in its quadrants.

*Faughaballagh*, he thought, that is what the boys had shouted at the Wheatfield; *Faughaballagh!* Clear the way! But the rebels did not clear the way so easy that day.

He remembered the regiment waiting in the still, stifling shade in the road behind the Wheatfield; under the trees waiting, the sun shining through the leaves in pinpoints, just like the road he was on now.

Father Corby had stood on a rock outcrop above the men, the purple stole around his neck peeking from under his long silky beard. He had blessed the regiment; given general absolution, and then into the field they went, and the chaplain with them.

Seamus' head started to ache. In his mind, the scene before the Bloody Lane came up and with it the knowledge that he had murdered Emily's husband

No! he thought, shaking again.

No! No time for that, follow the trail!

He reached a trembling hand into the inside pocket of his coat and withdrew his big silver flask. It was nearly empty. He fumbled with the screw cap, placed the flask to his lips. The rim of the spout clattered against his teeth.

He took a swallow and then another; the last. It burned. He choked. His eyes watered. He stopped shaking.

"There now," he muttered to himself, "medicinal purposes." He screwed the cap back on the flask and returned it to his pocket.

Concentrate, he told himself.

He traveled a few more rods along the road and came to the place where the game trail went off to the right. The spot was clearly marked by a thickening spatter of snake blood. A small cloud of green-bottle flies droned happily in the humid swelter.

That vision itself began to bring up another set of images for Seamus so that he quickly urged Sarge onto the game trail. A dozen yards into the woods, he slowed Sarge to a walk. He crouched low in the saddle and searched the path for tracks.

The ancient trail was plainly visible as a parting of the trees ahead. The leaves on the ground had been flattened by the regular passage of the native deer. In places, round darkened circles appeared were the small hooves had kicked up little piles of leaves and pine needles.

Seamus continued along slowly, but saw no sign to indicate that either human or horse traffic had passed. The trail meandered generally east and north toward South Lake. After a few minutes he came to a glade overgrown with bright green fern and just beyond, the upper reaches of the stream which drained the lake and which eventually flowed into the Kaaterskill gorge. He stopped on the south side of the creek and surveyed the opposite bank. He saw that after crossing the water, the deer trail branched to the west, toward the Falls, and to the east toward the lake.

He crossed the stream and halted Sarge. He dismounted and stooped down. Someone, or possibly an animal, he reminded himself, had splashed through the stream and had continued on the east fork of the path. The leaf litter was still damp to the touch where the trail entered yet another patch of fern.

He remounted and hurried along the eastward fork. In a few more minutes the woods opened onto a coach road at right angles to the game trail. He emerged onto the road and found it to be disappointingly well-traveled. Indeed, the sound of a horn greeted his arrival as a red tally-ho coach bore down on him from the left. The coach passed, and the guest who was acting as assistant driver smiled and waved a long shinny trumpet at Seamus in boozy, good fellowship. The passengers all appeared to have benefited from a champagne picnic, and each joined in the chorus of boisterous cheer with waves and shouts directed at Seamus.

Dust billowed up from the massive wheels of the vehicle and Seamus, unsmiling, waved back.

So much, he thought, for any sign of interesting tracks on the carriage road.

He sat astride Sarge in the middle of the road and watched the coach disappear in the direction of the Mountain House. He crossed the road and noted that the game trail continued into the woods on the other side in the same line to the north. He dismounted and walked the deer trail for a short distance, but found no sign of the type for which he was searching.

He returned to the carriage road and decided for no reason other than growing hunger and thirst to follow the road in the direction the coach had taken and thereby to return eventually to the hotel.

He remounted and traveled along. Presently, the western end of South Lake came into view on his right through the trees. There were now few boats on the deep blue waters, and those which were, had pointed their prows toward the boathouse on the distant eastern shore.

The blue of the lake merged with the blue of the sky, interrupted only by a stand of dark green pine and hemlock forming the jagged horizon behind the boat house.

The road followed the north shore of the lake and continued toward the east. Seamus kept Sarge at a walk, allowing all other traffic to pass. He studied, each passer-by, but found none to resemble the person he had seen running on the deer trail.

At the point where the shore of the lake took a turn to the south, the carriage trail merged with a broader, more developed road also headed south to parallel the shore.

Seamus noticed to his left a charcoal burner's pit, now in a derelict state; testimony to the decline of industry in these mountains which, he had read, once centered on the tanning of hides. That business had supplied leather for the war, perhaps the very leather for the boots he was wearing, but was now virtually halted due to the depletion of the hemlock. The bark had provided tannin, and as a result that species of tree had been nearly wiped out.

The industry was a small loss, he thought, it would not hurt for the forests to be allowed to grow back. The woods were beautiful in their own right, as could be seen by the lands around the hotel which had been spared the ax. There was no need for wealth to be wrung from them to enrich the few. Seamus' guide book had told him that Mr. Beecher had strictly conserved those woods which he owned.

The shore of South Lake was growing farther away to the right as Seamus rode along, and very close now to the left another body of water ranged toward the east. The road hugged the very shore of what Seamus could recall from his guide book was North Lake. The Lakes, according to the book, were not very large; South Lake thirty-three acres and North Lake, twenty-six acres, but they were perfect gems in their setting.

I am, thought Seamus, between the two lakes now, traversing from the north shore of South Lake to the south shore of North Lake. He laughed aloud at the thought, and at the idea of the kind of military monkey show which could have evolved were such directions to be found in a set of orders during the war.

"Lieutenant," he said, "you will advance the company from the north shore of South Lake to the south shore of North Lake." He laughed again, and then silenced himself in mid-laugh.

He heard voices coming to him from across the water.

There was a murmur of men's voices on the left; low and rapid, angry voices.

Sarge stopped almost in anticipation of Seamus direction. Seamus dismounted and led the horse off the road into the shoulder high brush by the shore. A line of cedar trees grew above the brush at the very edge of the water, and he tied Sarge to one of the trees. He stood sideways to the tree, removed his hat and placed it upon the saddle and sighted around the trunk across the angle formed by the north shore and the western shore upon which he now stood.

About one hundred yards distant, on the rocky north shore, a small group of men stood before a towering, dark grove pines. Seamus could hear the voices but could not distinguish what was being said.

He had learned over the years that sounds, particularly the human voice, traveled exceedingly well over bodies of water. He had learned that even accents could be discerned by a careful listener, if not always the content of conversations. The question of accents had been an important consideration, for Seamus, on some memorable occasions along the Potomac, the Rappahannock and at Sailor's Creek.

Seamus himself normally spoke with a soft west of Ireland accent, having in it a touch of the southern counties of his distressed homeland. He had an especially good ear for tone and pitch and was a natural mimic. This sometimes caused people to think he was mocking them when he unconsciously fell into the cadence of their speech. He was also something of a linguist.

During the war, his Irish accent had stood him in good stead since it was neutral as to the north or south of the American continent because the sons of Erin could be found serving in both armies. At will, however, he could converse in the English language in a variety of accents from all parts of the British Isles as well as from various regions of North America.

What Seamus heard now, was barely restrained anger.

The men who spoke were plainly striving to keep their voices down, but the fervor of emotion would sometimes overcome restraint and a voice would rise dripping with contempt. Seamus heard the word; 'fool!' distinctly, followed shortly by the words; 'goddamned Yankee!', and this in the accent of northern Virginia or possibly of Maryland.

He carefully slipped his small brass telescope out of his deep coat pocket, quietly extended it and raised it to his eye. He marveled once again that although he was on vacation, he still could not bring himself to stop carrying most of the equipment, or at least the pocket-sized items, he had carried on assignments in the past.

He steadied the instrument against the tree, viewed the scene across the lake, and was glad that he had not broken the habit of carrying the equipment.

Four men stood in a circle; on the left a man of stocky build. He wore a dark brown, broad brimmed hat with a round crown, a brown jacket and gray trousers. Down the length of the outside seam of the right pant leg, Seamus could distinguish a crimson pinstripe. The man was facing to his right oblique and his face was visible only in partial profile. Curly dark, greasy-looking hair almost covered the man's ear and the chubby cheek had been free of the ministrations of a razor for several days.

Across from the man, two others could be seen in full face. They both appeared to be speaking at once at the moment and their faces were contorted and flushed red. Each of them was dressed as a gentleman, with tall black silk hat, black frock coat, and black trousers. Heavy gold watch chains crossed their black waistcoats and each held a silver toped walking stick. The shorter of the two was gesturing violently with his stick as he spoke.

Although the men were dressed alike, there the similarity ended. The shorter man on the left appeared to be in his forties, and was coarse featured. His flabby jowls were now shaking with indignation. His thick black eyebrows were complimented by a thick black mustache.

The man on the right was tall and erect and appeared not to have an ounce of unnecessary flesh on him. He was clean-shaven, and, while he did not appear to be over fifty years of age, a pure white mane of hair reaching to his collar and bushy white eyebrows gave a cold aspect to his handsome face.

Looks like a military man, thought Seamus.

The jowly man was quieted by the white mane, who raised his voice with a few sharp words.

A Scottish accent, thought Seamus. No, he considered, not exactly Scottish.

Facing the two, and to the right of the man in the gray trousers, stood a man with his back to Seamus. He too was dressed as a gentleman in a tall hat and dark suit of clothes. He too, carried a walking stick and appeared to lean upon the stick which he held in his left hand. Dark, curly hair grew down the back of the man's neck and tufted out to the sides beneath the brim of his hat. He appeared to be of average height and of slight but wiry build.

He raised his hand, and the others turned to him.

He continued to hold his left hand raised. The skin of the hand was pale. The man appeared to be speaking, but in so low a voice as to be inaudible to Seamus.

The man pointed at the man in the brown jacket and pointed abruptly into the dim woods. Brown jacket nodded and departed in the direction indicated, disappearing in an instant beneath the pines. A flight of passenger pigeons arose from the trees like a bush of lavender lilacs taking wing.

The pale hand pointed at the short jowly man and the white haired man and they nodded in unison and departed together stepping along the curving shore toward the east. In a few moments, they were out of sight.

The pale skinned man waited and Seamus held him in the lens of his telescope hoping he would turn his face to the south.

He did not, however, and shortly set off in the same direction as the two whom he had just dispatched. As the man half-turned, Seamus caught sight a dark down-turned mustache beneath an aquiline nose. After that Seamus could see only the man's back going out of sight at the curve in the shore. The man limped slightly on the uneven ground, favoring his left leg.

Seamus held his position for a time to see if anyone returned and to ensure that his own departure would go unobserved.

At length, he backed away from the tree which had sheltered him. He returned the telescope to his pocket, unhitched Sarge and led him back to the road. He donned his hat mounted and paused to give some thought to his next movements. He could see no point in attempting to follow brown jacket into the pine woods. He was more interested in the well dressed gentlemen with whom he had seen brown jacket conversing and particularly in the man with the pale hand who appeared to be giving the orders.

Seamus decided to follow the road he was now on in hopes of seeing the three again in the environs of the Mountain House as they completed their circuit of the lake.

He coaxed Sarge into a walk and soon crossed a log bridge over the stream which joined the two lakes. A short way further along the road and he came to a great angular boulder lurking in the gloom of the hemlocks. A carved sign nailed to a tree at trailside labeled the boulder; 'Alligator Rock'. At a time in the remote past, some mighty convulsion of nature had deposited this specimen and had fractured it in such a way as to leave a gapping maw in profile.

In a more recent time, some energetic persons had enhanced the reptilian effect by placing pointed blocks of bluestone along the lower 'jaw'. Above the corner of the toothy mouth, a stony eye-socket stared at Seamus.

He spurred Sarge into a trot and hurried up the trail away from the monstrosity.

In yet a few more moments he emerged into the common

before the stables. He left Sarge with the younger Van Bronc, the older being nowhere in evidence, and walked to the rear of the hotel. Few guests were about, and Seamus assumed that most where in their rooms preparing for the evening meal. He walked down the central corridor, ascended the oval staircase and returned to his room. He did not see any of those upon whom he had . . . yes . . . spied by the lake shore.

He entered his room in his usual wary fashion, and felt a sudden exhaustion of body, mind and spirit. He hung his hat on the hall tree; fell onto the bed fully clothed and closed his eyes.

# III

# An Evening's Entertainment

Seamus awoke with a start in the dim light of his room. At first he did not recognize his surroundings. When he remembered where he was, he was still confused by the darkness.

When he had closed his eyes, the sky was blue outside his window and now it was gray in the gathering dusk. Surely he had only shut his eyes for a moment or two, he thought, how had it gotten so dark so fast?

He took out his watch. Oh no! It was already ten past seven. He must have lain down at about half-past five and slept for over an hour and a half. His stomach growled with hunger, and the dinning room closed at seven. Perhaps, he thought, I can go to the kitchen and forage.

He jumped from the bed and was suddenly dizzy. He held the bedstead and allowed his balance to come back. He sat in the cane-seated straight backed chair by the door and peeled off his knee length cavalry boots.

They had fairly well protected his trousers from the mud and wet of his afternoon ride. The tail of his coat needed a thorough brushing however and he quickly set about the task.

This was his only suit of respectable civilian clothes; another gift from the Secretary via Brooks Brothers of New York City. If he could not make this suit presentable, he had no other clothes appropriate for the dining room and other public rooms of the hotel.

Hunger hastened his hands. Not real hunger though, he

thought, real hunger made you scream.

As he worked, he remembered that he had been dreaming about his mother again.

He hardly ever dreamed about her anymore; only when he went to sleep hungry. The dream was always the same. He awoke in the 'scalp'; the primitive shelter of branches roofed with furze by the side of the road to Tuam in the County Galway. His father, weak as he was, had thrown up the scalp after the police and soldiers had evicted them; his mother, his two sisters and Seamus, from their cabin for failure to pay rent. It was the time of the Great Famine in Ireland.

In the dream, he woke feverish, and his mother put her cool hand on his brow.

"Sleep now, Seamus, *agrah*", she said, "your daddy is just after going on to Tuam to get us some food. He will be back with us before long." In the dream she spoke to him in Irish, as she had in life.

Seamus turned to his sisters lying next to him, quiet now, eyes closed too weak to scream with the hunger anymore. Little Seamus fell back to sleep, his mother's hand on his brow. He never saw any of them again.

The dream would always run its course and he would awaken as he did this time. The dream no longer disturbed him. It was more like a friendly visit than a haunting as was the specter of the Bloody Lane. He had been eight years old when the Famine took his family and except for the dream, he had scant memory of them.

"Ireland," he said to the four walls.

Ireland was not his country anymore. America was now his country. Still, he thought, it would be good to go back sometime.

To settle the score, a voice within him said.

No . . ., no revenge, just to go back to visit, his other internal voice answered.

He shook his head. This nonsense is not getting me supper, he thought. He examined his coat by the remaining daylight coming in through the window, decided it would do, quickly donned the garment and was out of the room locking the door behind him.

Seamus hurried down the hall to the central staircase and descended to the ground floor. He turned into the passage to the dining room and saw that the doors to that chamber were closed. He approached and tried the handle on the right door and found, to his encouragement, that it was not locked.

He entered the vast dining salon and saw that it was empty of guests. A few waiters were carrying trays of dishes toward the kitchen entrance at the left rear of the
room. The elderly waiter he had seen coming out of the private dinning room earlier in the day stood by a large sideboard against the far wall. The man was counting and polishing the silver plate knives, forks and spoons and arranging those treasures in one of several massive dark wooden chests.

When the waiter looked up and saw Seamus, he ceased his activity and hurried over, wiping his hands on his apron.

"Good evening, Colonel, may I help you." He smiled pleasantly, his strong features wrinkling between long white mutton chops, which ascended the sides of his face to join the equally white fringe of hair circling his bald crown.

"It seems," said Seamus, "that I took a nap this afternoon, over-slept and missed supper."

"Well, Colonel," said the waiter, "I am sure that we can find for you an order of trout *almandine*, with fried potatoes and peas, if that will suit you."

"It will suit me down to the ground." Seamus could already taste the flavor of fresh tout.

"I am Levi," said the waiter as he led Seamus to the same window seat he had occupied at lunch. "Can I bring you something to drink?"

Seamus hesitated. Yes, he thought.

"White wine, if you please." he said.

Levi nodded and crossed the room to the wide swinging doors of the kitchen.

Seamus looked out the window and down into the depths of the Hudson Valley and at the mountains beyond. The Berkshires of Massachusetts were turning deep purple in the twilight, and the sharp points of green and red running lights could be distinguished on the boats on the river. An owl, under wings pink in the last rays of the sun, swooped silently across the scene and disappeared over the ledge.

Levi returned through a door to the left of the one by which he had departed. He carried a silver ice bucket on a stand which he placed beside the table. He took a dripping bottle of Chablis from the bucket, wrapped it in a towel, uncorked it and poured a taste of the straw colored wine into a tall glass.

Seamus sampled the vintage, nodded, and Levi filled the glass. Seamus emptied the glass in a swallow and held it up to be refilled. Levi obliged and Seamus gulped the second glass. He held it up again and Levi, betraying no surprise, filled the glass for the third time. Seamus sipped half the third glass and set the remainder on the table.

There, he thought, that's better.

Levi replaced the bottle in the ice bucket and withdrew to the kitchen.

He returned shortly with Seamus' dinner and asked if there was anything else needed.

Seamus thought to order another bottle wine, or at least a half-bottle; thought better of it, and instead sent Levi on his way with heartfelt thanks.

He ate slowly, savoring the meal. The trout tasted like nothing he had ever had before; like something even better than trout. As he ate, he thought about the day, but came up with nothing but questions. He was sure of one thing, however; Emily needed protection, and he needed more information if he were to protect her, and protect her he would. Who else, he asked himself, was there to do the job?

The place to get information, Seamus knew, was the bar.

He finished the wine and, as he arose from the table, Levi returned. Seamus assured the man that the meal had been perhaps the best he had ever had. He thanked Levi again, offered a gratuity which was declined, and left by the door through which had entered.

He walked to the staircase and turned right. At the end of the long central corridor, beyond the front desk, the rear entrance door was open and a cool breeze swept the hallway. The breeze made his face feel hot and flushed.

He walked slowly and let the other guests pass as they hurried toward the door to the casino, where Professor Smith had promised a musical evening. On his right he passed three tall windows which let onto the grassy confines of the north courtyard.

Seamus paused at the entrance to the casino. The room was assuredly not a gambling den, but rather, a kind of drawing room for small entertainments. Within, the porters had begun to augment the last glow of day by lighting the chandeliers. The room was painted a pale shade of peach, which along with the lighting, gave the entire space a warm and welcoming air. Groups of guests were arranging themselves at clusters of round tables.

He considered that he might join them later but for the present he would go to the bar. The entrance to that room was the next on the right.

He stopped by the barroom and looked out the back door. The setting sun turned the sky blood red beyond the shadowy stand of pines. The crimson fire reflected in the water of the lakes and set aflame from below the dark blue and gray clouds floating above the mountains.

Out of the corner of his eye, he examined the men standing by the front desk. One was the night porter dressed in hotel livery, and the other was a most striking personage.

That man stood apart from the porter gazing also at the sunset. His face seemed to be carved of ebony, the eyes rheumy and distant. His close cropped hair was sprinkled with silver. The cheeks were clean shaven and three parallel scars ran down both sides of his face from the corner of each eye to the jaw line. His large, powerful hands hung at his sides, extending from the cuffs of his blue, waist-length cavalry shell jacket. The jacket bore neither insignia nor emblem of rank, but the three rows of brass buttons on each side of the breast beneath the stiff white collar were polished to a high luster. Dark trousers and shined shoes completed the man's attire. He seemed to Seamus to be detached from all around him and stood simply . . . waiting.

Seamus realized that he was no longer peeking at the man

surreptitiously but was now openly starring. The man appeared not to notice, and Seamus turned to enter the bar.

He pulled the handle on the left of the two heavy, oaken doors and noticed that each had a round window at eye level set with colorful stained glass. Each window was identical to the other except that the one in the right door depicted the Mountain House in summer, with the appropriate green foliage of the forest surrounding the white building on its craggy perch, while the window on the left represented the hotel in the fall, against the blazing orange, yellow and red of autumn. The light from within the bar illuminated the images seared in the glass.

Seamus entered the barroom and found it to be nearly empty. There was a haze of tobacco smoke beneath the low ceiling. The smoke gathered into a halo around the twin green glass shaded lamps hanging above the substantial mahogany bar on the left. The light in the windowless room was provided by these and other small lamps, also with green shades, which were set on each of the round tables along the right wall.

At the far wall was a double door, the match to the one through which Seamus had just passed. That doorway let into the casino, where the band could be heard to be tuning up.

He stepped to the nearest corner of the bar and rested a foot on the rail. Three gleaming brass cuspidors were stationed one about every ten feet along the rail and crisp linen bar towels hung from silver clamps about every six feet along the front of the bar.

A square carved pediment, supported by dark stained Corinthian columns, crowned the back bar. Between the columns, shelves of bottles alternated with panels painted of mountain scenes, executed in oils apparently many years before. On the counter of the back bar, casks of various sizes lay on their sides on semi-circular wooden stands. Rows of polished glasses in a variety of shapes waited to be employed.

At the moment, the barman was occupied at the far end of the bar in filling a line of small stem glasses from a cobalt blue sherry bottle. In front of him, a hatch opened to the casino, where waiters were just now coming and going; placing orders and picking up trays of drinks. As quick as the barman would place the filled glasses on the counter which formed the lower edge of the hatch, they would be snatched up by the hurrying waiters.

He looked back at Seamus and smiled making a helpless gesture indicating that he would tend his new customer as soon as possible.

Seamus returned the smile and shrugged. There was no rush; he was content to continue his visual survey of the room.

Though elegant, it nonetheless had a snug, homey, permanent quality about it, which reminded him of Mr. William McSorley's newer, but far less stylish establishment on 7th Street in Manhattan.

That respectable workingman's ale house had literally been a home to Seamus when he had first come to America. Mr. McSorley had put him to work as a porter the day after his arrival at Castle Garden on the Battery. This employment had been arranged before Seamus had even sailed from the Cove of Cork and he had at first slept in the kitchen of the place until space became available in the boarding house his Aunt Kate; Felim's mother, kept on Fifth Street.

In due course, Mr. McSorley introduced Seamus to his great friend, Peter Cooper; the inventor of modern steel processing, builder of the first locomotive in the United States and founder of the Cooper Institute; a free engineering college around the corner from the ale house. Mr. Cooper had then employed Seamus as porter at the college and later engaged him in progressively more responsible positions. Eventually, Seamus was able to attend courses of engineering, architecture, trigonometry and the calculus at the Institute. Later, he took courses at the Jesuit college in the city.

He remembered McSorley's as it was in those days. The copper boiler on top of the stove in the barroom was always well stocked in winter with steaming clam broth. A brass spigot on the boiler provided the nectar, gratis. He remembered Felim and himself and some other young men, warming themselves with bowls of broth on the freezing February evening when they had returned from the Institute after hearing Abraham Lincoln speak. Mr. Cooper had requested their attendance to help ensure Mr. Lincoln's safety. Seamus, looking back, could see that his life had changed that night. There had been something so strange about Lincoln; he inspired.

Seamus had been to the ale house the week prior to his arrival at the Mountain House, and when he had returned after the war, he found little changed at Mr.McSorley's. Peter Cooper's personal chair still stood in its usual place, but one of the boys who had survived Andersonville had come back to hang his leg irons on the wall behind the bar. A Zouave fez hung near the chains, the thick dusty tassel drooping down. A handbill, offering a reward for information leading to the capture of the President's assassins had been framed and screwed to the wall at the end of the bar by the entrance to the back room.

Seamus returned to the present.

Only two other patrons were in the room. To the right, a man sat alone in the first table by the hall door.

The man was dressed in a black gabardine suit, a tall silk hat, cocked to one side, upon his head. He played at solitaire; his pale, thin fingers flashing slowly, rhythmically in the lamplight as he dealt the cards. A thin cigar was stuck in the corner of his mouth. A cut crystal decanter stood on the table at his right hand and with it, a brandy glass.

As Seamus looked at him, the man put down his cards and with his right hand removed the cigar, picked up the half-glass of brandy, looked straight at Seamus, drained the glass and set it down.

The man held Seamus in his gaze, his dark eyes burning out from somber hollows. His cheeks were emaciated and a small, down turned mustache made his colorless face seem even thinner.

Without looking away from Seamus, the man picked up the decanter, filled the glass, drank off half of it, and set it down. He returned the cigar to his mouth, and favored Seamus with a smile which, far from being cheery, gave the whole face the aspect of a mustachioed skull. He continued to regard Seamus with his ghastly grin, and then took a deep inhale on his cigar. He uttered a profound, rumbling, controlled cough, and returned his attention to his cards.

Consumptive, thought Seamus. As if in affirmation, the

man rumbled deeply again and inhaled once more on the cigar.

Seamus turned his eyes to the other end of the bar, having determined that he might not be able to stand another smile from the solitaire player should such be offered. He was pleased to see that the barman had dispatched the last tray of drinks to the casino.

The only other bar patron was sitting at the far end of the room at a table in the corner by the entry to the casino. He sat with his right foot drawn up on the rung of his chair, his left leg stretched out to the side. He was dressed in an elegant black suit and he too wore a high silk hat squarely on his head. A dram glass stood on the table before him. The man's face, however, was buried in the pages of a newspaper which he held in both hands. The skin of the hands was a pasty white.

The masthead of the paper read; *The Zephyr*, and the headline shrieked; 'Fenians Disarmed At The Border!'

Dear God, thought Seamus, the Fenians. He turned his eyes instinctively from the report of the latest exploits of the Movement.

His attention was drawn to the low, square Steinway piano standing against the center of the wall and the large framed Untied States flag hanging above it. The flag, he thought, though, tattered at the edges, was generally well preserved considering its age. He counted twenty-four stars in the canton.

"That is the first flag to fly over the Mountain House, it was used at the opening ceremonies for the hotel on July 4th, 1823." said the barman, who now stood across the counter from Seamus.

"Of course," he went on, "that was a few years before my time, and the country has grown a good deal since then. So has the hotel for that matter. Back in those days, or so I'm told, the building was only about sixty feet across the front of the ledge and twenty feet deep centering mostly about this barroom. It was only three stories tall, but it grew steadily and will keep doing so as long as we get some successful seasons now that the war is ended. But it is a fine old flag, is it not?" He beamed up at the framed ensign.

"It is indeed," said Seamus, "and I would lift up my glass in its honor, if I had a glass and something in it to drink."

The barman's face flushed rosier, matching more closely his wild shock of red hair and the fiery muttonchops which all but concealed his ears. He was a beefy, broad shouldered man.

"Please excuse me, sir. Here I am talking on and you have been waiting so patiently. I am Rolf van Zand, at your service, sir. What can I get for you?"

Seamus considered whiskey but decided that he better go light.

"A large glass of beer, if you please," he said. "And there is no need to apologize, I am in no hurry."

Rolf went to the center of the bar, where he drew a generous goblet of beer. He returned and set the glass before Seamus, who quickly picked it up and held it toward the flag. He had an idea.

"Will you join me in toasting our country's banner?" he said to Rolf, but in a voice loud enough to be heard throughout the room.

"I don't take strong drink while I am working", Rolf replied," but . . .," he brought up a pitcher of lemonade from behind the bar. Clinking chunks of ice floated in the pitcher. He filed a short glass for himself and held it up in salute.

"Now then," said Seamus loudly, "Gentlemen, I give you our country's flag!"

The solitaire player rose to his feet with difficulty and leaned against the table. He raised his glass and intoned, in the accents of northern Virginia or perhaps Maryland, "Our country's flag!"

The newspaper reader did not move.

"Mr. Tompkins?" said Rolf, and the man put down his paper, rose, also with some difficulty, and stated in the accents of northern Virginia of perhaps Maryland, "Our country's flag."

They all drank, Seamus nearly choking.

Booth! he thought. The newspaper reader; Mr. Tompkins, had the face of John Wilkes Booth.

Seamus set his drink on the bar and Rolf returned to the hatch to greet a waiter returning with a tray of empty glasses. Mr. Tompkins and the solitaire player resumed their seats and Seamus stared into his beer and remembered.

He remembered the night when he, just back from

Appomattox, and his comrades were celebrating the surrender of General Lee in the tap room at Willard's Hotel in Washington; that cold, rainy night in April, little more than a year before. A courier from the War Department had arrived with the news that the President had been shot and with orders for Seamus and some of the others to report to an address only blocks away, near Ford's Theater. In a few moments, Seamus was standing, dripping wet, before Secretary of War Stanton in the front parlor of the residence while the President lay dying just down the hall in a small bedroom.

Seamus had been one of the few people in the city that night who had not been surprised to hear that it was the actor Booth who was believed to have shot Mr. Lincoln.

After his wounding at Antietam, Seamus had been sent to Georgetown to recuperate in a military hospital there which had previously been a girl's school. When he had recovered sufficiently, he had been assigned to the Provost Guard in Washington. At first he had simply helped to round up drunken soldiers and deserters and return them to their regiments. Eventually, he was assigned more serious and delicate duties. Later he rejoined the Irish Brigade, but after being wounded at Gettysburg, he went back to the Georgetown hospital and in time resumed the duties which included, between periods of service with the Brigade, the surveillance of the agents who plotted to abduct or to kill the President.

Seamus had long known, and had reported to higher authority, the fact that chief among the plotters was the agent John Wilkes Booth. The orders sent in reply to Seamus' reports had always been the same; to maintain surveillance, never to take action. Could that have been, he used to wonder, because Booth, while involved with half a dozen other women, was engaged to the daughter of a United States Senator?

Seamus had since heard that Booth had boasted that at the time of the President's second inauguration, he had stood in the audience on the Capitol steps above Lincoln and could have shot him then had he "wished." Booth would have been surprised to know that at that time and place, he himself was in the sights of a very competent marksman stationed behind a tree below in the park. That marksman had been Seamus, and he had held Booth's face centered in the telescope sight of a heavy barreled Sharp's rifle. If Booth had made an attempt on the President's life that day, he would have been both unsuccessful and dead in an instant.

Later, on the night of the assassination, Seamus had, as he stood before Secretary Stanton, cursed mightily within himself with regret that he had not simply violated orders and launched a bullet into Booth's arrogant face on Inauguration Day.

After the President had expired, Secretary Stanton had assigned Seamus to the 16th New York cavalry as a guide and had dispatched him to the trail of the assassin. There followed days and nights of pursuit through the back roads and hamlets south of Washington which Seamus knew so well. At various times, Seamus had trailed Booth before the assassination and he knew that face. He had seen Booth performing in plays, and at the Capitol and near the Soldier's Home on the previous St. Patrick's Day. In the end, he had seen Booth close to for the first time when Lt. Doherty had brought their quarry to ground in a tobacco barn near Port Royal. Booth had looked different with his mustache shaved.

Seamus had watched Booth die, after the assassin had been shot in the neck by one of Doherty's sergeants; Corbett. Corbett, thought Seamus, now there was a truly dangerous character, with his weird high-pitched voice and his rantings and his devilish face. Corbett had said that he had shot Booth at the direct order of God. The orders more likely came from the infernal regions in Seamus opinion. Or perhaps, as some said, Booth had attempted suicide with his revolver and had, at the last moment funked, lowering the muzzle from his temple to his neck. But then why were there no powder burns around the wound? Either way, Seamus had watched Booth die, watched for nearly two hours, without a glimmer of fellow-feeling or remorse.

And that is the point, thought Seamus, now angry with himself, Booth is dead and this newspaper reader; this Mr. Tompkins, has a face only *like* that of the assassin. He is not, could not be, Booth.

Seamus took another sip of his beer and grimaced. He did

not particularly care for the taste of beer, nor the flavor of whiskey either. He drank only to join in the conviviality of his fellows or for medicinal purposes, he told himself.

He could not help looking back in the direction of Mr. Tompkins, but the newspaper was again in front of the man's face. The shocking resemblance Tompkins bore to Booth had almost caused Seamus to forget to evaluate the results of his tactic in saluting the flag and getting the others to do the same.

Right, he thought, by their looks and accents, either of them could have been the man who had been giving the orders to the three men on the lake shore this afternoon. Either of these two, or one of the scores of other men presently at the hotel today could fit the hazy description, or even someone who was not staying at the hotel. The grounds were, after all not closed, but open to any in the world who cared to ride or stroll them.

Seamus could not get away from his thoughts of Booth, or rather his impotent loathing of the man. He had watched Booth die and had felt a cold pleasure, which, as he tried to live the life of a Christian, filled Seamus with regret, but could not be denied. By April 26, 1865, he had seen too many brave and good men and women of the North and of the South, of the white and of the black, suffer and die in the war to waste much sympathy on the back-shooting coward Booth. And too, Seamus had learned to look coldly on death and life as well. Still, he lusted to take Booth's life himself. He sometimes wished Booth could somehow come back to life so that he could hunt him down and kill him.

This kind of thinking will drive you mad, he said within. It is absurd and un-Christian. How much killing, he asked himself, do you want in your life? It occurred to him that he had not seen any one die since he had witnessed Booth's unlamented demise, but that today death again had been very close.

As if on cue, and by prearrangement to lift Seamus from the dark place in his heart where he was just then dwelling, Professor Smith's musicians pitched into a spirited rendition of the jaunty and popular tune, *Columbia, Gem of the Ocean.*

Seamus looked up from the schooner of beer where he had sought, yet again, to relive the past and perhaps divine the future.

From where he stood, he had a good view of the band through the hatch and of the Professor leading it.

The casino appeared to be an 'L' shaped room with its entrance up the hall eastward from the bar entrance and wrapping around the right wall and the back wall of the barroom. The band was formed in front of the French doors to the left of the hatch along the west wall of the hotel.

Professor Smith directed his musicians vigorously with a thin baton in his right hand and a resplendent silver coronet in his left. As Seamus watched him, he put down his baton upon his music stand and joined in playing his instrument with the rest of the ensemble.

Seamus could see Mr. Beecher sitting with a party of ladies and gentlemen at a table across the floor from the band but could see no more of the audience.

The professor finished the first piece with a flourish and to the enthusiastic applause of the guests. He turned, bowed and gestured to share the applause with his musicians. When the clapping subsided, he adjusted his spectacles on his nose.

"Thank you, ladies and gentlemen," he said, "thank you most kindly one and all, and welcome to our evening's entertainment. I would like to announce that tomorrow's traditional sunrise service will commence at five o'clock on the main floor piazza. The Reverend Schyler Van Wyck; dominie of the First Dutch Church of Brooklyn, who is visiting here at the Mountain House along with his good wife, has consented to preside at the service. The topic of the sermon will be 'The Sepulcher in the Garden'. Thank you for your kind attention; we will now resume our musical offerings with *I Dream of Jeannie with the Light Brown Hair*."

These announcements were met with restrained applause and the band continued playing in the hushed and gentle style appropriate to the soulful character of the tune.

Rolf returned and Seamus placed a few coins on the bar to cover the cost of his beer. I t occurred to him to inquire about replenishing his now empty flask against future emergencies and he did so.

"Well, yes sir," said Rolf," we have a fine selection whiskies as you can see." He pointed to the back bar. Seamus recognized the popular imported Irish products, Cork Distillers, with the map of Ireland on the bottle, Jamieson's, and Bushmills. Whiskies of Scotland and Holland were also represented as well as Overhalt and other American ryes and bourbons. Seamus had had his fill of bourbon at the South.

"Or perhaps," said Rolf, "you might wish to try something new, something a bit different, sir." He brought up a half-gallon crockery jug from behind the counter. He set the jug on the bar; it was light brow on the bottom and darker brown at the top.

"And," said the barman, "Mr. Tompkins is just the man to tell you all about this new liquor."

At the mention of his name, Mr. Tompkins put down his paper, rose, picked up his dram glass and crossed the room to join Rolf and Seamus. As he approached, Seamus noticed that he favored his left leg slightly.

Mr. Tompkins placed his glass on the bar and smiled.

"Surely, if I can be of some small assistance," he said in cultivated tones.

"This gentleman," said Rolf, "may be interested in purchasing a quantity of the product which you have brought us from far off Tennessee, sir."

"Why," said Mr. Tompkins, "thank you for drumming up some business for me, Rolf." Turning to Seamus he said, "But I am sure that once you try this Tennessee whiskey it will sell itself. Mr . . . ?"

"Delaney," said Seamus offering his hand and concealing the distaste he felt, albeit irrationally, at contact with this person who still seemed to him to be Booth.

"Pleased to meet you, Mr. Delaney," said Mr. Tompkins. "You may have become familiar with the bourbon whiskies of the South. This product is similar in many ways to those liquors but because it is filtered through charcoal as a part of the distilling and aging process, it is different from bourbon; lighter and smoother. In our opinion it is an altogether superior and more pleasing beverage."

Mr. Tompkins seemed to Seamus to be the about the same age as himself and yet in actions and speech there was a youthful, even boyish quality. The enthusiasm, he thought, of the born drummer. Tompkins had dark eyes and exceptionally dark eyebrows which added a certain earnestness to his features.

"I wish to let you know," said Tompkins, as if reading Seamus thoughts, "That I am not a salesman, Mr. Delaney. Rather, I am the sole dealer of Tennessee whiskey outside of that state. I have embarked upon this enterprise on my own and traveled to Tennessee and invested in the shipment which I have conveyed by rail and by riverboat to Catskill. There the balance of the cargo, save the wagon load I brought up the mountain last week, rests in Mr. Beecher's warehouse. If I can create demand for this charcoal filtered spirit up and down the Hudson Valley, I may be able to expand the market to the east to Boston and north to Canada. And toward that end, I will, if I may, offer you a sample of Tennessee whiskey."

Seamus accepted with thanks and Rolf poured out from the jug a dram of the tawny liquid. Mr. Tompkins held up his glass in salute, Seamus reciprocated and took a sip. As advertised the whiskey was smooth, lighter and far less fiery than many of the spirits to which he had become accustomed in recent years. He still did not care for the taste, but this whiskey would serve the purpose, he thought, and with less burning and choking.

"Excellent," said Seamus and Tompkins smiled broadly.

Seamus placed a five dollar greenback note on the bar, took his flask from his pocket and passed it to Rolf. He offered to buy Tompkins a drink and the man accepted. Rolf replenished the glass and filled the flask with the aid of a copper funnel. When he was finished he returned the flask to Seamus, took the money and returned in a moment with the change.

"To your very good health, sir," said Tompkins, "it is a pleasure to meet a patriotic gentleman like yourself who is a judge of fine whiskey and, I take, it a veteran of the late War for the Union."

"Yes," said Seamus, "I did serve."

"I, alas," said Tompkins, "was unable to do so because of an injury which I suffered in a riding mishap in my youth. I do feel that I did my best to help the cause, however, through my activity in commerce."

And made a tidy penny for yourself as well, no doubt, thought Seamus.

Mr. Tompkins proved to be a loquacious companion and regaled Seamus both with tales of his efforts to bring creature comforts to the soldiers of the North in the Border States during the war, and with predictions of the prosperity to come, now that trade could blossom between the formerly antagonistic regions of the country.

Seamus was perfectly content to be the good listener while he continued to survey the barroom and to observe the exertions of the Professor and his band through the hatchway. He was feeling quite relaxed and ignited the third of his daily allotment of cigars.

The band had progressed through a series of ballads and concluded a medley of marches with *Marching through Georgia.* The Professor announced that the musicians would take a short rest and a number of the male guests entered the bar from the casino.

The first through the door was a distinguished looking gentleman who appeared to be in his fifties. He sported a head of wiry gray and brown hair and a spade beard with curled mustaches. He stood at the bar very erect and held his chin high as if to balance the gold framed pince-nez spectacles on his nose. The man's right hand was scarred and clenched permanently into a claw with the middle and index fingers protruding in a hook-like fashion.

As Seamus watched, the man produced a short cigar and inserted it into his hooked fingers. He lit the cigar with a lucifer match from the stand on the bar and exhaled a cloud of smoke toward the ceiling.

"Good evening, Doctor Duboise," said Rolf, "The usual, sir?"

"Good evening, Rolf, yes, the usual, if you please," said the doctor to the barman, who was already pouring out a brandy.

"And are you enjoying the music, doctor?" said Rolf as he set the glass on the bar.

"I am indeed," said Doctor Duboise. "Especially that last tune; one of my favorites." He hummed a few a few bars of the chorus.

"Marching through Georgia! Marching through bloody Georgia! Are we never to hear the end of it?! Suppose it was marching through Pennsylvania, or marching through Maryland or marching through Washington City, as it should have been, how would they like that?!" This declaimed in a vehement stage whisper, came from the casino door, and caused Seamus and the others in the barroom to look in that direction. Entering through the door were the jowly man, just finishing his declaration with a guttural grunt and, at his side, the white-manned man, the pair of whom Seamus had last seen at the lake shore that afternoon.

Mr. Tompkins glanced in the direction of the two and quickly looked back to Seamus with an expression both bemused and rueful.

The white-haired man guided his companion by the arm and directed him to a table near the framed flag. He seemed to be embarrassed by the other's display. Seamus heard him say in a placating tone that he would get them some drinks.

"Right!" was the loud reply of the jowly man. "Some of that fine Southern whiskey." His slurred speech told that he already had drink taken.

"Fine Southern whiskey, here in Yankee-land," he said more loudly still, his face twisted into a truculent smile. "They have taken our country and stolen our whiskey, and now maybe they want to steal everything else too."

With this last, his unfocussed eyes found the end of the bar, and he continued to stare in Seamus direction, while his associate retrieved two whiskies from the bar.

The jowly man gulped his drink.

"Well, they may have maneuvered us into defeat with their blockade and their diplomats, but Southern honor will not be kept down. We know what it takes to defend our honor," he said still staring at the end of the bar. "The fight is not over yet . . . isn't that right, Captain?"

"Clay! That is enough!" the white-haired man growled.

Is this jackass speaking to me? Seamus wondered. And if he is, I will let him know right now that it is colonel, not captain. He stepped back from the bar and was on the point of imparting to Clay that information, as well as some intelligence regarding the outcome of the war, when he was stopped by the sound of a chair being suddenly and violently scrapped against the floor.

The solitaire player rose in his place and pounded his boney fist on the table amid a clattering of lamp, glass and decanter. He fixed his eye on Clay and rumbled within his chest. Then in a voice low and threatening, deep and resonant as if coming already from far down in a burial chamber he said; "You speak of Southern honor, I saw but little of that vaunted honor at Andersonville Prison. I know your type just by looking at you and by your speech, sir. You talked of honor as the poor farm boys of your army threw themselves on the guns with the greatest of valor in battle, while you and your kind carefully took your slaves and the rest of your 'property' and your precious selves further to the south, further away from the war front, is that not right, sir?"

Clay had no answer. His face had gone pale.

The solitaire player was relentless. "You never saw a battlefield," he rasped, "unless it was the day after the battle, when you came to rob the dead, isn't that so?'

Still no answer and Clay's jowls began to shake almost imperceptibly.

"Please, Major," said Rolf standing nervously at Seamus corner of the bar.

The cadaverous Major went on his voice never rising in volume, but increasing in force. "You talk," he said to Clay, " of your 'country' when the only country you ever had was, and is, the United States of America, beneath whose flag you now sit and whose honor you have besmirched as you have attempted to defile the honor of all those who served on both sides in the late war. I tell you, sir, that I have never before involved myself in an affair of honor with one who was not a gentleman, but in your case I will make an exception. I tell you, sir that you are a poltroon and a liar, and I will wait upon your pleasure for you to name your seconds."

My God, thought Seamus in utter amazement, the solitaire player, the Major, is challenging Clay to a duel!

"Dueling is illegal in New York State, Major," said Rolf,

tremulous desperation creeping into his voice. "Please, Major," he said "please sit down!"

"I will sit down, Rolf," said the Major, never taking his glittering eye off of his prey, "when this coward tells me the names of his seconds and his choice of weapons."

The fact that dueling was illegal in New York seemed to interest him not a whit.

Still, Clay had no reply.

"I will meet you," the Major addressed him again, "at the place and time of your choosing. I will meet you tomorrow at dawn, or by the living God, I will meet you here and now, but as I am a son of Virginia who fought for the Union, I will have satisfaction."

With this last, the Major's voice rose and the heads of persons in the casino could be seen, through the hatchway, to turn toward the barroom.

"Please, Major," Rolf spoke again, "this is a respectable place, please sit down or I shall have to call Scipio."

"Call whomsoever you may, Rolf," said the Major, 'but I will have satisfaction from this . . . this . . ." The remainder of the man's sentiments were lost; sunk into a fit of coughing. He pulled a stained handkerchief from his sleeve and put it to his mouth. Heaving silently, or almost so, he doubled over and fell back into his chair. His eyes bulged and he appeared unable to breathe.

Seamus stood transfixed as the door to the hallway opened and the wraith-like figure of the black man in the shell jacket, whom he had seen earlier near the rear entrance, appeared. The man went quickly to the Major's side. He picked up the half-glass of brandy from the table and held it to the Major's lips. His movements were marked by a tenderness which Seamus found incongruous in a man who was so clearly a . . . warrior.

With the sip of brandy, the Major caught his breath.

"Scipio," he said, "my old and dear friend." On his face was a look of suddenly dawning recognition.

"Scipio, my dear friend," he said again, as if, thought Seamus, the Major had not seen Scipio in years.

The effort at speech started another fit of coughing.

"Mayjah, you must come now." said Scipio in a deep and strangely accented voice. He delicately lifted the Major by his arm.

"Doctor, if you please," said Rolf.

"Of course," said the doctor. He went to the stricken Major and took his other arm. With his good hand, he took the decanter of brandy from the table and he and Scipio left the room supporting the heaving, wheezing Major between them. The interest in the occurrences within the bar had grown to the point where some guests had approached the hatch and were peering in.

The Professor was, however, equal to the task of creating a diversion to return the evening to a more cheerful and genteel course and he struck up the band. The rollicking tune, *Kingdom Coming*, played rather more loudly than usual, filled the casino.

Seamus noted that the coronet band was not limited to brass, or even to woodwind instruments, as this number was being presented along with a pair of fiddles with a banjo and guitar joining in. The medley continued through *Old Rosin the Beau* and *The Minstrel Boy*. As the music played, most of the men in the bar returned to their tables in the casino.

At the conclusion of the set of three songs, the Professor again addressed the audience.

"Ladies and gentlemen," he said, "after our next set of tunes, we will be asking that some of you come forward and share with us your singing talents. So please be thinking about the songs you may wish to sing, and do not be shy! I must warn you that Mr. Beecher, our illustrious host, has advised me that if there are no volunteers, I may draft singers for service. So come along and volunteer, before you are caught up in the draft!"

This last was greeted by hearty laughter and cheering as the band swung into *We Are Coming Father Abraham 300,000 More*.

In Seamus mind, however still echoed the words of *The Minstrel Boy;* ' in the ranks of death you'll find him.'

Seamus looked at Clay. The man had not moved since the Major had begun his assault. He looked to Seamus to be among the ranks of death; looked to be mortified. As Seamus watched,

Clay attempted to take a drink of whiskey. His hand shook so that he spilled half the glass as soon as his trembling fingers touched it, and he gave up the attempt.

Rolf drew near and poured Seamus and Tompkins a replenishment of Tennessee whiskey. Seamus noted that Rolf too had a tremor in his usually steady hand.

"On the house," said Rolf. He continued. "That gentleman who was so eager to duel," he said in a low voice meant to be heard by Seamus and Tompkins only, "is the notorious Major Thaddeus Savage."

Seamus knew of the Major by reputation. He had fought in the Border Wars in Missouri and Kansas which had formed the brutal prelude to the Rebellion. The Major was known to have ridden with John Brown on the border and was widely believed to have been involved with the Abolitionist zealot at Harper's Ferry in 1859. Later, during the war, he had led his Federal raiders in campaigns at the South which had become notable for their destructiveness of property, particularly of plantations. Captured by rebel cavalry, he had been imprisoned at Andersonville. The wonder was not only that he had survived, after a fashion, in that hell hole, but that he had not been hanged outright. The fact that Savage was an old and respected name in Virginia may have saved him.

"The Major," said Rolf, "apparently came out of his imprisonment with tubercular lungs, and, sadly, it would seem that he has not much time left. Each night since he came to stay here last month, he has sat at that table and drunk brandy. Scipio always waits for him in the hall and seems to know when the Major needs to be helped to his room. The Major, I am told, personally liberated Scipio from a plantation in Mississippi. Scipio joined the Major's troop and they rode together until they were captured. The Major was put in prison and Scipio was returned to slavery, but he escaped

"At the end of the war, he sought out the Major and found him in a hospital in Alexandria, Virginia. He has stayed with Major Savage ever since. They are devoted friends and he is now the Major's nurse. They share a two room suite on the third floor. We do not ordinarily have this kind of behavior here."

Rolf seemed relieved to have delivered himself of this information.

Seamus looked at Tompkins out of the corner of his eye and saw that the young man appeared to be shaken by what had just transpired.

Seamus glanced at Clay and saw that the man had recovered enough to be able to convey his dram glass to his fleshy lips.

The hall door opened and in walked Luther Van Bronc. He was dressed in the same fashion as he had been earlier in day, with the exception that he now wore a gray sailcloth jacket against the evening chill. He held his hat in his right hand and in his left a ring of keys. He greeted Seamus with a nod, and stood next to him at the very end of the bar. Rolf bade him good evening and hurried to the far end of the bar where there was a safe situated below the counter of the hatch. The safe had the word 'EXCELSIOR' imprinted in ornate yellow letters on its green door above the dial and the handle.

Rolf bent to the dial, carefully shielding with his body the combination as he worked it. He returned after closing the safe, and placed two sacks on the bar in front of Luther. The one sack rustled and jingled slightly as Rolf gently laid it down, the other thumped softly. Seamus figured that sack held a pistol.

A large caliber revolver, he estimated, with some pride in his talent for discerning the size and shape of concealed weapons. He noticed that Clay had again more or less focused his eyes on the end of the bar.

Rolf brought the pitcher of lemonade up from behind the bar, poured out a large goblet and set it before Luther. Luther thanked Rolf, took a deep drink of the glass and replaced it on the bar.

"Are we now expected to drink with these specimens of unbleached humanity!" came the thick and loud voice of Clay from his side of the room.

"My God, Clay!" said the white mane sitting next to him.

"Please, sir," said Rolf, "it is only lemonade, Luther is an employee here . . ."

Seamus turned toward Clay and dropped his right hand to his side. He could see that Clay had regained his rosy color quite suddenly, and that Tompkins had turned ashen.

"You . . ." was all that Seamus could get out before Luther cut him of.

"I'll deal with this, Colonel," he said quietly.

Luther pushed the sacks on the bar away, stepped back from the counter, placed his cap on his head, lowered his hands to his sides and faced Clay.

"Are you speaking to me, mister?" he said.

Clay got unsteadily to his feet, pushed back his chair and stood with his fists clenched at is sides.

"There has been," he slurred in a venomous voice, "a time and place when one such as you has been shot for having far less effrontery than to drink in a white man's bar. And I have never had any fear in shedding blood to defend the God-given superior position of the white man."

In a level and emotionless voice Luther made his reply.

"And if I were to shed blood in order to defend myself, or my family, or my comrades or the God-given rights which this country now upholds for all, it would not be the first time."

Silence enveloped the room. Luther held Clay in his steady gaze.

Seamus could see the color again drain from Clay's face and the jowls begin to tremble once more.

The big old-fashioned Dutch case clock on the back bar could be heard distinctly;

. . . tick . . . tick . . . tick . . .

A single violin started to play in the casino; the long, slow notes wafted into the bar; the introductory notes of *Lorena.* Seamus turned toward the hatch, and there, standing before the band, was Emily.

Beautiful, thought Seamus, beautiful.

She seemed to be a part of the very atmosphere of the casino; warm, bright, sparkling. She wore a peach colored dress of watered silk, the neckline cut low, a necklace of gold and coral against the skin of her throat. Her hair was parted in the center and white ribbons hung down from the masses of curls at her temples. Her hands were clasped at her waist and in them she held a closed ivory fan.

Beautiful, thought Seamus again.

Now she tilted her head and began to sing in a clear and poignant style the first words; "The years creep slowly by Lorena . . . The snow is on the grass again . . . The sun's low down the sky, Lorena . . . "

She is an angel, thought Seamus.

"She is a whore!" bellowed Clay. And he made for the casino.

"A Yankee soldier's whore!" he screamed. With surprising quickness he was at the double doors, and by the time Seamus had shaken off his paralyzing shock and covered half the distance to them, Clay had slammed through.

Seamus broke into a dead run and crashed through the heavy, wildly swinging doors, in time to see Clay heading straight for Emily.

Clay bellowed again; "You whore! How dare you sing that defeatist song in front of these goddamn Yankees!" He strode toward Emily his right hand raised in a fist and Seamus sprinted around him and stood before Emily. The rest was simple.

Seamus raised his left forearm, blocking Clay's right, and stepped in with a lightening right to Clay's ample breadbasket. Clay immediately went down on one knee and actually clung for an instant to Seamus leg. Seamus took a step back to allow the man to fall on his face.

Emily was, in an instant, at the stricken man's side.

"Fenton!" she said, "Fenton!"

"Fenton?" said Seamus, sounding to himself to be rather stupid, "I thought his name is Clay."

"His name is Fenton Clay," said Emily now putting her hand on the gasping man's shoulder. She looked up into Seamus eyes.

"He is my husband," she said and looked down again.

"Your husband?" Seamus thought that he now sounded even more stupid. He looked around the room, all eyes were riveted on him. Some looked away. He found that to be even worse. His face burned.

The white manned-man emerged from the bar and lifted Clay to his feet. Clay roughly pushed Emily's hand from his shoulder. Seamus fists clenched.

"Please withdraw, Colonel Delaney." The voice came from behind and Seamus turned to see Mr. Beecher approaching, his face severe.

"I feel it would be best", he said, "if you would kindly withdraw from the room for the present."

"Yes, of course, sir," Seamus mumbled as with head down he made his way past Clay.

Clay had regained some use of his voice.

"That's right, go!" he hissed. "But this does not end it. Our empire is not visible, but it is real. It will make itself felt again . . . the circle is intact . . . the camellia will bloom once more . . . !

"Clay, shut up!" growled the white mane.

Seamus hurried out of the casino and through the barroom. Tompkins and Rolf looked away as he passed. Luther, Seamus noticed, was gone.

Out the door and into the hallway, he went and left toward the oval staircase. He decided to go up the back stairs. He did not care to meet anyone at the moment. He turned right at the central staircase and passed, on his left a door marked with a brass plaque stating 'Lounge.' He thought of sitting in the room alone for a time in the dark, but there being no guarantee that he would be alone, he pressed on to his own chamber.

His mind's voice kept cadence with his rushing feet; her husband . . . her husband . . . her husband. He entered the stairwell and climbed to the second floor.

He picked up a candle in an old-fashioned iron candle-stick from a rack of candle-sticks on the opposite wall and fished in his pocket for his match case. He lit the candle took his key and let himself into his room. He glanced at his watch. It was half-past nine.

He set the candle on the washstand and emptied his pockets, placing the contents on the chiffonier. He set down his wallet and his purse and some lose change, his cigar case and the match safe. He lit his last cigar of the day from the candle. He took off his frock coat and from the deep left pocket took his telescope and his long, flat, German-made Mercador folding knife, and lay them on the washstand. From the right pocket he took his .36 caliber Colt's New Model Police Pistol. He held it up and admired the blued steel in the candle light. He valued this revolver, which he had carried as a pocket pistol throughout the war. He liked the half-fluted cylinder and the short barrel which looked like the future of firearms. Mostly, however, he valued it because Felim had given it to him. Had given it to him on the night of Lincoln's speech at the Cooper Institute. Seamus had intended to be a policeman. Felim had said, "Here's a policeman's pistol for you then!"

Felim's face came up in Seamus memory; not the dead face, but the live smiling one, crowned with red curls, shinning white teeth, the laughing face.

"Ah, Seamus," he would say, "you’re too serious."

Hush now, Felim, Seamus said within himself, I'll be with you in a bit. I've other things to think about now.

He looked at the pistol again in the candle light.

How would it have been, he thought, if Mr. Fenton Clay had known that I had this small engine of death in my pocket, and was ready to use it? How would it have been if I had just shot him?

He put the pistol on the chiffonier and placed the extra, loaded cylinder, which he took also from the right pocket, next to it. With the spare cylinder, he could, if necessary, make a five shooter into a ten shooter by quick disassembly of the revolver frame, removal of the expended cylinder and replacement with one already loaded. With practice he had become very adept at that exercise, both with this pistol and with his six shot Army .44.

Soon, he thought, all pistols will fire metallic cartridges and will not require the laborious loading of each chamber with loose powder, balls, or bullets and individual priming with caps. Not yet though, metallic cartridges were not, in Seamus opinion, reliable enough for the life and death situations which arise in fights with handguns. They will be some day soon, he thought, but until then, he would prefer to use a pistol, if he had to use one at all, which he knew would discharge as planned.

Intruding on his thoughts his mind said, her husband . . . her husband.

From his left coat pocket Seamus took his flask and set it on the wash stand. He hung the coat on the hall tree. He unloosed his galluses, took off his collar and tie and shirt and hung them on the side of the mirror. He took a dented silver tumbler from his carpetbag pulled the arm chair up to the wash stand, and poured a large whiskey into the tumbler.

Her husband . . . her husband . . . her husband, he thought.

"Her husband," he said aloud, and took a deep drink of the whiskey.

He sat in the arm chair bare-chested and looked out the window at the stars above the river. He put the big flask on the stand and looked at it gleaming in the candle light.

It was a souvenir of St. Crispin's Day in 1854; a day when there had been four separate cavalry charges in the Crimea. Seamus, along with his fellow dragoons serving with the British Expeditionary Force had met with glorious disaster charging batteries of well-laid Russian artillery. Walking back to his lines that day, after his horse had been shot out from under him, Seamus, who had felt sick and feverish even before the charge, now thought that he would choke to death in the heat and blinding smoke and dust before gaining safety. He had espied this flask glittering in the shimmering air on the ground before a destroyed Cossack gun emplacement. Seamus, unsophisticated youth that he was at the time, took it for a fancy Russian officer's version of a canteen. He had picked it up, uncapped and it placed it to his lips. His palette, which had not been accustomed to spirits, had been prepared for a draught of water, instead the fiery liquor the Russians called bodka had seared him down to his innards. He had gasped, tears had run down his begrimed cheeks, but he had drunk and drunk again. He had reached his lines in a calm, even jovial state and collapsed in fever at the feet of his quartermaster sergeant.

Seamus chuckled to himself at the child he had been before that day. He regarded the flask as he poured another drink. It was curved to fit the body, and held more than a pint, reflecting, most likely, some Russian measurement. The Russians, it seemed, always went in for large dimensions. The front of the flask was overlaid in a gold representation of a unit insignia which incorporated the two-headed eagle of the Romanoff dynasty and the Orthodox multi-armed cross. The numeral '20', written in script, appeared at the bottom of the insignia. On the back of the flask were words engraved in seven lines in the curious blocky alphabet of the Russian language. Seamus had no idea of what the inscription meant, but always intended to obtain a translation.

Seamus thought back again on the quartermaster sergeant who had saved the flask for him and had sent it along with the rest of his kit to him at the General Hospital in Scutari. Sergeant Bloomfield, possibly the most profane man Seamus had ever known, certainly the toughest, but he had thought of all of the troops in the command as his sons. The sergeant had grown tired of seeing Seamus, who did not enjoy fighting and who in fact had been raised to be a priest, being pushed around by the company bullies.

One afternoon, before the dragoons had sailed from southern Ireland to Turkey and thence to the Crimea, Sergeant Bloomfield had taken Seamus out behind the barracks and taught him how to end a fight quickly. They practiced particularly the uppercut which could render a man senseless in an instant and the right to the midsection which could render one defenseless, though not necessarily unconscious. Later, when the occasion arose, Seamus demonstrated what the sergeant had taught him to some of his brother dragoons, as needed, and thereafter he was not bothered by them again.

It was important, however, to remain strong in addition to practicing the tactics of boxing. Exercise must be a daily routine. Seamus rose, went to his trunk and took out the two Hotchkiss rifled cannon shells which a friend in the Ordinance Corps had disarmed and converted into dumbbells for him. The conversion had been accomplished by defusing and removing the powder from the hollow shells, taking the lead bore-riding sabots from the outside of them, melting the sabots and filling the shells with the lead.

Seamus sat and exercised; pumping the weights up over his head and alternating roundhouse punches and jabs.

He thought about the hospital at Scutari, a cesspit if ever there was one. There was a night, though, when he had awakened in his fever, a lady's cool hand on his brow. She stood by his bed, an old army lantern in her other hand.

"If he lives through the night," she had said, "he will, I believe, survive."

He did, and never again in his life had a serious fever.

Seamus was breathing heavily and stopped his exertions for the moment.

He could faintly hear the band playing far down below. The tune was *Home Sweet Home*. Was there a woman's voice singing along? He could not be sure.

Now he heard footsteps ascending the backstairs. Two, perhaps three people were climbing from the floor below. Indistinct murmurs and then the word; 'bitch' was spit out distinctly. It was Clay.

"Shut up," came a harsh whisper in the voice of the white-mane.

A soft, delicate tread passed up the stairs behind the wall of Seamus' room, the two heavy sets of footsteps behind. Seamus followed the sounds with his eyes. A key turned in the lock of the door directly above the ceiling. The light footsteps passed across to where the ceiling joined the wall. Another door opened and closed and the latch on that door was thrown.

A two room suite, thought Seamus still gazing upward.

The heavy footsteps stomped to the middle of the room above and a body dropped ponderously onto squeaking springs. In a few moments the air was being sawed with sonorous snoring.

Her husband . . . her husband . . . her husband, Seamus mind spoke in his ear.

Clay is her husband. Coltrane was her husband, but he is now dead.

I killed him, thought Seamus, concentrating with difficulty. She never mentioned being remarried when we spoke in the gazebo at the Falls this afternoon, he thought. Well, that was not your ordinary conversation, in fact there seems to be nothing ordinary at all about this lady.

But, you have made a drunken, foolish, music hall version of a brawling Irishman out of yourself tonight, haven't you, he said to himself inwardly. You will have to leave this fine hotel at the first opportunity tomorrow morning to spare yourself the added embarrassment of being ejected by the management.

He took another swallow of whiskey.

What of it? he thought. You don't belong here anyway.

How did I get involved in this? Infatuated with that strange lady?

A runaway horse, how many times does that happen all over the country every day? A snake in the road, it is unusual, but not impossible. No proof the creature was ever in that sack. No wonder Luther gave me such an odd look. He must think I am mad. Everyone must think so now after tonight. Man in a brown jacket running in the woods. So what? Maybe he was poaching rabbits or grouse or whatever they hunt around here. But, he met with the others. If that was the same man in a brown jacket. They were angry, they shouted. Damn Yankees! they said. So Southerners don't all love Yankees. I wonder why that is? Could it be because Atlanta and Richmond and other locales in the South are still piles of rubble to this day? Why this strange animosity at the South? Not to mention too the dead generation of young Southern men. Why say damn Yankees? Have we of the North offended?

He laughed; a short grim bark. He finished the whiskey in the tumbler and poured another.

So, he thought, I determined over my wine glass at dinner that I must protect Emily from, as it turns out, her husband.

And then I think I see the dead murderer Booth in that young whiskey drummer Tompkins; truly, the cap and bells of folly. Tompkins, despite a superficial resemblance in the physical sense, is nothing like Booth, behaves nothing like the dead, yes dead, assassin did in life.

Other men resembled Booth. Seamus remembered a report that the rebel secret agent, Captain Hines, had nearly been killed by a mob as he sat in a saloon in Detroit two days after the assassination, when he was mistaken for the murderer. Hines, 'The Fox', had used his boots, his fists and his clubbed pistol to extricate himself from the barroom, commandeered a ferry boat and slipped into Canada. Tompkins is not Booth!

So Fenton Clay is an obnoxious boor, he thought, but I could not let him strike the lady. Wife, or not, he has no right to insult her and strike her, not in public. Not in private, either.

Seamus looked up at the ceiling. Clay's snoring had softened to a deep, steady breathing.

If he was going to strike her, thought Seamus, or was he just waving his fat fist in the air?

And what was this nonsense Clay was babbling about the blooming camellia and the circle. The empire cannot be seen. The fight is not over. Was there something to that? What was it? Seamus could not remember.

Well then, Clay is an obnoxious boor and a drunken lunatic and too bad for Mrs. Fenton Clay for marrying him. It is not my fight, he thought with finality.

And I am becoming a drunken lunatic too, he thought, I should stop this drinking. And I will, for tonight anyhow.

Seamus rose unsteadily. He placed the tumbler on the chiffonier, extinguished the cigar butt, and put the pistol close at hand on the washstand in another unbroken habit from the war.

He got on his knees at the side of the bed to check the location of the chamber pot for future reference and, while he was in a kneeling position, said his usual evening prayer; "God help me!"

He stood took off his shoes and trousers, blew the candle out and opened the top window. He slipped under the quilted coverlet. The night air was chill but fresh.

He lay in bed for a time, knowing that he would not be able to sleep. His mind kept going over the day. His accusing conscience raced between his murder of Emily's previous husband and his buffoon-like assault on her present one.

Down in the casino, the band played *Beautiful Dreamer*; a signal to all that the evening's gaiety had come to an end.

For a while, Seamus heard the voices and movements of the guests returning to their rooms, the staff closing up for the night.

Presently, all was silent in the darkness.

Below, on the river, a boat whistle sounded, like the whistle of a boat which had sunk years ago, the sound so far away, so smothered that it might not have been heard at all, it might have been imagined.

Seamus was just falling asleep. He knew this because his thoughts had become even more nonsensical.

There were footsteps behind the wall. The stairs creaked, steps coming up, steps going down, muttering voices, indistinct. One of the voices said; "center the door" or something like that.

Seamus slept.

# IV

# Sunrise Services

A shot. Seamus was awakened by a shot. A shot far away, far down the side of the mountain, now echoing across the valley in the darkness outside the window.

He sat up in bed suddenly and reached for his pistol. He pulled his hand back and put it to his aching forehead. Last night's whiskey was exacting its toll. He gingerly rested his head back on the pillow. He thought to look at his watch, but did not. He had a pretty good idea of the time. He always awoke suddenly, shot or no shot, at about four o'clock in the morning when he had been drinking the night before. Since he drank every night, it was his usual routine to be jolted into wakefulness at that hour and to be unable to return to sleep. His painful conscience would then torture him and his head and stomach would make him pay the price in discomfort for the previous night's imbibing.

In Seamus reckoning, it was a transaction. Since he could not get to sleep without drinking, the alternative was to stay awake all night and relive innumerable episodes which he would rather forget. If he drank, he slept. Sometimes even the dreams would be held at bay by the liquor. The price he paid was to be snapped into consciousness at the miserable hour of four in the morning.

He got out of bed and went to the window. There was nothing to see but the thin gray line of pre-dawn above the Berkshires. An owl began abruptly to hoot beneath the ledge and stopped.

He sat in the arm chair and pressed his hand to his brow. He remembered that he had been dreaming just before he had awakened. It had been Antietam again. He had taken aim at the Confederate officer and then had seen that the officer was Emily; Emily Coltrane or Emily Clay. He remembered that he had found it remarkable how pert she appeared in the uniform; the collar high around her neck, the cap at a saucy angle, the gold braid sparkling in the sun. He had fired. Her face had exploded in blood, and he had awakened.

No more of that, he thought.

He shook his head and it hurt even more, but the pain took the image from his mind. He thought of going for a run around the lakes. He had started doing road work to strengthen his leg while recuperating from the wound he had received at Antietam. He looked down at the thick ridge of scar running across the heavy muscle of his right thigh.

He remembered waking up behind the lines, shells screaming overhead, other wounded men all around, a woman's cool hand on his brow. She was a plain looking woman, but her smile when he opened his eyes was angelic. She had given Seamus a drink from her canteen and moved on to the next man. As she rose, he had seen that the hem of her skirt was sodden with blood.

An Assistant Regimental Surgeon of the 33rd New York, himself a native of Ireland, later told Seamus that the prompt ministrations of that female nurse in cleaning and dressing the wound had saved the leg.

Later still, when assigned to the Provost Guard in Washington, Seamus had shared quarters in a commandeered house in Georgetown after his release from the army hospital there. In the early morning hours, he would don his knickerbockers with his knee length maroon and white and gray banded stockings and matching scarf of the Jesuit school in New York, place on his head his baseball player's cap, venture out and jog slowly along the canal into Washington City and back. He had continued running in the mornings after his leg had regained its full strength as he found that the exercise helped him overcome the physical penalties of a night's drinking. The road work had become a daily routine as his drinking was a nightly one.

As Seamus sat he considered the shot which had awakened him. He wondered if someone had been out hunting at this hour and at this time of year.

Unlikely, he thought.

Raccoon, he knew, were hunted at the South at night, but usually with dogs. He had heard no dogs baying.

He could now hear people moving along the stairs and hallways. He rose, lit the candle and looked at his watch. It was twenty minutes past four. He heard still more people moving about and wondered why so many of the guests would be arising so early in the day. He heard footsteps in the room directly above and remembered that sunrise services, as announced the previous evening, would be commencing shortly. There were hushed murmurs and the hasty scurry of feet converging on the central staircase and thence to the lower piazza. A gong sounded softly through the corridors and the muffled chant of a porter's voice repeating; "Sun rising, sir . . . sun rising, sir."

Seamus gave up the idea of going for a run, since, although he considered that he cut a rather dashing figure in his gray and maroon stripes and ball player's cap, he preferred not to be observed by too many people while he was thus attired. Further, he felt that his jogging about while divine services where in progress would be disrespectful. Instead, he decided that he would attend the services himself, and he set about washing up in preparation. He knew that he had no chance of getting back to sleep and the prospect of sitting in his dim room waiting for the sun to come up was really too gloomy. He decided that he could benefit from some type of worship and the fact that this would be a Protestant service, deterred him not at all. He was sure that God heard all sincere prayers, and had determined that those who believed would be better off to cooperate rather than to dispute with one another.

The question of sectarianism had been settled for Seamus for once and for all on an afternoon spent in a division hospital in Virginia during the Valley campaign. He had gone to visit a fellow member of General Sheridan's staff who had been mortally wounded. In fact, Seamus had inherited his wide-brimmed cavalry hat from the young officer. On that occasion he had recited the Lord's Prayer with his dying friend, who happened to be a Presbyterian. In the next bed, one of General Franz Sigel's youthful corporals, an immigrant like Seamus, lay dying. Rabbi Schwartz, the Jewish chaplain, was helping the Lutheran boy recite the same prayer in German; "Unserer Vater. . ."

Seamus decided that he would allow time for most of the congregation to gather and then slip in at the back of the crowd. He would join in worship, return to his room pack and leave. He hoped that he would be able to do so without having any extended contact with anyone.

He finished dressing and looked at himself in the mirror. He needed a shave but that could wait until later. He figured that in any case he looked better than he felt. He consulted his watch again. It was now five minuets to five. He tended to his trunk and carpet bag as was his habit, left the room and locked the door behind him. Some of the wall lamps in the hall had been lighted and Seamus chose the back stairs in order to limit his chances of being seen by anyone. As he stepped out of the stairwell on the ground floor, he saw that the lobby was filled with guests slowly making their way through the double doors to the lower piazza.

He walked along the hall toward the throng filtering through the doors. When he reached the door to the lounge on his right about halfway to the lobby, he tried it and found it unlocked. He entered and paused to let his eyes focus in the dim glow from the windows. He walked around the big table in the middle of the long narrow room, went a little farther toward the center of the building and found a door exiting onto the piazza which also proved to be unlocked. He stepped through the door and hearing movement behind him, turned to see some of his fellow guests coming through the door from the hallway. They apparently had observed him and decided to take advantage of the same shortcut. One of the ladies at the forefront of the group smiled in a conspiratorial way at Seamus as he held the door for her to enter the piazza.

He made his way along the porch toward the center of the building. There he found those assembled had spread themselves out on both sides of the double doors leaving an open space around the worthy dominie; the Reverend Van Wyck. Seamus edged up behind the group with his back to the eastern facing wall. He found himself standing almost next to the doorway which he had exited after signing the register the morning before. Considering that he intended to leave immediately after the service, it occurred to him that his vacation would prove to be one of less than twenty-four hours duration. He shook his head ruefully. To his right front, stood the back wall of the exterior staircase which descended from the upper piazza, where he had first seen Emily.

The dominie stood facing the congregation with his back to the brightening eastern sky. He was a well set up man in his late thirties, clean shaven except for the curly Burnsides framing his round face. His stiff collar and black cravat accentuated his serious mien, but he gazed at the assembled worshipers with benevolence, a slight smile upon his lips. In his right hand he grasped the Book.

When all shifting about had ceased, he nodded to Professor Smith who stood to his right and the Professor came forward and raised his coronet. The instrument caught the first rays of the dawn just breaking above the black ridge of mountains far across the river and sparks of gold reflected on the people. The clarion call to prayer sounded over the valley and echoed back in long slow notes; *Nearer my God to Thee*, a moving and lonely hymn, the only sound in the world at this moment it seemed to Seamus.

He heard a sigh and looked to his left. The lady standing next to him was Emily, and to her left, in front of the door was her husband and beyond him the white-manned man.

Oh, my good God, no, thought Seamus. Retreat however was out of the question as he was hemmed in by the lady and her party who had followed him through the lounge. He turned his face to the front and tried to pull his head turtle-fashion down into his shirt collar.

The music stopped and the Reverend Van Wyck cleared his throat and addressed the congregation.

"In the words of the psalmist," said he," ' I wait for thee, as they that wait for the eyelids of the morning.' "

He continued, "And again to refer to the Psalmist: 'I will lift up mine eyes unto the hills, from whence cometh my help. My help cometh from the Lord, which made heaven and earth. He will not suffer thy foot to be moved: he that keepeth thee will not slumber. Behold, he that keepeth Israel shall neither slumber nor sleep. The Lord is thy keeper: the Lord is thy shade upon thy right hand. The sun shall not smite thee by day, nor the moon by night. The Lord shall preserve thy soul. The Lord shall preserve thy going out and thy coming in from this time forth, and even for ever more.'"

Amen to that, thought Seamus.

"Let us bow our heads and pray," said the dominie.

BOOM! A thunderous explosion blasted through the hall of the great hotel.

THWACK! A familiar sound in Seamus' left ear. A spray of crimson spattered the wall in front of Seamus and Fenton Clay slammed face first onto the porch floor.

Seamus turned to Emily and grabbed her roughly by both of her shoulders. He lifted her in pirouette around to his right. With her back to the clapboard wall of the building, he looked directly into her wide eyes.

"Look away," he said, "Look away." He knew exactly what had happened and he knew too that if Emily were to look down at her just shot and now dead husband, she would never get the image out of her memory.

"Close your eyes," he said. She did, and he handed her to the lady who had been on his right.

Seamus turned back toward the double doors. Out of the corner of his eye, he saw the white-manned man kneeling on the floor at Clay's side. A dark puddle was widening across the gray floorboards and sending up a liquid reflection in the early morning light.

Seamus hazarded a quick peek around the edge of the doorway, and just as quickly pulled his head back. He had seen a man at the back entrance door. The man had been framed in the doorway at the far end of the hall, standing, barely visible, behind a cloud of smoke which hung in the still air inside the back door. The cloud was illuminated by the orange rays of the rising sun shinning all the way through the building.

Seamus peeked around again and quickly withdrew his head. The man was still there, more visible now in the dissipating smoke. He was a black man.

The scene on the piazza had become chaotic now that the rest of the congregation had gotten the idea of what had happened. Screams mingled with a babble of questions, shouts of alarm and a shuffling and scuffing of feet.

Seamus looked back down the hall and saw that the man was still standing in the doorway. It was Luther Van Bronc.

Seamus pulled his head back behind the doorframe and looked down to see that the white-mane was still at Clay's side and that Doctor DuBoise was at Clay's head. Tompkins was now at the other side of the body, crouched awkwardly, his far leg stuck out stiffly. Tompkins lifted Clay's head and Seamus looked back down the hall. Luther stood at the back door his hands at his sides.

Seamus took a deep breathe and let it out. He stepped into the lobby and started the long walk through the hall toward the back entrance. He purposefully held his hands low and slightly outstretched palms forward. He never took his eyes off Luther who in turn never moved. As Seamus grew closer to Luther he could see that the man held an object in his right hand; long, bulky, darkly glinting metallic blue and gold in the glancing light. A revolver, Seamus was now sure; a large heavy revolver, maybe a Colt's Dragoon. It hung loosely in Luther's hand, the muzzle pointed to the floor.

With a will, Seamus commanded his right hand not to go to his pocket, where the weight of his own pistol and spare cylinder hung comfortably.

No, he said within himself, no more gunplay, no need to make bad situation worse. If Luther wanted to shoot me, he could have done so by now, he thought as he reached the end of the hall.

He stopped before the man and looked up into his face. The face wore a puzzled expression.

"What happened, Colonel?" said Luther, squinting in the

sunlight.

"The pistol, Luther, if you please," said Seamus as evenly as he could. He held out his left hand to receive the weapon.

"The pistol?" said Luther. He looked down and seemed surprised to see the revolver in his hand.

"Can I have the pistol, Luther?"

Luther transferred the weapon to his left hand and carefully handed it to Seamus butt first, the puzzled expression never leaving his face.

"What has happened?" he said.

"You mean you do not know?"

"I do not, Colonel. I was outside, I heard a shot and I came to the door . . . "

"It is the killer!" a shrill voice came from the other end of the hall.

"He has the killer!" A group of stalwart male guests were leaving their safe vantage in the doorway to the piazza and rushing to help Seamus with the now disarmed Luther.

Seamus took Luther by the arm and stepped back to the entrance to the barroom. He tried the door and found it to be locked.

"The killer is a colored!" the shrill voice sounded again now coming closer.

Seamus looked around for some place to go with Luther, knowing that the situation, as unpleasant as it was, could become even more unpleasant in just a few moments.

"Gentlemen, please," came the commanding voice of Mr. Beecher from the rear of the band of stalwarts.

"Your presence here," he said for all to hear, “is not required, Colonel Delaney has the situation well in hand. I suggest you see to your wives and families and return to your rooms, breakfast will be served shortly. Thank you for your interest in the matter, but as you can see there is no further need for your assistance."

As he was speaking, and as Seamus watched with mounting relief, Mr. Beecher worked his way around to the front of the group effectively blocking their progress down the hall. Mr. Beecher was accompanied by the muscular young porter

Sampson.

It was plain to all present that Mr. Beecher was simply not one to be argued with, especially not within the confines of this great building which in every sense was his castle. Nor did any of the stalwarts seem inclined to dispute the issue with Sampson, who stood peaceably enough by his employer's side with his arms folded across his chest, but with his body bladed left side toward the group his massive shoulders flexed in what Seamus recognized as a ready fighting stance.

With a few murmurs and mutters, the band of braves dispersed, drifting in ones and twos back in the direction from whence they had come.

Mr. Beecher and Sampson joined Luther and Seamus at the barroom door. The master of the house produced a small ring of keys and opened the door. They entered and Sampson set about lighting the two lamps above the center of the bar. When that task was completed he turned to Mr. Beecher who spoke rapidly to him.

"Sampson, if you will," he said, "take this key and return to the piazza, open the lounge, and have the body taken in and placed on the long table. Ask Doctor Duboise if he would please tend to the body there. Ask Levi to have the kitchen staff begin serving breakfast as soon as possible. Then I want you yourself to ride as quickly as you can to Haine's Corners, to the Constable's house and tell him there has been a shooting and that he must come immediately."

Luther appeared stunned and suddenly out of breath. He dropped into a chair at the first table by the door.

Seamus stepped to the bar and laid the Dragoon pistol upon it. He stood with his back to the counter, the pistol behind him.

"Excuse me, sir," he said addressing Mr. Beecher, "but the lounge with the long table at the front of the building was open this morning before the service began; both the hall and porch doors."

"Odd," said Mr. Beecher, "In any case, go now Sampson and once the body is taken to the lounge be sure the doors are locked. Post one of the staff in the room to admit no one with the exceptions of the doctor, the Reverend Mr. Van Wyck, who can doubtless do more good for the unfortunate Mr. Clay than can any physician, Mrs. Van Wyck and, of course, Mrs. Clay and Mr. Clay's associate; Mr. McCain. I will accompany the Constable to the lounge when he arrives."

Sampson hesitated.

"Mr. Beecher," he said, his eyes flitting to those of Luther, "if Luther is to be accused of anything then I hope that he would be afforded proper legal counsel." The last words were spoken with a hard look at Seamus.

Luther, who now appeared to have recovered himself fully interrupted.

"Go ahead now, Sampson," he said, "I will be all right, you are not a lawyer yet you know."

"Rest assured, Sampson," said Mr. Beecher, "that I am not accusing Luther of anything, and that he has, as always, my utmost faith and support."

Apparently satisfied, at least for the moment, Sampson departed, with one last stony glance at Seamus.

"You will have to pardon Sampson, Colonel," said Luther, "we are very proud of him. He works here during the season to earn enough to support himself while he reads law with an attorney of Mr. Beecher's acquaintance in Poughkeepsie during the rest of the year."

Mr. Beecher addressed Luther.

"Can you tell us what happened?" he said.

"All I know, Mr. Beecher," said Luther, " is that I had just finished driving the meat wagon up from Catskill, had stopped by the kitchen store room door, as usual, and was about to rouse the scullery boys to unload the provisions, when I heard a shot. The sound seemed to come from the area of the back entry door, so I ran around from the north side of the building. I slowed as I approached the door, but I saw no one around so I went to enter the building. As I stood in the doorway, I could see that something was happening at the other end of the hall on the piazza. I was at a loss as to what to do, so I just stood there until the Colonel walked up to me. He can tell you that I had to ask him what had happened. The fact is Mr. Beecher, I still do not know exactly what took place except that it is plain that Mr. Clay must have died."

Mr. Beecher explained to Luther what had happened on the piazza.

Seamus looked carefully at Luther and said; "When I looked back through the hall, I saw you standing at the door and as I came closer, I could see that you had this." He indicated the pistol lying on the bar. Seamus did not want to be the one to accuse Luther of the murder of Clay, could not think of what else to say, and so left the question hanging unspoken in the air.

"Colonel," Luther responded to the unasked question, "when I heard the shot and started around the corner, it occurred to me that I might need to defend myself or someone else, and so I retrieved the pistol from under the seat of the wagon and then, at the double, proceeded to the door. Yes, I had the pistol in my hand, but, as I suppose I must now say, I did not shoot Mr. Clay or anybody else."

"The pistol, Colonel Delaney," said Mr. Beecher, "is mine. I have insisted that Luther take it with him whenever he travels down the mountain, particularly when he carries the week's receipts down to my office in Catskill each Friday night."

Mr. Beecher was silent for a moment, gazing at the painted mountain scenes on the back bar.

"Back in the twenties," he continued," when my father first opened this business as a simple traveler's lodge, there was never a need to so much as latch a door. The country people were the very soul of decency and would never have dreamt of theft or any harmful act. Our guests, in addition to representing the finest class of persons in the Republic, were, for the most part, scholars, *artistes*, and poets; the gentlest of souls.

"In these more recent decades, I fear a level of brutality has spread throughout the life of our nation. During the fifties, before the war, slave-catchers, some from the South, and some of local vintage, increasingly plied their evil trade in the Hudson Valley; capturing escaped salves, even kidnapping free-born blacks and carrying them off to bondage. The divisive effects of that time, and of the late war itself, have served to focus the hatred of some of the lower class of whites in the valley against black people. There are some today who would assault and even kill Luther, and other members of our staff, not simply in the course of robbery, but out of sheer envy for their position with me, and out of the distilled wickedness of race hatred. Added to this atmosphere has been the economic distress since the end of the war which has created a mass of idle workers, some quite desperate.

"Therefore, Colonel, when my staff go abroad, I insure that they are prepared for any eventuality, most especially if they are carrying anything of value which might entice a robber. It is regrettable, but it would seem that this new era which is coming upon us, is bringing, along with many benefits, many new ills."

Seamus considered for a moment and it occurred to him to check the pistol to see if had been discharged. Prior to Mr. Beecher's statement, Seamus had taken it for granted that when he had seen Luther at the end of the hall, the man had just fired the fatal shot and had obtained the pistol solely for that purpose. In view of Luther's denial, and Mr. Beecher's corroboration, Seamus took the weapon from the bar.

He pointed it away from himself and the others and brought the muzzle up to his nose. The sharp odor of burned powder on steel evidenced a recent discharge. Seamus half-cocked the revolver and rotated the cylinder. An empty chamber gapped up at him. He placed the pistol back on the bar and looked at Luther. He was still reluctant to be the accuser and so said nothing.

Luther again wore a puzzled look on his face. Then his eyes widened and is face dropped.

"Yes, Colonel," he said, "the pistol has been fired this morning, and by me. I had almost forgotten." He turned to Mr. Beecher.

"Do you remember, sir," he said "last month when I told you that the old she-bear with the two cubs had followed the meat wagon on the mountain road after the turn above the Short Level near Featherbed Hill, and how finally I had to fire a shot over her to scar her away?"

"I do," said Mr. Beecher.

"Well, the same thing happened again this morning and in just about the same place. I suppose she just could not resist the scent of a wagon load of fresh beef and pork."

Luther was silent for a moment.

"I guess," he said, "that the fact that the pistol was fired this morning, of all mornings, makes it look bad, does it not?"

No one answered Luther's question.

A knock came to the door which let on to the casino. Mr. Beecher took out his keys, went to the door and unlocked it. Levi entered shouldering a tray covered with a large white linen napkin. He carried the tray to the center of the bar and placed it delicately on the counter with a soft clatter of crockery. The seductive aroma of fresh coffee filled the barroom.

"I thought some coffee and sweet rolls would be welcome, gentlemen." said Levi.

"Thank you, Levi," said Mr, Beecher, "but why did you not use your own key to unlock the door?"

"Because, sir, the staff keys are no where to be found. I let myself in from the servant's wing this morning through the kitchen as usual, crossed the casino and opened the butler's pantry with my key and the ring of keys was not hanging on the hook behind the pantry door as it is supposed to be. Perhaps, Rolf forgot to put the keys in the pantry last night after Luther gave them to him, what with all the excite . . . ," Levi looked quickly at Seamus and caught himself.

Seamus jumped in to relieve the man's embarrassment.

"Yes, Levi," he said, "coffee would indeed be welcome."

He lifted a corner of a napkin and took a cup and saucer.

Levi continued.

"Mr. Beecher," he said, revealing the true reason for his foray into the barroom, "Sarah would appreciate a word with her husband."

"Certainly," said Mr. Beecher, "please ask her to come in."

Levi departed and Mrs. Van Bronc entered the room almost immediately. She bade all a good morning, went to the bar, poured a cup of coffee and brought it to her husband.

"How are you this morning, Luther?" she said.

"Not bad, Sarah, not bad," her husband replied. "I will have to wait here for a time to speak to the constable when he comes. There seems to be a misunderstanding about what happened on the piazza. I am sure that the matter will be cleared up to everyone's satisfaction, and I will join you as soon as the constable leaves."

"Of course, Luther," said Sarah, "well, then, I will be going now, we will all be very busy today, some of the guests have already decided to depart in view of the . . .ah . . situation. Mr. Twilling is beside himself. He is issuing orders in all directions. He just spent ten minutes hectoring Levi and me about dishonesty among the staff, because when he took his morning inventory of the silver chest he found a spoon missing. Can you imagine that, Luther? After all that has happened here today, Mr. Twilling can see nothing but a missing spoon."

She started to laugh and the laugh died in her throat. Tears came to her eyes.

Luther was at her side in a moment and accompanied her to the casino door. He stood outside the door with her, embraced her and spoke a few soft words. She departed and Luther returned to his coffee. He sat with his eyes downcast. The other men looked away. Luther sniffed once and cleared his throat.

Silence hung in the room.

The hall door opened and Rolf entered with his key in his hand, surprise evident on his face.

"Gentlemen," he said, "I did not expect to find the door open."

Mr. Beecher greeted Rolf and apprised him of the morning's events. Rolf stood in mute astonishment. Seamus poured a cup of coffee and handed it to him. The barman sipped at it absently.

"By the way, Rolf," said Mr. Beecher," do you have the staff keys with you."

"No, sir," said Rolf, "I placed the key ring on the hook behind the pantry door last night, just as I always do, before I lock up and go home."

"Might you have forgotten in view of the . . . ah . . . excitement, last night?" asked Seamus. He figured that he might as well broach the subject himself and spare anyone else from having to reference his assault upon the late Mr. Clay.

"No, Colonel," said Rolf, "the routine is always the same. Almost all the produce which we serve in the dinning room is grown here on the mountain top. Of course, we have potatoes, turnips and other less perishable vegetables and apples in storage in the root cellars. Likewise, we serve chicken, eggs, trout and game which we can obtain for the most part locally and we smoke our own bacon and ham and bake our own bread. But the fresh beef and pork and lamb has to be brought up daily by wagon.

"It takes about three or four hours, as you know, to get from here to Catskill, and at least a half hour to load the wagon and perhaps three or four hours for the return trip. Every night about eight or nine o'clock, Luther, or one of the other experienced drivers, will come to the bar and give me the ring of pass keys which Sarah returns each evening. The keys are used mostly by the chambermaids during the day. I go to the safe and give the driver Mr. Beecher's pistol . . . ," Rolf's eye strayed to the weapon on the bar, " …and I take the key ring and keep it on my belt until I close up and I lock it in the butler's pantry. Levi retrieves it in the morning when they start to get the breakfast and the keys are returned to Sarah.

"Last night was the same as always . . . ," Rolf's voice trailed off.

"You were standing right here, Colonel," he said, pointing to the corner of the counter, "when Luther placed the key ring on the bar . . . I . . . I put the sack with the pistol in it on the bar . . . and the money bag, as it was a Friday night, and . . . " His voice trailed away again. He squinted into space in consternation.

"I did go to the pantry and lock it . . . I cannot remember hanging the key ring on the hook." Rolf's face was even redder than usual. He shook his head, his hand went to his belt.

"No, of course I don't have them on me . . . "

He looked to his employer.

"I am sorry, sir, I don't know . . . "

"Not to worry, Rolf," said Mr. Beecher, "it is a matter of but little consequence. The keys will turn up and if not they can be replaced. We have rather more serious considerations to deal with this morning."

The hall door opened, and Sampson entered accompanied by two other men. Each of the other men was wearing upon his breast a copper shield enclosing a cutout star.

Mr. Beecher introduced the constable to Seamus. All the rest of the men in the room were clearly acquainted with one another.

"Colonel Delaney," said Mr. Beecher," permit me to present to you our resident Constable; Mr. Humphrey Wyncoop. Constable, Colonel Delaney."

"Good morning, Colonel," said the Constable, "this is my deputy; Sylvester."

The constable was a burly man, perhaps in his mid-forties, with big blue eyes and a ruddy complexion. His cheeks were grizzled with several days' growth of beard. Dark, silver-flecked curly hair stuck out from under the wide brimmed hat on his head. He wore an old brown jacket and waistcoat but no collar on his white and blue pin-striped shirt. Black twill trousers and heavy boots completed his dress.

Sylvester in some ways resembled the constable except that he was a pale, beardless, and slender youth, who, Seamus guessed, had not yet reached his twenties. He was dressed in a fashion similar to that of the Constable, with the exception that he wore a broad-brimmed hat of yellow straw. He was tall but stoop-shouldered and his mouth seemed to hang open constantly, allowing him an orifice through which to breathe other than his large, bent and apparently non-functioning nose. The open-mouthed arrangement also afforded one an excellent view of Sylvester's protruding upper teeth.

He nodded acknowledgment and uttered a nasal; "Mornin'," upon being introduced.

"Sorry for the state of our attire, Mr.Beecher," said the Constable, "but Sampson found us on the road along the creek, half-way to Haine's Corners. That's how we got here so fast. We were on our way to go fishing. He said we better come right along and so we did."

Mr. Beecher described to the Constable the events of the morning, while the agent of the law listened responding with an occasional shake of the head or a discreet 'tsk' through pursed lips.

Luther then told his story, including his confrontation with

Clay on the night before.

When he had heard all that was to be told, Constable Wyncoop turned to Seamus.

"Well then, Colonel," he said, "I understand that you and the dead man had a fight last night."

Sampson, Seamus could see, had already been at work on the ride here with the Constable laying the ground work for Luther's defense.

Good man, Sampson! thought Seamus.

"It was not much of a fight, but, yes we did have an altercation." he said.

"Do you, Constable," Seamus continued, "see a connection between the altercation of last night and the tragedy of this morning?"

"I see that Luther was not the only one to have had words with Mr. Clay. There might be more than one person who had something against the man, on to it."

On to it? thought Seamus.

"So in theory," he said in response to the Constable's veiled allegation, "I could have had a reason to shoot Mr. Clay. And that would be an excellent theory, except for the fact that I was standing practically next to him when he was shot from behind."

The Constable puzzled the logic of the statement for a moment and then responded.

"Now," said he, "I wasn't making an accusation, I just figured there might be more here than meets the eye, on to it."

On to it? thought Seamus, a local colloquialism, no doubt. The people of these mountains had their own regional dialect. Indeed, Seamus had noticed that on the previous morning below in the little hamlet of Palenville, at the base of the mountain road, the farmers gathered at the toll gate were conferring with one another in what sounded like Low Dutch, and this hundreds of years after the British had taken the Valley from Holland. More power to them, he thought, and to the people of the west of Ireland, as well, where the Irish language was still alive some hundreds of years after the British had made their presence felt there.

The Constable stepped to the bar and stood next to Seamus.

He picked up the pistol.

"I take it," he said, "that this is the revolver which was in Luther's possession at the time of the shooting."

Mr. Beecher nodded.

"I am going to have to keep it as evidence, for the time being." The Constable sounded apologetic.

Mr. Beecher nodded again.

Constable Wyncoop thought for another moment and spoke again.

"Well, I expect we better go and see the body," he said. "Luther, would you please stay here with Sylvester while we go down the hall."

"I will," said Luther, his voice firm.

"Should I get the shotgun from the buggy, Uncle Hump?" said Sylvester.

"No, Sylvester!" said the Constable his face suddenly flaming. "And don't call me Uncle Hump! Luther is not going to give you any trouble, are you Luther? Just stay here with him!"

"My sister's youngest," he muttered to Seamus and then addressed him in full voice.

"Colonel," he said, "if you would please accompany us to the piazza so that you can show me where you were standing when the fatal shot was fired."

Seamus had no desire to view again yet another in the long series of cadavers he had seen in his life, nor did he wish to revisit the killing ground. Nonetheless, he followed the constable, Sampson and Mr. Beecher out the door and into the hall. He looked toward the piazza and back toward the rear entry. It suddenly became apparent to him that Luther was, of a virtual certainty, and despite all appearances, innocent, and that he would rather be the man's defender than his accuser.

The party proceeded to the piazza door with the Constable in the lead. There they were greeted by a team of porters armed with mops, buckets and cleaning rags and a ladder.

"I posted these men here," said Sampson, "to be sure that no one disturbed the scene until the Constable had a chance to see it."

A thickly coagulated stain marked the spot on the porch

floor where the victim's head had come to rest. Flies buzzed in the bright morning air.

Seamus raised his eyes and as his hands began to tremble, thrust them into his pockets. In front of him, a spattered trail of gore ascended the back wall of the exterior staircase. The constellation of blood spots climbed the wall as high as the ceiling, and the ceiling itself had not remained free of stain. A trail of spots, diminishing in size, spread back along the whitewashed boards to a point directly above where Clay had been standing when he had been shot.

All the men on the piazza stood gazing silently upward, transfixed by the devastation which had been wrought by the fatal round.

Seamus broke the spell.

"Yes, well, Constable, he said, "I was standing here, just here, when I heard the shot."

He recounted the details of Clay's murder, as he knew them, and described how he had taken Emily out of the line of fire. He told how he had peeked around the edge of the doorway several times before venturing to the rear entry to confront and disarm Luther.

"So," said the constable, "you didn't really see Luther fire the shot."

"That is right, Constable." said Seamus

The constable nodded.

"We've seen enough here," he said, "let's go into the lounge and see the body."

"The doctor is in there at present, Constable," said Sampson. He asked Mr. Beecher if the porters should commence with the cleaning and his employer agreed that they should.

"I shall see to it personally," said Sampson and he set about assisting one of the men in placing the ladder against the staircase wall.

The party was admitted to the lounge by the porch door. Sunlight flooded in through the tall windows. Dr. Duboise stood wiping his hands on a towel at the far end of the long table. The body, covered by a sheet, lay before him. The victim's highly polished shoes stuck out from the end of the sheet nearest

Seamus and the others. Stacks of magazines; *Harper's, Frank Leslie's,* which usually rested on the table had been transferred to the side tables or were piled on the seats of the wicker arm chairs. The three men joined the doctor at the table.

The dead man's head was outlined beneath the sheet, a brown-red smudge on the white cloth were the right eye would be.

The doctor tossed the towel on the victim's chest and extracted a cigar from a tan pigskin case, inserted the corona-corona in his hooked fingers, struck a lucifer and inhaled deeply. He exhaled with evident relish and with his good hand lifted the sheet.

In unison, and as if by some silent command, both Mr. Beecher and Seamus looked away.

The constable examined the face of the corpse for a moment and signaled for the sheet to be lowered. The doctor dropped it and took another inhale of his cigar.

"Well, doctor," said the constable, "what can you tell us?"

"Little more than the obvious, Humphrey," replied the doctor, squinting in the smoke of his cigar. "The man was shot from a distance; no powder burns around the wound. He was shot with a firearm of about .44 or possibly .45 caliber, surely no smaller. My examination has, of course been cursory, and I would not be held to my results without a full postmortem, but as best as I can see, the ball, or perhaps an actual conical bullet, entered the cranium approximately in the region of the left occipital squama."

The doctor paused, glanced at Humphrey and saw that he was lost in the Latin.

"More or less behind the left ear," he continued. "The projectile apparently transited the left cerebellum and most likely the medulla oblongata. It exited the cranium in the region of the juncture of the right maxilla and the right frontal zygomatic process causing a protrusion, as you saw Humphrey, of the right eyeball. I noticed that the exit wound was not directly in line with the entry wound and I would attribute that to the likelihood that the head, at the instant the shot was fired, was inclined downward slightly and turned a few degrees to the left."

Seamus thought of the last words Clay was ever to hear; the good dominie's voice intoning; "Let us bow our heads in prayer."

"And," said the doctor," there was most likely some deflection of the bullet within and upon exit of the skull case."

"So the bullet did not stay in the body." said the constable.

"No indeed," said the doctor, "and this is why I postulate that the projectile in question may have been a conical bullet. I am expert neither in physics nor ballistics, but I have a vast wealth of experience with gunshot wounds and usually a conical bullet or elongated ball, such as the minnie ball, will develop more energy in a rifled bore than will a round ball. That at least is my assumption, because I have found that generally a conical bullet will create a more penetrating wound. This is one of the reasons why all the world is going over to the conical bullet. Of course, matters of range, the size of the powder charge and so forth are all variable factors, but in this case I had the feeling, however unscientific, that I was looking at the work of a conical bullet."

The constable pulled the Dragoon pistol from his belt, rotated the cylinder and looked into the remaining loaded chambers, each was packed with grease. He took a pen knife out of his pocket and dug away the grease in one of the chambers. He closed one eye, peered into the chamber, and then removed the grease from the other unfired chambers. He wiped his knife on the towel on the victim's chest and showed the pistol around, chambers upward, to the others. Each chamber was loaded with a conical bullet.

He read aloud the inscription stamped on the barrel of the weapon; "Colt's Patent, .44 Caliber."

"And the whereabouts of the fatal bullet?" he asked the doctor.

"God knows." the doctor replied. "Given where the deceased was standing and the fact that the projectile passed entirely through his head, the bullet, which it seems to me was likely still traveling at great velocity, must have cleared the short distance to the ledge and beyond and now probably rests somewhere far below in the forest on the slope of the mountain."

"Conical bullets for pistols is kind of a new idea, especially for this neck of the woods," said the constable. "I wonder if there is another pistol in the county loaded with such bullets?"

"Well, perhaps," said Mr. Beecher. "My gunsmith is Mr. Ishmael Phaestus of Kiskatom, down in the valley, with whom I know you are acquainted, Humphrey. When I brought to him my problem of preparing my staff against malefactors, he recommended the use of such bullets for the very reasons which the doctor has enumerated and in fact he sold me the bullets, the powder and the pistol itself."

"Maybe he'll be able to help us in this investigation," said the constable. "In the meantime, can we think of any others who could be considered witnesses; anyone else I can question this morning?"

"Mr. McCain," said Mr. Beecher, "is . . . was . . . Mr. Clay's business associate and was traveling with him. He was standing with Mr. Clay when the poor man was shot and Mrs. Clay was also standing next to her husband at the time, but I should not care to disturb her at the moment. The Reverend and his wife were also near as was Professor Smith. I recall seeing Mr. Tompkins at Mr. Clay's side as he lay prostrate on the floor. There were many others on the piazza and some may have had a view of the tragic happening, but we must remember that most, if not all, were facing away from the doorway toward the dominie and the rising sun. Few would have seen what happened until after it had already happened."

"I can't really order anyone to stay," said the constable, "and I understand that some guests have begun to leave, but I would appreciate your spreading the word, Mr. Beecher, among your guests that if any of them have any information regarding this incident, I am asking that they remain here until an inquest can be held. Of those you mentioned, where can they be found now?"

"I take it," the doctor interjected, "that Mr. McCain is the tall man with the long white hair. He and Mr. Tompkins, the whiskey drummer helped carry the body in here. That is Tompkins tried to help, but I fear it was more than he could stand. He was white as a ghost and begged off as we were lifting the corpse. He gagged and limped away clutching at his liver as if he had sampled too much of his own merchandise last night. He hobbled to the edge of the piazza, took a few deep breaths and said that he needed to go to his room. After we brought the body in here, he went into the lobby. He seemed to be so distressed that I even stepped into the lobby to see if he might need medical assistance himself. The last I saw him he was struggling up the steps. Mr. McCain said he also would go to his room, but he, on the other hand, seemed to be calm and in full possession of himself. Neither was the Professor, who also helped with the body, in any way disturbed by the experience. When we were done, he stated that he would go and get some *breakfast!* One could certainly tell the veterans from those who had never served." The doctor smiled a wry smile.

"I believe," he continued, "that the dominie's wife, in whose charge the Colonel placed the victim's wife after the shooting, accompanied Mrs. Clay to her room. The Reverend himself performed the Last Rights for the deceased here and then went to join the ladies in Mrs. Clay's room. I expect that he and they are still there."

"Humphrey," said Mr. Beecher, "how soon will it be before an inquest can be held? I shall have to know because the guests will certainly ask."

"That's the problem, on to it," replied the constable, "Judge Livingston is not in Catskill. He left last night for a fishing trip to the Adirondack Mountains."

"Well," said Mr. Beecher, "surely the county coroner could hold a preliminary inquiry without the presence of the judge."

"He could, Mr. Beecher, indeed he could, except that he has gone with the judge on his fishing trip, along with Sheriff Cass."

There was silence in the room for a long moment, and then the constable continued with apparent reluctance.

"And," he said, "that's another problem, on to it. The way things stand, Mr. Beecher, I am going to have no choice but to charge Luther with the murder of Mr. Clay and take him into custody. I do not want to lodge him in the county jail at Catskill because with these guests leaving here and traveling through Catskill, the story is bound to get out that a black man killed a white man. There is enough riffraff around the docks down in the town to make a nasty mob, especially on a Saturday night. With the sheriff away, I just do not think Luther will be safe in the jail. I have no place to incarcerate anyone here on the mountain top. Usually, all I have to take into custody are drunks who get into brawls at Brenner's Saloon and then I just shackle them to a stall in my stable until they sober up. It would not be hard for some of the lay-abouts up here on the mountain to form a mob either, my house is very close at hand to the low characters of Haines Corners and Tannersville, and again with only Sylvester and myself to defend him, I fear for Luther's safety. I have known Luther a long time and I don't want to believe that he did this . . . by thunder! . . . I don't believe it! But I am an officer of the law, on to it, and with all the evidence I have seen pointing to him, well I just don't know what else I can do. I must take him into custody but then I 'll be responsible for his safety until justice can be done and I am not sure if I can protect him."

The constable appeared to be genuinely miserable.

Mr. Beecher appeared to be in a like state of mind. He thought a moment and then brightened.

"Would it be acceptable," he said, "to keep Luther under arrest here on the Mountain House property?"

The constable considered very briefly.

"I think I can approve that arrangement," he said, "He will really have to be secured and under guard though, both for his own protection and in order to be within the requirements of the law."

"How would it be," said Mr. Beecher, "if he were to stay in one of the root cellars. The cellars are sturdy; stone built. He would be cool during the day and we could supply him with blankets at night. A padlock could be applied to the door if necessary."

"Yes, a lock would be necessary and Sylvester and I could guard him in shifts until the judge can be recalled from his trip. Sylvester will have to take the first shift as I must go to Catskill and report to the deputy sheriff what has happened and see if I can recruit some deputies to help us. We must also make arrangements to contact the judge and have him return as soon as possible."

"We can use the telegraph machine in the front office here to communicate with my office in Catskill," said Mr. Beecher. "That is our private wire, but my office in the town is right down the street from the Western Union office and will be able to relay our messages. From there, we should be able to reach the judge wherever he may be. With Mr. Field's impending completion of the Atlantic Cable, we could reach him were he in Europe."

"Might I suggest, gentlemen," said Seamus, "that we maintain secrecy about these communications as they leave here and as best we may when they are relayed in Catskill. I will speak frankly, Mr. Beecher, we should not let any who may wish to do harm know of Luther's circumstances, nor the progress of the constable's work, nor the movements of the judge, nor of any of the principals in this matter."

All present nodded in agreement.

"Mr. Twilling," said Mr. Beecher, "who is our telegrapher, as well as day desk clerk, will, I am sure, use the greatest discretion."

Seamus had his doubts about Mr. Twilling, but said nothing. Am I still angry with that man, he asked himself in his mind. Yes, came the answer, I am.

Sampson entered from the porch and approached his employer.

"Excuse me, Mr. Beecher," he said, "but Rolf has just sent down the porter, young Terwilliger, who was helping him with the morning cleaning, with the news that Major Savage has come to the barroom and demanded to be served even though the bar is not yet open for business. Rolf has given the gentleman a drink of brandy, but he asks that you come along as soon as convenient because of the awkwardness of the situation with Luther and Sylvester there . . . sir . . . a . . .," Sampson ran out of words at about the time Mr. Beecher was ready to reply.

"Oh my," he said, "the Major's behavior can be most vexing!" He stroked his white beard nervously and shook his head. He looked to the constable.

"Should we go back to the bar then?"

"Yes, sir," the constable replied. "I want to speak with Major Savage anyhow."

Mr. Beecher ascertained from the doctor that his work with the body was finished, at least for the time being, and he instructed Sampson to have the corpse removed to the ice house.

Mr. Beecher and the constable then lead Seamus and the doctor out of the lounge through the hall door.

"I am astounded," said the doctor quietly to Seamus, "that Savage is awake at this hour. He must have the constitution of an ox, despite his consumptive condition. I gave him a hefty dosage of laudanum last night once we got him to his room. What time is it now?"

He reached for his watch, fumbled it, and it fell the length of its chain and then fell off the chain and onto the thickly carpeted floor.

"Damn!" said the doctor.

Seamus quickly stooped to retrieve the time piece and in picking it up felt that the carpet was damp. In the slanting light from the lobby further down the hall, Seamus saw that the rich turkey red rug showed faint spots of dampness traveling across the hall from the door of the lounge to one of the hotel rooms. He looked up to the brass numeral on the door. Room number four, he read.

"No harm done," said Seamus. He rose and held the doctor's watch out to him.

The case of the watch was embossed with a shield on which appeared the image of a human right hand, the palm outward. The Red Hand of the Irish province of Ulster, Seamus thought. The shield was surrounded by the words 'Ulster Guard' and 'N.Y. Vols.'

"So," said Seamus, "you too are a veteran, sir."

"Yes, Colonel," said the doctor," a rather old one. But when the war came and the boys of Ulster county were all joining the regiment it occurred to me that I had delivered about half of them at birth and cared for most of them as they were growing up, at least those from Saugerties township, so I felt obligated to do my best to see them through the dangers they were then facing. I signed on as assistant regimental surgeon.

"I was working in the field hospital behind Meade's headquarters at Gettysburg, working on a head wound as a matter of fact, on the third of July, when General Lee's batteries opened up. A bit of case shot went through this," he held up the claw that had been his right hand, "and cut short my budding career in surgery. No matter, I always preferred general practice anyhow."

He thanked Seamus for rescuing his watch, clenched his cigar in his teeth, deftly returned the watch to its chain with his left hand, and opened the case.

"Sixteen minutes past nine." he read.

Mr. Beecher and the constable, unaware of the mishap with the watch, had proceeded to the lobby and now stood by the staircase, where Seamus and the doctor hastened to join them. The party reassembled and all turned to the hallway and headed toward the barroom. At the end of the hall, framed in the doorway of the back entrance stood a black man. Seamus kept his eyes fixed on the man as he walked along with the others, and as he grew closer he could see that the man was Scipio. He was attired as he had been the night before; his cavalry jacket spotless, his shoes and buttons gleaming in the sun-filled passage. He regarded the approach of the party with neither expression nor acknowledgment. He seemed to gaze through them.

They entered the bar and found the Major lounging in a chair at the table by the piano, below the framed flag; the very chair which Clay had occupied on the previous evening. His back was to the wall and he was fully dressed, except that his feet, propped on a chair in front of him, were clad only in carpet slippers. He wore no stockings, and his bare, knobby ankles protruded from the cuffs of his trousers. The skin was purple and ridged with interlaced scars.

"Good morning!" he said in raucous tones. "Good morning, gentlemen! And good morning to you too, doctor, as you can see I have survived your ministrations of last night."

The doctor did not rise to the bait of the double insult.

The Major appeared to be in the very best of good humor.

Rolf, on the other hand looked miserable. He stood behind the bar wearing an expression which combined embarrassment and exasperation.

"I understand," the Major continued in full voice, "that we have dispensed with that fine example of Sesech manhood to whom I made my proposal this past evening. More's the pity. I would have preferred to have met with him myself, but if it happens to have fallen to a brave son of Africa to have the honor of dispatching that worm to join his fellow worms, well so be it." He lifted his glass in the direction of Luther in his seat by the door. Luther was not rising to any bait either.

The constable stepped forward.

"Major," he said, "I am Constable Wyncoop, I would like to speak to you about your conversation with the deceased last night, on to it."

"Pleased to make your acquaintance Constable, I suspect that you know as much about what transpired in this room last night as do I. Put simply, the late lamented deceased was, I found, rather offensive. I offered to take his life, in a fair contest to be sure, and he, not surprisingly, coward that he was, declined . . . on to it."

A look of irritation crossed the constable's ruddy features.

"Can you tell me of your movements at the time of the murder," Humphrey managed to get out before the Major interrupted.

"My movements, if any, took place within the sweet embrace of Morpheus. I was sound asleep until about one-half hour ago when I found it necessary to arise and come here for a portion of medicinal stimulant."

"Do you have," said the constable, his tone becoming increasingly officious, "either on your person or in your property at this hotel, a firearm."

"I do indeed, Constable," the Major responded a broad smile on his pinched face, "it is a souvenir of the late War of the Rebellion. It is a rebel Dance Brothers revolver of Texas manufacture, and there is an engaging story goes with it.

"When captured, I was at first put in Andersonville even though I was an officer. It was my Southern brethren's way of telling me that I was not, in their august appraisal, a 'gentleman'. Later, I was transferred from Andersonville to another prison where I was eventually liberated by our army. On the morning of my deliverance from that prison, I was being carried out of the front gate on a litter, and they had some of the rebels who had been our hosts lined up to bid us *adieu.* I asked the bearers to halt when we came abreast of a bright young lieutenant, who, while we had been at Andersonville, had taken particular delight in delivering the *coup de grace* to those prisoners who were wounded by the guards in escape attempts. I asked if his pistol had been taken and I was informed that it had been. I asked one of my liberators if I could have it as a memento. The weapon was produced and was given to me as I lay flat on my back on the litter and I promptly cocked it and shot the young lieutenant in the belly. He died late the next day, which was about what I had in mind when I shot him. It was the very pistol, don't you see, which he had used to finish off our poor boys. Do you see the perfect symmetry of it?"

The Major smiled even more broadly with his death's head grin.

Madman, thought Seamus.

The constable went pale.

"But that was murder!" he said.

"Was it?" said the Major. He seemed honestly puzzled. "The war was still on, as indeed it still officially is at this very moment."
His smile diminished only slightly.

"Sir," said Humphrey, "shooting an unarmed prisoner, whether in time of war or not, is murder."

"It is?" said the Major. "Oh, well, no one thought to charge me with murder, so I suppose it was not. My valiant liberators were all very shocked at my behavior, wanted to take the pistol away from me, but they could not. I had cocked it again and told them I would shoot them too. I kept it until I got to the hospital.

"Once there, a doctor wanted to cut off my feet. They had festered because I had been kept in irons all the time. I told the doctor that I would shoot him too if he tried to cut off my feet."

Major Savage paused and looked directly at Doctor Duboise.

"I did faint eventually," he went on, "and they got the pistol away from me, but I must have frightened the doctor, because, as you can see, he did not amputate my feet. Instead, he treated them with caustics over a long period of time. Painful, but effective. Really it was Scipio who saved me."

The Major was silent, his eyes grew moist. At length he continued.

"When he took me out of the hospital, they had to return the pistol to me."

"Of what caliber is that pistol Major?" the constable inquired off-handedly.

Savage's eyes narrowed.

"Do I stand accused of this murder?" he asked.

"No, sir," said Humphrey, "you do not. But if you would cooperate with this investigation it would be appreciated. Would you be willing to show us the pistol?"

"No, I would not. I am a gentleman and if my word is not good enough, too bad. And I know the law too. I was reading for the law in Virginia before I started my illustrious military career. Even after I had begun my life's work in Missouri and Kansas, I returned to the practice of law to help prepare the briefs for the defense of John Brown at Charlestown. John Brown . . . John Brown . . . hanged for treason against the sovereign commonwealth of Virginia. That was when I yet hoped that the world could be changed by democracies and courts. His execution, his murder more accurately, proved that mine was a vain hope. The world cannot be changed by such means, you know. The only truth is that which issues forth from the cannon's mouth.

"The war was the thing," the Major's eyes were distant, glittering, "the war, so right, so pure, so beautiful, but the fighting ended too soon, ended before all secessionist slavers could be wiped out . . . " He eased into a deep, rumbling fit of coughing.

Savage drank off his brandy, stopped coughing abruptly and stood up. He took his glass and the decanter from the table and limped to the door. He turned and addressed all in the room.

"Do you know how I got the pistol back from the superintendent of the hospital? I threatened to bring suit against him!"

The Major laughed heartily.

"Here the man had just been through a war and he was afraid of my bringing a lawsuit against him!" He laughed again and coughed deeply. When he recovered himself, he continued.

"And so, Constable, I bid you good day. And if you want to look at my war souvenir, you may get yourself a search warrant. Or attempt to, for I will fight you in court. 'Fight you in court', as if a court action really is a fight."

The Major left the room roaring with laughter. His laughter could be heard diminishing down the hall. After a time, deep coughing could be heard far off, and then more laughing.

Silence reigned in the barroom for a full minute after his departure.

Rolf said, in an absent way, "There's your murderer, Humphrey."

"If I only had some kind of evidence," said Humphrey in an equally absent way.

All in the room were still gazing at the door through which the Major had left.

"But I don't have any evidence against the Major, on to it," said the constable with finality. He turned toward Luther.

"Luther, I'm afraid that I am going to have to charge you with the murder of one Fenton Clay, at this hotel, this morning between five o'clock and half-past five. I have spoken to Mr. Beecher and agreed that you will be kept under guard here on the property until the judge can hold a hearing and the coroner an inquest. I'm sorry to have to do this Luther, but it is my duty."

"I understand what duty is, Humphrey." said Luther. He appeared serene.

The constable spoke to Mr. Beecher.

"Could you, sir," he said, "have this Mr. McCain sent for so that I may talk to him before I go to Catskill."

Mr. Beecher asked Rolf to cross the hall and so instruct Mr. Twilling.

When Rolf returned the constable went on.

"Luther," he said, "I hope you understand; you were seen at the end of the hall right after the shooting holding a pistol which had been discharged. Now, I know you said you fired to chase off a bear earlier in the morning, but is there anyone could back up your story, did anybody hear the shot, onto it?"

There was no response.

Then Seamus said, "I did . . . onto it."

All heads turned toward the speaker.

"I beg your pardon, Colonel." said Humphrey Wyncoop.

"At about four o'clock this morning," said Seamus, "I heard a single shot far down the side of the mountain, probably coming from the road at about where Luther said he fired. In fact, I believe the shot actually awakened me from sleep." Seamus looked directly at Luther as he made his statement to the constable.

"Well," said Humphrey, "that is interesting, but it doesn't change what I must do for the moment. We will have to ask others if they also heard the shot at that time. With all due respect Colonel, your testimony will need corroboration, as the judge always says. Speaking of the judge we can't afford to loose any time in contacting him and his party and telling them that they have to return as soon as possible. As far as I know, the first leg of their journey was to take them north to a hotel in Albany. I believe they were to travel on one of your steamboats, Mr. Beecher. From Albany they were going to Whitehall by coach and staying at a lodge. Then they were taking a Lake Champlain steamer still further north and spending the rest of the week traveling by canoe and fishing the upper Hudson River and the Adirondack lakes and steams with a guide. If we don't catch them with a telegraph message either to Albany or at Whitehall, there will have to be riders sent out to locate them and Heaven alone knows how long that may take, so we must not tarry."

"If they booked aboard my Friday night boat to Albany," said Mr. Beecher, "we will have a record in Catskill as to which hotel their baggage was forwarded. And if they went to Whitehall via coach, they traveled on one of my coaches, and again we will be able to trace them. Knowing the judge as I do, I would say they most likely stayed at either the Phoenix House or the Clinton House. As you say, Humphrey, we must not tarry, but must attempt to notify them before they enter the wilderness."

With that the constable, Mr. Beecher, Doctor Duboise and

Seamus crossed the hall and caught the flappable Mr. Twilling in the midst of arranging transport down the mountain for a group of guests who were plainly in a great hurry to depart the site of the morning's murderous occurrence.

Mr. Twilling was directing his shrill, excited voice at one of the porters, when Mr. Beecher cut him off in mid-tirade and peremptorily advised him that he must now don his telegrapher's hat. The clerk appeared pained, but nonetheless, all crowded into the small office behind the front desk, and Mr. Twilling unlocked the cabinet in which was housed the electric telegraph.

Mr. Beecher dictated exactly what was to be sent and also informed the clerk of the importance of secrecy in the traffic of the messages to and from Catskill regarding the matter in question.

After making what appeared to Seamus to be a great show of preparing the telegraph machine to transmit, Mr. Twilling began to send the message as instructed. Seamus figured that he could do a quicker and better job of it himself, but did not say so. The slight aroma of the acid in the batteries on the top shelf of the cabinet reminded him of the hours he had spent in the telegraph wagons of the Army of the Potomac.

Once the message had been sent, the party returned to the barroom. As they crossed the hall the doctor spoke to Seamus in a low voice.

"I could have done a quicker and better job of telegraphing that message myself." he said.

In the barroom, the constable detailed to Sylvester his duties for the next several hours. The constable, Mr. Beecher, and the deputy then left the bar and accompanied Luther to his prison in the root cellar.

Seamus had no desire to see anyone imprisoned in any way, especially not a man whom he considered to be innocent of the charges against him. He therefore stayed in the bar with the doctor and Rolf and young Terwilliger. The skinny, tow-headed youth had returned from the piazza and resumed assisting Rolf with the cleaning by polishing the brass spittoon at the end of the bar near the door to the central hall.

"Rolf," said the doctor wearily, "is the bar still closed?'

"Doctor," said Rolf, "if I must perforce serve a raving lunatic like my first customer, then I willingly and happily serve a decent man such as yourself."

He poured a large tumbler of brandy and the doctor smiled brightly.

The thought of strong drink crossed Seamus mind as well. He let the thought keep crossing however, and opted instead for a cup of now tepid coffee from the pot still set on the center of the bar. It occurred to him that his morning drinker's malaise had left him entirely and that he had missed breakfast and was hungry. He took a sweet roll and then another and another from the tray and crossed the room to join the doctor who had left the bar and was sitting and savoring his brandy in the chair just vacated by Luther.

Seamus sat next to the doctor and ate his sweet roll and thought how excitement was as a good a cure for the effects of a night's drinking as was road work. It had happened before. On some occasions in camp during the war the early morning sound of the drummer's long roll, and of the bugler's *officer's call*, followed by the shriek and boom of in-bound shot and shell would literally snap one right out of the physical and mental doldrums which had resulted from an evening of comradely carousing.

The rising of the blood must clear the system, he thought. Of course, the cure could be an expensive one.

"Well," said the doctor to no one in particular, "I have known Luther and known him for a very long time, and I would never expect him to shoot someone from behind. It is simply not in the man's character to do so. Savage would, in my view, rather more likely be the man for that kind of work. There again, however, it would seem that last night he was offering to Clay a challenge for a fair fight. His account of his exit from the rebel prison, though, if true, would indicate that his hate has twisted him so as to make him capable of anything."

The doctor took a sip of his brandy and then went on.

"The factor which clears him of the murder of Clay, I think, is that which I know at first hand, and that is that last night, after Scipio and I got him to his room, I administered to the Major a dosage of laudanum calculated to make him sleep until about noontime today. I still cannot see how he was awake and in the barroom this morning even at nine o'clock, let alone at the very crack of dawn when Clay was killed."

The doctor shook his head and Seamus devoured his last sweet roll and pondered whether or not it would appear gluttonous of him to go to the bar and take two or three more. He decided that it would, and so kept his seat.

"I am surprised that the Major had already run out of medicine."

This unsolicited comment came from the young Terwilliger as he rose. He had polished the cuspidor to a high gloss.

"Mind your own business!" said Rolf to the lad, his complexion igniting. "Don't be butting into the doctor's conversation and get on about filling the lamps!"

"No, Rolf," said Doctor Duboise," let the young man speak. Tell me son, what medicine do you mean?"

"Why, that laudinium, doctor." said young Terwilliger, his big innocent green eyes opening wide.

"Laudanum," the doctor corrected.

"Right, sir. The stuff you have been speaking about. I was surprised to hear you say that you had to give the Major some, because I went to the pharmacy in Tannersville and got him his week's supply on Thursday, just like I did on the Thursday before. Major Savage gave me two bits to go to the store for him and the money to buy that medicine this past Thursday and I would not of thought that he would use up the whole quart bottle by Friday night, sir."

"And you are sure, son that it was laudanum you got for the Major," the doctor asked.

"Oh, yes, sir, I read real good, and the bottle is marked laudinium, I mean laudanum, and under that the label says; 'Tinct. Opium' and under that; 'E.R.Durkee Inc., New York.' Anyhow, sorry to interrupt, sir, but it having to do with medicine and you being a doctor and all, I thought you knew that the Major had his own supply."

"No need to apologize, my boy," said the doctor, "you have done very well. Yes it is a matter of the Major's health and you have done the right thing. I thank you for your concern, you need not tell the Major that we have had this little talk. I will consult with him about his dosage of the medicine."

Young Terwilliger smiled and turned to the casino end of the barroom where he began filling the lamps.

The doctor turned to Seamus and whispered.

"There you have it; the Soldier's Sickness, I should have thought of it, given the patient's military record. I estimated what I thought was a correct dosage based upon the Major's apparent height and weight, his tubercular condition and the fact that he had been drinking, as well as upon the assumption that he had probably not been eating very well, if at all. I never thought to include in my equation the possibility that he, like so many of our poor young veterans who were wounded in the war, may have come away from the service with an addiction to opiates. If he is habituated to taking laudanum in the quantities described by our young friend here, his system has almost certainly developed a resistance to the effects of the drug and my dosage of him last night may have had little or no effect on him with regard to inducing sleep. He may well have been capable of physical activity at an early hour this morning."

Seamus responded in a whisper also.

"To paraphrase the good constable," he said, "that is very interesting, onto it, but it was Luther, who I saw at the end of the hall after the fatal shot was fired, would that I had not, and he standing there armed with a pistol. Any number of people, opium addicts or not, may have been up and about at that hour, but Luther was the man in the place and at the time. We must think about what can be proven in court under the rules of evidence. Being physically capable of firing a revolver, and indeed being a homicidal maniac, are conditions which do not, in and of themselves, prove that a particular individual is guilty of a particular murder."

After a pause Seamus concluded.

"Still and all," he said, "it is something to think on."

Having decided not to continue eating rolls, Seamus extracted his cigar case from his inside coat pocket, took out his morning cigar and lit it. He sat smoking in pensive silence.

In a few minutes, Mr. Beecher returned to the barroom and took a seat at the table with the doctor and Seamus. He appeared drawn.

"The constable," he said, "has departed for Catskill after Mr. Twilling sent word with a porter that Mr. McCain was not in his room and had not been located anywhere in the hotel. Humphrey said that he hoped that Mr. McCain would stay on until the inquest or hearing could be held and that he would interview the gentleman upon his return from Catskill, but that he must hurry down and report this matter to the deputy sheriff in person. He said that he would see about securing a search warrant or more likely, an order to produce, regarding the Major's pistol, but that he was at a loss as to how to obtain such a document in the absence of the judge who grants such processes.

"Luther, sad to say, is ensconced in the root cellar on the north side to the rear of this house under guard of Sylvester. By the way, Colonel, Luther asked if you would come to see him at your earliest convenience."

Seamus stood and said, "My earliest convenience is right now, sir."

He walked to the door and, as he was about to exit, the door opened and Sampson came in. He looked, if possible, even more serious than usual, and he spoke to his employer.

"Mr. Beecher," he said, "would you please come with us to the piazza, we have made a discovery."

Mr. Beecher rose and turned to the doctor and Seamus.

"Please join us, gentlemen," he said.

"Uh, sir," said Sampson speaking to Mr. Beecher and looking straight at Seamus. Words were not necessary; Sampson did not want Seamus to accompany them to the piazza.

"Sampson," said Mr. Beecher, "Colonel Delaney is on our side."

Sampson appeared not to believe this, but neither was he inclined to argue. The four men went to the piazza together.

The place were Clay had fallen had returned largely to normal. All traces of gore had been removed from the floor boards, and most of the back wall of the staircase had been cleaned. The porters had arranged some of the porch furniture as a barricade to the left and to the right to keep the curious at bay and out of their way while they worked. The few guests now on the lower piazza had taken the hint and had situated themselves at the farthest ends. Occasionally, a surreptitious glimpse would be stolen from a distance.

One of the porters was perched on a ladder propped against the wall of the staircase. Sampson pointed up past the porter, and the man placed his finger below a spot at the very top of the whitewashed wall where it joined the ceiling.

"Do you," said Sampson, "see where Jacob is pointing, sir?"

"Yes," said Mr. Beecher, "that blood spot."

"That is the place, sir, but that is not a blood spot. I thought it was too, so did Jacob there, but as much as he scrubbed at it would not come clean. What it is, sir, is a hole."

"A hole," said Seamus, "a bullet hole."

"Allow me," he said and quickly replaced Jacob on the ladder. He climbed as high as he could so that his head was touching the ceiling. He could feel, through the top of his head, the footsteps of strollers on the upper piazza. He placed his face into the angle formed by the wall and the ceiling and saw that the spot was indeed a hole; black, round and deep. It seemed in size to be of .44 caliber, or possibly .45 caliber, certainly no smaller. Seamus put the tip of his little finger into the hole and puffed the cigar which he had clenched in his teeth. He took it out of his mouth and blew on the glowing end to provide a light source which he then held up to the hole. A metallic spark glowed amber in the reflecting light about three inches deep into the hole. He spoke quietly to those below him.

"I believe there is a bullet wedged in the hole. The heavy beam behind the top step must have stopped it. I am going to dig it out and I want you all to witness this."

Seamus again clenched his cigar in his teeth, took his folding knife from his pocket and began to carefully cut the wood away from the edges of the bullet hole.
He worked carefully and after several minutes was able to free the bullet from the surrounding wood.

He held the silver-gray lump in the palm of his hand. It was a conical bullet, the point now flattened. The striations of the rifling grooves in the bore of the weapon from which it had been fired were clearly embedded along the sides of the cylindrical missile.

Seamus descended the ladder, the others gathered around him in a tight circle, and he displayed his find to them.

"The bullet," said the doctor, "in passing through the cranium, must have been deflected as much as forty-five degrees up and to the right." He looked up at the hole and then back at the bullet.

"We should all keep this discovery secret." said Seamus, and all murmured their ascent.

"Too bad the constable is gone," said Mr. Beecher, "I could send someone after him . . ."

"No, sir," said Seamus, "he has enough to do. Can we speak someplace where there is more privacy?"

"My office," said Mr. Beecher.

Sampson instructed the porters to complete their work and admonished them to keep quiet about what had just happened. He joined Seamus, the doctor, and Mr.Beecher as they entered the lobby, turned right and started to ascend the left side of the oval staircase. Seamus slid his hand along the banister, which followed the curving wall, felt an oily substance on the wood, took his hand away and found his fingers smeared with thickened blood.

He called the attention of the others to the blood on the railing, while he wiped his hand on his handkerchief. Sampson produced a cleaning cloth and ran it along the banister as they continued to mount the stairs.

"That," said the doctor, "may have been Tompkins who left the blood stains there. As I told you, he had attempted to help with the body and I recall he lifted the victim's head from the porch floor, he could have gotten blood on his hand. The last I saw him he was going up these steps, leaning heavily on the banister here and dragging his bad leg."

At the second floor landing, Sampson found another spot of blood and wiped it up. Killing, thought Seamus, always creates such a terrible mess.

The party continued to the third floor and then turned into

the corridor in the north wing. They walked to the very end of the wing, passing numbered rooms on both sides. Mr. Beecher stopped at the last door on the right, unlocked it and entered. He welcomed the others into his office which proved to a spacious corner room with high windows facing both north and east. Two normal sized rooms had been combined to make the large chamber and a door centering the south wall gave Seamus to believe that a bedroom lay beyond. A partners desk was situated in the middle of the room at which Mr. Beecher seated himself after motioning the others to the cluster of captain's chairs opposite.

Seamus sat and looked at the bullet in his hand. There was something odd, yet familiar about it. What? he wondered. He studied it a bit longer and then passed it to Doctor Duboise.

"That could have done the job all right." said the physician, and he passed the bullet to Sampson.

"It seems different in some way," he said, "from the bullets that were loaded in Mr. Beecher's pistol, but that may be because of the nose being flattened."

Sampson, in turn, passed the bullet to Mr. Beecher, who looked at it and set on the desk.

"I confess," said Mr. Beecher," that I know but little of firearms. I left the whole matter of providing the weapon and the training of the staff in its use to Mr. Phaestus. He instructed them at his shop down in Kiskatom. Sampson here was one of those who were trained, as he sometimes took over Luther's duties as principal driver."

Mr. Beecher was silent for a moment and then went on.

"Gentlemen," he said, "I am very worried about the ramifications of what happened here this morning. Someone killed Mr. Clay and I am certain it was not Luther. I have faith that an inquest or a hearing or even a trial, should the matter go that far, will prove Luther innocent, however, I fear that mob violence may occur long before the legal process can be brought into play.

"I have no idea of how we can defend Luther from such violence as may be visited upon us by twenty or fifty or a hundred of the local 'element' and so I think we must do all in our power to find out who really committed this crime and expose the true murderer as soon as possible.

"To that end, I will ask each of you to cooperate with each other to the fullest. I ask you Doctor because you are my old and good friend and likewise a friend to Luther.

"Sampson, I do not have to tell you why I need your help, but I want you to know that Luther asked me to tell you that he had the fullest faith in Colonel Delaney's intentions and that you should work with the Colonel to discover the truth of this matter.

"Colonel, I ask your help because I feel that your special talents will be of the utmost importance in our efforts in these next hours and days."

By way of reply, Seamus almost inquired as to what the good man knew of his 'special talents' and, for that matter, why it was that he was Mr. Beecher's 'special guest'
at the hotel. Instead, Seamus told his host that he would help in any way he could.

"Thank you, Colonel," said Mr. Beecher, "I knew that I could rely on you. And again, I must emphasize my concern that we work as quickly as we may.

"This is a great nation, and the people herein equally capable of greatness, but when matters of race arise, it seems that sanity often departs them. If what occurred in the hallway this morning immediately after the shooting can be taken as an example of how the more educated and refined strata of society can react when confronted by what appears to be an inter-racial killing, I dread what may befall us when the idlers and ne'er-do-wells of the surrounding towns make up their collective 'mind' that they must avenge their race."

Seamus, although he preferred not to, could not help but recall what had happened in New York City only three years before, almost to the day. Then too, many of his fellow Irishmen, forgetting their own history of persecution, and while their brothers were covering themselves in grim glory at Gettysburg, joined in an orgy of hate and violence directed at the black people of Manhattan. The rioting spanned a week and included the burning of the African Orphanage and the hanging of black men from lamp posts. Some of the Irish, God forgive them, thought Seamus, who still sought respectable citizenship for themselves and decent treatment in this country would deny even life to those unfortunate people. What came to be called the Draft Riots were still a sore point for Seamus.

"I believe," he said," that this bullet could be the key to the question of who shot Clay. Sampson just said that it looks different from those which were loaded in the pistol. The constable took the pistol with him, of course, but do you have here any of the other bullets which you got from your gunsmith to which we can compare this bullet?"

"Yes," said Mr. Beecher, "Mr. Phaestus gave me a pouch of bullets and a flask of powder as well as a tin of percussion caps with which to reload as necessary."

He unlocked a drawer in his desk and withdrew a leather pouch. He opened the pouch and spilled the contents on the desk. About two dozen round, .44 caliber balls rolled out of the upturned pouch.

"But, I thought the pistol had been loaded with conical bullets." said the doctor.

"I think I can explain," said Sampson. "When Mr. Phaestus had us down at his place in the spring, he had us practice loading and shooting with conical bullets. At the end of the day, he realized that we had used up just about his entire supply of conical bullets, save seven. And so he loaded the six chambers with the last of the conicals and gave Luther the pouch filled with round balls and the one odd, left-over conical that he had handy. He said that he would cast another batch of conicals the following week, but in the meantime, we would be able to use the round balls to reload if we had to and it was better than having no ammunition at all. It is not like we have done any shooting since then and nobody remembered to go down and get a new supply of conical bullets from Mr. Phaestus.

"When Luther had to reload the one chamber after he fired over the bear last month, he must have used the one remaining conical in the pouch since it was the best ammunition available."

"Mr. Phaestus may or may not be able to tell whether or not he molded this particular bullet," said Mr. Beecher indicating the partially flattened slug, "but we should certainly have him take a look at it. Colonel, since you undoubtedly know more about arms than any of us, would you be willing to make the trip down the mountain, perhaps this afternoon, and take the bullet to him to examine?"

"I am at your service, sir." Seamus replied.

"Good, I will write you a letter of introduction." said Mr. Beecher and he took a pen and paper and passed a pencil and paper to Sampson, asking as he did so that the young man draw a map and write down directions for Seamus.

Seamus felt a sudden restlessness. He stood and walked over to an east facing window. He thought aloud.

"We have no way of knowing for sure," he said, "whether or not the actual killer is at the hotel either as a guest or as a member of the staff, and yet as Luther rounded the corner after hearing the shot, he saw no one running away over the open ground behind the building. A number of people have departed since the murder and there is no way to say that the killer was not among them. Still we must do what we can with what we have. Mr. Beecher, are there other firearms in the building that you know of, sir?"

"I have three fowling pieces in that locked cabinet." Mr. Beecher replied, pointing over his shoulder to the glass fronted case situated between the two north facing windows.

"And I have an old Pennsylvania rifle in there as well," he went on, "but no other pistols or firearms in the building. The staff, naturally, are not in the habit of possessing firearms, however the guests are free to bring such pistols, rifles or shotguns as they may choose. Some bring shotguns with which to shoot pigeons and, in the season, some do hunt grouse and pheasant on the grounds. In short, any number of guests may have any number of firearms in their rooms, or even on their persons, at any time."

"And," Sampson interjected, "we have a little coehorn mortar, a relic from the War of 1812, that we discharge on the 4th of July, but no real bombs just paper ones."

Seamus considered this information silently for a moment and then walked back to the desk.

"Good enough," he said, "If we can, I think we must find the gun which fired this bullet." He picked the projectile up from the desk and held it up to the sunlight.

"I therefore propose," he went on, "that we enlist all the staff, particularly the chambermaids, to surreptitiously search the rooms of the guests with the object of discovering the true murder weapon."

Seamus suggestion was received with what he perceived as stunned silence.

At length Mr. Beecher responded.

"Colonel," he said, " what you intend for us to do would be not only dishonorable, but contrary to the principles of trust upon which this business was founded and upon which it thrives, further it is almost certainly illegal."

Sampson nodded in ascent to that legal opinion.

"However, sir," Mr. Beecher continued, "you need not argue the point, you need say no more." He made a dismissing gesture with his hand. "I know that Luther's life may depend upon what action we now take and that is, to be sure, the higher good. Sampson will you please so instruct the staff and consult particularly with Mrs. Van Bronc. As the chief of the chambermaids, Sarah will have to coordinate their efforts."

Seamus was quietly astounded that an old-fashioned man of character, such as Mr. Beecher, would so quickly accept his nefarious suggestion.

"Very well," he said, "please see to it that the staff are provided with paper and pencils. They should copy any writing, or initials or trademarks of manufacturers which they find on any firearms they may locate. For the sake of speed, they need search only the rooms which are occupied or were occupied at the time of the shooting. If they could make a sketch of any such firearm, that would also be of help. Perhaps most important, they should be instructed to trace or make an impression on a piece of paper of the muzzle of each weapon they encounter. This will help us eliminate those which are not in the likely range of calibers; .44 or .45."

"Most of the staff," said Sampson, "are able to read and to write. Sarah and Levy teach a school in the evenings in the servant's wing for both the children and adults. The majority of the chambermaids and other staff will be well able to carry out your instructions, Colonel."

"Good," said Seamus. "They should not remove any firearms from the rooms and should be careful to avoid detection. If the guilty party is still in residence, we do not want to give alarm which may result in flight. The staff should report back as soon as possible and note the number of any room where they find a weapon."

Sampson placed his hand-drawn map and directions to the gunsmith's home on the desk and departed to set in motion the newly founded network of *videttes.*

Seamus decided that he should provide Mr. Beecher with some silence as he composed the letter of introduction. He therefore picked up the bullet from the desk, put it in his waistcoat pocket and stepped to an east facing window.

The Hudson Valley spread out before him and the Berkshires merged blue into the sky above Massachusetts. A haze was forming over all the valley; the harbinger of the humid heat of mid-day. Below the window, on the ledge, an old man sat on a camp stool. He wore a long linen duster and his white locks hung on his shoulders under the round straw farmer's hat on his head. His face was hidden beneath the wide brim, but a long white beard could be seen to flow down upon his chest. An easel stood before him and an open box of colors was at his feet. He dabbed at the canvass, looked to the valley and dabbed again.

Seamus walked along the east wall toward the next window. Between the two windows was mounted a framed engraving. On close inspection, it proved to be a rendering of a middle-aged General Winfield Scott, so recently deceased. He was one of the great military heroes of America's history. He had served with distinction in the War of 1812 and the Mexican War. Although he had been called 'Old Fuss and Feathers' by some at the beginning of the Rebellion when he commanded, at the age of 75, what there then was of the Union Army, he had known from the start what it would take to win the war. In the end it was his plan, Seamus reflected, the Anaconda Plan, which had strangled and destroyed the South. The Plan however had been carried out by other, younger leaders.

The old print depicted the General as a laurel-wreathed and heroic Roman, still at the peak of his powers. Seamus squinted at the fine print at the bottom of the portrait; Asher B. Durand; engraver, he read.

The print was inscribed in brown ink; 'To Mr. Chas. Beecher, the finest and most loyal friend whom God has vouchsafed to this sacred Republic and to this old warrior, with deepest gratitude and highest regard, Winfield Scott, Genl. USA.'

Mr. Beecher, thought Seamus, has had *some* connections, and he moved on passing the next window.

Before the corner where the east wall joined the north wall hung another, much larger engraving. Seamus read the caption; 'The surrender of General Lee and his entire Army to Lieut. Gen. Grant, April 9th 1865. This memorable event terminated the Great Rebellion. pub. by John Jones Phila. 1865.'

Clearly, John Jones had not, as had Seamus, been at Appomattox when Lee capitulated to the inevitable. In the print, both Lee and Grant were pictured in full dress uniform. This was more or less accurate as to Lee, but Seamus could still see, in his mind's eye, Grant entering McLean's house, scruffy as usual in a private's blue blouse with the springtime mud up to his knees. Even Lee's best had not been as fine as that portrayed in the print. The two were pictured standing outdoors, under a tree, their armies in the background facing each other in perfectly ordered ranks. Absurdity compounded as the rebels were shown as fully equipped, plump, cheerful and exquisitely uniformed, as if on parade the day before the war started. The Confederates' commissary wagons were shown in exact order, in columns stretching to the horizon.

Seamus recalled the grimy, ragged but fierce and wolfish rebel soldiers at Appomattox. Did any two of them have uniforms that matched? By that day, the rebels having been blocked from reaching their ample supply trains at Danville and other locations, the Confederate commissary consisted of one handful of parched corn in the pocket for privates, two for officers and something in between for sergeants.

The face of Grant, as pictured did resemble the Union general, but it seemed that the artist had never seen even a picture of Lee. The head on top of the gray dress uniform in the print looked like the bust of Homer which Seamus had seen in the library of the Jesuit school in Georgetown.

Strangest of all, the flags, incongruously un-tattered, which floated over the ranks of the Southerners, resembled none of the series of secessionist banners. None had the canton of circled stars, nor was the St. Andrew's Cross inspired battle flag to be seen. Each was simply a dark bar above and below a central bar of white, looking more like the flag of Holland than anything else. On reflection though, Seamus considered that this particular inaccuracy was most likely intentional. Who, in the North at least, would want to buy a representation of a secessionist flag to hang in his or her parlor or business place? As Seamus had recently witnessed in the barroom, fights had started over far less. There was too much bitterness, hate and violence attaching to that symbol for it to be a popular sight for any time in the future which Seamus could foresee. And in that future Seamus envisioned that the public at large would have a false idea of war. Only those who would go to a photograph gallery, like Mr. Brady's, would ever have a view of what war really looked like. Since photographs could not be printed in magazines or books, fanciful woodcuts and engravings such as this one would forever counterfeit reality for most people. Further, Seamus knew that Lee's surrender did not immediately end all hostilities, many died long after that day.

Seamus looked out the north facing window. To his left were the lakes and behind them the green forested ridge of the mountain, sharp against the blue of the sky. Below was the head of the mountain road. Directly under the window rose the cruciform shape of the first telegraph pole, the glass insulators gleaming in the late morning sun. The wire lead to the next pole down the road, and then to the next. Seamus lost sight of the poles as the road disappeared into the trees.

The old painter came into view where the ledge ended and a path lead through the woods to the road. He slowly strolled down to the road, his box of colors, with the folded camp stool tied to it, on his back, his easel carried over his shoulder like a rifle. As the old man entered the woods, Tompkins strode up from the road, his tall hat cocked to one side, his walking stick beating cadence in the dust. Tompkins walked around to the rear of the hotel out of Seamus line of sight.

"Mr. Beecher," said Seamus, "can you find out for me who is occupying room number four?"

"Colonel, I can tell you without the need for research that no one is occupying that room at present. The window of number four lets only onto the south courtyard. None of those rooms are rented this early in our season, nor are those on the north courtyard. They are the least desirable and though they are cheaper, no one is interested in renting them until we are full up at the height of the season and no other choice is available. With the present downturn in the economy, I do not know if those rooms will be rented at all this year."

Presently, McCain came up from the road and walked out of Seamus view to the left behind the building.

Seamus looked to the gun case between the windows. Three high quality, double barreled shotguns were lined up standing on their butt plates. One was a beautifully detailed 12 gauge and the other two were of about 8 gauge. Even if loaded with a solid ball instead of buck or bird shot, none of them could be considered as a likely murder weapon in the present matter. A fine old Pennsylvania rifle stood at the end of the row and it appeared to be above .50 caliber in the bore. Again, a very unlikely prospect for the murder weapon, in Seamus' opinion.

Above the gun case hung a framed, color tinted print of the Hudson River steamboat; *Mary Powell.*

This, at least, was an accurate portrait as Seamus could attest having seen the actual vessel off the Battery in New York Harbor on the previous Thursday evening. He had been told that after renovation in recent years, she was now the longest steamboat on the River. She was faithfully portrayed in the engraving with side-wheels churning just forward of amidships and with flags and pennants flying. Seamus recalled the original speeding along the waters of the harbor, the great diamond-shaped walking beam above her topmost deck tilting fore and aft, the piston rod and connecting rod pumping up and down, and the whole scene heroically illuminated in orange by the setting sun.

He had resolved to take trip on the rakish craft should the opportunity present itself, but at that moment he had contented himself with travailing on the rather more prosaic night boat.

Seamus finished his turn of the room passing portraits of President Lincoln and William Lloyd Garrison on the inside wall above the black marble fireplace. On the mantle stood a plaster copy of the bust of Colonel Shaw which had been executed by the American sculptress; Edwina Lewis. Miss Lewis, Seamus recalled, despite being a woman of African and Ojibwa-Chippawa descent *and a Catholic* was now enjoying well earned success as an artist, although she had in the past to endure mob violence and, more recently, to travel to Rome in order to do so.

Seamus stationed himself at the side of Mr. Beecher's desk just as his introductory letter was being blotted. Mr. Beecher put the letter in an envelope, handed it to Seamus, and took out his watch.

"It is nearly eleven o'clock," he said, "and I take it that neither of you gentlemen has eaten. There is little more that we can do now until we get reports from the staff and until you, Colonel, make your trip down the mountain this afternoon. I suggest you get yourselves some lunch. I insist that you use the private dinning room where you will be able to converse without fear of being overheard."

He rose and stepped to the bank of speaking tubes on the wall next to the hall door. He lifted one of the tubes from its hook, removed the brass stopper, blew into the mouthpiece and put it to his ear. When he got a response, he spoke.

"Yes," he said," if you please Levi make sure that the private dinning room is available for Doctor DuBoise and Colonel Delaney, they will be down directly. Thank you, Levi."

The doctor and Seamus rose and met their host at the door as he replaced the tube on the hook. A framed salt print photograph hung above the bank of tubes. The picture had been taken out of doors before a grove of trees and in front of a platform. A banner above the stage read; 'The American Anti-Slavery Society.' A group of men and women stood in the foreground. It looked like a camp meeting. Seamus immediately recognized among the group the renowned faces of Frederick Douglass and

William Lloyd Garrison. He also recognized the less famous countenances of Mr. Luther Van Bronc and Mr. Charles Beecher.

Seamus turned to Mr. Beecher. There was the hint of a smile on the man's lips.

"I will meet with you again after you have dined." he said and showed the doctor and Seamus out the door.

As they walked toward the central staircase, Doctor DuBoise spoke.

"The struggle against slavery," he said simply, "started in this country long before Fort Sumter was fired upon, and my friend Charles Beecher has been a long campaigner in that struggle. If ever the government awarded medals for that bitter and secret war, he would justly be among the first to be so honored."

When they reached the ground floor, the two men turned to the left and walked the few steps to the open doorway where Clay had met his fate a few hours before. All was in order as if nothing out of the ordinary had happened that morning.

They turned into the passage and found the excellent Levi standing by the private dining room. He greeted them, ushered them in, seated them and presented each with a bill of fare. The room was the essence of warmth and intimacy; paneled in rich walnut wainscoting and hung with curtains of red velvet.

From a sideboard against the far wall Levi brought a silver tray of relishes; spiced watermelon, sweet and sour gherkins, pickled onions and piccalilli. Seamus chose the loin of veal *demiglace*, mashed potatoes and succotash. For a beverage he selected Dr. Welch's grape juice punch, considering that it was too early for him to safely start with ardent drink.

The doctor ordered the same meal with the exception that he chose a glass of hock as his beverage, possibly considering, Seamus supposed, that he had already started with ardent drink earlier in the morning.

After taking their orders Levi advised them of the progress of the *videttes*.

"Sampson and I," he said quietly, "have instructed the staff as you requested, gentlemen, however, since the rooms are usually made up while the guests are at breakfast, the chambermaids had mostly finished their work in the rooms before we could tell them what to look for. It does not seem to be a good idea to revisit too many rooms as that might arouse suspicion, so it does not appear that we will have very many reports until after breakfast tomorrow. By the way Colonel, it is our understanding that each and every occupied room will be . . . ah . . . investigated, is that not correct?"

"Yes," said Seamus, "each and every occupied room without exception."

Levi nodded and departed.

As they awaited their meal, Seamus remembered a comment the doctor had made after they had viewed the body and left the lounge earlier in the morning.

"Doctor," he said, "I too was in the hospital, in truth a large farm shed, as I recall, behind Meade's Headquarters when the rebel cannonade commenced on the last day at Gettysburg. I was there as a casualty. I had been knocked out by a glancing minnie ball in the Wheatfield the day before." He held up the lock of hair by his right temple and showed the scar.

"I did not awaken," he said, "until the blast of a shell, which must have thrown me to the floor, brought me back to consciousness. I vaguely remember crawling along the ground outside the shed after which I must have again fainted. The next I knew I was in the hospital which had been set up on the Lightner Farm a few miles below the town on the Baltimore Pike. I stayed there a while, lapsing in and out of wakefulness and was eventually sent to the same hospital in Georgetown where I had been after Antietam. There I recovered fully."

"Colonel," said Doctor DuBoise, "we may well have met before."

He held up the thick wave of hair at the side of Seamus face and gave the scar a closer look.

"The pattern of those sutures," he said, "appears to be my handiwork or half of them at least. I recall that I was about half-way through stitching just such a gash, when a shell blast interrupted my virtuoso performance and rendered me unconscious. It looks as though another hand finished closing the wound and, may I say it, did not do so neat a job as would have mine. I never knew, but often wondered, what happened to the young officer upon whom I had been working at that moment, and I will take it that you are he, and now that we are reacquainted, tell you that I am glad that you are alive"

"Thank you, Doctor, I am happy that you too survived General Lee's bombardment."

Their meal arrived shortly and they did it good justice, while their conversation turned to more light-hearted reminiscences.

# V

# A Ramble in the Afternoon

After finishing his dinner with a dish of bread pudding and fruit sauce, Seamus joined the doctor on the piazza for coffee and a cigar. They parted then, the doctor expressing his intention of taking a midday *siesta.* Seamus returned to is room and found that Levi had, as promised, dispatched a pitcher of hot water. Seamus promptly stripped, lathered his face and shaved. When he finished he examined his face in the mirror and dashed on some witch-hazel. He wet and soaped a hand towel, bathed and dried himself. He donned clean drawers and bent to his trunk. He looked before opening it for the single strand of his hair he had affixed with spittle across the seam between the lid and the left side of the trunk before leaving the room that morning, and found it to be missing. Seamus figured that the porter or chambermaid Levi had sent with the water had taken the opportunity to carry out his order to the letter; to search each and every occupied room without exception.

No weapon would have been found. Seamus' other possessions were presently divided between his Aunt's boarding house and the regimental headquarters in Manhattan. The only firearm he had with him on this trip was the police revolver now resting in his coat pocket on the bed.

Well so be it, thought Seamus. It was encouraging to see that the staff, whom he now thought of as his *videttes*, were doing a thorough job.

He opened the trunk and took out a short gray jacket with three rows of brass buttons down the front and three gold bars at the collar. It was the uniform of a captain in the 9th Virginia Cavalry. It brought back memories of Chancellorsville and of a time later, in the winter of '64-65, when Seamus and Sergeant McCabe and Archie Rowand and some of Sheridan's other scouts would dress as Confederates and cross rebel lines along the Blue Ridge to capture Southern generals.

Two such generals were in fact captured and both McCabe and Rowand were eventually awarded the Medal of Honor. They richly deserved the decoration, as the forays into rebel territory bordered on the suicidal.

This jacket could have gotten me hanged, Seamus thought.

Spies wearing the enemy's uniform had no need to worry about how they would get along in prison. Their term of incarceration invariably lasted only until a tree of appropriate height could be found.

Seamus set the jacket aside, wondering what his *vidette* had thought upon discovering it. He set aside also a small leather dispatch case and then found that for which he had been searching, a white linen jacket. It had been given to him by a surgeon in the hospital at Georgetown.

The other guests at the hotel, Seamus had noticed, generally observed a rather more relaxed style of dress, especially in their rambles around the countryside during the heat of day. He thought that he too might therefore dress in a more informal and comfortable way on his trip down the mountain. He stood, faced the mirror and put the jacket on. The surgeon had been taller than Seamus by half a head and the skirt of the garment came down to mid-thigh. The sleeves were too long also and there were dark stains at the cuffs which Aunt Kate's best remedies could not completely expunge. But the cuffs were designed to be unbuttoned and could simply be turned up to both shorten the sleeves and hide the stains. He rolled the cuffs and took off the jacket.

He dug further into his trunk and came up with a pair of brown checked trousers he had worn on a recent trip to Canada when he was playing the role of an itinerant photographic *artiste* while gathering information for the Secretary.

Although the flashy trousers were not Seamus' style they

had been convincing as authentic fashion for an *avant garde* photographer. As his present wardrobe was limited Seamus decided to wear them, at least for the afternoon.

He dressed with a clean shirt, collar and plaid necktie. He transferred his possessions to the ample pockets of the linen jacket, donned the jacket and bent again to the trunk. He took out a narrow brimmed straw hat and removed the brass 'bursting bomb' insignia from the front of it. He put the insignia back into the trunk and set the hat on his head. He looked at himself in the mirror.

"Hoo-rah," he said aloud.

Anyway, he thought, I'll be cooler.

Seamus tended to the room and his luggage as was his custom, exited and locked the door behind him. He walked quickly to the central staircase and descended to the ground floor. He walked to the very spot on the piazza where Clay had been standing when he had been shot and suppressed the image in his mind of the dead man and the puddle of blood.

He stepped behind the door post and took out his watch. While holding it in his hand, he turned about with both hands held in front of himself. He paused, turned back to the doorway, peeked into the hall and looked back to the piazza floor. He peeked around the door post and looked back to the piazza floor two more times and then looked at his watch. He looked back into the hall a final time and again consulted his watch.

An elderly lady in a near-by rocker looked at him aghast.

Seamus tipped his hat to her, smiled warmly and put his watch back into his waistcoat pocket. He entered the building and walked all the way to the rear entrance. He faced about and stood looking down the hall to the piazza doorway and the blue sky beyond. It was long way, over fifty yards as he had just paced the distance, better than one hundred and fifty feet.

How to shoot someone, he thought, at that range with a pistol?

Difficult shot, he answered himself, aim for the widest part of the body.

He stood and considered, turned and looked through the entry toward the lakes. He faced back toward the piazza and noticed that Mr. Twilling was staring at him from behind the front desk

Seamus chose to ignore the man's existence. He looked at his watch again and started back toward the piazza, but turned right at the front desk. He walked along the corridor which lead to the south wing of the hotel. On his right, he passed the door of the office behind the front desk where the electric telegraph machine was installed. The next door on the right was marked with a brass plate reading; 'Trunk Room'. On the left side of the corridor was a row of large windows affording a view of the south courtyard. The wall to his right was uninterrupted by doors and he assumed that the storage area occupied the space behind that wall to the end of the corridor.

When he reached the end of the passage, he turned left and continued at a brisk pace, passing the numbered guest rooms on both sides of the hall. Those on the left, 12, 10, 8, he knew faced onto the south courtyard and were, according to Mr. Beecher, unoccupied. At the end of the hall he turned left again and passed, on his right, rooms 5, 3, and 1, the windows of which, he knew faced the valley. On his left he passed rooms 6 and 4. He stopped for a moment and again read the time on his watch. The door to the lounge, where the post mortem had taken place, was just to his right. He walked to the lobby and stood in the doorway to the piazza for a moment. He walked the central hall, passed the windows of the north courtyard on his right and, on his left, the reading room, where the bust of Daniel Webster still stood guard. As Seamus approached the desk, he could feel Twilling's eyes on him, but he continued to ignore clerk.

I am, he thought, driving Twilling mad with curiosity. Good!

Seamus turned left into the south corridor and this time stopped opposite the

door to the telegraphic station. There a door on his left let, he was sure, into the south courtyard. He tried it and found it to be unlocked. He entered into the cool, grassy space.

The sun was now high and illuminated the upper stories of the walls surrounding the court yard. A line of bright light cut an angle across the white painted clapboard wall across from him.

Below and to the right, all was in shadow. The grass below the windows on the ground floor rooms was just now beginning to get the benefit of the glancing sunlight. A gravel path lead to the right to the center of the court where a white painted iron bench, wrought in a floral pattern, was set amid a bed of purple and yellow iris. He looked about, and saw that the door through which he had passed was the only door to the court.

He started to walk toward the bench when he noticed something shinning in the patch of sunlight on the ground below the far left window in the opposite wall. He left the path and headed toward the object. He found that the grass was still wet with the evening's dew as his shoes and stockings became immediately damp. He plodded on through the grass until he reached the object and stood looking down at it. It lay immediately below the sill of the window and looked like a highly polished hook. Seamus bent and picked it up and found that he had discovered the whereabouts of the missing spoon which had so concerned Mr. Twilling. Not only had the utensil been purloined, it had, he could now see, been vandalized. Someone had exercised considerable force to bend the spoon into the shape of the letter 'S'. The handle had been twisted into a tight curve and then bent again. Drops of dew stood beaded on the silver plate. Seamus dried it with his handkerchief and put it into the inside pocket his coat.

He thought of Sarah VanBronc's comments on Mr. Twilling's apparent inability to grasp the relative insignificance of a lost spoon on a morning when a murder had been committed. Thinking of Sarah reminded Seamus that Luther had asked to see him and he turned and left the courtyard.

He passed the front desk and successfully fought the urge to present the still staring clerk with the prodigal spoon. He exited the building by the rear entrance. A coach and four was parked in the circular drive and Seamus recognized Jacob among the porters loading a large trunk on top of the vehicle. Seamus asked, and was given directions by Jacob to the root cellar where Luther was imprisoned.

As instructed, Seamus walked to the right along the gravel of the drive. On the broad lawns behind the hotel, were groups of ladies in bright dresses and gentlemen in white playing noisily at the popular new game of croquet. To the right, Seamus came abreast of the corner of the building and the scullery entrance to the kitchen where some of the staff were unloading boxes of provisions from a small wagon. That was the spot he reminded himself where Luther was standing when he heard the shot that took Clay's life.

Luther could have just stayed where he was and minded his own business and he would not be in his present predicament, thought Seamus. But then Luther was a soldier. He could not just stand by, he would always pitch in. And that was the difference; Luther could not shirk even if it ever occurred to him to do so.

The midday heat was mounting as Seamus continued along the drive to the point where it began to circle back to the left toward the flagstone walk in the middle of the lawn. He stepped off the gravel and onto the shale paved common. He skirted around to the right where a steep trail lead down to the head of the mountain road. Before the beginning of the trail was the entrance to a straight drive which lead back through a stand of ancient pines and hardwood trees to the scullery entrance. The drive was lined by a number of out building. Just inside the shade of the trees sat Constable Wyncoop's nephew and deputy; Sylvester.

He sat before the gable end of a cedar shake roof which seemed, strangely, to be lying on the ground. As Seamus got closer he could see that the roof was not capping a collapsed building, but was covering a low wall of dry laid stone. The building was intact but appeared to be only waist high. Most of the structure was built underground or more accurately cut into the living bedrock on the northern edge of the vast shelf upon which the hotel and all of its ancillary buildings stood. The land fell away behind the root cellar where the trail connecting to the mountain road descended.

A few paces beyond the root cellar was an identical low building and beyond that what appeared to be an ice house constructed of gray painted beams.

The temporary resting place of Clay? Seamus wondered.

The last building in the line was a little brick building with smoke rising from its chimney. An errant breeze wafted back the aroma of fresh bread, confirming Seamus suspicions that this was the bakery.

Seamus approached quietly so as not to disturb Sylvester who was guarding his prisoner while seated in a plain old rush seated chair tipped back against the front wall of the root cellar. The brim of his straw hat was pulled down over his face. A vicious looking double barreled shot gun, sawed of at both ends, was balanced in his lap. Both hammers were cocked. Sonorous emanations escaped from under the hat.

Seamus was recalling how dangerous it could be to awaken an armed sentry when he took one more step and his foot settled on a fallen branch on the path. It gave way with a sound like a derringer being fired. Sylvester awoke instantly and threw his head back against the stone gable of the cellar with a hollow sounding thud. He swung the chair forward and came to a standing position with the shot gun leveled at Seamus midsection, the great hat still over his eyes.

Seamus side-stepped nimbly behind the thick trunk of a pine.

"Lad!" he said, "Would you ever be careful where you are pointing that street howitzer!"

"Oh," said Sylvester, pushing up the brim of his hat with the muzzles of the gun, "it's you, Colonel. Hadn't ought to sneak up on a man like that, sir." Sylvester shifted the gun to his left hand and rubbed the back of his head with his right.

Seamus stayed behind the tree.

"Sylvester," he said, "in my considerable military experience, I have found that it is more difficult to sneak up on a sentry when he is awake. For God's sake and mine as well, point the gun at the ground and un-cock the hammers."

Sylvester complied and Seamus stepped around the tree.

"Please be so kind as to let me visit with Luther, alone." he said.

"Yes, sir." said the deputy juggling the gun and a ring of keys as Seamus danced around to avoid the cavernous muzzles which were alternately aligning with his face, chest and feet.

"Uncle Hump, I mean, the constable told me that you would be around and that I should let you in, sir." said Sylvester.

He eventually succeeded in unlocking the big, heart-shaped lock which secured the oaken door of the cellar. Seamus ducked into the low doorway and stepped down the four steps. The place had a pleasant earthy smell. His eyes grew accustomed to the dim light and he saw Luther standing bareheaded before him.

"Good afternoon, Colonel." said Luther.

"Good afternoon, Luther. How are you getting on?"

"Tolerably well, Colonel. I have had worse accommodations, as I am sure you have had yourself. It is cool and dry hear at least. Please pull up a potato sack and be seated."

Seamus sat across from Luther. The root cellar was lined on either side and at the back with sacks and barrels. Stenciled letters on the containers indicated parsnips, potatoes, apples, turnips. A lamp stood on a low keg between the men along with a stack of magazines and books, *Les Miserables* on the top of the pile. Luther took two big red apples from a peck next to his improvised table and offered one to his guest. After each had taken a bite, Luther continued.

"Back before Emancipation," he said, "many an escaped slave found refuge in this very cellar and thanked God for shelter on free soil. This property was a station on the Underground Railroad and Mr. Beecher was a station master. He could have lost everything if he had been prosecuted under the Fugitive Slave Law, including his own freedom, but he is a man of courage and did not fear to violate an unjust law.

"Many of the refugees were brought here by my good wife. She had been purchased out of bondage by the abolitionists, who set her up in her own little home in Peekskill. It was there we met when I put into the harbor on one of Mr. Beecher's sloops. I have worked for him for most of my life. Sarah was a seamstress by trade but made extra money by selling fruit along the docks of the town. And so we met and married. Since then we have worked for Mr.Beecher doing any number of jobs, but Sarah showed me that our real work has always been to better the lot of the African people in this country. To that end we have taken every opportunity to educate ourselves and devote our skills to that higher cause.

"Sarah said that the life of a slave was no life at all and she was better than her word. She became a conductor on the Underground Railroad and made many trips
to the South, following the path of the great Harriet Tubman, who did the same. She brought out many of our people and there were wanted posters offering rewards for her capture from the Carolinas to Canada

"I, of course, was fearful for her safety, and told her that I wished to go to the South with her. She laughed and said that my accompanying her would guarantee our capture since I had never been a slave and did not know how to act like one. My bold demeanor, she said, would be a flag to the dullest slave-catcher in the South and we would all have the devil to pay. I was born a free man on a farm up near Coxsackie at the north end of the county.

"So we worked together for Mr. Beecher on his properties and with him in the abolition movement. We traveled to Boston, to the African Meeting House and helped with anti-slavery speeches and newspapers. It was not an easy life but it was a free one and we gained much. Our son came to us on the Underground Railway.

"Sarah had strict rules about not taking the sickly to the North. She could not take the chance, you see, of slowing down and have everyone caught. But one woman who was very ill, Frederick's mother by birth, begged and pleaded. The boy's father had been sold down the river and she feared that her son would be sent further south as well. Sarah is a very strong woman, but she has a compassionate heart. She relented and took the boy and his mother. The poor woman died along the way, and we have taken Frederick for our son. We did not even know his name so we named him for Mr. Douglass.

"When the war came and the 54th Massachusetts was formed I was among the first to join those free men of color and escaped slaves to take the necessary steps to put an end forever to the great evil of slavery. It broke my heart to leave my wife and my son but there was never any question of my duty."

Of course not, thought Seamus. He listened amazed at how

imprisonment had so freed the tongue of this man whom he had thought to be preeminently taciturn.

"I thank God that our cause has, so far, been victorious," Luther continued, "and that I have been returned in good health to my family. As I said Colonel, my wife is strong, but each person has a breaking point. I feel that since the welcome end of the brutal war and with it slavery, Sarah has allowed herself to let down and repose. This sudden turn of events, the murder and my being accused, has caught her off guard, with her defenses down. I therefore wish to see the matter cleared up as soon as possible so as to relieve her mind of anxiousness.

"Now, I am usually a man of very few words, but I needed to tell you all this because I could see this morning that you somehow are as sure as I am of my innocence. Tell me Colonel, how do you know that I did not kill Clay?"

"I know that you are innocent of this crime," said Seamus, "because I consider myself to be an excellent judge of the character of men, especially in trying circumstances, and I have formed the opinion that you would never be a back-shooter and I heard your shot over the bear."

There was another reason as well but Seamus did not think it necessary to say more at the moment.

Luther was silent for a time.

"Colonel," he said at length, "I have no fear of the law in this matter, and I have faith in God. I am sure that a proper court will find me guiltless in this case. But, Colonel, I do not expect that I will get to stand before a legitimate court. I have been concerned since this murder happened and since I was accused, that a lynch mob would form and come here to take me. You are familiar with the term 'lynch'.

"Yes, Luther, the term, sorry to say, was invented in Ireland and the practice is not unknown there." Not unknown here either, he thought.

"There again," said Luther, "I do not really fear being lynched either because I do not intend to let that happen. Long before any lynch mob had me in its power I will have taken that shotgun from Sylvester and made my escape. It would not be hard to do. I know it would not be fair to Sarah at this stage of life to have to become the wife of a fugitive, nonetheless I will do as I have said."

Seamus leaned closer to Luther.

"Please," he said, "do not think about escaping. As it stands now you are only accused. If you were to do as you describe, and especially if the deputy were to be . . . injured, you would be guilty of crimes. For your sake and the sake of your family, please do not take any rash action."

"The time is getting short," said Luther. "The scullery boys went to Tannersville this morning and when they returned just now, they visited me here and told me that a bunch of idlers on the porch of Brenner's Saloon in Haines Corners cursed them as they passed. One of them yelled that I would pay for killing a white man. I would rather be a fugitive than have my wife a widow and my son an orphan. But best of all I wish to be cleared entirely of this false accusation and so I put it to you, Colonel that you will have to find the true culprit as soon as possible. My friends here and I will help in any way we can."

I have been assigned a task, thought Seamus, issued marching orders.

"Very well," he said, "what can you tell me that is not already generally known?"

"Not very much. Sampson visited me here also and told me that no one in the hotel has yet been found, except yourself, who heard the shot I fired over the bear, not even the scullery boys. They, as usual, were sleeping on pallets by the door in anticipation of my arrival with the meat wagon, and had not heard the shot. It is possible that some of the guests who checked out this morning may have heard it but, as they are gone, we may never know."

Both men sat in silence staring at the pool of daylight on the dirt floor that streamed down from the barred window in cellar door.

"There is one thing," Luther said suddenly, "I don't know if it means anything as to the murder of Mr. Clay, but when Sampson came to see me I was reminded of what he told me last week. When he drove the hotel coach down to Catskill to meet the steamer from New York City, there was a cattle stampede in the street above the dock and Mr. Clay's wife was very nearly trampled. Sampson had run into the street and split the herd by waving his coat and saved the lady."

"I have heard of that incident," said Seamus, "but was Clay also in danger of being trampled at the time?"

"No," said Luther. "Sampson told me that Mr. Clay had hurried across the street to the coach, leaving the lady to pick her way across the mud with lifted skirts. Later, when Sampson found out that the two were married to each other it struck him that the man was singularly ungallant not to assist his own wife across the street. Within the week, we had all come to know Mr. Clay well enough to see that he never had anything to do with being gallant toward anyone."

Seamus nodded.

"The reason I bring this up, Colonel, is that the stampede did not happen accidentally."

"Yes, I understand that a drunk fired a pistol into the air causing the cattle to break from their pen".

"That is just it, Colonel. Sampson later noticed that the latch on the pen was not broken. It must have been left unsecured. And Sampson recognized the drunken man. It was Leander Skhutt; known hereabouts as 'Reb'. He was a notorious Copperhead at the beginning of the war. Before that, he was suspected of being a slave-catcher, although we never found him at it. If we had . . ., well. Anyhow, he disappeared from the valley in '63, as best we could tell and believe me, we kept pretty good track of him. The rumor was that he had gone to the South to join the rebel army. He had always been a loud supporter of the Secessionists. That was how he got the nickname 'Reb'.

"So, Colonel, Sampson told me that Reb was back in the valley and I did not think too much of it. His shooting a pistol in the air in town while drunk would not be considered unusual behavior on his part. Hard to believe that he ever fought in the war though. A fair fight was never to old Reb's liking. But it occurred to me that he would fit the description of the man you told me you saw running away in the woods when Mrs. Clay's horse bolted because of the rattler.

"If Reb had intentionally tried to harm Mrs. Clay or her husband that day by the dock, maybe he then tried to harm the lady yesterday by putting the snake in the road. You said the man was stocky and Sampson described Reb as being dressed in a brown coat and gray trousers that day in Catskill. Sampson also said that he had heard from Jubal, a friend of ours who works as a porter and sometimes banjo player at Brenner's saloon. Jubal said that during this last week Reb had returned to the bar, one of his old haunts, and with plenty of money to buy rounds of drinks. He was full of stories of his exploits as an artillery man in the rebel army, and damning Abe Lincoln to hell and the South will rise again and all that.

"Jubal said that Reb wore gray trousers with a red stripe like a soldier's uniform, so whether he had been a soldier or not, he did have soldier's pants. If Reb had something against the Clays, maybe he is involved in the murder. Finally, the man who was on the porch of Brenner's when the scullery boys passed who said that I would pay for killing a white man was, they tell me, Reb himself, so we know that he was up here on the mountain top this morning."

"Well, there may be a connection. We will look into it." said Seamus. What he did not say was that he had seen Reb, if that was who the man in the brown coat in fact was, meeting with Clay and the other two on the shore of the North Lake after he had left Emily with Sarah on the previous afternoon. At that meeting Clay had been angry, but had he been angry with Reb?

Seamus stood.

"Luther," he said, "I will do everything I can. Please give me time, do not make matters worse."

Luther stood also.

"Colonel," he said, "the amount of time available is not in my hands, but I will not be the helpless victim of a mob. If I must die, it will be as a man and after a good fight."

Seamus had no more words. He bade Luther a good afternoon and knocked on the door for Sylvester. The lad arrived and repeated his juggling performance with the shotgun and the ring of keys. He released Seamus from the root cellar and locked the door again.

Seamus walked to the common and crossed in the glare of the mid-day sun. The dust rose at each step on the crunching shale chips. With gratitude, he entered the cool, leather and horse smelling stable. Young Frederick hurried up to him out of the dimness.

Frederick Douglass Van Bronc, thought Seamus, like me, raised as a foster child.

"Frederick," Seamus smiled down at the lad, "would you kindly saddle Sarge for me as soon as you can."

He handed Frederick a bright new silver three-cent piece.

But the young fellow seemed distracted.

"Yes, Colonel, thank you, sir," he said, "my mother said that I should tell you when I see you that you must go to her right away. It is very important. She said that she will be in the kitchen. Please hurry, Colonel."

"I am on my way; please send for me when Sarge is ready."

Seamus walked with lengthening stride back across the common and onto the walk between the lawns. As he hurried toward the back entrance, he noticed a group of people standing near the south corner of the building. The three of them were engaged in animated conversation. Seamus recognized the Reverend Mr.Van Wyck, and the lady he now knew to be the dominie's wife. They were speaking with Major Savage's associate; Scipio.

Seamus paused at the entrance and watched yet another coach being loaded. As he stood, he kept an ear cocked to listen to the conversation of the three at the south corner. To his irritation, he found that although he could hear the voices clearly, he could make no sense of what was being said.

He gave over his eavesdropping as useless and entered the hotel. He stopped in the hall for a moment and determined that the quickest way to the kitchen was through the barroom and the casino.

Rolf manned his post behind the bar and Seamus thought of an ice cold glass of beer, but allowed as he might more safely quench his thirst with a lemonade. He asked Rolf for one and it was quickly provided. He also had a question for Rolf.

"Last night," said Seamus, "you told me a good deal about the history of Major Savage. Can you tell me how you came by that information?"

"I can, Colonel, I got the information from the Major's man, Scipio. That is, not directly from him. I did not talk with him, he doesn't exactly speak much English as you and I understand the language. He talks a kind of mixture of English and Indian and maybe French and the African tongues that some of the black folks down in Carolina, I believe it is, speak. 'Gulla', it is called. Luther's wife, Sarah is the only one of our staff here who understands Gulla and can speak it. She has been talking to Scipio. He was born in Africa, she says, and was a prince among his people. The scars on his face are a badge of his royal rank. Sarah was the one who told me about the Major's . . . adventures. Scipio has been very worried about the Major, about his drinking and the . . . uh . . . state of his mind, if you know what I mean, Colonel."

Rolf made a circular motion with his index finger next to his temple.

"Yes, Rolf," said Seamus, "I know just what you mean."

"Well, Colonel, I asked to see you as soon as possible, and here you are standing at the bar." This came from Sarah as she entered through the casino door.

"Would you come with me now, please?" she said. It was not a request.

Seamus gulped the icy lemonade, which cause his eyes to ache and water. He put the half-full glass on the bar and followed Sarah into the center of the empty casino. The room was dark, save for the sunlight glancing from the lawns beyond the French doors in the west wall.

"My son," said Sarah, "sent one of the stable boys over to the kitchen" she gestured to the wide doors on the opposite side of the casino, "to say that you were on your way over. I waited and waited and you did not come and so I thought you may have been thirsty . . ." She let the accusation end there.

Seamus thought that he should feel angry at being portrayed as a typical Irishman who would find his way to a bar at all hazards and despite any obligations to the contrary. He decided that he did feel angry, but had no opportunity to express his feelings to Sarah who continued to speak in hushed, urgent tones.

In her hands she held a fringed paisley shawl folded like a package. She opened it to reveal a pair of hair combs, elegantly wrought in Spanish silver.

"Colonel," she said, "I spent much of the day with Mrs. Clay after the unfortunate occurrence of this morning. I helped her to change her clothes which had been stained with blood. Mrs. Van Wyck also was with us most of the time and left Mrs. Clay's room about an hour ago. After that, Mrs. Clay said that I could leave too because she felt quite well now. Before I left she took out these combs and told me how much they meant to her. They were given to her by her late father who had brought them back from one of his trips abroad. She wore them at her wedding to her first husband. She wrapped them in this shawl, which she said had been a wedding gift from her first husband, and then, Colonel, she gave them to me. I told her that I did not want to take these treasures from her. But she pressed them on me and told me that I was the only friend she had in the world, because of the confidences which we had shared since yesterday when you brought her back from the Falls. She said she wanted someone to remember her when she was gone and that she would 'rest easier', . . . that is what she said, 'rest easier' . . . knowing that these things would be used by someone who would have kind memories of her. I thought her actions and words strange, but she seemed cheerful when I left. She even smiled as she closed the door. Then, perhaps twenty minutes ago, I was out on the upper piazza and saw Mrs. Clay enter the trail to the cliff walk. I was filled with fear for her safety.

"Colonel, that lady has suffered so much, you do not know. I am afraid she will harm herself. So I sent for you. Colonel, she thinks very well of you. You must hurry and go and find her!"

Seamus felt the growing coldness in his chest sink into his stomach.

"Where . . . where is the trail?" he said. His voice sounded to himself to be far off.

Sarah took him past the door to the butler's pantry next to

the bar entrance, through a door in the back wall of the casino and into the deserted dining hall. The tables were all set for supper and sparkled with silver, crystal and porcelain. They hurried through the room, their footsteps echoing, and out past the private dinning room. They stepped onto the ground floor piazza and rushed to the ledge. Sarah pointed Seamus to the trail which began at the south end of the cleared ground around the hotel where the ancient forest resumed.

"For pity sake hurry, Colonel!" said Sarah.

Seamus mumbled that he would and walked quickly along the ledge to the trail head where a carved board proclaimed; 'Trail to Boulder Rock'.

Boulder Rock, he thought, how far to Boulder Rock? He took out his watch as he entered the shade of the trees, passing between the trunks of two tall pines which formed a gateway to the trail. It was a quarter to four.

What does that tell me? he thought. What?

Nothing. That is what, he answered himself. Nothing. Sarah said Emily entered the trail about twenty minutes ago. What does that tell? How far did she go? How far do I have to go? I do not know.

"Hurry." he said softly to himself.

The trail went almost immediately up hill. The pine needles were slippery beneath the soles of Seamus' dress shoes. He scrambled up and up through the pines. The sun dappled down through the canopy and the light played tricks in the dark woods. Huge out crops of bed rock stood upon the side of the ridge and the trail meandered between them. The terrain reminded Seamus of the reverse slope of the Little Round Top at Gettysburg where the men of Maine had held the flank.

Sweating, Seamus reached the summit where the trail ran level for a piece and then descended between two rocky crags. He followed along to the south. Through the trees to his left he could see the blue sky above the valley. He saw a flash of deep pink to the side of the path ahead and hoped for a moment that he had seen Emily, but soon could see that the pink was the clustered flowers of an alpine shrub. Others of the same species stood out like rosy beacons in the shadows beneath the fir and hardwood trees.

A few more steps and the trail lead upward again and was blocked by a wall of conglomerate rock the height of Seamus head. It was green with moss and wet with moisture and slick as well he discovered when he tried to take the barrier by frontal assault. His foot slipped and he landed on his right knee. He shredded a hole in both his stylish trousers and the skin under the fabric on the pebbles imbedded in the puddingstone. Seamus climbed around the obstruction more gingerly on his second attempt.

Hurry, he thought. Hurry!

The trail descended again toward the daylight above the valley and he stumbled over a network of roots and pressed on to where the path was paved with bed rock. There, two great evergreen trees were joined together by massive exposed roots which formed a natural bench. The wood of the bench was polished by constant use and a carved sign on the nearer of the two trees read, 'Lover's Retreat.' Seamus stepped out onto the ledge in front of the bench.

Across the valley, the Berkshire Mountains had all but disappeared in the gathering blue haze. The air as increasingly hot and close. He took off his hat and mopped his brow. With hat in hand, he crossed to the edge of the cliff, and looked down. Below, he estimated about four hundred feet below, was the bright green dome of tree tops on the lower slope of the mountain. Seamus thanked God that he saw no sign of Emily. He put out of his mind the thought that he was looking only at the forest canopy and could see nothing of the forest floor, perhaps another fifty feet down.

He turned back into the dimness of the woods. He pressed on and saw that the mountain laurel was just beginning to blossom at this latitude and altitude. The pale flowers were barely showing themselves amid their shinning green leaves at the side of the trail.

Seamus thought of the Blue Ridge and of the two forks of the Shenandoah. The laurel would already be in full bloom there, looking like a great convoluted thunder cloud which had bowed down from the sky to rest under the trees.

The Shenandoah Valley of Virginia, where Jackson had destroyed one Union army after another. Soldiers, hardened Union veterans, would blanche at the mention of the name of that beautiful, deadly valley.

Would any other river valley in the world, Seamus wondered, ever be so deservedly feared by troops of the Republic? He fervently hoped not.

He pushed on through the thickets of laurel which partly overgrew the trail. The path continued south and he soon came to a sign which announced 'Eagle Rock.' A broad slab of stone angled horizontally, resting upon other flat monoliths in a glade. From the side it appeared as a profile of the raptor for which it was named, reminding Seamus of the figure head on a clipper ship. It resembled something else, too, something in Ireland. He could not remember what.

The trail made another deliberate turn toward the cliffs and Seamus took out his watch. He was surprised to see that he had been traveling for no more than thirty minutes. He felt he had been searching forever. Now he could see that his search was coming to an end. On the right side of the trail, a lady's wide brimmed straw hat hung upon a low cedar branch. A sudden breeze came up and stirred the branch.

Seamus took the hat and found that it had been secured to the tree by a long pin. There was a blue satin band around the crown of the hat and in the band was stuck a folded sheet of pearl colored note paper. Seamus took and unfolded the paper. Written in a fine feminine script, the note began without preamble:

I am dead by my own hand. None should be accused of my murder. No longer on earth can I stay.

Emily (Mrs. Robert) Coltrane

"Please God no!" said Seamus quietly to himself. He hurried another few yards along the path and stopped.

The forest opened again to the eastern cliff. On this ledge however, a caprice of primordial cataclysm had left perched a great block of sedimentary rock. It was trapezoidal in shape and the size of a coach, perhaps ten feet high. It sat poised on the very rim of the cliff, framed in the center of the hemlock bows at the limit of the woods. The clear sky rose above the haze across the valley beyond. Emily, her back to Seamus, her gauzy white dress cinched at the waist by a blue satin sash, stood atop the rock, her hands clasped behind her. A breeze came and made her dress and her hair, which was completely undone, float about her like a shimmering halo.

Seamus, careful not to startle her, quietly dropped Emily's hat to the ground and dropped his own as well. He silently slipped of his jacket and placed it on top of the hats. He absently tucked Emily's note in his pocket and took two steps forward. His feet were quiet on the pine needles.

She does not hear me, he thought, there is still a chance.

He took another step and was on the ledge itself.

Emily took a step along the boulder toward the cliff edge.

Seamus advanced two more steps, and Emily looked up to the sky, dropped her hands to her sides, and took another step.

A gust of wind came up and rustled the upper branches of the trees. Seamus took advantage of the covering noise to sprint to the giant rock. Emily was now out of sight above the top edge of the boulder.

Stay there please Emily, said Seamus within himself. He searched the back of the rock for a way to climb up.

How DID she get up there? he thought.

He looked carefully around to the left and then to the right side.

There! Part way along the right side of the rock a combination of natural and man-made hand and footholds pocked the boulder. Seamus crept around and looked up. He could just see Emily's right shoulder and the side of her face.

A strong gust of wind rushed through the trees and blew her long brown hair around her face. Seamus again used the covering sound and climbed up one foothold and then the next, his hands reaching for the carved handholds. His feet slipped and he was let hanging by his fingertips.

How I wish, he thought, I had time to change into my doe-boy's boots, before beginning this impromptu woodland jaunt.

But those accouterments of the infantryman were resting in his trunk in his room and did him no good here.

He suppressed a grunt and peddled the air until the square toes of his shoes again found purchase on the rock face. The wind died and Seamus hung in a crouch below the flat top of the boulder.

Emily, still gazing toward the heavens took another step.

Please, God, Seamus prayed silently.

The wind suddenly roared from the west across the ridge of the mountain and Seamus flexed the muscles of his arms and legs in practiced coordination and leapt cat-like to the top of the boulder. He landed crouched on toes and fingertips, his eyes focused on the center of Emily's back. The wind again died.

Emily took one more step and then had no steps left. Her next move would be into the sky above the Hudson River Valley.

Seamus estimated that he was at about the middle the rock; ten feet, at least, behind Emily.

One chance and one chance only, he thought, to cover that distance.

All was silence, and then a hawk screamed high up in the air. A piercing sound, like an iron nail drawn across a pane of glass. A sound meant to frighten a hidden rabbit into making its last move.

Out of the corner of his eye, Seamus saw the mass of a towering black cloud growing above the mountain ridge to the southwest. The rest of the sky remained clear, blue and sunny.

A tremendous gust of wind blasted down the mountain. It hit Emily with force and tipped her balance. She lifted her arms like wings, and Seamus was up and springing forward. Two vaulting steps and his chest slammed into her back. He threw his arms around her waist and the momentum of his lunge bent them both over double, dancing on tiptoes at the brink. The dome of the woods far bellow and the distant horizon changed places in Seamus eyes again and again as he strained against gravity.

He rocked back on his heels, dug in and flung himself rearward taking Emily with him. He fell back on the flat of the boulder and Emily on top of him. She struggled against him.

"Please, please be still." he choked.

"Oh, it is you," she cried, "let me go, I must die, I wish to die!"

"No!" he screamed as loud as he could next to her ear. "No, you do not wish to die! You do not wish to die, and if you did, I would not let you! Our lives are not ours to throw away, they belong to God!"

Emily stopped her struggling, and all was silent again.

Minutes passed and they lay atop Boulder Rock, the blue sky above them, Emily's cheek against Seamus cheek. He felt her warm tears streaming down. Her body shook with silent sobs and his own eyes filled up. He closed his eyes and they overflowed down his cheek, the two streams of tears mingling.

Thank you, he said within himself to heaven.

The sunlight glowed orange through his shut eyelids. He felt bathed in pleasing warmth. A shadow crossed his face and then another.

Seamus opened his eyes to see three vultures circling down out of the clear sky. One was closest, another farther up and the last still higher above, but they were all coming down. They wheeled about with immense patience, looking to see what was not moving atop the Boulder Rock. Their frayed black wings reminded Seamus of other times and places where their evil-looking brethren had feasted full.

"Not today." he said aloud.

Not today, he thought, we have cheated you today, you gloomy sons of perdition.

"What?" said Emily sleepily.

"Nothing," he said, "we are getting out of here. Up now, and carefully."

He rolled Emily up into a seated position, her legs hanging over the edge of the boulder. Without letting go of her hand, he lowered himself over the side and felt for the footholds, sliding down and drawing her down with him. When he was standing on the ledge, she slipped down into his arms. She held him and he her. Her face rested against his chest and he rested his face against her hair. Her hair smelled like lemons.

"No," she said, "I do not want to die."

A tremendous peal of thunder crashed down from the highest ridge of the mountain. Seamus looked to the southwestern sky and saw a boiling, black storm cloud bearing down on them. Another great rush of wind scoured the forest, blowing leaves and twigs and dust at them. They sheltered in each others embrace a moment longer.

"We are going to get drenched with rain," said Seamus. "We had best be making our way back to the hotel."

"I do not care if we get drenched." said Emily simply.

"Yes, well you see where there is thunder, there is lightening also. You are just after saying that you do not want to die and neither do I. This open ledge on the top of a mountain is hardly the safest place to be during an electrical storm, so we must hurry. I have noted that the Mountain House is equipped with the very latest in lightening rods, which is not something that can be said for the trees beneath which we will have to travel."

They turned to the trail, and as they entered the woods, another great explosion of electrical force shuddered the very air around them. The sun suddenly disappeared, swallowed by the mass of dark clouds climbing the sky above the western ridge. The rain began in a torrent, as if poured from a titanic bucket.

Seamus took Emily by the hand, and after retrieving their hats and his jacket, led her quickly along the path to the hotel. The trees offered some slight protection from the rain at first, but before long Seamus prediction was fulfilled and they were soaked to the skin. The air rapidly turned cold, and the sky above became completely obscured with black churning clouds. To the north though, through the trees before them, they could see that the sky was still bright. They hurried toward the promise of the dry comfort of the Mountain House.

As they approached the Eagle Rock, Seamus caught a glimpse of the valley and the lightening belching clouds marching up from the south to the north. The blue of the northern sky was being enveloped by the gray, black and violet of the storm line. The trail led back toward the ridge of the mountain, where the floor of the forest was now almost as dark as night. The rain lashed straight down through the trees.

Seamus felt the hair on his head rise up and the world was

blasted with pale blue light. He dropped with Emily to the ground amid the deafening thunder clap, his face in the mold smelling leaves.

Again, a blinding flash of light and an immediate explosion, but now accompanied by the scream of rending wood. A tall pine not three rods away took a direct hit, the top third of the tree shattered. Giant splinters whipped through the air. When the last of the great fragments landed, Seamus was up with Emily's hand grasped in his, sprinting toward the ledge called the 'Lover's Retreat.'

They reached the ledge and stopped a moment beneath the bows of the twin fir trees. To the north and east the sky was still bright, but the encircling clouds where constantly gaining and the rain lashed down. Seamus reckoned this an uneasy place of shelter. At any instant the fir trees which formed the lover's bench could themselves attract the fatal bolt.

They stepped out onto to the ledge just as the last of the light faded in the north. The clouds now swept around from the northwest ridge of the mountain.

"We are being flanked," said Seamus. "No hope now of getting to the house before the storm is all around us."

A flash of lightening illuminated the air accompanied immediately by the impact of thunder just behind the ledge on which they stood. Seamus ducked and looked back to see three soldiers in blue erupt into a fountain of bright red gore. Their shattered rifles cart-wheeled through the forest as did an infantryman's boot with a splintered, bloody white shin bone sticking out of it; strips of flesh and shredded pant leg streamed behind the severed limb.

Seamus straightened up and turned to Emily.

"We must find a bombproof." he said. A bombproof, he thought, as we had when we were before Petersburg.

"What?" she said, her eyes wide, her voice rising against the roar of the wind.

"A bombproof, a bombproof," he said. "A place underground or a hole covered with logs and earth to protect us from their artillery; a bombproof." But he could see that she did not understand. No, of course not, he thought, how could she?

His eyes darted about, searching the ground.

There, he thought, by the side of the ledge to the right, the hint of a path down the steep slope before the land dropped off sheer.

He jumped down into the wet leaves and pulled Emily behind him. She held back against his apparently suicidal course but he pulled on her wrist the harder, pulled her down off the side of the ledge. They slipped on the sodden leaves and slid down to where the cliff began its straight fall to the treetops far below.

Seamus broke their descent with his heels and with his free hand grasped an exposed root. He locked his grip on Emily's wrist and worked his way up and to the left until he entered the cavity beneath the ledge upon which they had been standing. He dragged Emily in behind him. They sat themselves together on the broken slabs of rock within the shallow cave and looked out toward the valley. Little could be seen beyond the walls of cloud and rain.

When they stopped moving they began to shake and shiver. They held each other for warmth. Seamus knew that his own tremors were not just from the cold and the wet.

Emily, her head on his shoulder spoke softly in Seamus ear.

"I must thank you again, as I did yesterday, for saving me. Will you always be there to save me?"

"Yes."

"After this morning," she said, "I became sure that death was looking for me, I thought I should go and meet it."

"You must not think that way." he said.

"With Fenton dead I thought I had nothing left, not that I loved him, quiet the opposite. It is just that I felt all alone in this world. Everyone who was of my family is now dead."

"But you mentioned your aunt in Georgetown who nursed you back to health." said Seamus.

"Aunt Margaret, dear Aunt Margaret. She was my father's sister, but older than he. I had lived with her during the school years after my mother had died with the ague when I was nine. Aunt Margaret was like a mother to me. Father insisted that I get a full education, so I went to school in Georgetown at Miss

English's Seminary and lived with Aunt Margaret. She was very bright and was father's partner in his import and export business. She taught me the workings of the company which they had incorporated in Washington where it is chartered through Mr. Cooke's First National Bank, even now.

"After I lost my Robby, father made me a partner too. He wanted me to be independent. He knew that the South was changing no matter how the war ended, and that a young lady could not afford to be dependent in the world that was coming.

"No," said Emily sighing, "Aunt Margaret is dead now too. Her body was found one morning in the canal in Georgetown. She had gone to do her usual errands and the marshal of the town said that he assumed she had a spell of dizziness crossing the little bridge by the canal lock. But the marshal had known Auntie for years and knew her to be of vigorous constitution, she simply never was sick. He seemed amazed that she should have had such a spell. Still she was over seventy . . ."

Emily's voice trailed off.

"After the funeral," she continued, "Fenton insisted that we come north. He said that the mountain air would be good for my recovery and he had business in New York with his associate Mr. McCain, who was on the porch with us this morning.

"Auntie never liked Fenton, few people did. He had done business with father, bringing in medicine and other needed things during the war through the Yank . . . I mean through the Federal blockade from Europe and Canada. After Robby and then father were killed in battle, Fenton was so kind and seemed so attentive to me, and I felt so alone at that time. Well, he proposed and we were married. And then I found that he was, in truth, a man of the lowest degree."

Emily held Seamus the stronger and whispered into his ear.

"Colonel," she said, "I must tell you something, but do not look at me while I tell you. Instead look out at the storm, and . . . here . . . hold my hand tight, tighter.

"When I married Fenton, I was living at our family town house in Raleigh. The Union troops held our plantation near the coast, I expect they still do. The night of our wedding . . . Fenton became so drunk that he could not . . ."

"You do not have to say this!" Seamus interrupted.

"Yes, I do. Please let me tell you. He could not perform the functions of a husband . . . he was so drunk. Do men's real characters come out when they are drunk? Is it really *in vino veritas*, or is a decent character and disposition corrupted by drunkenness?"

A good question, thought Seamus, but he said nothing. At that very moment he had been considering reaching for his flask but now dismissed the impulse.

"That night," said Emily, "Fenton fainted from the drink. I left our room . . . slept in the guest quarters. The following morning one of the servants of our neighbors came to me. I had known her since I was a child. She is a dear woman and very brave. If her master had known that she was 'meddling' in white folk's affairs, it would have gone hard for her. She had no fear, and revealed to me that it was known in the town . . . in certain districts . . . that Fenton was afflicted with an unspeakable malady and that had she not been down at her master's plantation before our marriage, only just returning that day, she would have risked whatever penalty to tell me that I must in some way . . . avoid Fenton.

"That night, when Fenton, slightly less drunk, came to our room, I showed him Robby's pistol which his men had brought back to me, and told him that I would kill him before I would let him . . .

"I still have that pistol in my room, I kept it with me always. He never did bother me that way again. He was, like most bullies, a coward. He laughed at me that night, and told me that he could get what he wanted, and at less of a price than his life, from women who he found to be much more interesting than me . . ."

"Emily, please . . ."

"I must tell you this, Seamus." she said.

She called me by name, he thought. He felt suddenly warm, stopped shivering completely.

"I must tell you this," she said, "Thereafter, while he never approached me in that way again, he usually treated me contemptuously. He told me that he had married me only to take over father's business. He had assumed that I would not, as a female, have been able to inherit father's property. When he found out that it was not a matter of inheritance, but that I was a full partner, and that Auntie and I *were*, along with a few small shareholders; the company, he became transfixed with rage. At times he would relent in his behavior toward me, but now I can see that it was only when he wanted me to cooperate with him in some way.

"I was still in law, and before God, his wife, and I could not bare the humiliation if all the world could see what a sham our marriage was, so I tried to keep up appearances. Today, after he had been killed, my feelings were so . . . so . . ."

Emily shook her head as though to clear her thoughts.

"I had told him," she continued, "that I would shoot him if he ever . . . and I know that I would have too. And God knows that I had, at the worst of it, wished him dead. Here he was shot standing next to me. And all the blood . . . , I just did not know but that God had answered my wish. As a Christian, I have no right to wish someone dead, ever."

She sobbed once.

"So I came here to the cliffs . . .," she said and her voice was lost in weeping.

Seamus held her until she stopped crying.

"Emily," he said into her hair, "I want you to freely swear to me, that you will not again attempt to take your own life."

"I do so swear." she said.

"I want you to give me time to work on this," he said. "I have learned some things from what you have told me."

One of the things was that Emily was yet another person on the mountain top who had threatened to take Fenton Clay's life and who possessed a pistol, but he did not say that.

"You," he said, "ever having wished Clay dead is not what killed him. A bullet did that."

He reached into his pocket for his handkerchief to dry Emily's tears and came out instead with her note. It was damp and the ink running. He handed it to her without a word and she silently tore it into small pieces.

The wind and the rain had subsided, with just a light shower coming down. The clouds across the valley above the Berkshires were the color of indigo dye. The rain slowly stopped entirely and suddenly the sun came out, low over the ridge behind them. The valley was lit in verdant patterns of field and forest. The little white houses and the church below in Palenville glowed orange in the declining light. Against the angry clouds at the eastern horizon, two mighty rainbows appeared side by side, spanning the distance from the city of Hudson in the north to Poughkeepsie and beyond in the south.

Emily tossed the tiny bits of torn paper up like a handful of confetti and the mild breeze swirled them down the cliff. Her eyes followed as the bits were borne away and she smiled as Seamus watched her. She turned to him.

"Do you think," she asked, "that there is a hope for things to get better?"

"Yes." he replied wondering if he were being truthful. He changed the subject.

"I want you to promise," he said, "that you will be careful, and not wander about alone, and that you will stay near the hotel and among people."

"I will." she said.

"At night I want you to be sure that you lock your door. Promise me." he said.

She nodded her head in the affirmative.

"Good." he said as he rose, stooped over in their snug refuge. "We had better go before we catch a chill."

He helped her up and onto the ledge and held her hand as they walked along the path through the dripping, glittering, sunlit woods toward the distant clearing where the Mountain House stood.

They passed the tall stump of the pine tree which they had last seen exploded by the lightening. Seamus saw no mangled remains of soldiers. The underbrush did not look as though a company of firemen had filed their engine with crimson gore and sprayed the bushes with it as would have been the case had a real artillery shell struck a group of men; had the scene been real and not just imagined at the time by Seamus. The fallen leaves and pine needles were littered, far and wide, with long splinters of wood, not with severed arms and legs.

It had looked real enough at the moment though, thought Seamus. Yes, there is always hope that things will get better, but am I not getting worse? Nightmares in the daytime now, while I am awake. This is not a sign of improvement. Am I loosing my mind?

The thought had occurred to him before but this vision was a new refinement in horror.

He held Emily closer and helped her down the wall of puddingstone which had cost him the knee of his trousers on his outward journey. He slipped this time too, damaging the seat of the beleaguered garment. Emily laughed her two hands clasped to her lips. He rewarded her at first with an indignant look, then with a shake of the head and then he laughed as well. They negotiated the final slope down through the woods with slips and slides on the wet leaves and pine needles until they were at the edge of the clearing at the trail head.

He let go her hand as they crossed the lawn toward the hotel. Its white walls gleamed with a coral tint in the cloud filtered sunshine. Torrents of water rushed out the downspouts and fell from the cornices round about. The Mountain House seemed to Seamus like ship which had just put into port after weathering the tempest. Crowds of people were gathered on the upper and lower piazzas, and at the cliff all looking to the east were the twin rainbows shown steadily. From above, a man yelled.

"The light is secure!" he said. Seamus looked up and there was Sampson on the flat roof of the south wing standing next to a big canvass covered object. Sampson looked down and caught sight of the approaching couple.

"Colonel and Miz Emily," he said, "oh, it is good to see you both! We were worried . . . about the storm I mean . . . Sarah will be so glad." He turned to the doorway in the wall of the central wing.

"Jacob," he said "tell Sarah that the Colonel and Miz Emily have returned."

Presently, the people turned their attention from the rainbows to the odd looking pair crossing the lawn. Seamus whispered in Emily's ear.

"We have a way, you and I, of making an attractive entrance." he said.

Sarah appeared on the upper piazza and fairly raced down the steps. She paused at the foot of the staircase, collected herself and came forth at a statelier pace.

"Well, Colonel," she said when she had reached them, "every time you return with this lady, she is soaking wet and covered with mud." Her eyes smiled through the feigned reproach. As in the past, she took charge of Emily and the two disappeared into the building through the door to the lounge.

Seamus, left standing alone on the path before the cliff, became the sole object of attention for his fellow guests. He doffed his sodden straw hat, executed a Shakespearean flourish and bow, straightened up and intoned:

"Ladies and gentlemen, I bid you a good afternoon!"

As one, they instantly looked away.

Give the curious, thought Seamus, something to be really curious about and they immediately loose interest

A few brave souls chanced to glance back at Seamus and he promptly treated them to a few quick capers from a step dance, his arms stiff at his sides. The brave souls looked away even faster than they had before.

Why is it, Seamus wondered, that the Irish have such an undeserved reputation for being mad?

When he had assured himself that no one had any further interest in him, he slowly ascended the stairs to the second floor piazza, entered the hall and turned toward his room. Sampson, just descending the central staircase, fell in step with him and accompanied him.

"If I hurry," said Seamus, "I may yet have time to go down the mountain and visit the gunsmith before dark."

"No, Colonel," Sampson replied, "Mr. Beecher has had some disturbing news and has asked me to convey his request that you not leave the mountain top tonight and that you meet with him in his office as soon as possible."

"Very well." said Seamus. They had reached the door to his room; he opened it and turned to Sampson.

"I will leave these clothes in the hall. Would you please see what can be done with regard to mending and cleaning them, and please inform Mr. Beecher that I will wait upon him as soon as I have changed and gotten myself cleaned up a bit."

"I will, Colonel." said Sampson and he was off down the hall.

Seamus entered and quickly inspected the room. Finding no evidence that anyone had intruded in his absence, he set about washing up and changing. He was now back to his Brooks Brother's suit. Before donning his coat, he searched in his trunk, found and put on the shoulder holster which he had purchased in New York City. He wore the uncomfortable item with its leather harness only when he thought that there might be a good chance that he would have to get to his Police Pistol in a hurry. He considered that Mr. Beecher's disturbing news, whatever it was, could forebode of such an eventuality.

He left his room and hurried to the central stairs. He climbed to the third floor and just before he reached the top step, the door to room 217, directly across from him, opened. Out stepped Mr. McCain. He was in shirtsleeves, his long black coat draped over his crooked arm. He walked past Seamus without acknowledgment. He began to descend the stairs, resting his right hand upon the banister level with Seamus' eyes.

A primitive blue tattoo; short, jagged, saw-tooth lines, was inscribed on the edge of the man's hand behind the small finger.

Seamus turned left toward the office, but quickly and quietly back-tracked to glimpse, at an angle, down the stairwell, McCain passing the second floor and reaching, at last the ground floor. He could not see which way the man turned, but guessed that he may have been going to the dinning hall. As if in confirmation, the notes of the supper gong floated up from below. The sound reminded Seamus that he was hungry and he hoped that his meeting with Mr. Beecher would not take long.

Seamus reached the office door and knocked.

The door was opened by Sampson, who directed Seamus to a chair in front of the desk in the center of the room.

Mr. Beecher rose from his seat behind the desk and welcomed Seamus in his old-fashioned, courtly way. When they both were seated, Mr. Beecher began.

"Colonel," he said, "I am delighted to see that you came through this afternoon's storm without any injury befalling either you or Mrs. Clay. The cliffs can be especially dangerous during violent weather. We are happy that our prayers have been answered and that you are both back safe and sound. It would have been particularly tragic had any . . . accident . . . happened to Mrs. Clay."

Seamus was sure that Mr. Beecher missed nothing of what transpired in his vast domain.

"While you were out," Mr. Beecher continued, "I received a telegraphic message which Constable Wyncoop had sent via a messenger to my office in Catskill. The constable reported that he was unable to leave the county jail, where the sheriff's office is located in Catskill, as he and the deputy sheriff were virtually besieged by an unruly mob composed of the lower types of the town. The crowd began to form, as predicted, as soon as the story was circulated that a black man had killed a white man at the Mountain House this morning. The deputy sent his brother, a youth of some sixteen years, out the back door of the sheriff's office, with instructions to take the constable's message to my telegrapher and to find some reliable citizens who could be deputized to defend the jail.

"In the meantime, the deputy and the constable are playing a dangerous game not letting on that Luther is *not* in the jail. The constable feels that the jail is far more defensible than is this hotel and he would rather that the hot heads of Catskill stay there instead of coming up to the mountain top to join their like-minded brethren here and take Luther from us. Of course, the constable knows that it is only a matter of time before it becomes general knowledge that Luther is being held here and the mob directs its attention to us. Humphrey believes that such a turn of events could occur as early as tonight. He views the mob's arrival here no later than tomorrow evening as a virtual certainty, given the continued exodus of guests and the fact that it was impossible to keep secret the removal of Luther to the root cellar. We can at least hope that by that time the judge will have returned and the truth of the crime can be established.

"The constable has therefore asked, Colonel, that you take

whatever measures you may be able in order to be on the alert against the possible action of the mob."

Mr. Beecher concluded his report and looked searchingly across his desk at Seamus.

Seamus thought that little or nothing could be done to defend the hotel from a mob which would, presumably, be armed and possibly well armed, but he saw no need to give the old gentleman that gloomy assessment.

"Yes, sir," said Seamus, "I will see what can be done."

"I am sure that you will, Colonel," said his host, "and I thank you for myself and on behalf of all of us here at the Mountain House."

Mr. Beecher continued.

"I have," he said, "received all of the reports from the staff who have been . . .ah . . . . examining the rooms in search of firearms. I have compared the numbers of the rooms which have thus far been seen against my copy of the guest register for this week. I have a list of all the rooms in the hotel with the names of the occupants next to their respective rooms as of this morning. There is a check mark in the left margin to denote rooms in which firearms were found, along with a short note written to the right.

"In this pile," he said, indicating a short stack of note papers on his desk, "are the slips upon which the staff have recorded details regarding what firearms have been found. As you know, Colonel, the search remains essentially incomplete, but we will have finished with all the rooms which were occupied at the time of the crime by late tomorrow morning."

Mr. Beecher handed the papers to Seamus.

The list was arranged by room number starting at the lowest. The rooms around the interior court yards were unoccupied and had not been searched. The ground floor rooms which faced the valley and some of the others downstairs were occupied and most had been searched. A check appeared next to the name of the occupant of room number 7 directly below Seamus' room. An explanatory note indicated that a Mr. Cazewell owned a shotgun. It was found in his closet in a case. Seamus picked up the corresponding slip of paper where there appeared a simple but creditable sketch of a double-barreled shotgun, signed by a *vidette*/chambermaid named Sally. She had made the picture and had impressed the muzzles on the paper tracing the outside dimension. Seamus estimated the inside dimension to be about twelve gauge. Sally had also copied the word, 'Purdey' along with, 'gunsmiths London', and some numbers.

Good job, Sally, thought Seamus, but Clay was not killed with a shotgun.

He continued reading down the list. Mr. Tompkins room, number 28, had been searched without result. Skipping down the list Seamus saw that his own room had also been examined and no firearm found.

That, thought, Seamus is because I never leave a gun in a room but instead carry it. He considered a moment and looked up from the list.

"Mr. Beecher," he said, "where is room number 28?"

"It is located, Colonel, at the rear-most end of the south wing. Not one of our most desirable rooms, but it *is* a corner room with windows both to the west and the north. Of course, the north facing window affords a view only of the circular drive and the back entrance. The room no doubt fills the needs of Mr. Tompkins as he is a . . . um ... commercial traveler."

Meaning, thought Seamus, that Tompkins is a traveling drummer with high ambitions but most likely with little remaining of the capital he probably amassed during the war and it is surprising that he can afford even a cheap room in this elegant hostelry. It is where, however, the clientele he hopes to cultivate comes to spend the summer. Mr. Beecher was far too decent a sort to put it that way, but those were the facts of the matter.

That corner of the building was, Seamus recalled, where he had earlier noticed the Reverend and Mrs. Van Wyck conversing with Scipio.

He perused the list further. A Mr. Sutton of San Francisco, currently occupying room number 101, directly below the office in which they were sitting, was the owner of a pistol found in his dresser drawer. Seamus leafed through the stack of notes and came up with another work by Sally. The pistol in question was an old six-shot pepper box. Sally had done a nice depiction of the multi-barreled handgun, and had impressed the six muzzles into the paper and traced the outside dimension, leaving an outline vaguely like that of a six-petaled flower. Seamus estimated the caliber at about .25 or perhaps a bit more. Not a likely murder weapon in this case, let alone the fact that these pistols had never been designed for long range work, more likely the width of the captain's quarter deck on a clipper ship in the event of mutiny, or the breadth of a poker table in the event of dishonesty. Pepper boxes were the favorites of those defending their claims back during the gold rush of '49 and of the claim jumpers as well.

Well, thought Seamus, did you make your fortune, Mr. Sutton in the gold fields of California and do you keep this old pistol as a memento? Were you a claim defender or a claim jumper? Perhaps you were both.

He continued studying the list. A few more firearms of various descriptions had been found, but none that would match the weapon which had killed Clay.

A thought came suddenly to Seamus and he looked to room number 217 on the list. It was described as being unoccupied. Room 219, next door, was listed as being occupied by Mr. Ian McCain of New York City. That room had been searched and no weapon found.

Of course! thought Seamus. More thoughts came to him in a rush.

"Mr. Beecher, Sampson," he said jumping to his feet, "the unoccupied rooms must be searched also!"

The two looked at Seamus with dismay.

"And we must start right now with room 217!" he said heading toward the door.

"Sampson, you have a pass key? Good. Let's go. There is no time to lose! By your leave, Mr. Beecher."

Seamus was out the door and running down the hall and Sampson following.

"I was a bloody fool," said Seamus over his shoulder to Sampson, "a *bloody*, fool to have only the occupied rooms searched."

They came to the door of the room McCain had exited and which was officially listed as being empty of guests. Seamus restrained his desire to enter. He checked around the lock and the door frame for telltales. He had seen McCain leaving the room without apparently setting any such warnings but Seamus was resolved to make no more amateur mistakes. When he was satisfied, he signaled Sampson to use his key.

As Sampson opened the door, the sounds of Professor's Smith's band rehearsal could be heard from below. Seamus reminded himself that he needed to have a few words with the professor.

Seamus and Sampson entered the room and began a thorough search. The edges of the rug, the wash stand, the closet, the dresser, the bed, the window sills, every conceivable hiding place was examined. After about fifteen minutes, it was clear that there was nothing to be found.

Seamus stood in the middle the room staring at the floor.

"Room number 4," he said suddenly. "Room number four, we must search there right now." He was out the door and descending the stairs in an instant with Sampson hastily locking the door behind them.

Seamus stopped when he reached the ground floor, and waited for Sampson to join him. A steady stream of guests was crossing the lobby, traveling to and fro between the dining hall, the piazza and the central corridor. McCain came out of the lounge across from room number four. He turned in Seamus direction, and Seamus faced about and spoke to Sampson in a low voice.

"I do not wish to attract attention," he said, "if you go into the room it will not be remarked." McCain passed them, heading toward the dinning hall, his long black coat now on his large, trim frame.

"Please go now," said Seamus to Sampson, "and search the room as we did number 217. I will wait for you in the lounge."

Seamus watched Sampson go to the door of the room and nonchalantly examine it for telltales before letting himself in.

Good man, Sampson, thought Seamus, you are a quick study.

Seamus walked to the door of the lounge and found it to be slightly
ajar. He started to enter but halted. An angry voice came from within. Three people were sitting opposite the door in front of the tall windows which looked out upon the valley.

"Damned! Damned by God for all eternity!" said the voice. It was, to Seamus astonishment, the voice of the Reverend Mr. Van Wyck. The same voice he had heard at the morning's prayer service, but no longer sweet and dulcet, but rather now growling, raspy, barely contained into a harsh whisper from breaking into a veritable bellow.

The good dominie stood up from where he was sitting with his wife and Major Savage. As he rose, so did his voice.

"Damned, I tell you, sir, damned!" he said and he turned from the maniacally grinning major to rush past Seamus in the doorway and head for the back stairs.

Mrs. Van Wyck got up as well and trailed after her inflamed husband.

"Schyler, Schyler, please!" she clucked.

The Major, for his part, remained in his supine position on the chaise, his eyes following the retreating couple, the mad leer on his face fixed.

Seamus turned away and closed the door as the Van Wycks disappeared into the stairwell at the end of the hall.

Sampson emerged from the room across the passage, a look of dismay upon his face.

"I did not find a thing of importance in the room, Colonel," he said. "The room is clean and empty. There was a dead ant on the floor below the window." He held up cleaning cloth with the flattened insect on it. In life, it had been a large black ant. Seamus examined the carcass briefly.

"I had hoped you would find more, Sampson." he said, not without irony.

Still, he thought, how had the ant met its end? Someone had apparently stepped on it. Who? When?

Levi approached from the direction of the lobby, greeted Seamus and handed him a small, delicate envelope. Seamus opened it and immediately recognized the note paper and the hand. He read to himself:

'Dear, Colonel, would you be so kind as to dine with me at seven o'clock tonight in the private dinning room. Please give your reply to the bearer of this note.' The signature was Emily's.

Seamus was again wrapped in the warmth he had last felt in the cave that afternoon when she had called him by name. He stood smiling at the note.

"Your reply, Colonel?" said Levi at length. He was smiling also. "The lady is presently waiting in the private room as it is nearly seven."

"Yes," Seamus roused himself. "The reply is yes, Levi. Please tell the lady that I will join her directly." Levi departed still smiling broadly and Seamus turned to Sampson.

"Thank you for all your help," he said. "The unoccupied rooms should be inspected as soon as possible."

"We will be working on it, Colonel."

"Very good. I see, Sampson, that Mrs. Clay's room has not yet been searched. You should do so now."

Sampson gave Seamus a very strange look indeed and left for the backstairs.

Seamus walked the few steps to the oval staircase and paused. A notice had been pinned to the placard which stood upon an easel facing the lobby:

Ladies and Gentlemen;

Due to the tragic events of this morning, and out of respect for the deceased, this evening's hop has been canceled. The band however will be providing suitable, refined and soothing music on the upper piazza this evening to accompany the viewing of the river boats, commencing at half past eight o'clock. Thank You, Prof. O.S. Smith

Seamus mounted the stairs two at a time and turned into the ballroom on the second floor. He hurried to the back of the room where the Professor was standing in front of his ensemble and waited until they had finished playing a rendition of *I Dreamt I Dwelt in Marble Halls.* Then he took the band leader by the arm and spoke a few earnest words to him. Professor Smith signaled the musicians to rest and Seamus walked him to the French doors behind the band. He stepped through the open doors onto the balcony above the rear entrance and looked to the reddening western sky. He glanced for a moment down to his left to the window of Tompkins' room on the edge of the circular drive as he talked with the professor and then looked back to the west. Beyond the trees, each of the lakes burned with the reflected crimson of twilight.

The professor went back to the doorway and called out the names of three of his bandsmen. When they had come out on the balcony he introduced them to Seamus and hands were shaken all around.

Seamus gestured toward the isthmus between the lakes as he addressed the men. Then he pointed straight toward the west behind the stables and then down in the direction of the mountain road. When the conversation had ended, the professor and his musicians went back to their rehearsal and Seamus remained for a time on the balcony watching the glow in the cloudless sky. The coolness in the air, which had begun with the afternoon's storm, lingered. The whole mountain top seemed to be awash in refreshment.

The band smoothly slid into *Flow Gently Sweet Afton* and Seamus took his leave exchanging nods with Professor Smith as he went. He descended the stairs to the lobby and crossed to the private dining room. He knocked and Levi ushered him in.

Emily was seated at the table in the center of the room. She was dressed as she had been when he had first seen her, but with her hair up and arranged on the top of her head. The candles on the table and on the sideboard had been lighted and Emily radiated beauty as she smiled at him. Seamus felt his throat tighten. He seated himself as Levi held his chair.

# VI

## In the Cool of the Evening

"Colonel," said Levi, "Miz Emily has ordered for you both. Lamb cutlets in wine and rosemary sauce with our assorted fresh vegetables, potatoes, rolls and butter and mint jelly. The wine is one of the premier *crus* of the Medoc, Chateau Lafite 1856, and if you are ready to dine, I am ready to present your meal."

"Levi," said Seamus, "I am ready."

"Very good, Colonel," said Levi as he set about his tasks. When he had laid out the food and drink, he left, and Emily at last spoke.

"As you are from Ireland," she said, "I thought it no harm to order lamb, as I understand that it is a popular dish there."

"Indeed, Ma'am," said Seamus, it has always been one of my favorites."

This was true and he did not think it necessary to add that he had seldom seen lamb or any other meat as a child growing up in the land of his birth. Usually, at home, he had lived on potatoes and milk, and for a while on Trevelyan's Indian corn in a thin gruel and then it seemed for the longest time on nothing at all.

After he had been taken to live with Father Healy and Aunt Mollie, in later years after the worst of the Famine had subsided, they sometimes had lamb, or mutton really, maybe at Easter.

Seamus and Emily each took a sample of the meat. It was delicious. He reached for his wine glass and hesitated.

Oh, he thought, it is just a drop of wine with dinner. It couldn't hurt.

They picked up their glasses together and inclined them

toward each other. The candle light made rainbows in the faceted crystal. Emily took a small sip and Seamus set his glass down half empty.

"Mr. McCain," said Emily, "like you, is from Ireland."

Seamus choked on the last drop of wine in his throat and put his napkin to his lips. He hacked and coughed and tried to regain his breath.

Of course! he thought, it was not a Scottish accent in which McCain had spoken. It was rather the accent of the Province of Ulster in the north of Ireland, and something else as well, some other tincture of clipped cadence and tone.

"My goodness!" said Emily. "Are you all right Seamus?"

"Yes, yes," he managed to say, "Pardon me, please." Once again her using his given name had its recuperative effect and he settled back to normal respiration.

I could, he thought, never tire of hearing her say my name.

"Yes," Emily continued, "As I was saying, Mr. McCain is from Ireland, but left there quite some time ago and lived in Canada for many years although he traveled to many places on business or at least that is my understanding.

"I only know about him being from Ireland because Fenton used to jibe him that he did not drink like an Irishman even though he was from there, and he does not. He is very moderate in his drinking."

She looked up suddenly from her plate, her face reddening.

"Oh!" she said, "I did not mean to imply that . . . the Irish . . . drink immoderately."

She blushed right down to the collar of her dress.

"It is all right, Emily," he said, finding her blush quite charming. "Many of the Irish do drink a good deal. It is a fact, and facts must be faced."

Seamus found her embarrassment incredibly attractive. He could think of nothing about her at the moment which was not attractive. He emptied his glass in illustration of his last statement.

"Were you and Mr. Clay friendly with Mr. McCain for some time?" he asked.

"Friendly is not a term which fits Mr. McCain in any way.

He was always polite to me," she said, "and in some instances intervened on my behalf when Fenton would become just too beastly, but I have always felt that Mr. McCain looks down upon me and perhaps upon women in general or maybe upon people in general. He is very reserved but seemed to have considerable influence with Fenton. Even at his worst, Fenton would not usually argue for long with Mr. McCain. I felt that Mr. McCain tried to make Fenton improve his behavior simply because he was himself sometimes embarrassed by Fenton's loudness and outrageous actions and because Mr. McCain had no choice but to continue the association since it was apparently profitable.

"That is, I felt that way until this morning when Mr. McCain came to our door and insisted that Fenton accompany him to the sunrise service. He told Fenton that the experience would do him good. I was particularly surprised as I had never known Mr. McCain to be in the least bit religious. I was astonished when Fenton, after some feeble protest, agreed to come with us to the service.

"Mr. McCain had come to our suite last night, keeping Fenton under a degree of control as usual, and after Fenton had fallen asleep in the parlor, he had left. This morning he told Fenton that last night he had agreed to attend the service.

"Now, I doubt whether Fenton could remember much of what anyone said last night, but sometimes after a bad bout of drinking he would seem full of regret and for a short while would resolve to change. He never followed through with such intentions but I understand that such a pattern; regret and backsliding is not unusual with drunkards."

Not unusual, at all, thought Seamus.

"In any case," Emily continued, "I was pleasantly surprised to see that Mr. McCain might really help Fenton to turn a new leaf. I was always hoping that there would be some hope. Who could have known how the morning would turn out?"

Someone knew, thought Seamus.

Levi returned, and refilled Seamus' glass. Emily's was down only by about two sips, Seamus noticed. Levi inquired if all was well and whether or not anything was needed and again departed.

"Now," said Emily looking over the top of her glass, "tell me all about yourself Seamus."

He was lifting a forkful of potatoes to his lips and quickly shoveled them in so as to give himself a few moments to think how to get out of complying with the request.

No, he decided, it was not a request, it was an order. He looked up smiled and pointed to his mouth, chewing away assiduously. Could not talk with his mouth full, he tried to communicate without speaking. He smiled again.

She did too, but ironically. She saw right through him.

"I can wait." she said and put down her glass. She folded her hands on the table.

Tell her about me, he thought. I can't do that. I never told anyone about me, Felim excepted, and maybe Mick Dolan. Felim knew everything about me but he was family, and Mick a comrade. His mind raced. As panic set in he swallowed his food and drank half his glass of wine.

"There is," he said touching his napkin delicately to his lips, "but little to tell."

Little, he thought, which I could tell to an American lady or to a civilian that would be understood. But this Southern lady understands loss, he thought. She knows about loss. Suddenly, he wanted to tell her.

"I was born in Ireland, as you know. The year of my birth was 1838. I grew up in a small town in the County Mayo. Really in a tiny hamlet called Island outside the town of Ballyhaunis. My father was a farmer. He farmed conacre, which means he was a kind of a tenant farmer. Very few of our people actually *owned* any land. I do not remember very much about my family, just the odd picture in my mind.

"When I was about seven years old, the potato crop began to fail. A blight came over the plants and they turned from green to black overnight. We could not eat the potatoes, so we had nothing to eat. Year after year things got worse. Corn imported from America barely kept us alive. We could not pay our rent so the army and the police and the bailiffs came and put us out on the road.

"I had two sisters, one younger than I. I remember them and my mother standing in the road crying. My father cried too. I remember the red uniforms on the soldiers. Before they left, the soldiers set the thatch of our roof on fire so that we could not later move back into the little stone cabin."

Seamus stopped his throat dry. He took a drink of wine.

"I was told," he said, "some of what I now know of those days many years later when I was reunited with some of my relatives. I understand that we set out from Ballyhaunis toward the town of Tuam in County Galway because my father had a cousin there who farmed on the estate of Mr. Charles Cromie of Annefield House. Mr. Cromie had reduced his rents in response to the Famine and distributed all the oats and grain grown on his property to his tenants to be ground to make meal and flour to keep them from starvation. Few were such examples of Christian kindness on the part of landlords in those days, but they have never been forgotten. In the end it did no good for my family. We never got to Tuam. Weakened by hunger and fever, we children and my mother could not go on. My father put up a shelter for us and tried to get help, but he must never have made it. My mother and sisters died by the roadside."

Seamus paused for a moment and went on.

"Although the potatoes had failed, other crops did well and the landlords kept exporting food stuffs to England throughout the Famine years. Of course, the food had to be moved under guard. Until they become too weak, starving people can commit desperate acts. I was found and rescued by an English soldier who was escorting carts loaded with grain. The cart man was from Ballyhaunis and recognized my people. He told the corporal, Watson was his name, who I was and the soldier wrote my name and the names of my parents on a slip of paper and pinned it to my shirt. He was a very brave soldier, because when he found me I was sick with fever and he could have caught the sickness too. He kept me with him and nursed me as best he could all the way until we reached the Cove of Cork, a harbor city some people now call Queenstown, in the very south of Ireland. He could take me no farther as he and his company were being sent back to England possibly to face court martial.

"He took me to the home of a parish priest just outside the town. There he found Mary Healy, who I later knew as Aunt

Mollie. A maiden lady, she lived with her brother Father Patrick Healy and was his housekeeper. They were originally from Tralee in County Kerry. Well, Corporal Watson told Aunt Mollie that she would have to take me in and take care of me as there was nothing else he could do. Before he had rescued me, he and his company had been detailed to evict starving peasants off an estate owned by a man named Walshe near Nephin, above in Mayo. The troops had grown heartily sick of putting these dying people out onto the road in the teeth of a storm in the midst of winter. The soldiers as much as mutinied and gave what money they had to the people as had some of the Scottish Highlander regiments earlier in that year. Corporal Watson's commander had invented a ruse to get them out of doing Walshe's filthy work for him and now they were all in trouble. Could not Aunt Mollie do something for the sick little boy?

"Well to be sure," Seamus smiled across the table, "she did which is how I am here now to tell you this story.

"There was no shortage of half-starved, feverish children anywhere in Ireland and the fear of contamination was real, but she took me in and the good soldier went on his way to Spike Island in the harbor and the fort there and then on to England. Years later, Aunt Mollie told me that when her brother came home that day from making his rounds of ministering to the hordes of refugees in the town, he was very cross with her for having taken me in. Aunt Mollie told me that he said that they could not take in every child who was brought to the door. Aunt Mollie told me what she had said in reply:
'Patcheen . . . , I mean Father, it is not every child in starving Ireland, it is just this one. And would you have had me put shame on our race by telling the English soldier, who had saved the lad that we, *we ourselves*, would not take care of one of our own. And finally Patcheen what would the Master do, what would Jesus do, put the child in the street?'

"He had no answer of course, and so I grew up there in the poor, frugal little parish house. I regained my strength eventually after a rather long time when I would get well and then sick again, recover and get sick yet again. Father Patrick was a truly saintly man and took great delight in being my teacher. I learned arithmetic and reading and learned English too. As a child at home I had spoken only Irish. He taught me the rudiments of Latin and Greek and history and classical literature, philosophy and doctrine. I was his acolyte and assisted him at Mass and in his rounds of the parish, up and down the steep streets of the port.

"I fear he was very much disappointed that I did not go into the priesthood, but as a youth I became enamored of the idea of traveling the world. At first, I worked handling livestock and cargo on the boats plying the rivers and canals of Ireland. I saw much of the country that way and I always hoped to go to sea. When England entered the war in the Crimea, they were looking for recruits to join the dragoons, particularly those who had experience with horses. I 'took the Queen's shilling' and before long I was on my way to Turkey and then up the Black Sea. Poor Father Patrick must have thought I was really lost then. But he told me I could always find a home with him and Aunt Mollie.

"Well, I was in the Crimea for a time, got sick and they sent me home. I recovered from the fever, but did not get back my strength right away so I was invalided out of the service. I came back to the parish house in Cove for a time but it became clear to me that as much as I love my homeland, and I still do, there was nothing there for me any more. Father told me that in my absence one of my relations from Mayo had come looking for me. The man had heard by chance that I had survived the Famine. He himself had removed from Ballyhaunis to Mayo Abbey during the worst of it. So I went to meet him, my older cousin James Delaney, at Tuam. Together we went to visit the mass grave beyond the town where my family is believed to have been buried. In the Famine years, the dead were gathered in from the fields and roadside ditches where they had fallen and given a decent, if anonymous, burial in holy ground."

Seamus paused. In his mind he was far away kneeling in the rain by that graveside.

The room was silent. Emily looked into his face her eyes moist.

Seamus cleared his throat.

"So," he said, "James Delaney gave me the address of my mother's sister, Kate.
She had married a man named Duffy and had emigrated to New York along with their son, my cousin Felim, just before the Famine reached its most deadly stages. So I said farewell to Aunt Mollie and Father Healy. He made me promise that I would continue my education, and wrote me letters of introduction to the Jesuit schools in New York and in Georgetown too where he had distant relatives who were also priests. So I came to my cousins in this country. Felim and I served together in the late war and he died, and that is all there is to tell." Seamus finished in a rush, and the room was silent again. He noticed that his glass must have been filled again. He was thirsty after so much talking and took some wine. He replaced a half-empty glass on the table. Emily's glass was still three-quarters full.

She reached across the table and took his hand in hers.

"Thank you," she said.

It was extraordinary, thought Seamus, he had never spoken just this way to anyone, except Felim, and even that was different. Felim had known about the Famine and they had spoken rarely of the loss of Seamus' family.

"It is I who should thank you," he said, "for listening to me. I must confess that I feel somehow . . . lighthearted . . . now that I have told you my story."

Or, he wondered, is it the three glasses of wine? No, this IS different, he concluded.

Levi entered and asked if they were ready for dessert. They said they were and Levi produced a portion of Peach Melba for each of them and poured the coffee. He placed a folded slip of note paper next to Seamus cup, and left.

They savored the Peach Melba without conversation. The twilight outside the window behind Emily's chair had now faded almost to darkness, just the faintest rosy afterglow in the sky across the valley.

The band began to play on the upper piazza. The music was familiar and Seamus soon recognized it as a medley of Thomas Moore tunes. When the band started, *Believe Me If All Those*

*Endearing Young Charms,* he sang along softly in a clear baritone of how even if her youth and beauty were to fade instantly, the lady to whom the song was addressed would still be adored.

Emily smiled and then laughed and they laughed together.

"Let us go up on the piazza," she said, "and listen to the music. Perhaps you can sing more songs to me."

"I think not in public," he said. "You do not mind being in the eye of . . . the throng . . . tonight, after . . . this morning?" He immediately wished he had said nothing to recall the morning.

"There is no need to worry," she responded at once, "People may think what they will. I simply will not mourn. It would be hypocritical and I am through with being false in any way, not least of all to myself. We will go and listen to the music."

That, Seamus could see, was all there was to be said on the subject. They rose and left the room. Seamus held the door for Emily and as he did so, took a quick look at the note which he had taken from the table. He slipped the note into his waistcoat pocket. Luther wished to see him.

They crossed the lobby, climbed the stairs and stepped out onto the piazza. Groups of guests lined the rail of the porch or sat in small circles of wicker armchairs. The band occupied the south corner of the grand promenade, their music drifting up to the overhead two stories above and rolling down into the still darkness of the valley. The musicians finished the songs of Thomas Moore and launched directly into *My Old Kentucky Home*, by Foster, the famous American Troubadour, who had so recently, and untimely, died.

The sky above the valley was now entirely dark and the brightest stars were visible. Seamus and Emily found a place by the railing and both looked up to see the Milky Way directly overhead. The course of the river could be traced below in the valley by the starlight shinning faint silver on the water and by the lights of the towns along its banks. The beacons of the lighthouses swept the darkness at wide intervals from south to north.

The music played on, blending without seam or interruption

into *Old Folks at Home*.

"Poor Foster," said Emily, "although he was from the North, his music captured so much of what the South used to be. Poor man, to die so young. When he died in '64, it was almost as if he too were a war casualty."

Emily was silent for a time. The band played a restrained version of *We've a Million in the Field.*

"Seamus," she said suddenly, "Sarah is so concerned for her husband. Do you think he killed Fenton?"

"No, I do not."

Emily began to speak again, but all conversation ceased when the shriek of a steam whistle rent the cool night air of the valley. The band abruptly concluded *We've a Million in the Field* in mid-stanza and began loudly with *Row Thy Boat Lightly*.

A sharp snap was heard from above on the roof of the south wing and a powerful lime light ignited. The solid shaft of harsh blue light pierced the darkness and grazed the treetops as it played down the side of the mountain. The shaft ended in a bright circle of white on the valley floor. As Seamus and Emily watched, the circle roamed the valley briefly and then settled on the river. It followed a more or less straight line until it came to rest on a great steamboat churning up from the south.

Seamus took out his spy-glass and focused on the boat. The lime light was reflected brilliantly on the white painted sides of the steamer and sparkled in the foam around the side wheel turning in its paddle box. The walking beam amidships flickered up and down and the red and green running lights shown before the rows of lighted cabin windows. He passed the glass to Emily.

The boat responded to the probe of the Mountain House search light by training its own light up the mountain. Seamus imagined that this 'handshake' of lights must have been a tradition of long standing. The boat sounded its whistle, piping up a variety of notes.

"It is the *Drew,*" said someone nearby, "the newest night boat. No two boats have the same whistle and if you know the river, you can tell each one by her own voice."

The band finished its tune and was silent.

Up from the river came the thin sound of the boat's band repeating the same tune.

Seamus turned to Emily and laughed and she did as well, her eyes glistening in the steamer's search light which bathed the piazza in the brightness of day.

The boat continued up the river and house and boat held each other in their lights for as long as they could. Professor Smith struck up the *Boatman's Song*, and the guests on the piazza sang along. Seamus and Emily joined in the chorus and when they finished, Emily put her lips close to his ear.

"See," she said "you have sung to me here on the piazza and in public too."

Seamus could not respond before another steam whistle sounded. The light atop the building quickly caught the boat and a few more sharp whistles arose from below.

"The *St. John*!" several voices said as one. The band struck up *The Belle of Mohawk Vale*, honoring the great Hudson River tributary and the boat responded by caressing the house with her searchlight.

Seamus thought with admiration of how superbly the band was playing despite the absence of three of its members, and recalled that he must go and visit Luther.

He did not in the least wish to leave Emily's company, nor to leave her alone, but he knew that he must go. As he thought of how to take his leave the Reverend and Mrs. Van Wyck approached.

"Oh!" said Mrs. Van Wyck, fairly dragging her clearly balky husband across the piazza from the second floor entrance, "there is Emily and . . . and the Colonel. Good evening Emily, forgive me for calling you by your given name, but after this morning, why I feel as though we have known one another for a lifetime, and good evening to you Colonel."

Mrs. Van Wyck's good natured effusion ground to a halt. Her husband said nothing but stared at his feet.

Emily embraced Mrs.Van Wyck.

"Thank you so much for looking after me this morning." she said.

"Oh, not at all child, why it was the Colonel who . . . handed you to me, we are Christians and on this earth to serve Him by serving each other. Why, everything happened so quickly, the first I knew I had you in my arms and Mr. Tompkins, I believe that is his name, was pushing past me to try and help poor Mr. . . . the poor man."

The Reverend lady's discourse ground to a halt again.

"You did not know Mr. Tompkins?" asked Seamus. "Did he not cut through the lounge with us, Mrs. Van Wyck, when I found the door to be open this morning?"

"I was not acquainted with Mr. Tompkins," replied Mrs.VanWyck, "prior to this morning. In fact we have yet to be introduced. After he attempted to help Mr. Clay, someone, I believe it was you my dear," she said turning to her husband, "told me that the man's name was Tompkins.

"You see, when I got to the piazza early this morning, I found that it was rather more chill than I expected so I went back to our room and got my light shawl. By the time I was coming back, I realized that the doorway to the piazza was so crowded that I might have trouble getting near the service and I do so like to hear the Reverend, even after all these years, as he is going about his Father's business. When I saw that you, Colonel, had apparently found a short cut to the piazza, why I just followed along as did a small group of other latecomers behind me. I was not to my knowledge acquainted with any of them. We were not a party, but just by happenstance came to be together when the service commenced."

Mr. Van Wyck continued to stare at the floor and wore upon his face a distracted and generally miserable expression.

Seamus took advantage of the momentary lull in the conversation to turn to Emily.

"If I might," he said, "I will again leave you in the pleasant company of the Reverend and his lady. I have some errands to run, but will join you here again within the hour."

Both Emily and Mrs. Van Wyck looked surprised but agreed. Seamus bowed.The Reverend nodded, mostly to the floor, and Seamus left.

He crossed the porch, entered the building and descended to the ground floor. As he turned into the central corridor, he thought of the deadly bullet in its flight this morning through the very hallway in which he now stood. It was all a matter of time and the dimensions of space. During the war, a peaceful cow pasture could one morning become a killing ground of flame and shot and shell, and in a few hours all would be silent again and would remain so for another hundred years. It all had to do with when one was there.

Had I, he thought, been standing where I am now, at that precise moment when the shot was fired, it would have been I, and not the unfortunate Clay, who stopped the bullet.

Sampson walked up to Seamus and awoke him from his philosophical ruminations.

"Colonel," he said in a low voice, "the staff have finished searching all the rooms which were occupied at the time of the murder and we have also searched the remaining rooms which have become vacant since the crime happened. We have turned up nothing of interest."

Sampson came closer to Seamus and looked up and down the hall, hesitated for a moment and then led the way to the reading room on the left side of the corridor. He opened the door and held it for Seamus to enter. When both were within the darkened room and the door closed behind them he continued, still speaking in a near whisper.

"Sally," he said, "examined Miz Emily's room and found a pistol." He handed Seamus a slip of paper.

Seamus quickly unfolded it and held it to the light coming through the window in the door.

"Thank God," he muttered.

He looked up at Sampson and found the man to be giving him, once again, a very strange look.

"It is all right, Sampson. This is not the pistol which killed Clay. Miz Emily has, I can tell from this very good rendering, a Model 1851 Navy Colt. From Sally's rubbing of the maker's inscription and from her tracing of the muzzle it is certain that this particular pistol is in .36 caliber; not of the size of the murder weapon. I see too that she took a rubbing of the decorative engraving on the cylinder; and of the presentation plaque on the grip inscribed to Lieutenant Coltrane from his men; very commendable, Sampson, very commendable, very thorough."

Seamus was now speaking distantly, absorbed in thought.

"The ornamental carving is a pictorial depiction of the battle of Campeche, if I remember correctly, where the Texas Navy was victorious over Mexico in the War for Texan Independence . . . yes, the Navy Colt was a favorite of General Lee. This is very good, Sampson; Clay was not shot with Miz Emily's pistol."

Which is no proof, Seamus thought, but did not say, that Clay was not shot at Emily's behest.

"I would not have thought of her as a suspect," said Sampson, his voice mixing irony and irritation, "since she was standing next to Mr. Clay at the time of the shooting, as were you Colonel."

Seamus looked up from the slip of paper and considered that he should not have been thinking aloud.

"One never knows," said Seamus looking away from Sampson's eyes. "But at least no one can accuse her of having supplied the murder weapon. And I am not saying that she wished Clay dead by any means, Sampson."

Although she had wished him so, Seamus knew.

To Seamus' relief, Sampson changed the subject.

"Mr. Beecher has asked me to inform you," he said, "that he has received further news, via the electric telegraph, from the constable. The 'standoff' at the jail in Catskill continues, although the crowd seems to have diminished slightly. The deputy sheriff, through his younger brother was able to round up three citizens willing to be deputized, all of them relatives of the deputy, and so the jail has been reinforced to that extent. The deputy also thought to have his younger brother call around to the Armory to see if any help could be expected from that quarter. However, the militia company has yet to return from the border, where it was dispatched last month to support the Regular Army in its mission to halt the Fenian raid into Canada and to disarm the Fenians. The only soldiers at the Armory are a veteran captain and a sergeant of militia who, of course, are under orders to keep the building secure and could not leave."

"Thank you, Sampson," said Seamus, "if not for the bad

news, then for your excellent style in reporting it."

They smiled ruefully at each other in the dim of the reading room and briefly discussed what few security measures could be taken for the Mountain House during the night

"Now," said Seamus, "I must be off to visit Luther."

"I will let Mr. Beecher know that I have found you and that I have given you the information," said Sampson as they stepped back out into the hall. With that they parted, Sampson heading to the stairs and Seamus to the rear entrance.

Seamus exited and paused to take a deep breathe of the cool night air. The sky was clear overhead and the stars blazed in distant glory. The Milky Way was bright across the center of the dome of the sky. All was silent, the band apparently taking a rest. While still in the circle of light by the door, Seamus took out his watch and checked the time.

Twenty minutes past nine o'clock, he read. The first bars of *The Garryowen* chiming from the timepiece encouraged him to whistle up the remainder of the tune as he marched along the flagstone walk toward the root cellar bastille where Luther was held.

Whistling at night is the Devil's delight, Aunt Mollie's superstitious verse echoed in Seamus memory. He whistled another few bars regardless.

The Fenian Brotherhood invading Canada, he thought and shook his head. And Sweeny leading them, and was not Sweeny still an officer in the U.S. Army?

It had taken four long years, hundreds of thousands of men, millions of tons of munitions, fleets of ships, gun boats and steam boats, leagues of supply wagons, whole railroad lines, thousands of batteries of artillery, untold quantities of treasure, diplomatic machinations, international networks of spies and agents and the sustained effort of an entire nation to defeat the Confederacy.

How, Seamus silently asked the night sky, were a few, perhaps fifteen hundred, Irish rebels of the Fenian Brotherhood, brave lads, and seasoned Civil War veterans of both the North and South though they were, and nobly lead though they may be, going to vanquish all or even any part of Canada, while armed with left over muskets, pistols and shotguns? Canada, which, after all, was itself within the British Empire, the most powerful political entity on the face of the earth.

Well, he thought, God bless them anyhow. He understood full well their motives, but the only way to fight a war or even a battle was simply to *overpower* the enemy and fifteen hundred Fenians were not going to *overpower* the British Empire with all the courage in the world on their side and even in a just cause.

He kept whistling *The Garryowen* as he walked along, both to honor the poor Fenians and on the principle that it would be best if the well armed Sylvester were aware of his approach.

Nonetheless, as Seamus turned into the path in the grove of trees, he was greeted by the chilling *click-click* of the two hammers of the shotgun being cocked. He nimbly slipped behind the stout trunk of a tree and considered how his wartime skills at seeking cover, which had been blunted by peace, were rapidly becoming as sharp as they had been of old. He also reasoned that at least the fellow was no longer sleeping with the gun cocked in his lap.

"Sylvester," he called, "it is I; Colonel Delaney."

"Oh, Colonel, is that you?" said the deputy constable.

"Yes, Sylvester, I just said that. Now un-cock the gun, Sylvester."

"Yes, sir."

"All right, I am coming in now." said Seamus.

Seamus came out from behind his tree and advanced to the root cellar. The glow of a light could be seen about the planks of the door. Sylvester gave an encore performance of his act of juggling the gun and the keys and Seamus again danced about to avoid the view down the gapping muzzles.

Luther met Seamus at the entrance and they seated themselves together at the back of the cellar. Seamus asked if he might smoke without giving offense and at the same time offered Luther a cigar.

"I smoke only on rare occasions, Colonel," said Luther, "but I think tonight will be one of those occasions." Luther accepted the cigar and Seamus lighted it for him, and then lighted his own. They smoked silently for a time.

"Very nice," said Luther, "Habana?"

"Habana." said Seamus.

The smoke curled around the soft light of the lantern on the improvised table between them. At length, Luther unburdened himself.

"Colonel," he said, "I asked that you come here because of new information that I have received which I feel you must know. Earlier I told you of Jubal, our friend who works at Brenner's Saloon down the road in Haine's Corners?"

Seamus nodded.

"Well, Colonel, I have heard from Jubal again through one of the scullery boys. Jubal has overheard conversations at Brenner's and has witnessed comings and goings which convince him that there will be a major assault mounted by the followers of Reb Skhutt directed at the Mountain House in order to take me. There will be no less than fifty and possibly more than one hundred in the mob. They will strike if not tonight or in the small hours of tomorrow morning, then certainly Sunday night or after midnight in the early hours of Monday morning."

"But surely, Luther, the mob seems to be turning all its attentions to the jailhouse down in Catskill."

"Jubal is very reliable, Colonel. He escaped from slavery before the war and struggled with us here in the valley against the slave-catchers. He knows how to play the ignorant servant, but he is cunning and, I must admit, vengeful. If those at Brenner's knew him as he really is, they would fear him. It has been said that when he took his freedom from slavery along with it he took the life of his overseer. And Jubal is sure, Colonel, that the mob activity in front of the jail is a feint or a diversion meant to confuse us as to their real target and to keep the deputy and the constable and any forces they can muster off the mountain top thereby keeping us completely vulnerable."

"But I thought," said Seamus, "that the mob assumed you were in the jail."

"That is just the point," said Luther, "they know perfectly well where I am. It was no secret to the people at the hotel when I was put into this 'cell' and the word of my whereabouts must have become common knowledge along with the accusation that

I killed Clay. Also, according to Jubal, we are being watched. Skhutt himself seems never to have left the mountain top and Jubal suspects that either he or his associates circulate around the property under cover of the woods to observe our movements."

"Luther," said Seamus, hoping he did not sound condescending, "are you not giving this mob more credit for organization than it deserves?"

Luther shook his head slowly and puffed his cigar.

"Colonel," he said, "believe me, I have fought these people for many a year. The individuals themselves may be uneducated, drunken idlers, but there is an intelligence behind them. Skhutt may be a brute, but he is wily as a fox and shrewd. Most of these men have no particular affiliation; they are just ready for any kind of mischief, especially if it is carried out against those who are defenseless. There is a chain of command above them however, and they are connected with the secret societies and powers which extend up and down the valley, throughout the state and across the country. You have no doubt heard of the Native American Party; the Know-Nothings."

Seamus, like all other Irish Catholics in America, had heard of the Know- Nothings. They were the sworn enemies of those who could not trace their American ancestry back before the days of the Revolution. Of course, membership was not open to Black Americans, some of whom served in Washington's army, nor to American Indians who could trace their ancestry back to a time well before the arrival of the *Mayflower;* quite the opposite. Terror and political action were the specialties of the party, whose members, if caught in the former activity, were very disciplined indeed. Having been sworn in great, deadly oaths, they would state under interrogation that they 'knew nothing' about the party's illegal actions. The popularity of the party had declined since the war, but it was not that many years before that a chapter of the Ancient Order of Hibernians, normally a social and benevolent society of Irish Americans, had to arm itself and fight off a rifle attack by the Know-Nothings on old St. Patrick's Cathedral in Manhattan. The dead assassin Booth had been a Know-Nothing.

Oh yes, thought Seamus, I am familiar with the Know-

Nothings. He nodded and Luther continued.

"That organization," he said, "is very active in this area and in turn is connected with other societies, some with slightly different goals, but all sharing similar ideas. Oddly enough, there were some Abolitionists in the party before the war, but now there has been an overlapping membership and leadership among the old slave-catchers, the Know-Nothings, the Copperheads and other groups of rebel sympathizers and such groups as the Knights of the Golden Circle."

Seamus knew of that group also. The Knights had been active in the cause of slavery before the war, the rebel cause during the war, and since the war, the persecution of Freedmen and the resurrection of the Confederacy from its ashes. Booth had been Knight of the Golden Circle as well.

"I assure you, Colonel," said Luther, "the leaders of the mob are capable of gathering together a force, at least for a short time, which will overwhelm any defense we can put up."

Seamus was silent. The cold grip of fear began to circle his heart. He peered at Luther through the cigar smoke. Finally he spoke, his throat dry.

"You say they are coming tonight."

"It is possible, Colonel, but Jubal thinks it more likely that they will not be able to gather a sufficient force until tomorrow night or early Monday morning before sunrise. Although they do have financial support from some source, since the war ended, it seems that much of their income has disappeared."

"That portion which had come in the form of Confederate gold, no doubt." said Seamus.

"No doubt," echoed Luther. "Providing transport is a problem for them. Their people will be coming from around the valley, some from pretty far away. Most of them are too improvident to own a horse, so they will likely come on foot and it will take them time to congregate in the vicinity of Brenner's. When they do come here, there may be at least some advantage to us in that all or most of them will not be mounted."

"Well, then Luther," said Seamus suddenly brightening, "if we cannot out-number them or out-fight them, perhaps we can out-run them. When we are certain that they are close, and we *will* be watching, we can simply transfer your incarceration to the saddle and whisk you away into the woods or down into the valley."

"Colonel, when they come here they are going to be liquored up and set on hanging a black. If they do not find me here, what do you think would dissuade them from taking out their wrath on another convenient black, or any number of blacks? Are we going to whisk Sarah and Frederick, Levi, Sampson, Jacob and all the rest into the woods? For that matter, the mob and its leaders despise Mr. Beecher, as his efforts on behalf of Abolition, the Underground Railroad and the Union are now well known by all. What would stop them from burning the Mountain House itself, if they chose to do so? Sampson told me about the lack of militia at hand in Catskill, we are indeed defenseless."

Seamus mind raced grasping for a strategy, alternatives. He could find none.

"Any ideas?" he asked.

"Just one," replied Luther, "when they come, release me, arm me, give me a horse, and I will take them on. If they do not kill me outright, I will try to draw them away from this place. If I am to die, I will take as many of them with me as I can." As he spoke, he held Seamus in his unwavering gaze. The flame of the lantern reflected in his dark eyes.

Up on the piazza, the band was playing *All Quite Along the Potomac Tonight*. Seamus thought, 'Greater love hath no man than to lay down his life . . .'

"It will not come to that, I promise you Luther, it will not come to that." he said.

"Colonel, you know my feelings on the matter and you know that I will do what I must. I will arm myself with Sylvester's shotgun if need be. But I did not ask you to come here to repeat our last conversation, but to be sure that you understand what it is that we are facing and the need for us to take some action soon."

"I do understand, Luther. But we are not beaten yet, and believe me when I tell you that you will not have to fight alone as long as I am still breathing." Seamus held his own gaze steady now on the former sergeant's eyes. After a long moment Luther spoke.

"Very well, Colonel." he said.

They sat in silence until Seamus started suddenly and looked at his watch. More than an hour had gone by and he had told Emily that he would return to the piazza within that time. He excused himself and told Luther he would keep him informed of any further intelligence he might receive and Luther said that he would do the same.

Sylvester opened the door and Seamus retraced his steps to the walkway where he ground out his cigar butt with his heel and turned toward the rear entrance. The back of the building was almost entirely dark. No light showed behind the French doors of the casino and neither did any light show in the ballroom above the back door. A few lights burned in the windows of the servant's wing. The great house was outlined in silhouette by the glare of a search light. Another steamer had found the old hotel on its rocky shelf and was holding it in a brilliant embrace. As always, Seamus marveled at the intensity of these magnified lime lights, they literally turned night into day. The band was serenading the steamer with the popular new song *We Parted at the River*.

He hurried up to the door where he again consulted his watch to be sure that he had read it right. Something more like an hour and one half had flitted by since he told Emily that he would be back with her within the hour. He entered the hotel and as he passed the door of the bar it opened and Mr. Tompkins stepped out.

"Oh, Colonel, good evening. Would you do me the honor, sir, of joining me in a drink." said the young drummer, who showed signs of having already taken a drink or two or perhaps more. He took Seamus by the elbow and ushered him toward the barroom.

"Uh, good evening," Seamus began to make his excuses, "I was just on my way to, . . . um." To what, he thought to himself, join the widow Clay? Better left unsaid, he decided.

"Please. Colonel," Tompkins was insistent, "I will not detain you more than a moment, but after the events of this morning, . . . what we have both been through, . . . terrible, terrible, . . . let us at least have a drink together."

They entered the barroom and stood at the end of the mahogany counter.

"Rolf, if you please," said Tompkins, "whiskey for the Colonel and me."

Rolf responded, as always, with alacrity and precision.

"Your health, sir," said Tompkins and he tossed off more than half his glass.

Seamus did the same or almost the same. He took slightly less than half his glass before returning it to the bar.

"What a tragedy, this morning," said Tompkins, "what a tragedy. I tried to help, but I fear I was just unable to bear up."

Seamus thought it remarkable that despite the harrowing exploits in bringing comforts to the soldiers during the war which Tompkins had recounted the night before, the man had never gotten close enough to the front to become familiar with dead bodies. On the other hand, Seamus considered, he himself had become familiar with dead bodies at an early age, had viewed them by the thousands and had never gotten used to the experience. Hardened to it, but not used to it. Now more than ever, he found it best that he look away from such sights least they return to haunt his sleeping and, recently, his waking hours. Indeed this was hardly a topic upon which he wished to dwell.

"So, Rolf," said Seamus, "how has business been this evening?" He looked around the empty barroom.

"Sparse, Colonel," replied Rolf, "sparse. The doctor was in for a bit and Mr. McCain and Major Savage for a while. The Major was on his good behavior. They left before you came in Mr. Tompkins. The three of them played a few friendly hands of poker. Mr. Beecher does not allow gambling, but if the gentlemen want to test their skill in a sociable game, he has no objection if they just play for matchsticks, say."

In other words, as long as there is no money on the table, thought Seamus.

"No, sir," said Rolf rubbing his chin, "it has been very quite. Lots of folks have left, of course. In fact, when Mr. Tompkins was just leaving, I was about to close up. Not that there is any hurry, on to it." Rolf discretely covered the beginnings of a yawn.

"We certainly do not want to keep you." said Seamus quickly. He was grateful for the opportunity which Rolf had presented for a quick departure from the lugubrious company of Tompkins who stood staring into his glass and seemed intent upon the dreary happenings of the morning.

"Therefore, Rolf," said Seamus putting vigor into his voice, "let us have one more, a quick one, and then you can go about closing up. Will you not join us in a drink yourself?"

"Well, thank you, Colonel, I ordinarily do not drink while I am working, but since I am closing . . ." He put three fresh glasses on the counter and filled each from the crock of Tennessee whiskey.

Seamus finished his first drink, put the glass down and turned to Tompkins.

"Here," he said, "drink up now and we will let Rolf go home."

Tompkins finished his drink, but seemed still to be stuck on the previous conversation.

"Terrible tragedy," he intoned, "terrible. I am afraid I was not much help although I tried. You soldiers, you are the ones who know what to do in such cases, but I…, I am just a traveling businessman . . ."

"There was not much could be done," said Seamus, "To your good health."

He held up his glass and Rolf and Tompkins did the same. Again Tompkins took about half and returned his glass to the bar. Seamus did likewise and Rolf took a sip and kept his glass in his hand.

"You veteran soldiers," Tompkins continued, "you will be a great help to this country in the future with the experience you have had. I understand that a veteran's organization, the Grand Army of the Republic, is forming and I feel sure you will all keep in contact with one another. No doubt each regiment will have its own veterans' corps, as they do in England, and you will have mess nights and reunions and I will be proud to serve the boys as I have in the past."

Tompkins turned to Seamus and seemed more cheerful. He

took from his vest pocket a pasteboard card and pressed it into Seamus hand.

"Colonel," he said, "keep me in mind when your regiment has such a function. I will be happy to supply your needs at cost."

Seamus glanced briefly at the card. It read:

Edwin Tompkins
Purveyor of Tennessee Whiskey
Imported Wines and Spirits
Bel Air, Maryland

Seamus pocketed the card realizing now that he had been waylaid into the bar more for a business proposal rather than to commiserate with poor Tompkins over the shocking affair of the morning.

Nothing stands in the way of business, thought Seamus. He remembered the sutlers, with their wagonloads of wares and their tent saloons. They were always on the battlefield as soon as the firing had ceased and were the last to leave before it should commence again.

Tompkins had hardly paused to take a breath.

"I will be ready," he said, "to supply any quantity to any locality, and at the shortest notice."

Seamus had decided that he was more than a bit irritated at being thus buttonholed, when the case clock behind the bar began to chime.

Oh no, he thought, and looked at the time; eleven o'clock Emily!

He drank up.

"Good night, Rolf," he said and turned to Tompkins.

"Good night, sir." he said curtly to the salesman who was still in mid-oration.

In an instant, Seamus was out the door and hurrying through the hall. He was growing even more distressed, but with himself more than with Tompkins. Tompkins was after all, he reasoned, what he was. No one forced me, he thought, to go into the barroom. Why did I go in, when I would have much preferred to be with Emily?

Seamus reached the circular staircase and vaulted one step after the other. He noticed that the band had stopped playing. When he got to the second floor he saw that the lights in the hall were being dimmed. Sampson and another of the staff were extinguishing every other wall sconce. Any elderly couple and a young mother with two small girls; one asleep in her arms, the other trailing on her skirts, were walking along the southern corridor.

Seamus stood by the door to the piazza. A handsome, youthful couple stepped in from the porch and turned into the northern corridor. When they had passed he went out onto the piazza and found that the concert was over. The piazza was deserted except for a few of the band packing up their instruments in the far corner. Emily was no where to be seen.

I could hardly have expected her to wait forever, he thought, infuriated with himself. She must be exhausted. How more difficult a day could anyone endure? He wished bitterly that he had come directly back from his visit with Luther.

He leaned on the railing and peered into the dark of the valley. A light flickered here and there among the farmsteads and villages widely separated by seas of blackness. Beacon lights still burned along the river at great intervals from south to north.

"Colonel?" a voice came from behind.

Seamus turned. It was Professor Smith, his pince-nez in hand.

"Colonel," said the professor, "Mrs. Clay asked me to convey to you her apologies. She had waited for your return, but said that she felt quite weary and really needed to retire. She instructed me to tell you that she understands that you were no doubt involved in some important business or you would have returned as you said within the hour. She said that you are not to worry, she is not put out at all and hopes to see you tomorrow at breakfast."

"Thank you," said Seamus. I would like to see her tomorrow at breakfast, he thought, but that cannot be, I will be far away by that time.

Sampson stepped up and Seamus greeted him.

"We have arranged," said Sampson, "for someone to be on duty at the desk all night long, Colonel. If there is any alarm or disturbance, you will be awakened immediately."

For all the good that will do, thought Seamus.

"Very well, Sampson." he said. "Would you kindly send to the stable for them to have Sarge saddled and ready for me by six o'clock tomorrow morning?"

"Certainly, Colonel." said Sampson and departed.

"Colonel," said the professor. "You know, sir, my boys are at your disposal and ready to help at any time."

"Thank you, Professor," said Seamus, and thought to himself that the two dozen or so bandsmen, armed with their ten-keyed bugles, saxhorns and piccolos would hardly make much of an impression on the mob of gunmen which was, according to Luther, likely to descend upon the Mountain House within the next forty eight hours.

"Thank you," said Seamus again. He smiled gamely, trying not to appear as desolate as he felt. He looked the band leader in the eye and shook his hand.

The professor left the piazza with his remaining musicians.

Seamus stood alone a few moments longer and then entered the building. He turned left toward his room. When he reached his door he checked his telltales, used his key and entered. He lit the candle, quickly determined that the room had not been tampered with in his absence, opened the window and set the armchair near it.

He emptied his pockets and took off his jacket. He hung the pistol in its shoulder holster on the hall tree. He removed his tie and collar, sat in the chair in his waistcoat and shirtsleeves, and peered out the window into the darkness of the valley. He thought of the professor and the brave and resolute look he had worn at their parting just now on the piazza. Smith was a Zouave through and through, he would never shirk, but courage alone was not enough.

Seamus thought back to the Crimean War, and how he had stood on the deck of a British troop ship and watched the allied French forces on shore. Spearheaded by the original and elite

Zouaves d'Afric they climbed the precipitous path across the face of the sheer chalk cliffs. That day, dragging their cannon with them, they had outflanked Menshikov's Russians at the Battle of the Alma. Much later in the war the Zouaves went on to storm the Malakoff Fortress at Sebastopol effectively bringing the miserable war to a merciful end. Thereafter, the Zouave became the beaux ideal of soldierly virtue in all the western armies. All soldiers wanted to be Zouaves and every army wanted to boast of at least one crack Zouave unit on its roles.

One memory lead to another and Seamus now saw himself standing on Broadway in Manhattan watching the old 69th march off to war before Bull Run. His cousin Felim had stood with him. They had applied for enlistment in the regiment and had been turned down. The ranks and the officer corps had been filled in short order after Sumter. Meagher's Zouaves, Company K, of the 69th Militia had passed on the avenue, *The Girl I left Behind Me*, ringing out from drum and fife. How grand they had looked with their short blue jackets trimmed in red brocade. Each man wore a white cap with white havelocks fringing the headdress to shoulder length to protect the neck from the searing sun of the South. The little drummer boys pounded out the marching cadence on bright green instruments emblazoned with the gold harp of Erin. Seamus had felt the beat of the drums in his chest.

The 69th fought well at the Bull Run disaster, perhaps too well. A rebel officer later said that they had resembled a rock, steadfast in the stream of Union soldiers who retreated all around them. After Bull Run, there were plenty of vacancies in the Irish Brigade. Seamus and Felim were given their commissions through the good offices of Felim's paternal cousin, a captain in the Brigade and himself a veteran of the Mexican War. That Duffy, too, would die at Antietam.

"Felim," Seamus said softly to the dark, "here I am thinking about you once more. I put you off last night, but here we are again."

I spoke to Emily of you tonight, he said silently within himself. I didn't tell her everything, of course. I didn't tell her how Mr. Plunkett was going to use his influence with the

Democrats at Tammany Hall so that you and I would perhaps be among the first Irish policemen in New York City; strange idea, Irish policemen. The Irish were usually the passengers in the paddy wagon, not the conductors of the vehicle. I didn't tell her how you and I dropped that plan, at least temporarily, in favor of joining the Brigade. I tried to talk you out of it, but you knew there was no use in my talking, and if you went, then I went. I didn't tell Emily how worldly I thought you were when we had renewed our childhood friendship. You had grown up in America, your boundaries were endless.

As he spoke to Felim in his mind, Seamus tried to hold in his memory the picture of his cousin as he had looked standing beneath the gaslights at the entrance of the Winter Garden Theater on Broadway. They had gone together to see Joe Jefferson in *Rip Van Winkle* on Christmas Eve in 1860. It had been a marvelous evening, crisp and cold, the steam of their breath lively in the illuminated air. Jefferson had been perfectly hilarious in the role. No thought of death or grief intruded. As always though, the image of Felim's pale dead face as he lie on the green before the Sunken Road came back. And tonight there also came back the dank and clammy thought that he, Seamus, had murdered Emily's beloved husband at that same Bloody Lane.

He leaned back in the chair, opened his flask and filled the silver tumbler. He drank the whiskey down and poured again. He took a sip and set the tumbler on the washstand. He lighted a cigar and blew the smoke out into the dark valley.

With an effort, he tore his thoughts away from the Sunken Road.

You have enough to think about in the present, he told himself. How to defend this place against the mob which is almost surely coming? When is the judge coming back so that we can get to the bottom of who really killed Clay? Maybe the truth alone will divert the mob. But maybe the mob is acting under some form of order, as Luther says, and will act regardless of the truth. And who really killed Clay? Well, at least he was not killed with Emily's pistol, which is not to say that someone would not kill him as a favor to her either at her request or not.

Hell, last night, I myself pummeled the man in her defense, he thought.

He poured another drink and found the flask to now be empty. He had neglected to get it refilled during the day.

Just as well, he thought.

No, he said within himself, Emily had not caused Clay to be killed. She was standing on the porch next to him when the shot was fired. She was in the doorway, in the line of fire. The shot could even have been meant for her. She was the only person on the mountain top Seamus knew of upon whose life an attempt had been made prior to the shooting. He was now certain that what had happened on the trail to the Falls on Friday had been a murder attempt. Emily could have just as easily been hit by the pistol shot at that range as had Clay.

For that matter, Seamus continued to speculate; maybe the intended victim was McCain. He had been standing next to Clay as well, and was the only other person, as far as Seamus could surmise, who would have been visible in the doorway from the point where the shot had been fired. Maybe the shooter had been aiming at McCain.

Maybe, maybe, maybe, Seamus thought.

"No," he said softly to his faint reflection in the half open window.

That shot was meant for Clay, and no one but Clay, he told himself. There was no proof and there was no proof of anything except that Clay was dead, but deep in his heart Seamus *knew* that someone, to his mind someone other than Luther, had coolly and calmly taken careful aim and placed that .44 caliber bullet into the back of Clay's head. He took the round out of his vest pocket and held the weight of it in his palm.

It had been a sharpshooter's shot, he thought, fired with murderous intent. The kind of shot that sometimes during the war had laid low the highest ranking officers; the shot fired at the victim's head and neck. It was the kind of shot meant to kill immediately and for sure, before the victim could speak again and perhaps get out the order which could spell the difference in a battle. A shot like those that had killed the gallant General Reynolds at Gettysburg and the beloved General Sedgwick at

Spotsylvania.

The same kind of shot, thought Seamus, that I made at the Sunken Road.

He looked at the flattened bullet in his hand. Held it up to the candle light and took another pull each of his cigar and his whiskey. There was something strange about this bullet.

What?

How many bullets have I seen, Seamus wondered. Hundreds? Thousands? Hundreds of Thousands? Minne-balls, round shot, conical, volcanic, buck and ball loads. How many? How many caliber's and gauges. Fired, unfired, just out of the mold, loaded into muzzles and breaches and cylinders. How many? Russian, English, French, Sardinian, Turkish, American. Embedded in trees and arms and legs, fence posts and artillery carriages.

In the Crimea, the spent bullets mounded in front of the trenches in long rows like gray hail stones.

Something about this one though, he thought, familiar, yet different. What? A question for the gunsmith tomorrow.

He put the bullet back into his vest pocket above his watch pocket, finished his whiskey and stubbed out his cigar in the candle holder. He stood and undressed for bed. He determined that he would jog around the lakes in the morning. A cure for this evening's drinking would most likely be in order. He removed his Colt from the holster and placed it on the washstand. He closed the bottom of the window to the cool night air and left the top open slightly. He extinguished the candle and lay on the bed.

Sleep would not come right away, he knew. His thoughts went to the image of Clay's bloody head being lifted from the floor. He shied away from that picture and replaced it with that of Emily standing in the sun atop Boulder Rock, and then his holding her in their wet embrace under the ledge at Lover's Retreat in the midst of the storm. His face grew hot at the thought.

TAP, TAP . . . TAP.

His eyes were suddenly open, his hand shot out for the pistol.

TAP, TAP . . . TAP. There was a tapping noise, soft but clearly heard directly above his face.

TAP, TAP, TAP, TAP. There was a pattern to it, a repeated pattern.

Morse! he thought, it was the Morse code tapping out from the room above. Emily was tapping the Morse code on her floor. He listened.

GOOD NIGHT, SEAMUS . . . GOOD NIGHT, SEAMUS.

He reached up and tapped with the pistol on the molding in the corner near the head of the bed.

GOOD NIGHT, EMILY . . .GOOD NIGHT, EMILY.

And that was all. She made no further reply, no more messages, just good night.

He put the pistol back on the washstand and pictured Emily in his mind. He fell asleep smiling in the dark.

# VII

# DIVINE WORSHIP

THWACK! The muffled sound reverberated in Seamus left ear. Emily crashed to the floor of the piazza next to him. He bent to her and rolled her over.

The bright, fresh blood spilled down on the gold thread of the high stiff collar on her gray military jacket. It splattered on the two sparkling bars of a Confederate lieutenant. The blood glistened wetly on the gold lace in the slanting rays of the dawning sun. He held his hand behind her neck and lifted her head. Her gold trimmed forage cap fell to the floor. Her eyes were opened wide, a great wound on her left cheek.

"Now I am dead," she said looking up into Seamus eyes.

"No! Emily! No!" he cried aloud and awoke.

The dim, leaden light of early morning glowed in the window of his room. His pistol was in his hand in an instant and he sat up in bed his body shaking.

A dream, he thought.

"A dream," he said.

"A dream," he said again, to be sure that it had not actually been Emily's bloody and dying face before his eyes. It had seemed so real. The worst nightmares were always the most believable when one was stuck in them.

But there *had* been a sound in the room with him, had there not? There had been a thud, or a thump or a bump or something. He looked toward the door and then toward the window. There was a lustrous bird in the window.

Seamus rubbed the back of his gun hand across his eyes and looked again. The morning mist flatly illuminated by the pre-dawn light hung beyond the window. The image of a large bird of prey, wings outstretched, appeared on the glass. One wing tip almost touched the upper right corner of the window frame and the other almost touched the lower left corner.

He got out of bed with his pistol held before him, hand trembling with unreasoning fear, and crossed the room. He sat in the chair by the window and examined the frozen picture of the bird. It was an owl, its form etched upon the glass as if with acid. He guessed that the creature had crashed into the window in full flight and at speed so that the natural oils of its feathers had pressed this detailed smudge on the lower panes. The representation was nearly perfect and spread across the six small panes interrupted only by the frames of the individual plates of glass. Each feather could be seen minutely and the owl's closed eyes and down turned beak conveyed the expression of surprise on the bird's face when its forward motion had been so suddenly stopped.

Seamus opened the window and looked down to the grass below. No sign of the bird could be seen on the ground. Although it had mostly likely been stunned, it seemed to have recovered and continued on about its business. He pulled his head back in, closed the window and sat staring at the specter on the glass.

"The Bird of Death," he heard himself say. He shook his head. The thought had entered his mind unbidden, as thoughts often do. He had been considering how glad he was that none of the more superstitious children of the Gael were present to suggest that the Bird of Death had tried to get into his room, when the very words were out of his mouth. He had said it for himself. The phantasm shimmered at him in the gathering dawn. He stood up and placed the pistol on the wash stand.

A useless instrument versus the Bird of Death, he could not help but think.

He looked at his watch on the chiffonier, a quarter to five.

His head ached and his stomach was sour from the night's whiskey. He had the usual morning regrets and now, he looked back at the bird frozen in flight in the window, now he had a pervasive feeling of doom as well. He decided that he was really in need of the exercise he had planned the night before.

He dug into his trunk for his rubber soled shoes and the knee stockings with the alternating maroon and white bands; the colors of the Jesuit school in New York City were he had studied rhetoric, philosophy and metaphysics before the war. He donned his knickerbockers and his stripped jersey. He slid his revolver into the shoulder holster and pulled on the harness, adjusting it until the gun rested under his arm. Over this he put on his Navy jumper. He had gotten it in trade from a sailor on a gun boat in the James River after the Battle of Malvern Hill at the end of the Peninsula Campaign.

The sailor had been a Maine man and a sharp trader. He had taken three twists of the best Virginia tobacco, a bright red and gold rebel artillery officer's kepi and the short cannoneer's sword that went with it before he would give up the blue jumper. But Seamus had been happy with the trade. He still was. The garment was ideal for exercise, loose and light. A fouled anchor was stitched in white on the breast.

Seamus sat and fastened his shoes, stood and put on his baseball player's cap. It matched his stockings with white and maroon stripes circling the flat crown. He looked in the mirror and adjusted the cap to the proper angle. He took up his Hotchkiss shell dumbbells and juggled them from one hand to the other. He looked into the mirror again.

"Ready." he said to his reflection and he passed out of the room without a backward glance at the ill-omened vision in the window.

Seamus locked his door in his usual way and cheered himself with the thought that at least nothing had transpired during the night or he would have been awakened by Sampson or another of the staff. He walked quickly to the central stair case and descended to the ground floor. The silvery light of early dawn was beginning to disperse the gloom of the central hall.

He saw that every other lamp in the hall had been left burning low in its wall sconce all night as a security measure. He strode through the hall and met Sampson at the desk by the rear entrance. At no time during the night had someone not been on watch.

"Well, good morning, Sampson," said Seamus, feigning a rather more sanguine aspect than he actually felt. "All quiet along the Potomac?"

"Yes, Colonel, all quiet along the Potomac," replied Sampson. He smiled broadly and indeed seemed to Seamus to be on the very edge of laughing out loud as he looked the Colonel up and down. Seamus suspected that the young man found his *ensemble* to be comical in appearance.

No matter, he thought. He felt himself secure in his own opinion that he cut a fine figure of a gentleman sportsman in his exercise costume.

"Have you had any sleep at all, Sampson." he asked.

"I did, Colonel, young Frederick spelled me." He nodded behind the desk where Seamus could see the lad sleeping soundly on a camp cot.

"And," said Sampson, "back in the office Dr. DuBoise is minding the telegraph machine for Mr. Twilling, who Mr. Beecher sent home to get some rest. Mr. Beecher himself is standing in for Deputy Sylvester in 'guarding' Luther while the deputy gets some sleep."

"Very well," said Seamus, "I am going for a run around the lakes and will be back in about an hour."

"Yes, Colonel," said Sampson, "Frederick has made sure that Sarge will be ready for you at six o'clock."

Seamus could see that Sampson was having difficulty containing his mirth, so he tipped his cap to the future lawyer and departed, breaking into a slow jog as he reached the flagstones of the walkway. He picked up speed passing between the lawns and crossed the macadam common where the roads all branched. He entered the road to Kaaterskill Falls. The coolness of evening persisted beneath the trees. A low mist hung in the forest and among the hollows, telling of moist, hot weather to come. He would not relish the trip down the mountain this day.

The fork to the South Lake boat house loomed ahead and the misty lake appeared in glimpses between the hemlocks and cedars. Seamus passed the fork and continued toward the Falls. A big gray hare lay comfortably in repose on its haunches and long forelegs sidewise in the middle of the road. It showed no timidity and gave way only grudgingly, hobbling slowly into the tall grass at the roadside after bestowing upon Seamus an insolent over the shoulder look.

Seamus sped up and took three deep breaths. The air had a silken texture to it at this hour and at this altitude. It was a positive pleasure simply to breathe. The road rose in a gentle hill and to the right a rusty colored bush appeared. On closer inspection, the bush proved to be a deer, or rather two deer, as one of them broke and bounded across the road in two graceful leaps. The other showed its white under-tail and vaulted into the lakeside woods. Drawing abreast of where the deer had stood, Seamus peered into the hemlock thicket and saw it still running along with him about two rods into the trees. A crunch of leaves to the left and Seamus turned and saw the other deer was also running along with him just behind the trees on that side of the road. The three, the two deer and Seamus, ran along for a time together and Seamus thought the experience marvelous. Shortly, the deer on the right decided it did not care to be in a herd with a human in it and veered toward Seamus. It crossed the road an arms length in front of him, leapt up into the woods to join its companion and the two turned straight away, lifted their tails and climbed into the deep forest. Seamus watched the two white tails bobbing from one side to the other as they rose up the slope through the dark of the tall pines and disappeared.

He felt more refreshed for the experience and began working his Hotchkiss dumbbells as he ran. He curled his arms, threw alternate jabs and upper cuts in cadence with his steps, and made round house punches and windmill motions.

Presently, he came to the spot where the rattlesnake had met its end on Friday afternoon. The rain of the previous day had washed the roadside clean. He turned to the right and onto the game trail he had followed in pursuit of the man in the gray trousers; the man who he was now almost certain was Reb Skhutt. He jogged more slowly on the rough footing of the deer trail. He passed the site where he had interred the carcass of the snake and found that the grave had been robbed, the reptilian cadaver removed.

By whom, or by what, he wondered. He thought he had put

heavy enough stones over the hole, but it *had* been a shallow pit. Surely a fox, a raccoon or more likely a family of raccoons could have been able to remove the covering of the grave in order to retrieve such a tempting morsel as rotting snake meat. In any case, Seamus could see as he paused, trotting in place, that the entire area had been scoured by the rain so that no tracks of any kind, neither animal nor human could be seen around the pit or on the trail.

He jogged on toward the road around the lake where he had emerged the day he had tracked Skhutt. He thought as he went that had he himself attempted and failed to cause Emily's death by placing a snake so as to stampede her horse, he might have gone and exhumed the body, had the opportunity arisen, in order to do away with that bit of evidence of foul play. Would the true perpetrator, Leander Skhutt, have done the same?

Another question, he thought, to which I have no answer.

He crossed the stream which drained the lake and found the level of the water to be just a bit higher than before. He got his feet wet but went on nonetheless. He came out onto the carriage road, turned right and in a few moments found himself on the western edge of South Lake.

The lake looked different at this hour, the water was still and glistening gray, a thin mist suspended just above the reflective surface. The rocks and trees on the shore were mirrored in the smooth waters. A great blue heron rose out of the reeds, its vast, slow wings lifting it across the lake, its alter-ego reflection flying along upside-down beneath it. Further on, a pair of mallards burst from the wild rice growing out into the water. They shot straight across the water, the drake's gleaming green head, iridescent in the dawning of the day.

No other sounds were to be heard, there seemed to be no one abroad at this hour. The lakes were not full of the chatter and laughter of the vacationers as during the day, but were full instead of the long silences they had witnessed for the eons before humanity had discovered them.

Seamus traveled on and overtook a young porcupine struggling frantically to out race him on its stubby little legs. He gave the creature a wide berth as it seemed never to occur to the spiny adolescent to simply walk off the trail into the undergrowth. He looked back to see the porcupine still creeping along at its top speed, oblivious that the danger had passed.

Seamus worked the dumbbells as he went and came upon a twisted old maple tree at a turning in the road. A large bole bulged from the trunk of the tree and he paused about two rods before it, took the bole for his target, wound up his arm and threw the weight in his right hand as hard as could underhanded. The shell struck the bole with a thump at dead center.

He shifted the other shell to his right hand, threw it overhand and again hit the target in the center. He jogged to the base of the tree picked up the dumbbells, returned to his original distance and repeated the exercise. This time he threw the shells by whipping his arm out to the side. He had found that this last method of throwing gave him the utmost speed, force and accuracy. He had developed this way of exercising to help improve his ability to throw when he played baseball in the army. He had played rounders, a game like baseball, as a child in the streets of Cove, and thrown the shot in the game of road bowling along the country roads of Cork as a youth. He had found that if he threw his Hotchkiss shell dumbbells as fast and as hard as possible at a target, he could gain skill with the much lighter baseball. He practiced a few throws more and went on.

Soon the first salmon-colored rays of the rising sun tinted the waters of South Lake and he came to the isthmus where the carriage road turned into the wider road and passed between the two lakes in it is return to the hotel. The abandoned charcoal pit stood on his left and he jogged across the road and found a path beginning next to it which continued on toward the shore of North Lake. The path dropped into a grove of pines and then merged with the shore of the lake at about where Seamus had seen Skhutt, McCain, Clay and . . . who? . . . he wondered on Friday.

The shore here was made up of flat slabs of bedrock, which though uneven in spots made generally good footing and Seamus picked up his pace, speeding toward the east where the sky was brightening the lake water to a rosy hue. The wooded brow of the mountain ridge ascended on his left and, in the distance before him, he could see the eastern end of the lake. There a forest of evergreens, described in the guide book as the Pine Orchard, fringed the shore. The tops of the towering pines were inclined, each and every one, toward the east by the prevailing winds. Beyond the tree tops was the wide open sky above the valley, a pale orange mist rising against the blue.

Seamus circled around the eastern shore and entered the trail into the cool cathedral of Pine Orchard. The path turned parallel to the cliffs at the edge of the mountain and headed toward the hotel. In a few more steps Seamus could see that the path intersected the top of the road to the valley, the same mountain road he had ascended in the coach on the day of his arrival, and the same road down which he planned to travel this morning after he finished his run. Coming near the intersection he heard a deer, or perhaps two, the sound was that heavy, crashing away down through the woods. Seamus eyes followed the sound without seeing the animals. Instead the saw a line of telegraph poles, the wood bright and new, marching down the right side of the road. The wire shown a burnished red in the morning light far down into the dimness of the trees. Seamus could still hear the hooves loudly crushing the leaves and the occasional crack of a branch retreating away down the side of the mountain.

His attention was caught by the second pole from the top of road. A slender strand of copper wire hung from the line near one of the glass insulators.

Sloppy work by the men who installed the telegraph line, he thought, and he resolved to more closely examine the installation on his ride down to the valley.

He had run harder then he had at first intended, but was feeling first rate. His head was clear and his stomach in fine shape. Indeed, he now felt hungry but knew he must continue his fast until the afternoon. He sprinted up the road through the Pine Orchard and up the steep path off the final rise of the coach road toward the north end of the hotel. He emerged from the woods at the top of the path where, late on the previous morning, he had watched from Mr. Beecher's office as the elderly artist had gone down and Tompkins and then McCain had come up.

Seamus sprinted around the servant's wing past the kitchen

and scullery entrance, retracing Luther's route of the last morning around the corner of the house. The scullery boys, just closing the doors of the storeroom, waved to him. Their wide smiles were full of mirth; at his expense Seamus was sure. The big spring wagon, now empty of provisions, was lumbering off through the grove of trees to the right, passing the row of outbuildings, among which was Luther's cell, and heading toward the stables. Seamus slowed to a walk as he neared the back entrance. He folded his arms, holding his weights in his fists, breathed deeply, and thought of how healthful the air was at this altitude. Everyone knew this fact and no one could be sure why. The unspoken truth was that those who could afford to do so came to these mountain top resorts to avoid the fever laden air of the cities in summer. No typhus, nor ague; known also as malaria, nor cholera, nor yellow jack, nor bilious fever nor black and bloody flux ever tainted these alpine aeries. Such contagion seldom came to the northern reaches of the Hudson River Valley although sometimes it did.

Seamus had been told by a friend who lived in the area, a comrade from the 69th, that in '49 and again in the summer of '54, the cholera had reached as far north as the Village of Catskill and people would be walking the streets in the morning and a few hours later would be dead in their beds. Yet even then the mountain tops had remained untouched. Seamus, who himself had survived more than one epidemic, had great respect for such horrors, but no particular fear of them. He had suffered no serious fever since returning to Ireland from the Crimea, and felt in his bones that when he died it would be in some other way. He believed that he had been spared from fatal sickness both by the grace of God and by the precautions he took. He drank only water to which had been added the purifying tinctures of either coffee or tea, or which had been mixed with whiskey, except in regions such as this where the pure mountain springs where know to be wholesome. Also, he was careful about the foods he ate and he kept his person as clean as was generally possible. He had learned these lessons over years of campaigning. The Irish Brigade as a whole shared the knowledge of how to stay healthy in the field, as many of the officers and men were veterans of other wars and knew how to live in camps while practicing a high degree of sanitary care. As a result, unlike most of the Union Army, more of the men of the Brigade were killed in battle than by disease.

The skills of how to stay healthy had been in the back of Seamus mind since the day he had left New York City earlier in the week. The first cases of cholera had been reported and the citizens were bracing for the first new epidemic of that disease since the terrible outbreak which had reached Catskill in 1854. Though he had concerns for his friends and relations in the city, he knew that aside from taking the usual measures of caution, not much else could be done except going to a high altitude. He thought too of how medical men where baffled as to the source of such pestilence and how some were even grasping at straws, saying that some of the illnesses, like ague and yellow jack, were caused by the bite of an insect such as a mosquito.

Seamus could not see how such a small creature could contain so much venom as to kill a full grown and vibrant man. A snake could inject much more venom yet a healthy adult could survive such a bite. Further, there were mosquitoes on these mountain tops and people got bit. He scratched a fresh welt on his elbow just obtained most likely, he thought, as he crossed the stream at the bottom of South Lake. But no one up here ever got sick with any of the deadly fevers.

Rather than insects, Seamus thought it more likely that the cold damp air of swamp lands caused some of the sicknesses so that it was a good idea to smoke tobacco and thereby warm the air before it entered the lungs. He had observed that among the soldiers he had known, those who smoked were less likely to get fevers than those who did not use the weed. Women, who never smoked, succumbed more often.

Well, I am no doctor, he thought, and looked up to see Doctor Duboise standing at the back entrance, smoking a small cigar and smiling at him. Still another, thought Seamus, who thinks I present a comical aspect in my sporting attire. The doctor bid Seamus a good morning as he joined him in the shade by the back door.

Mr. Beecher came out of the door with a yellow slip of

paper in his hand.

"While you were out," he said to Seamus, "the doctor received momentous news for us from the constable via the telegraph."

"The telegraphic code," said Doctor Duboise, "has been a hobby of mine for twenty years or more." He seemed delighted to have received an actual message.

Mr. Beecher held his spectacles before his eyes and looked to the slip of paper.

"The constable," he said," is still within the jail house in Catskill and he sent this through the deputy's younger brother. He says that the crowd before the jail has thinned considerably and is now down to about a dozen or so. He feels that with the help of the deputies he should be able to take those remaining into custody if they do not leave of their own accord. He says further that if they are still in the street by noon time, he will give the order to disperse and if they do not he will arrest them for unlawful assembly. He will lock them in the cells of the jail, will put two of the deputies in charge and will come, with the remaining deputies, to the mountain top as soon as possible, because the judge and his party have been located.

"They were caught just as they were boarding a Lake Champlain steamer at Whitehall. If they had not been reached by my courier at that point, they would have been in the wilderness and I do not know when we would have found them. They embarked as soon as possible by coach for Albany, and with that news, the constable said that he would proceed as planned. By that he means he will, as I instructed him to do before he left the mountain top yesterday, contact my agent in Catskill and advise him to arrange by telegraph to Kingston for Mr. Cornell at Rondout to do me the favor of running his steam boat the *Mary Powell* to Albany to return the judge and his companions to Catskill. *Mary Powell* normally runs from Rondout to New York, and never runs on Sunday, but I am sure that Mr. Cornell will oblige me. She is the fastest, or nearly so, on the river, and if she is able to get underway this morning and if the judge's coach can be met at the Port of Albany without delay, we may be able to get the judge here to the Mountain

House by midnight tonight."

Seamus, quietly impressed with the extent of Mr. Beecher's influence in the Valley, nodded his understanding. The very idea of Mr. Beecher's word having the power to dispatch the most celebrated steamer on the River from Rondout; Kingston's port, to Albany, contrary to her usual route, and on a day on which she customarily did not even sail, and at top speed, and empty of paying passengers, for the purpose of transporting three people to Catskill, was extraordinary.

Mr. Beecher continued in the face of Seamus' dumb response.

"We will," he said, "as you suggested yesterday, keep the intelligence of the judge's movements confidential, although I will tell the Van Broncs. They have a right to know. Now please, Colonel, you must exercise all haste in your business in the valley today and return to us as soon as you may. But by all means do be careful for your own safety. We are here involved in a most deadly affair."

Seamus nodded again and entered the doorway. The light of the sun streamed from the door of the piazza far down the hall precisely as it had on the morning before, when a bullet had traveled through the same space where Seamus was presently hurrying. Twenty four hours before, he thought to himself, and this had been a killing ground. Now it was again simply a hallway, just as the Cornfield at Antietam is again simply a cornfield and other murderous fields have gone back to being cow pastures. It was all a game of inches and seconds, space and time; you lived or you died depending upon where you were and when you were.

He took the central staircase as the quicker route to his room. There were still very few of his fellow guests about and the few who were regarded him, not atypically, with amusement. He gained the door of his room and entered. He stripped off his exercise attire and hung his pistol in its holster from the hall tree. He found warm water in the wash stand pitcher and poured some into the big bowl. As he poured he stole a glance at the window. He had averted his eyes from it since he had entered.

To his relief, whoever had delivered the water and made the

bed had also erased the unwanted image from the panes. He thanked God for the efficient porter who had done that good work.

Seamus shaved quickly but carefully, his hand now steady after his morning run. He bathed himself with a wash cloth and the remaining water and toweled himself dry. He waxed his mustache and dressed in a fresh collar and shirt and his Brooks Brothers suit. It had been cleaned and was none the worse for Friday's adventure at the Falls. He decided it would be too hot down in the valley for boots and instead donned his dress shoes and, in the manner of General Sherman who disdained thigh-length military footwear, attached his spurs to them. He loaded his belongings into his pockets, leaving the flask on the wash stand. He checked his wallet to be sure of his all his letters, maps and directions, and replenished his cigar case. He put aside the shoulder holster as the day would be hot and he might want to shed his outer garment. Instead he placed his pistol and the extra cylinder in his right coat pocket. He picked up the old cavalry hat dusted it and retrieved from his trunk an infantryman's canteen, with a strap and a sky-blue woolen cover. He hung his saddle bag over his arm, checked the room as usual and departed, locking the door behind him.

He hurried to the central staircase, descended, turned into the hall and headed toward the rear entrance. None of the guests he passed seemed to find him amusing now, nor even to notice him.

It is not, he thought, only a matter of space and time, of where you are and when you are, but also a matter of condition, of how you are, in this case of how you are dressed.

"Clothes make the man." he quoted aloud as he came abreast of the front desk.

Mr. Twilling was on duty.

"I beg your pardon, Colonel," he said, puzzlement on his face.

"Clothes, Twilling, clothes! They make the man!" said Seamus and he turned sharply into the barroom. It is getting to the point, he thought, where I really delight in confounding that man. He shook his head at is own childishness.

As Seamus' eyes adjusted to the dimness of the barroom, his surprise at it being open this early was answered by the sight of young Terwilliger going earnestly about the morning cleaning. The lad turned.

"Oh, good morning, Colonel," he said and propped his broom against the bar.

He came to Seamus at the end of the bar, took a small bit of colored paper from his pocket, unfolded it and presented it.

"Maybe you can help me, sir," he said.

Seamus took from the young man's hand what he immediately recognized as a United States Note in the amount of fifty cents.

"Colonel, I wouldn't for a minute doubt the honesty of the gentleman who gave me this money, but I don't know much about such things and I hear that sometimes this paper money can be fake. We don't see many of them up here in the country, on to it, usually just regular coins made of metal. I expect you know about such things. Is this a good one, Colonel?"

Seamus looked again at the little rectangle of paper currency. It was creased but fairly new. On the obverse was a portrait of President Washington surmounted by the phrase 'Fractional Currency' and ornate engraving of the numerals and words signifying the value of fifty cents. The reverse was printed in red ink and again complicated renditions of the value of the note were printed and overprinted. He held it up to the light and saw the fibers embedded in the paper. He smiled and handed the money back to young Terwilliger.

"It is a good one," said Seamus.

"Well thank you, Colonel. I would, like I said, never doubt Major Savage. He always has dealt square with me," here the youth lowered his voice, "even if he is a little strange. But it was just possible that he could have got a bad one and passed it on by mistake. He gave it to me for getting his medicine and another package from Brenner's saloon.

"Yesterday afternoon he gave me two envelopes with letters and money inside and I took one to Brenner's and one to the pharmacy on my way home. The pharmacist gave me the medicine right away and I took it home and kept it safe overnight. But the man at Brenner's told me to come back early this morning on my way into work and pick up that package. He said the package could be easily broken and he did not want me to take a chance of breaking it if I took it home overnight. I didn't see the difference. I'm very careful and never broke any of the medicine bottles before. Of course, the man at Brenner's wouldn't know that but the package turned out to be big and heavy and pretty solid, I'd say, in a wooden crate about a foot square. Must have weighed ten pounds. Anyhow, it was not my place to argue with the man at Brenner's, so I just did like I was told. I stopped by Brenner's on the way in and the man gave me the package. Again he told me to be careful with it. I just now brought it to Major Savage's room and he gave me this note. I sure am glad you could help me, Colonel."

"Happy to be of service," said Seamus.

Young Terwilliger returned to his sweeping and Seamus turned to the big stoneware crock which stood on a washstand at the end of the bar. The cooler had the words 'ICE WATER' etched in blue on the front and a porcelain lid fashioned like a blooming sunflower covered the brim. He had seen it on his first night in the bar and made note of it as a source from which to fill his canteen. This day promised to be a sweltering one in the valley.

As he uncorked the canteen, Sarah Van Bronc entered from the hallway. She placed a tray of dishes covered partly with a linen napkin on the end of the bar, and took Seamus' canteen from his hands as he began to fumble with the spigot on the crock.

"Here, Colonel," she said, "let me do that before you make a mess. You need a funnel."

She reached under the counter and came up with a small copper funnel, filled the canteen and corked it. She looked at the cover of the canteen and ran her hand over the embroidery on it.

The cover was stitched across its face with a large Harp of Erin, in golden yellow thread, half-encircled with a bright green wreath of shamrocks. Below that the name 'felim o'duffy', was writ in the simple and graceful curves of the ancient Gaelic alphabet and executed in letters of the same gold thread as fashioned the harp.

"That is beautiful work." said Sarah.

"My Aunt Kate did it for her son, my cousin Felim Duffy before we left for the South. We served together. He was killed."

Sarah looked up, her hand resting yet on the golden harp in its wreath.

"I can see that your Aunt worked with love." she said.

"Yes," said Seamus, "she did."

Sarah placed the canteen in Seamus' hands and picked up the tray. She spoke softly.

"I have just shared breakfast with my husband out in the root cellar. Mr. Beecher came out and told us the news about the judge. Luther and I appreciate all you are trying to do and we have faith . . .," she hesitated, her voice strained, "we have faith. Be careful on your journey today, Colonel."

She turned quickly and was off to the casino door.

Seamus stood and watched her go through the door way and cross the empty and echoing casino to the kitchen entrance. He slung his canteen on his shoulder and nodded in parting to young Terwilliger, who was now standing on a chair and replenishing the oil in the lamps above the center of the bar. Seamus went out into the hallway and stepped to the back door. An impulse made him turn back and look down the long hall to the piazza door.

He felt a chill in his shoulders and took in a quick breathe as he caught sight of a portly man in a tall hat standing in the center of the doorway, the light above the valley framing his broad figure in silhouette.

No, not a ghost, he thought, just a guest standing in the killing zone, unaware and at a non-killing time.

Seamus took the opportunity to raise his right hand, and sight out of his right eye as if holding a pistol.

One-hundred and fifty feet, he thought, or fifty yards. He could see the target, the back of the head beneath the tall hat, but he wondered if he could have hit it with a pistol. Perhaps holding the pistol with both hands, he thought.

He raised his other hand and sighted out of his left eye, then dropped his right hand and sighted along the top of his left hand.

As an officer he had been trained to shoot left handed and left eyed with the pistol while wielding the sword, an obsolescent weapon, in his opinion, with the right hand. Seamus was a good shot in all configurations and positions, but when he wanted to shoot his very best, in competition or at the Bloody Lane for example, he shot the pistol right handed and left eyed. But could he have made this shot?

He could not say. He shrugged and dropped his hands to his sides. The portly ghost at the piazza door moved on unaware that he had acted as a target.

Seamus now realized that Twilling had been staring at him from behind the front desk. He slowly turned his head toward the clerk, like the rotating turret of a monitor, smiling with lips and teeth while leaving his eyes cold. Twilling blanched and looked down at his ledger while Seamus slipped out the back door.

You are becoming infantile in your behavior toward that man, Seamus told himself, but he nonetheless smiled genuinely at the warmth he felt within. He found the doctor standing yet by the door.

"Colonel," said the doctor, by way of an excuse, "I could not tear myself away from watching the morning sun brightening the woods around the lakes. I have always found this to be a splendid time of day, haven't you?"

"Yes," said Seamus, "except for mornings like yesterday."

The doctor frowned.

"Quite so, quite so." he said and puffed his small cigar.

"I understand, Doctor, that you played a few friendly hands of cards with Major Savage last night. Hard to think of Savage or Mr. McCain for that matter being in any way friendly, but I heard that the Major was 'on his good behavior'".

"Melancholic would be a more accurate term," said Doctor Duboise. "I am not a practitioner of the 'dark arts' surrounding the treatment of the various maladies of the mind, nor of the types of excitements of the brain, but one does keep up with one's professional reading. I suspect that the Major is one of those who suffer from, among other things, the mind illness characterized by alternate behaviors ranging wildly from the violent and maniacal on the one hand to the depths of quiet despair on the other. Whether the effects of opiates and /or ardent spirits, both of which are factors, as we know, in his case, serve to ameliorate or to exacerbate the condition, either temporarily or for the longer term, is a matter of learned conjecture. As for the Major, he was, in my opinion, in the melancholic phase last night. His 'good behavior' merely a hiatus. Generally, these cases can result in very violent acts being committed by some individuals. As for Mr. McCain, he is, in my professional opinion, simply a very cold fish."

"That is your professional opinion," said Seamus, "a very cold fish."

"Quite," said the doctor, showing no sign of rising to the irony in Seamus comment. He went on.

"It seemed not to bother Mr. McCain an iota that he was sitting and playing cards with Major Savage, who, on the previous night had threatened the life of his now murdered associate; Clay. A very cold fish; McCain." The doctor concluded with a knowing look and a thoughtful pull on his cigar.

"Well," said Seamus, "I do not know about cold fish, but with regard to Savage, I have it on the very best of authority, in the form of young Terwilliger, that the Major this morning received delivery of a large and heavy package from Brenner's Saloon."

"Given Major Savage's drinking habits," said the doctor, "I would opine that a package received by him from such an establishment might very likely contain bottles of whiskey or some other distilled spirit." It was Doctor Duboise's turn to speak with irony.

"Why would he send out for liquor when he has access to the well stocked bar here in the hotel?"

"Because, Colonel, it is characteristic of those who become addicted to strong drink that they reach a stage where they become surreptitious about their consumption and become miserly about their supply of alcohol, purchasing in secret, religiously re-stocking, hiding bottles, drinking privately and so forth. Do not expect the Major's behavior, especially as regards his addictions to make any sense."

The doctor's words gave Seamus pause.

Drinking in private, he thought, restocking . . .

"Still and all," said Seamus, "we must remember that Brenner's is more than just any saloon in these present days. Why don't you, while I am gone, doctor, see if you can devise a way of discovering what was in that package."

The doctor nodded his ascent and appeared to immediately begin puzzling the question in his mind, his eyes straying toward the lakes.

"Well, I must be off," said Seamus.

"Be careful," said the doctor and he took Seamus by the hand.

"Be careful," he said again looking Seamus in the eye. He released Seamus hand and turned back into the hotel.

Seamus stepped off down the flagstone walk and headed for the stables. Frederick saw him coming before he had crossed the common and the young fellow ducked quickly into the barn door and just as quickly emerged leading Sarge all saddled and ready to go. He then took the canteen and saddle bag from Seamus and fixed them to the saddle.

Seamus took the proffered reins and pulled from his waistcoat pocket a silver quarter dollar which he pressed into the boy's hand.

"I don't know, Colonel, I don't know if my mother would want me to take this," said Frederick and he made to return the coin.

"Private Frederick Douglass Van Bronc," said Seamus as he swung up into the saddle, "you will keep that quarter dollar and that is an order!" And he gave one of his best hand salutes.

Frederick grinned and returned the salute.

"Yes, sir!" he said.

Seamus coaxed Sarge into to slow canter across the common toward the mountain road. He looked toward Luther's root cellar jail and thought that although Luther was passing through the dark valley at the moment, he was to be envied his fine son.

It must be a great thing, he thought, to have a son or a daughter. Today, he told himself, we will see what can be done to keep Luther alive to enjoy raising his son.

He slowed Sarge to a walk and headed down the road behind the row of out- buildings which included the root cellar and the ice house where Clay's body reposed. He unlimbered his canteen. As he had not paused to take a drink since returning from his circuit of the lakes, he was fairly parched with thirst and the heat of the day was already coming on. He took a long swallow and was pleased to find that the crock in the barroom had contained, as advertised, water which was truly ice cold. He took another greedy gulp and reminded himself of water discipline, corked the canteen and hung it again from his saddle. It occurred to him that the block of ice presently resting in the crock, may have come from the very ice house where Clay's corpse presently rested.

Seamus considered that such a proposition might bring pause to a civilian, but did not have any effect on him either one way or the other. He recalled that after a close and sharp engagement on the Peninsula, perhaps at White Oak Swamp, if memory served, he had relieved a moribund comrade of his canteen and mixed the contents with the last of the whiskey in the big Russian flask. He had then taken the bread bag from the body of a dead rebel corporal and discovered the contents to consist of Union issue-hardtack, probably captured by the Confederates at Savage Station and now recaptured by himself. The hardtack was only partially blood-soaked and Seamus broke that part off, moved up wind a few paces, sat and enjoyed the first meal he had eaten in three days of fighting and retreating.

Ice from the morgue did not bother him.

The carriage road lead across the eastern most shore of North Lake and Seamus savored the view of the still water reflecting upside down all around its margins the dark green forest. The surface of the lake was now tinted with the colors of salmon and coral and through the trees of the intersecting isthmus; he could see South Lake as it began to blaze and spark with the light of the rising sun.

He looked back down the road before him. The orange shafts of morning beamed from right to left through the woods. The sun was still low on the horizon out beyond the Berkshires, just breaking above the ridge of the distant mountains. The light grazed the trunks of the trees in its passing.

Nothing is straighter than a beam of light, he thought. Straight as a cannon shot flew, knocking down a tree here, gouging out a semicircle in another trunk there, and putting a hole through the man half-crouching behind it, further along, clipping off an arm, punching through an ambulance.

After Gettysburg, Seamus had lain in a stable with other wounded men behind the old center of the Union line. Looking up he could see where a shell had pierced straight through about twenty of the rafters which supported the loft. The shell had traveled from one end of the barn to the other and from one of the rafters hung, like a silvery crescent moon, the twisted lead sabot which the projectile had left behind before exiting the back wall to explode God knew where in the rear of the Army of the Potomac.

"The shortest distance between two points is a straight line," said Seamus to Sarge, who paid no apparent attention whatever to his Euclidean spouting.

Presently, horse and rider came abreast of the telegraph pole from which the curl of copper wire had earlier been hanging. There was no wire hanging from the pole now.

Seamus looked at the ground around the pole. There appeared tracks of horses and of wagons the whole width of the road, it was after all, a thoroughfare. One set of horse tracks, however, came right to the base of the telegraph pole.

Were the tracks at the base fresher than the others, he pondered. No way to tell for sure. He could see the tracks of his own rubber soled shoes and could hardly distinguish them as fresher or not than the others and he knew that his were only an hour old.

Still, had someone on horseback stopped here by the pole for a time?

Seamus lead Sarge closer to the pole and as the underbrush was parted by the horses feet a newly deposited pile of manure came into view beneath the ferns.

Seamus pictured in his mind a rider, half off the trail, his horse's hindquarters in the bushes, waiting. Waiting for what?

Perhaps, Seamus thought, the sounds he had heard retreating

through the woods down the side of the mountain when he had jogged by here earlier had not been those of deer. Had the rider heard him running through the Pine Orchard and departed the road in order to avoid detection?

Seamus side-stepped Sarge up against the pole.

"Steady old Sarge," he said and slowly pulled his feet from the stirrups and eased himself up into a standing position on the saddle. He grappled up the rough wood of the pole, which he figured was about twelve feet high. Standing on the horse's back he came to eye level with the cross beam where the telegraph wires were fixed. He had performed this exercise many times in the years just gone by, and suddenly a thought came into his head and he just as abruptly dismissed it.

"No," he said under his breath, "that cannot be."

He examined the wires, found them to be intact, and could see no evidence that any effort had been made to disable them. He slowly settled himself back down into the saddle, and thought for a few moments.

"I don't know," he finally said to Sarge, "but we had better press on."

He nudged the horse's flanks gently and continued down the mountain road. After a sharp turn to the right and a short, steep descent followed by another sharp left, horse and rider where on the portion of the road known as the Long Level running straight and slowly dipping down into the valley.

The further he went down into the valley, the more the heat and closeness of the day increased. He resorted to his canteen for just a sip. The embroidery on the cover summoned Felim back into his thoughts.

Seamus earliest memory of Felim was one of the very few memories he had of his own mother and sisters, one of the only memories he had of his father.

Felim, six months younger than Seamus was standing on a ruined old cart in the door yard of the cabin in Mayo, misting rain made the wall of the house and the ground glow in the thin twilight. The two cousins were pretending that the old cart was Cuchulain's war chariot. Inside the house the voice of Felim's father, John Joe Duffy, grew loud.

"You are a bloody fool!" he was saying to Seamus' father. "A *bloody* fool! Ireland is dying! *Dying!* The people are starving now by the hundreds here in Ballyhaunis alone, soon they will be starving by the thousands all over the country and England will do nothing. We are getting out of it now, before it is too late and you had better do the same."

It was the beginning of the Great Hunger.

Seamus father had replied in a small voice.

"But John," he had said, "Leave Ireland? How could we leave Ireland?"

Felim and Seamus had looked at each other each ashamed of his own father, the one to loud and strong, the other too quiet and weak.

After that day, Seamus had not seen Felim again until he had met him at Castle Garden, the immigrant debarkation point on the Battery, on the day Seamus arrived in New York.

John Joe had taken his family out of Ireland and to New York where they not only avoided the worst of the Famine, but prospered. Felim's father had a relative in the city and he quickly found work as a 'runner' steering other Irish refugees to the warren of squalid rooming houses in the Five Points slum near City Hall, where they were usually defrauded of their meager wealth. The fact that he was preying on his fellow Irishmen, had he stopped to consider it, would not have troubled John Joe in the slightest. He had been a subscriber to the dictum of the survival of the fittest long before the scholarly Mr. Darwin had codified it.

Felim's father had risen rapidly in the jungle that was New York City and soon owned his own hotel and saloon in Nassau Street and had an interest in another drinking establishment in Broome Street. More important, he rapidly made connections within the growing circle of Irish political power connected with the Tammany Hall Democratic Party. He used to tell his son Felim that the lad would be the first Irish Catholic mayor of New York.

Perhaps Felim would have been too, thought Seamus.

Shortly after the family's arrival in New York, Seamus' Aunt Kate had given birth to a daughter, Margaret, or Peggy, as everyone called her. Tough piece of work though he was, John Joe had been delighted with his daughter. By the mid-1850's the future had looked bright for the Duffy family, but in 1854, the cholera claimed both John Joe and gentle Peggy. Leaving Ireland had spared them the Famine, but pestilence could not be so well avoided, nor could war.

When Seamus had come back from Antietam without Felim, he had been astonished at how his Aunt Kate had aged since he had seen her on his last furlough, less than a year before.

Some of her own life must have left her, he was sure, when she had received the letter from General Meagher telling her Felim was dead. She had seemed to Seamus, as they stood in the front hall of her boarding house that day, to be all gray. Not just her hair but even her complexion, her lips, her eyes. When she tried to smile, she cried. She could not bear to look at the canteen cover over which she had labored, nor at any of Felim's effects and so Seamus had kept them.

The Famine had driven Felim's family out of Ireland, and Seamus' family had stayed and died, all except himself.

He had known little of the facts about the Great Hunger in which he had suffered until he began to study it, just as he had known little about the Crimean War in which he had served until he had studied that subject years after his service. Few who had survived the Famine cared to speak of it. His sources of information had included reports and documents in the archives of the Secretary, for whom he now worked, as well as texts and letters in the libraries of the Jesuit schools in New York and Georgetown.

His studies had revealed much to Seamus. He had learned how the Famine had been very beneficial to powerful interests in England and had succeeded in clearing great tracts of land of unprofitable small tenant farmers. He had learned how England's efforts at relief under the Irish Poor Law were so little and so late that it would have been far more merciful had she simply sent in her armies and put the people to the sword as she had in the days of Cromwell. That mighty empire's miserly efforts at feeding the starving had only prolonged the agony to be endured before death brought surcease to pain. He had learned how food stocks had been withheld from starving children until local taxes were paid. The taxes were not and never could have been paid and so the children died, slowly and horribly.

Seamus discovered how the biggest fear among the wealthy and powerful in the City of London in those days was that the distribution of free meal to the starving would depress the prices on the Corn Market. One of England's most revered economists had expressed the view that although a million Irish had died, it was not enough "to do any good" with regard to clearing all the land of the surplus population for more profitable enterprises.

But of all the things Seamus had learned from his study of the Famine, the most chilling was the evidence he had discovered deep within one of the Secretary's files which pertained to the source of the potato blight that had struck in those years.

The report in question had noted that Ireland had been spared the blight for many years and that when the first outbreak occurred there in 1845, the occurrence may not have been solely the fault of nature, but may have resulted from the intentional introduction of shipments of diseased potatoes imported from Nova Scotia. The implication was that entities which stood to profit immensely from the clearing of the land may not have been able to resist letting loose upon the population of small impoverished farmers so efficient a means of extirpation. In other countries the loss of a potato crop was a hardship, in Ireland, where the poor had nothing else to eat but potatoes, it was death wholesale. In other countries in Europe where the crop failed other food was available and the governments provided aid to the afflicted. In the case of Ireland, the English government did worse than nothing by permitting the continued export of food and providing, occasionally, a paltry aid program which guaranteed death by slow starvation. The Empire had made no genuine effort to save lives.

Regardless of the cause of the Famine, and despite the fact that many individuals and charitable groups among the English had tried to help, Seamus was convinced that from those terrible times onward the relationship between Ireland and England would never in the future be anything but one of the utmost enmity.

An explosion of drumming wings and feathers on the right and a grouse burst from the side of the road and shot through the hardwood toward the valley. Seamus started out of his reverie and in testimony to Sarge's coolness, the horse never flinched. Seamus patted him on his neck.

"You are steadier by far than am I, old veteran." he said.

Sarge nodded, the bit clinking in his teeth.

They had come to the end of the Long Level where it descended Feather Bed Hill. Seamus took out one of his hand drawn maps as supplied to him by Sampson and checked his location. All seemed to be in order and the slow progress down the steep hill began. Seamus remembered that on the way up on Friday morning he and his fellow passengers had been encouraged by the driver to exit the coach and walk; " . . . a piece to stretch the limbs and rest the poor horses." All had willingly complied. It was a wonder that the beasts could haul even an empty coach up the incline.

At the bottom of the hill, the road switched back to compensate for the slope and at the turn began the Short Level. At the very apex of the turn a game trail crossed the road where, in the moist black soil, Seamus saw the unmistakable tracks of a black bear. Or, he thought, more likely, of at least two bears. The paw prints of a small bear had been superimposed over the prints of a larger one.

"Luther's she bear and her offspring following," he said to Sarge, "She probably crossed again here this morning."

Seamus stood up in the stirrups and looked around the dense forest.

"Too much to ask," he said aloud, "that we could just find the tree which stopped Luther's bullet."

He looked and looked.

A hundred men, he thought, might find it in a hundred years.

"No," he said at last to Sarge, "we will have to find another way to prove the truth." And he nudged the horse's flanks and turned down onto the Short Level.

Presently, they gained another sharp turning to the right at a spot marked on the map as Cape Horn. There was a clearing in the woods to the side of the road affording a broad view of the valley to the right and the descending brow of the forested mountain to the left. The sun was shining brightly now and the heat of the day and the closeness were oppressive.

Seamus took off his coat and slung it carefully over the saddle bow in front of him. The portion of the road picturesquely named Dead Ox Hill dropped away and he and Sarge began to carefully pick their way down into the steamy shade of a vast grove of cedars. The flank of the mountain rose on the left in wooded crags and ledges. Seamus glanced again at his map.

At the foot of the hill, the road descended less steeply toward the clove of Stony Brook. In the dimness of the thick forest enclosing the road, he saw ahead the outline of a white clapboard shanty where the road crossed the brook. Seamus coaxed Sarge into a gentle canter down the easy slope. In a few moments the simple log and plank bridge thudded under the horse's hooves, the brook below was little more than the suggestion of a water course.

Seamus pulled up, dismounted and led Sarge to the left where a sink had been hewn of blue stone slabs to catch water from the brook for the refreshment of four-footed travelers. Just beyond the water trough and the shanty stood a small frame house where in the recent past refreshment for the lady and gentlemen travelers had been available although, according to Sampson, the business had not opened this season. The tiny establishment stood in the very crotch of the mountain with a wild ravine, strewn with jagged boulders beneath tall dark pines rising behind it and tumbling down before it. A signboard painted in a primitive style depicted a mossy, over-grown Rip Van Winkle with flowing white beard and battered hat stretching and yawning upon his rising from twenty years of slumber reputedly completed in this very glen.

*Rip Van Winkle's House*, said the lettering on the sign. On the side of the shanty itself was a more poorly lettered sign which invited the wayfarer to 'See the bones of Wolf; Rip's dog. 25 cents' and a cartoon of a hand with extended finger pointing up the ravine. Seamus smiled at the offer to view the mortal remains of a fictitious dog belonging to an imaginary personage.

"Perhaps, now," he said to Sarge as the horse drank, "I should go home to Ireland and put up a sign by the side of the road offering travelers a view of the bones of the Drumshallon Banshee at a shilling per each. Maybe the show business is the career for me. What do you think, Sarge?"

Sarge was non-committal, but finished his drink and looked up at Seamus who turned back to the trail and did not mount but led the horse along. The road switched back now descending the northern branch of the mountain and Stony Brook ran down to the right of the road in a deepening chasm. The road had been cut into the very side of the mountain, the rocky slope rising to the left.

Seamus thought of Rip Van Winkle and chuckled to himself remembering the first time he had ever heard the curious name.

While serving in the Crimea he had been told one morning that the military transport ship; *Rip Van Winkle* had been cast by the previous day's storm upon the rocks in Balaclava harbor and lost. He had known the great ship well and had been aboard her on more than one occasion and the news that she had perished with all hands had added yet more misery to the all pervading misery of that war. At that time he had never yet heard of the legend of the Catskill mountaineer who had played at nine pins and tippled with Henry Hudson's elfin crew, fallen asleep in the woods and waked to find the world changed. He had often wondered why a British ship should be called for whom? . . . a Dutch Admiral named Van Winkle?

Later, when he was returning to Ireland via England on a transport of convalescents he had availed himself of the on-board library which had been donated by the good ladies of London. There he had found a dog-eared copy of Irving's *Sketch Book* containing this and other charming stories.

"Ah ha!" he had said to himself, "So that is who Rip Van Winkle was." Although it seemed to make even less sense that a British ship should be named for a character of legend from the mountains of New York. In reading the shipping lists before departing the City this past Thursday, Seamus had seen that a twice weekly steamer between New York and the river port of

Saugerties was named the *Rip Van Winkle.* That at least made some sense, he thought.

He thought too of how coming back from the Crimea to Ireland, and more recently, from the Civil War front to New York, he had felt like poor Rip. Everything had changed; style, what passed for humor. He still felt that way. People his own age who were not veterans were particularly alien to him.

He made an effort to shake off these dreary musings and thought instead of the perfectly comical Joe Jefferson in his theatrical rendition of old Rip he and Felim had attended at the Winter Garden before the war. He smiled thinking of Felim the avid theater-goer and young man about Broadway. Felim had always behaved as if he owned New York City. "My town." he would say. Earlier that year, just after St. Patrick's Day, they had gone together to see the *Brides of Garryowen* at Laura Keene's theater.

Seamus frowned again. Laura Keene, the lovely actress, would always now remind him of the night the President was murdered as she performed at Ford's Theater.

He brought himself back to the present as the road passed over a small bridge spanning a dry stream bed.He looked again at the map. 'Black Snake Bridge' was marked at this spot. Looking at his watch he realized that he must make better time and he remounted and nudged Sarge into a comfortable walk down the gentle slope of the road.

His memory went back again to thoughts of Felim and evenings on Broadway, and St. Patrick's Day and again of the transport back from the Crimea. Many of his fellow passengers had died on that ship and were buried at sea before they ever came home to England or to Scotland or to Wales or to Ireland. Seamus used to read to the sick and wounded to help pass the time. Among the reading materials sent by the good ladies were back numbers of the *Times* of London and the magazine *Punch.* It was in those days that Seamus began to wonder what country was his.

It seemed that England claimed Ireland as its own but Mr. Punch never was able to portray the Irish as Englishmen or even as human, but rather as some species of gorillas from Mr.

Darwin's writings. The *Times* always looked upon the Irish as 'those people'. So, although Seamus was serving in the English army, it became clear to him that the English did not see him as one of their own. The Irish, on the other hand, did see him as one of their own, but Ireland did not belong to the Irish.

No, he thought, Ireland will always be the place of my birth, and I always think of Ireland as home, but America too is my country now.

When he had first landed in America, it was as a foreigner seeking his fortune. He would not have taken citizenship in a United States which countenanced the slaughter of innocents in the form of slavery. But after hearing Lincoln speak and after what had happened in his life and the life of the country in the last several years, he was now proud to call himself an American. He felt no less American than the superb General Hancock, whose antecedents had founded the Republic and who loved the Irish Brigade, and no less American than the annoying Mr. Twilling.

"American, yes American," he said aloud to Sarge who as usual paid no apparent attention. Still, he knew, there would always be in his soul a fondness for his native country and her people. A sliver of emerald, he thought, in my heart, aching, lodging deeper with each beat, *macushla macree*. And today he would be with some of his 'own'. He viewed the prospect with a mixture of anticipation and foreboding like any other home coming, the bitter commingled with the sweet.

He came to the base of the mountain road where the valley began and the forest opened up to cultivated farm lands. Waist high walls of flat stones laid dry, without mortar, bordered the woods and divided one field of tawny wheat from the next. Green vegetable gardens, all neat and trim, stood out among the grain fields.

The road led to a toll gate standing just beyond the shade of the forest. Beside it was a small shed where dozed the gatekeeper in an old rocking chair with high canned back. A little red barn stood behind the shed and across the road a white frame farmhouse. The single rail of the toll gate was open and a notice board announced the rates for passage down the road. The toll taker roused himself as Seamus brought Sarge to a halt.

The old fellow heaved himself off of his chair with some effort as he was fleshy of build. He tipped back his wide brimmed straw hat and squinted up at Seamus. A smile creased his round, ruddy face.

"Well," he said, "how be ya? You're up early. Don't see many travelers on a Sunday especially at this time of day, except the Mountain House wagon and that don't count. A little while ago though, did see a rider cutting back across the fields over yonder." He pointed across the road.

"What some people," he continued, "will not do to get around paying a ten cent toll for horse and rider. Pretty foolish if you ask me, coming down the mountain through the woods, over the ledges. Horse breaks a leg, onto it, where do you save the ten cents? Answer me that. But I guess he don't care much about his horse 'cause then he tore off over the field, jumped that wall there, and him a big hefty fella like me," he patted his ample girth," and then galloped down the pike toward Catskill. Maybe he figured I was going to try to stop him. Not likely, I ain't no fool and I wouldn't abuse my Queenie," he pointed to the old mare tethered by the shed, "to race her on a hot day like today anyhow, not for ten cents, no sir. So where you headed Mister? If you don't mind my asking."

Seamus got the impression that the toll keeper lacked for company and was starved for conversation, but he now knew that he could not afford to waste time in his business today. He took a dime from his waistcoat pocket and handed it to the old fellow.

"Toward Saugerties," he said in reply to the man's question.

"Go straight," said the gate keeper, dropping the coin in the pouch on his belt, and pointing east, "down the hill to the four corners and take the right where Bogart Road crosses the turnpike. Come to think of it, that fellow who cut through the fields may not have been headed to Catskill, on to it. If he went right, as you will, he may have been going toward Palenville or beyond to Saugerties too. See if you meet him on the road. A big fella, wearing gray trousers, a tan jacket and a brown hat. He will be riding a played- out roan, played-out I ‘d say, if he kept riding it like that."

"If I see him, I will let you know on the way back," said Seamus.

If I see him, he thought, will I have to shoot him? Will he see me first? No, if he wanted me dead, he could have made it so on the mountain road. Maybe.

"You do that, if you would Mister," said the old man, "I might just let the constable know if I can find out who the fella is."

Seamus bade the toll keeper good day and departed. The man seemed disappointed that his sole paying customer for the morning had not been disposed to stay and chat longer.

Sarge trotted down the pike between the fields and patches of forest. Tall old oak trees lined the road and the stone walls continued on both sides. When the road took a dip down into a curving ravine and he was sure he was out of sight of the toll keeper, Seamus shifted his coat on the saddle in front of him and took his pistol out of the pocket. He tucked the revolver into the left side of the waist band of his trousers, the handle to the front for a cross draw. He pulled out the tail of his shirt to cover the grips.

Now Seamus had no doubt concerning the identity of the rider the toll-keeper had seen. He himself would be sure to tell the constable as soon as he could of this sighting of Leander 'Reb' Skhutt, but in relation to what might be far more serious crimes than cutting the turnpike toll.

He reached the place where the town road crossed the mountain turnpike and turned Sarge to the right. The road wound through fields and forest glades and he consulted another of his maps. He determined that once he reached Palenville, he could either turn left through that tiny hamlet or gain Saugerties by a slightly longer route continuing parallel to the escarpment of mountains and reach his goal through the equally tiny hamlet of West Saugerties. He chose the latter as it appeared to be the less traveled and therefore the less likely route. If someone intended to lie in wait for him, Seamus would not give up the advantage by passing along the more obvious road.

This second map had been drawn for him by a comrade of the 69th who lived in Saugerties and it had been fashioned with military precision, depicting alternative routes, distances and landmarks.

"Good job, Mick," said Seamus as he returned the map to its envelope which also contained a recent letter from his friend.

He passed through a stand of tall tulip trees. The air was scented by their white flowers, the buds dropping from the branches individually and deliberately, like heavy feathers. He half expected them to thump when they hit the road. Beyond the grove of trees the fields opened again. To the right the mountain he had just descended rose in billowing wooded ridges to the top.

Seamus heard music playing, soft, hushed, far off, indistinct at first and then becoming clearer. A band was playing somewhere, and playing church music at that.

He looked about, left and right and then looked up to the mountain's crest. There, on its rocky shelf, stood the Mountain House, brilliant in the morning sunshine. A light breeze came down the slope and bore upon it the strains of *A Mighty Fortress Is Our God.*

Even the voices of the congregation could be heard singing with the accompaniment of Professor Smith's Coronet Band as it provided music for Sabbath services. The tune ended, Seamus entered a forest of hardwood trees and the great house passed out of his sight.

The grand old hotel was, he thought, a constant presence in this part of the valley. Always in view and frequently in hearing both night and day.

Before long, horse and rider reached another road and they were in Palenville. To the left Seamus could see the few homes and businesses of the sleepy hamlet which according to the guide book, was reputed to be the home of the likewise sleepy Rip Van Winkle. He turned to the left and went but a few rods before a small, white painted general store came into view. He looked at Mick's map again and found the store marked along with the narrow lane which passed through a grove of pines to his right. He followed the lane down to a log bridge where he crossed the Kaaterskill Creek, whose waters and name descended from the Falls, miles above, which he and Emily had visited on Friday.

Seamus followed his map through the back of the town

passing a number of pleasantly constructed homes and some rude cabins clustered about tree shaded alleys and streets. He threaded his way to the road to West Saugerties and took that route among woodlands and rocky passes, the wild flanks of the mountain ridge always on his right. The road lead him through increasingly less settled precincts where the forest was interrupted only occasionally by the odd cabin of squared logs amidst a stony field. All the while he kept alert, not letting his mind wander from the possibility of ambush. He kept his hunter's eye sharp, but saw no others about until he reached what he took to be West Saugerties.

No sign marked the limits of this hamlet which, if anything, appeared to be even sleepier than Palenville. He turned left as per his instructions and crossed a bridge over a deep gorge. A stream coursed beneath and a sturdy stone building stood below on the bank. A tall wheel, rising two stories at the side of the building marked it as a mill. The wheel was motionless as no industry was being carried on this Sunday morning.

A few houses framed the road, where passed groups of travelers, some on foot, some in buggies or farm wagons. All headed in the same direction and Seamus rode along among them returning the occasional nod of the head or curious wave. All, young and old, man, woman and child, wore, as they stared at Seamus, that inquiring expression, so characteristic of people who are unaccustomed to seeing others with whom they are not acquainted. In a little while all the traffic exited in the same direction toward the white painted steeple where stood, as described on Seamus' map, the Reformed Dutch Church of Blue Mountain. The bell in the steeple rang out, hastening the late comers to services.

He again had the road and the countryside to himself and he paused and took a long drink from his canteen, nearly emptying it. He reckoned he had not too much further to go and he pressed on passing a few more prosperous farms, until, in about another mile, he entered a turnpike which weaved among farms and bluestone quarries. One after another, appeared substantial stone built farmhouses constructed he was sure in the previous century or at the very beginning of the nineteenth.

On the left came into view a square, two story stone building, closed today and bearing a sign stating 'Quarry Office'.

Mick had told Seamus that the majority of their fellow Irishmen in this vicinity gained their livelihood either in the backbreaking employ of these quarries or from the dangerous work of the local gunpowder mills or through the backbreaking and dangerous work of the iron foundries.

Seamus passed an old stone farm house perched on a hillside to the left of the road. Just beyond spread away to the north broad, rolling fields below a smooth and gently slopping ridge of green pasture. The distant mountains shimmered blue in the heat of late morning. The whole prospect gave the impression of an immense amphitheater. He thought it looked to be excellent ground for battle, thought how batteries could be placed along the top of the ridge and rifle pits at the base. Supporting infantry could be dug in on the wooded hills to the rear. One would *want* the enemy to attack if one held such a position.

Seamus caught himself and questioned why he was thinking such war-like thoughts on what gave every indication of being a peaceful Sunday.

Habit, he thought to himself, a bad habit.

Why not, he questioned himself, think of this place as one in which a great religious camp meeting could be held or an inspiring concert of music with the audience reclining on the slope. Why not see this as a lovely bit of land for a peaceable and loving assemblage.

"Bad habits," he said to Sarge. The horse continued to keep his own counsel.

Ahead were the spires of the churches of Saugerties, and although the day had grown no cooler, he slipped on his coat in order to make a respectable appearance in this built up and clearly thriving town. He looked about to be sure that no one was in sight, transferred his revolver back to the right hand pocket of his coat, and tucked in his shirt.

He rode into the town proper, passing by the white clapboard toll house. The barrier of the turnpike was open and a sign on the wall of the gatekeeper's shed stated that no tolls were collected on Sundays. This, thought Seamus, was most likely out of deference to the collection plates of the various denominations. He passed between rows of neatly painted frame houses and entered the village center.

A young lad was standing in front of a new brick building which housed a hardware store. Advertisements in the windows offered for sale glass, nails and firearms.

Seamus inquired as to the location of the livery stable, and the boy directed him to make a sharp right on Main Street, just ahead, and then a quick left onto Bridge Street in front of the Congregational Church, and go down one block. He did as he was told and soon found himself to be the stranger and object of attention of the flock of Congregationalists exiting their substantial house of worship with its pure white walls and tall square bell tower at the front. The words 'First Congregational Church' emblazoned in stained glass stood above the door.

He nodded greetings to one and all and continued down the short block where he found the livery stable.

The building was modern and looked nothing like a stable so much as it did like another church. It was of board and batten construction, in Neo-Gothic style, the center portion rising to a pointy, curved cupola roofed in copper and surmounted by an ornate weather vane. All the windows were surrounded with carved frames, the woodwork painted green with buff trim. The ridges and gables of the roof were topped with soaring finials. Two long wings off the central section ran parallel to the street and the whole effect was to give more the impression of ecclesiastical pursuits rather then the boarding of horses and the renting of buckboards and buggies.

Seamus pulled Sarge up in front of the entrance and read the sign over the door: 'Michael J. Dolan & Son, Livery.'

"Mick," he said under his breath, "you have done well for yourself."

As if in response a bright young fellow opened the door and looked up at Seamus with a serious mien.

"Good morning, Daniel Patrick," said Seamus before the boy could speak. He had never met the young man, but had seen a Daguerre-o-type portrait of him taken when the lad was ten years old. The face was the same, and the same as that of the boy's father, a face which Seamus knew very well. Daniel Patrick appeared to now be about sixteen.

"You are the son mentioned on the sign, are you not?" said Seamus.

"Yes, sir," said Daniel Patrick, "and you are Colonel Delaney, sir. My father waited as long as he could, but had to go to church. He told me to watch for you. There is still a half hour until late Mass" the young man had a watch in his hand, "it is just a short walk across town if you wish to leave your horse here."

"I do so wish," said Seamus dismounting. He took a silver quarter dollar from his pocket and pressed the coin into the boy's hand.

"This is old Sarge," he said by way of introduction. "Like your Daddy and me, he is a veteran. Take good care of him; give him a good rub down and a good feed of oats, if you will young Daniel Patrick."

Michael Dolan's son looked open mouthed at the coin in his hand.

"It would not cost this much anyhow, sir, but my father said there would be no charge for you Colonel."

"No charge?" Seamus had known there would not be. "No charge? Well then Daniel Patrick Dolan, you will just have to keep that two bits for yourself."

With a smile and a wave Seamus stepped off for the church.

"But, sir," said the young fellow after him, "I couldn't do that."

Seamus stopped and turned.

"What is happening to the youth of this country? Have they no ambition to begin making their fortunes? I am just after having the same conversation with another smart young lad like yourself up above on the mountain. Do I have to order you to keep that quarter dollar?"

The boy hesitated and then smiled.

"No, sir. Thank you, sir."

"Very well then, I will see you later, with the help of God."

Seamus turned chuckling to himself and crossed the street.

A fine young fellow, he thought, and the image of his father.

Even all the freckles seem to be in the same location on the son's face as on the father's. He wondered for an instant what his own children might look like someday.

Depends on who you marry, he said silently to himself.

He strode along at good pace down the narrow street, the entrance of which was flanked on each side by fine old brick homes built, he guessed, about the time of America's second war with England. Black shutters framed the windows and the entrance doors were surrounded by small porticoes supported by Ionic columns on the one and Doric columns on the other.

Gradually, the street gave way to less impressive houses and by the middle of the block he was passing the back yards of small shops and then a row of little brick warehouses. The footpaths were paved with rectangular slabs of the ubiquitous blue stone. At the end of the block began the business district, and a rapidly growing one at that. Seamus counted no less than five new buildings in various stages of construction. A sign on the lamppost at the corner read 'Partition Street'.

Directly across that street stood a building which appeared to have just been completed. It was of a very modern design, offering a bowed front to the thoroughfare, the windows curved at the ends. The entry door between the windows was of highly polished and carved oak, the lintel above and the doorposts echoing the floral motif. The glass of the windows and door was etched in patterns which repeated those carved in the wood. Gas light globes hung above the entire length of the street frontage and they too were etched and cut with facets. When lighted at night they would offer a splendid display, thought Seamus.

Above the lights, the capital of the entrance ballooned in a Byzantine or Russian style, and above that rose a second story of sturdy brick work and a row of six large windows. The parapet over the windows was supported by heavy carved scrolls and brackets. The whole front of the building was painted a deep green with light tan trim. Altogether a very inviting aspect, made all the more inviting to Seamus' mind by the elegantly lettered sign in the window which proclaimed that this was the home of Hurley's Saloon. The blinds were, of course, drawn because, as Seamus reminded himself, it would be unusual for a saloon to be open on a Sunday.

Suddenly, an oily looking fellow ducked out of an alley next to the saloon. He mounted the stone steps to the front door, looked up and down the street, apparently without noticing Seamus, bent to the door knob and knocked. Presently, the door was opened and the oily fellow slipped inside.

A red faced man, with a long white apron tied up around his chest and a shock of white hair stood in the doorway and looked to the right and the left. He spotted Seamus who responded with his quick smile and a nod of the head. The man in the doorway returned the smile and the nod along with a wink and disappeared inside. The door closed and Seamus continued on his way.

The saloon is open, he thought, to a select clientele.

He crossed the street and took a quick reference to Mick's directions. Accordingly, he turned right and shortly came to an old stone cottage from the previous century and there turned left. He passed along the street and came to another marked Washington Avenue. A large church stood in front of him and its bells started ringing in the tall steeple, but this was the call to prayer for those of the Methodist persuasion. Seamus' house of worship was further on still.

He turned left at the corner of the appropriately named Church Street. Neat little brick houses lined the street on his left and to his right there fell away open pastures giving a long view down to the Hudson and the east shore beyond. He walked down the slope of the street to wide common before the grassy hill where he found St. Mary of the Snow Roman Catholic Church standing peacefully among ancient oaks within a walled graveyard.

The church, he knew from his conversations with Mick in years gone by, was the seat of the oldest Catholic parish between New York and Albany, having been founded in the early 1830's. The building itself had been constructed in stages over about twenty years, and reflected the slowly rising fortunes of the Catholic population which consisted almost entirely of immigrant Irish and their descendants. The present building was completed in '52 and was of Gothic style. The tall spire above the front door faced the east and commanded a panorama of the Hudson and the lower reaches of the tributary Esopus Creek.

A few farm wagons and buckboards were tethered at the bottom of the church yard, but the majority of parishioners seemed to be coming to Mass on foot. Seamus crossed the common and started up the walk as two young boys scurried around him and turned the corner to the back of the building.

Acolytes, thought Seamus, and tardy too.

He followed them around to where he found the door to the sacristy just closing behind them. He mounted the three stone steps and knocked. The door was opened immediately by a man dressed in a black suit with a long frock coat, white shirt, high collar and a loosely knotted black silk tie. The man appeared to be about Seamus height and about ten years his senior. He had a head of bright red curly hair. His level gaze emanated from pale blue eyes set in a sunburned face beneath a high forehead and heavy brows. Scars about the eyes and a large flattened nose gave Seamus the impression that before him stood a pugilist. The expression on the face was relaxed, the eyes intense.

"Good morning, what can I do for you?" said the man in the accents of County Cork, Ireland.

"Good morning, sir" said Seamus, "I was looking for the priest."

"Colonel Delaney is it?" said the man as he stuck out his hand, which Seamus took and found to possess an iron grip.

"Michael Dolan asked me to be on the look out for you. I am the pastor here, Father Michael Power. Do come in."

The priest ushered Seamus into the sacristy. He seemed to be a man full of energy. He spoke quickly and moved quickly. No time to waste, appeared to be his motto.

"Cornelius, Timothy," he said to the altar boys as they struggled into their white, lace fringed cassocks, "you are late, hurry now, " he clapped his hands, "go and light the candles."

He took two tapers from a box attached to the wall near the door to the sanctuary and gave one to each boy as he herded them out.

He turned to Seamus.

"Michael should be at the back of the church just now

getting ready to ring the bells." He looked at his watch.

"I am late myself," he said, "I celebrate Mass here at seven o'clock, then ride to our chapel of St. John the Evangelist at Fish Creek where we have Mass for the quarrymen and their families and then back here for late Mass. Thank God our community is growing."

He stopped speaking abruptly and looked at Seamus. The silence conveyed to Seamus that he had better state his business and quickly.

"Father, I would like to go to Confession before Mass."

"Of course," said Father Power, "no time to go out to the confessional before Mass."

He closed the outer door and bolted it and crossed to the sanctuary door and locked it as well. He pulled up a kneeler and an arm chair and sat facing away, his chin resting on his heavy fist. Seamus knelt and blessed himself.

"Bless me Father for I have sinned . . .," he began.

He stated the length of time since his last confession and then noted certain thoughts of a carnal nature which he had entertained since then. The priest asked whether Seamus was married , Seamus said that he was not, and was told in the words of St. Paul that, in the absence of a priestly vocation, it was better to marry than to *burn.*

Seamus broached the topic of the deadly action which he had taken at the Sunken Road, and was told that it was not a mortal sin to kill in battle in a just war. Father Power added that in his view that the war which had recently ended in victory for the Union had been fought in what was as just a cause as ever there had been.

Seamus was familiar with the killing in a just war doctrine. He did not say so, but it gave him no solace.

He mentioned his thoughts that his spirit had in some way accompanied that of the man he had killed to pass by that of the man's loved one on its way to the next world.

The priest responded with impatience that God had all the spirits sorted out and that souls went to Heaven, Hell, Purgatory or Limbo and made no side trips. He warned Seamus to stay clear of the ". . . Spiritualism Craze."

Seamus also confessed the murderous sentiments he had harbored toward Clay and in telling of this described briefly the happenings at the Mountain House since his arrival there. The priest, it seemed, was already aware of much that had transpired on the mountain top, as he moved Seamus along quickly through his story.

He asked if Seamus had been drinking on the night he had assaulted Emily's husband and when Seamus admitted that he had been, Father Power offered to give him the Pledge of Temperance.

Seamus declined and concluded his confession with mention of having used bad language and having missed Mass on one occasion while traveling.

Father gave Seamus his Penance and recited the Latin Formula of Absolution while Seamus recited the Act of Confession.

Both stood and the priest said, "There now," and told Seamus that he wanted to speak to him again after Mass.

The bells began ringing in the steeple and Father Power looked at his watch.

"Ten minutes," he said and took off his frock coat. He hung it on a hook next to a large wardrobe on the east wall.

"I understand," he said, "that you were raised in the care of Father Patrick Healy of Cove with whom I was acquainted before I left Ireland to go to seminary in France. As fine a priest as ever I have met. So I know that you are familiar with the liturgical vestments. Give us a hand then." He opened the wardrobe.

"The red then," he said, "it is the Feast of the Most Precious Blood of Christ."

He took off his collar and tie as he spoke. He fastened the white linen amice, like a little shawl, around his broad shoulders and tied the long cord of the garment about his narrow waist.

Seamus fell readily into the ritual which he had practiced daily during the years of his fosterage.

He brought from the closet the richly woven and embroidered crimson maniple, stole and chasuble, while Father Power slipped the long white alb over his head and smoothed the skirt of it which reached to his feet. Seamus passed over the cincture, the red cord with tasseled ends. The priest tied it about his middle and put the long red stole around his shoulders. Seamus helped him don the chasuble which, like a Mexican poncho, hung down before and behind, and draped the maniple on the priest left forearm. A representation of Host and a Chalice was stitched on the maniple in gold thread.

The priest busied himself with further preparations of the vessels used in Mass and brought the altar boys back into the sacristy.

"Thank you for your assistance," he said the Seamus, "I am sure you will find Michael in the back of the church. I will see you after Mass."

Dismissed! thought Seamus and he let himself out the door and hastened along the path to the back of the church. He climbed the high steep blue stone steps and entered through the heavy oaken doors. Standing to the right of the entrance, within the vestibule near the thick bell rope was Michael J. Dolan, former First Sergeant, 69th Regiment New York Volunteers.

The wiry little veteran turned and smiled broadly at the approach of his former commanding officer and his blue eyes danced.

Seamus noticed that his friend had let his hair grow a bit longer since they had last parted. He put out his hand and the two took each other by the shoulders in a near embrace. The small bell in the sanctuary by the sacristy door rang and the priest and the acolytes emerged for the beginning of Mass. Michael and Seamus' reunion was therefore limited to a few whispered greetings.

Father Power began the Mass, "In Nomine Patris, et Filii, et Spiritus Sancti. Amen. Introibo ad altare Dei."

The altar boy responded, "Ad Deum qui Laetficat juventutem meam."

The God of my gladness and joy, Seamus translated the ancient, musical Latin in his mind.

His eyes went up to the ceiling soaring overhead, its recesses and rafters highlighted by flickering candles in the traditional style and, more by up to date gas jets in cut glass lamps suspended part way up the wall on either side of the transept. The pews were filled with several hundred parishioners in their frugal Sunday best and the daylight shinning through the simple squares of stained glass in the tall windows dappled their heads and shoulders with glowing hues of red, gold, blue and green. Above in the choir loft an organ accompanied a choir of young girls who joined in signing the Latin responses to the priest intercessions.

Seamus had never yet heard the angels sing, but expected that when, in God's good time, he did hear the Heavenly Chorus, it would sound about like that to which he was now listening.

As this was the last Mass of the day, it was the High Mass and was sung at a stately pace. In due course, the Pastor ascended the pulpit, read the Gospel for the day
and prepared to deliver his sermon.

Father Power blessed himself.

"In the Name of the Father, and of the Son, and of the Holy Ghost," he said and paused.

Total silence reigned in the church.

"The Fenian Brotherhood," he commenced in a calm, slow, almost disinterested cadence, "as you may know, is considered by many to be among the secret societies which His Excellency, the Archbishop of Dublin, has condemned. He has set excommunication as the penalty for the Catholic Church's sons and daughters who join secret societies which advocate the use of physical force and violence in order to set right the evils which have beset and indeed are still being visited upon the poor people of Ireland; for many of us assembled here today, the land of our birth. To date, the Archbishop has not been successful in his efforts to petition the Holy Father in Rome to condemn, specifically, the Fenians and to excommunicate Catholics who join that society. Therefore, the ban of excommunication carries only within the Archdiocese of Dublin.

"On the other hand, our own Archbishop Hughes, here in New York, has noted that there are times wherein the Church may recognized an obligation on the part of Catholics to rise up and fight against tyrannical governments.

"Nonetheless, I, as your Pastor, must warn you that it is very likely only a matter of time before all who join such societies anywhere in the Roman Catholic world will be excommunicated. “Those who are presently involving themselves with the Fenians even here in St. Mary's Parish, are treading a very dangerous path with regard to the salvation of their souls."

Father Power's voice now took on a cold vehemence.

"No one here knows any better than do I the history of terror and oppression which has been the lot of our people. How they have been murdered wholesale, at times nearly exterminated by sword and by famine under the aegis of foreign power, pomp and greed.

"I know full well how hard it is to stand by and watch helpless as the weak and innocent are made to suffer. Further, I fully accept that at times it IS necessary for the good to use force to protect the powerless. Few in this valley more strongly and actively supported the cause of the Union in the late war for the just and holy cause of freeing men and women from bondage and of preserving this great and free nation than did I...."

The priest paused and collected himself. His face blazed red as could be seen easily even at the back of he church. He went on.

"But, it is one thing for the duly constituted and freely elected government of a nation to take military action to secure peace and freedom, and quite another for gunmen to take the law into their own hands. Ireland and the Irish are in God's keeping. The day will come when justice will be done for our native land, and we Irish in America can hasten that day best by building upon the contributions which we have made to the foundation and preservation of the United States. We will help Ireland best by minding our hearths and homes here in America and by insuring the prosperity of our families and the education of our children. As we grow in strength as a community in America, we will be able to reach across the sea and offer to Ireland our helping hand.

"Nothing," the priest's voice rose and echoed through the church, "NOTHING can be gained by going off on ill conceived and misdirected adventures which are guaranteed, AS THEY HAVE ALWAYS BEEN, to end in tragedy and failure."

He paused again and then softly prayed while blessing himself.

"In the Name of the Father, and of the Son, and of the Holy Ghost. Amen."

He stepped down from the pulpit, centered the altar and began to recite the Creed.

Seamus edged toward Mick's ear.

"What was that all about?" he whispered.

Mick half turned toward Seamus.

"Some of the boys from here," he rasped out of the corner of his mouth, "went up and raided Canada with the Fenians."

He winked and continued in his harsh whisper.

"They're just after getting back. You'll be meeting them later."

Mick's eyes sparkled as he beheld Seamus expression. He winked again and turned back to the Mass.

The Fenian Brotherhood, Seamus thought.

Taking its name from the Fianna of Irish legend, the elite band of warriors who had followed the mythical hero Finn MacCoole into battle in a time before memory, the Brotherhood drew its impetus from the myriad murders, evictions and injustices which had been heaped upon Ireland over hundreds of years. The most recent and nonpareil devastation of the Famine had forever put the sword of enmity between England and Ireland and in this generation that sword was taking the form of the revolutionary movement that was the Fenian Brotherhood. Their goal was to liberate Ireland by military force. They said that they would strike again soon.

As the Mass progressed, Seamus reminded himself to recite his penance and he did so in silence. He wanted to be sure to be in a state of grace at the time he received Communion. When that time came he and Mick followed the line of parishioners to the altar rail and received the Eucharist. He returned to his pew, kneeled and with tightly closed eyes prayed earnestly for God's help in what he had to do in the next hours. When he opened his eyes he felt secure in his purpose and calm in his acceptance of what the near future held.

The Mass concluded with Benediction. The litanies were

chanted and the priest held aloft the monstrance, like a great golden sunburst, the consecrated Host in its crystal window. Father Power blessed the congregation making the Sign of the Cross with the Host. The light reflected off the monstrance and small circles of gold played among the worshipers and on the walls and ceiling of the church. Clouds of incense rose among the shafts of sunshine, and the ancient hymns *O Salutaris* and *Tantum Ergo* were sung. Finally, all joined in singing *Holy God We Praise Thy Name*, one of Seamus' favorites, both for its vibrant music and for its lyrics, which placed the source of all earthly power where, in his opinion, it belonged; in the hands of God.

As the priest and the altar boys filed out, Seamus thought, I am home.

All slowly departed by the back and side doors. A few men with their hats in their hands and women in bonnets lingered by the banks of flickering votive lights. Seamus and Mick exited by the door at the back of the church passing through the vestibule below the belfry. They each squinted as they came out into the bright noonday sun. The door of the church faced east and commanded from this height a view down the wide Esopus Creek to where it emptied into the Hudson, about a mile away. The creek flowed slowly perhaps a hundred feet below at the bottom of the bluff upon which the church stood. Mills, warehouses and wharves lined both shores of the creek all the way out to the river. Sloops and small steamers were tied up, idled by the Sabbath. Thin columns of smoke rose from the tall brick stacks of the iron works, the fires banked against the renewed labors of Monday morning. Far out on a spit of land at the mouth of the creek was a lighthouse. Across the river, magnified it seemed by the blue haze of midday's damp heat were the dark green hills on the east side of the Hudson.

A cloud of black smoke rose above the trees on the south side of the creek. Seamus held his hat up to shield his eyes from the glare and saw the cloud move northward. Suddenly at the mouth of the creek there appeared the prow of a large steamer moving up the river. Seamus reached into his left coat pocket for his spy glass and then caught himself, remembering that he had given it to Emily the night before and had not rejoined her to retrieve it.

The pilot house of the boat appeared and shortly the wheel box and the walking beam smoothly pumping fore and aft. He squinted even more but from this distance could not make out the name of the vessel. Just forward of amidships, a white jet of steam billowed up and then another and another. The three blasts of the boat's whistle sounded up to Mick and Seamus.

"The *Mary Powell.*" said Mick, amazement in his voice.

"Thank, God." said Seamus taking out his watch. It was twenty-five minutes past twelve. There was a chance that the judge and his party could be brought to the mountain top before much longer.

"What?" said Mick turning to Seamus.

"I said, 'That's odd,'" Seamus equivocated. He kept looking at the steamer.

"That it is, Colonel," said Mick turning his gaze back to the river.

"The *Mary Powell,*" he went on, "never runs on Sunday and what is she doing heading north? She only runs between Kingston and New York. But that's her for sure, I can tell by the whistle."

As the great boat passed the mouth of the creek, her flags and pennants streaming, with three more blasts of her whistle she warned small craft to be wary of her wake and then she and her crowning cloud of dark smoke went out of sight beyond the lighthouse.

Seamus and Mick heard footsteps on the bluestone path and turned to see Father Power now attired in his black suit. He joined them and spoke to Seamus.

"Colonel," he said, "I need to speak to Michael for a moment, if you would please pardon us."

"Certainly, Father." Seamus replied and he wandered off down the hill into the graveyard.

# VIII

# The Brotherhood

As Seamus strolled among the tombstones, he read the names of the people of Ireland and the names of the places where they had been born. Many had come before the Famine and many had come since that time. He read the names Donnelly, Hackett, Kavanaugh, Donlon, Murphy, Sullivan, Flanagan, born in Sligo, Skibereen, Ballina, Killala, Listowel.

A whole nation, he thought, was being transported across the ocean, fleeing from there, finding their rest here.

"Colonel," the priest was walking down the hill.

Seamus took a few steps up the slope to meet him by the side door near the cornerstone of the church. It read '1833.'

The priest regarded the stone along with Seamus.

"We Catholics," he said, "have been in Saugerties for some time now and we are generally finding acceptance. I encourage our people to be industrious, courteous and neighborly. The great majority of the Christian community here is, of course, Protestant and for the most part, the salt of the earth. None of us are without our prejudices, but those of our Protestant brethren, who are worthy of the name Christian, are eminently tolerant.

"There is however a small but virulent clique of bigots of whom I am sure you have heard. It is that type who have been causing the disturbance at the Catskill jail and who threaten Mr. Beecher's foreman, Luther. They belong to their own secret societies; Know Nothings among others. Some of them were Copperheads during the war. I have no personal fear of them, but neither will I give them an easy target, so as you can see," he touched his bow tie, "I wear no clerical garb, no Roman collar, in my travels about the countryside. Their anti-Catholic zeal, I have found, is matched only by their avarice and they are astute enough know that I often travel with sums of money, both the weekly collection for the churches and the banking which I do for the families of the parish.

"I would not hesitate to meet any one of them hand to hand," the priest's expression remained quietly resolute as he paused to look Seamus directly in the eye. When he was sure he had Seamus full attention he continued.

"But they never come at you one at a time and never unarmed. I will not carry a weapon, as has been suggested to me by the local authorities. You, however, Colonel, do not have the same rules to follow as do I, so you must be ready to deal with these people in any way you can. God will help you in the just work you are doing. If need be He could send legions of angels to assist you, but you must be ready to recognized and accept this help when it comes."

Mick now came around the side of the church and walked toward them.

The priest spoke to Seamus in a low voice.

"Remember, you cannot, and need not, fight the whole world alone."

When Mick joined them the priest spoke to both of them in a louder voice.

"Now then," he said, "I must be on my way to visit some of the sick of the parish. If you will kneel gentlemen, I will give you my blessing."

So Seamus and Mick doffed their hats and knelt on the hard flagstone at the side of the church while Father Power traced the Sign of the Cross in the air above their heads, intoning as he did so; "In Nomine Patris, et Filii, et Spiritus Sancti. Amen."

The two men blessed themselves and echoed; "Amen."

They rose and Father Power said, "Good day" and disappeared around the back of the church with his hurried earnest tread.

"Be dad," said Mick quietly, "and what was that; the Last Rites?"

"I hope not," said Seamus, "but I will take all the help I can get."

Mick led Seamus around the front of the church and down the steps cut into the side of the hill. The graveyard rose on either side of them. They left the church grounds through the tall iron gate in the massive limestone retaining wall and turned left onto the road. As they walked along they spoke of the recent events at the Mountain House and in the village of Catskill. Mick was aware of much that had happened and said that he was acquainted with Luther.

"A finer man never lived," said Mick, "black or white. All the better class of river men think well of him, and even some of our fellow Irishmen who are prejudiced when it comes to matters of color respect him, especially for his war record. Anyone must admire a man with the courage to join in the assault on Fort Wagner, forlorn hope that it was. Nobody around here with more than half a wit thinks him a back-shooter."

As they walked along Luther and his predicament centered their conversation.

Mick paused a moment, took out a small note book and a pencil, wrote on a page, tore it out and handed it to Seamus.

Seamus folded the paper and put it in his pocket.

They walked on and in very short order Mick stopped again.

"Well," he said with a laugh, "here is Castle Dolan."

The neat white clapboard house stood on about two acres of land which sloped away from the right side of the road. A rail fence surrounded the property and another ran down behind the home, dividing the residence from the pasture where a pair of horses grazed in the far corner. A dozen or so sheep and a few frisky lambs loitered nearer the house. At the right of the pasture was a chicken coop. Far down at the back of the pasture another small shed served as a piggery, its two hefty residents rooting near the fence.

A little girl, who Seamus knew to be about age seven, was kneeling by the fence which separated the dooryard garden from the pasture. She was petting one of the lambs who had stuck his small round head through the rails. When the girl saw the men, she jumped to her feet, blonde curls bouncing, and ran to the kitchen half-door.

"Mama, mama," she wailed, "they're here, they're here!"

"Alright, Mary," came a woman's voice from within.

The door opened and a slight, handsome woman with red hair and big green eyes appeared. She held a little child on her hip.

Seamus remembered that the baby had been born while the Brigade was fighting before Petersburg, but he could not remember her name.

"Colonel," said Mick, "this is my wife Kathleen, and my daughter Mary and the little one is Susan. Kathleen this is Colonel Seamus Delaney."

Seamus doffed his hat and bowed. Kathleen and Mary curtseyed.

"You are welcome to our home, Colonel," said Kathleen and she smiled briefly.

Seamus recognized the clipped tones of a Dublin accent in Mrs. Dolan's speech.

"Michael has told us much about you," she said, "well come in so. Your dinner is on the table." With downcast eyes, she ushered the men into the house.

They entered a capacious old-fashioned kitchen, with rough hewn beams supporting the low whitewashed ceiling. A stolid brick fireplace occupied the entire wall to the left. A modern iron cook stove had been installed in front of the old hearth, the stove pipe angled back to the chimney. The mantle of the fireplace was a thick beam of oak and hanging from it were two of Mick's possessions which Seamus recognized from the old days, a rebel cavalry saber and below it a .52 caliber Spencer repeating rifle, the barrel burnished bright.

On the far wall, the windows let in the daylight and the back door stood open. There were white lace curtains in the windows and they billowed in the cool breeze from the river below the bluff upon which the house was set. The room was redolent with the aroma of boiled ham and cabbage and the perfume of fresh baked bread.

Mick's son Daniel came in through the back door carrying a bucket of water. He placed it on the soap stone sink beneath the window, nodded a greeting, and took the visitor's hat.

"God bless all here," said Seamus, in keeping with the ancient custom.

"Amen," said all the Dolan's except baby Susan in her mother's arms. She just laughed.

Seamus turned to her and took a silver dollar from his pocket. He held it up to the baby.

"Have you been a good girl?" he asked.

"Goo!" said Susan. She reached out her tiny hand took the coin and put it into her mouth. Her mother quickly retrieved it and Susan started to wail. Kathleen took her into another room.

As usual, thought Seamus, my dealings with families take on a bumbling character. Daniel Patrick and Mary stood in front of him. He gave each of them a silver dollar.

"Don't eat them." he said.

Daniel Patrick grinned and Mary giggled.

"Thank you, sir!" they said together.

"Colonel," said Mick, "you don't have to be doing that. You will have yourself bankrupt like the Confederate Treasury."

"Not at all, Mick, it is my pleasure. Besides, the Secretary has plenty more where that came from."

Mick's eyes widened.

"Still with the Secretary, is it?" he said with a rueful shake of the head.

"Apparently." said Seamus

Kathleen returned with Susan who was now smiling and chewing on a bit of wheat bread. The mother put the child into a highchair and pulled it up to he table.

"Please everyone, be seated," said Kathleen, "Michael would you ever cut the meat."

Seamus followed instructions and sat, but for a time was the only one seated as all others, with the exception of the baby, bustled about him until his plate and tea cup were filled. The best of blue patterned chinaware, linen and pewter had been set out. Grace was said, and eventually all, Kathleen last of all, had partaken of a solid and satisfying meal. Despite the clatter and talk, Susan, as everyone watched, slowly bowed down her head of short blonde hair on the tray of her highchair and, to the great amusement of one and all, fell fast asleep.

The hospitality of the Dolan home was such that even when Seamus, full to bursting, would decline yet another helping of food, it would be tossed on his plate
regardless.

Seamus thought of how the welcome which the Irish gave to guests, be they friends, relations or strangers, was legendary. The poorer a family was, the more they would share. It was thought to be the greatest sin not to give to the needy, not just from the surplus, but from the last of what one had.

During the Famine it was well known that families who were themselves starving would welcome into their poor cabins the dispossessed wretches who were wandering the roads, there to eat the very last of their parched corn. If a family had no food left, but still had a hut or a cabin, they would bring in the wanderers to at least share the roof and die with them.

And these are the people, he thought, who for centuries have borne the yoke of an empire built on greed.

Finally, his hosts took pity on Seamus and permitted him to beg off any further victuals beyond a last cup of tea and a wedge of warm apple pie with a bit of cheddar cheese on the side of the plate. The dishes were cleared and Mick rose, went to the shelf by the hearth and took down two short Glasgow clay pipes and a jar of tobacco. He lighted a taper at the stove and returned to the table. While Mick and Seamus smoked, Kathleen sat with them and replenished the tea. Daniel excused himself saying that he must go back to the stable and reopen the office after the dinner break.

"Good lad," said his father, "I'll be along directly to spell you."

Mary busied herself playing on a blanket in the corner with Susan who had awakened from her short tableside nap.

"Rather not keep the stable open on Sundays," said Mick to Seamus, "but we have no choice. We do most of our business renting gigs and buckboards to folks for Sunday drives, so we have to be there in the morning when they are leaving and in the afternoon when they return. With the depression the economy is in now, there are not as many commercial travelers during the week. When the war was on and Kathleen and Danny ran the business in my absence, there were hoards of government contractors, buyers for the military and Army inspectors coming to the iron mills and factories in the town and the powder mills up in Fish Creek. We did plenty of trade. Kathleen was able to build up the stable. Things are a bit sparser now, but I'm sure it will pick up. Anyway we have no complaints. We could have worked all our lives in Ireland and not have a tenth of what we have now."

Seamus knew how Mick's wife had worked at the family business after Mick had joined the 69th. As comrades they had discussed their lives with each other on many a lonely night during the war. They knew more about each other than did most brothers. This was particularly true as there was less class distinction between officers and men in the all Irish regiment than was the case in the Army as a whole, and because of the special service he and Mick had shared.

Seamus knew how between the birth of Daniel Patrick and that of young Mary, two other children, a girl and a boy had been born and were lost, one to scarlet fever and the other to the same plague of cholera which had taken Seamus' uncle John Joe and cousin Peggy.

Seamus recalled that Mick had recounted those dark memories to him on the miserable night after the colossal Union defeat at Chancellorsville as they huddled together under a square of sodden oil cloth with sheets of cold rain crashing down on them. It was that night that the great Southern commander Thomas "Stonewall" Jackson had been mortally wounded. It was commonly believed that Jackson's own pickets had shot him accidentally as he was crossing rebel lines.

Now as Mick talked on about his business and the potential of the town for renewed prosperity Seamus watched Kathleen.

She took all in silently. She had been the very soul of hospitality, but Seamus in his admittedly clumsy efforts to gauge the interplay among families had often seen that married ladies were usually reticent when it came to their husband's men friends. This, Seamus had found to be especially so when the men friends were bachelors.

At a pause in Michael's discourse Seamus sought to bring

Kathleen into the conversation.

"Those are three fine children you have, Mrs. Dolan," he said smiling.

"Why, thank you, Colonel," said Kathleen returning the smile.

"Might Daniel be named for Daniel Patrick O'Connell the Liberator of Ireland?"

"He is," replied Kathleen, "Michael chose the name."

"And little Mary for the Blessed Mother?"

"That's right, Colonel." Kathleen's pleasant smile never wavered.

"And Susan?" said Seamus. He turned to Mick who winced.

"Why for Susan B. Anthony, Colonel." The smile was fading.

"Susan B. Anthony? The abolitionist?" said Seamus.

"And suffragist." answered Kathleen. The big green eyes sharpened.

"Suffrage? Oh, votes for women," Seamus was trying to sound polite. To himself he sounded, instead, condescending.

"And why not?" said Kathleen, the Dublin accent like a knife in the air.

"Am I not," she went on "as well able as any man to choose between one blathering politician and another and them standing on a soap box gesturing like a child playing at Grand Mufti? Didn't I run the stable with little more help than what I got from wee Daniel all those years while Michael was at the war, and him only home on one furlough. And I kept the books and kept the house and raised the children and made do with little. Many a hard decision I had to make. Who can now tell me I do not deserve the right to make decisions about how the government will be run?"

She paused looking straight at Seamus awaiting a reply to her rhetorical question.

"Ah, no one ma'am." Seamus stammered. He looked to Michael who was extinguishing the remains of his pipe and who showed every sign of preparing a tactical withdrawal.

"Not that I begrudge America Michael's service during the war," Kathleen continued. "The poor black people had to be freed and must be given the vote just as all women must be given the vote. All I want is that which is fair and just."

Her voice mellowed and then rose again.

"And America could not have asked better service than Michael rendered, could she Colonel?"

"No ma'am, not at all." Seamus looked around for Michael. He was at the coat rack by the front door getting their hats. Kathleen spoke, an even harder edge on her voice.

"And the best service we Irish in America can render to Ireland is, as the good Father Power said at every Mass this morning, to mind our own families and homes and build and not destroy. Is that not right, Colonel?"

"Yes ma'am, absolutely right ma'am."

Michael was standing behind his chair now and as Seamus rose, his host took the pipe from his hand and gave him his hat.

"Here's your hat, Colonel." said Michael in a voice louder than necessary.

"Right, Kathleen," he said to his wife, "we must be going now. The Colonel has important business to occupy his time this afternoon. I will see him off and relieve Danny at the stable"

"Fine, Michael," said Kathleen smiling sweetly once again, "Colonel, it has been a pleasure to meet you. We have heard so many good things about you over the years. God go with you this day."

She turned to Michael still smiling.

"Remember," she said, "Daniel will be waiting for you," the smile dropped, "don't be spending too much time at Hurley's."

Hurley's? thought Seamus.

"Hurley's?" Mick dissembled, "Of course not, Kathleen."

He hustled Seamus out the door.

Little Mary, holding baby Susan, joined her mother at the door to wave good-bye.

Michael led Seamus out the gate and up the road going back the way they had come past the church yard.

They stopped for a moment at the top of the hill and faced toward the river. An osprey flew up the creek at them, its wings beating slow and steady; the black and white feathers flashing in the bright afternoon sun. The sea hawk soared high over their heads and as they watched, circled the steeple of Saint Mary's, wheeled and sailed in a long glide back down the creek to the river. Seamus spoke.

"For the second time today, Mick, I must ask you; what was that all about?"

"Oh, votes for women? Kathleen is very serious about that business. Ah, she might be right, what's fair is fair. But when it comes time for you to marry, Colonel, don't marry a Dublin girl, they have minds of their own. On the other hand, she does, God bless her, keep things interesting."

Michael smiled to himself gazing at the river, lost in thought.

"No, Mick, not the votes for women question, your wife was very clear on that. No, what was the other bit about rendering service to Ireland?"

"Oh, that," Mick replied. "Well, with all the news about the Fenians invading Canada and some of the local boys being involved, she probably thinks you're the Fenian Centre for New York City up here to reorganize the Brotherhood."

"Me! I am not a Fenian, Mick you know that!"

"Well I do, Colonel, well I do, more's the pity."

"Michael, you and I have had that out long ago. Me! A Fenian, and a centre at that." Seamus shook his head incredulous. "She thinks I am the leader of a Circle of the Brotherhood. Mick, you must tell her that I am no such a thing."

Mick continued calmly looking out over the river.

"I would, Colonel, but it would do no good. She would not believe me. She knows it's a secret society and that I do not discuss with her, or with anyone, who is and who is not a Brother. *If* I were a sworn Fenian, I would not admit it to any outsider unless he was a prospective member about to be sworn himself, even though here in America the society is not illegal."

"The Brotherhood might itself be more successful if all those who are Brothers were so faithful to silence and secrecy," said Seamus.

"Too true, Colonel, too true. But all this talk standing here in the heat of the day has given me a thirst." Mick cleared his throat demonstratively, and led the way back up the street.

They retraced the route Seamus had taken to Mass a few hours before, passing into Church Street and the cool shade of the maples, oaks and elms along the footpath. After a while Mick spoke again.

"When you wrote me," he said, "and told me you were coming up to the Mountain House and I wrote back and suggested you might want to come down to Sunday Mass and to visit with us, I thought we could stop for a quick one after dinner and you could meet some of the boys." He gave Seamus a wink and they shared a conspiratorial smile.

They turned in front of the Methodist Church and crossed to Russell Street. A distinguished looking gentleman in black coat and tall hat drove toward them in a pony and trap. He waved to Mick, his face crinkled good-naturedly.

"Good afternoon, Mr. Dolan." he said.

Mick tipped his hat and Seamus followed suit.

"Good afternoon, parson," said Mick as the trap went up the street.

"That," he said to Seamus, "is the Reverend Mr. Osterander, the Methodist pastor ridding out to tend his flock. He is a great gent, and one of our stable's best customers. The congregation hires his transportation from us."

When they came to Partition Street, they turned right and presently were standing before the entrance to Hurley's Saloon.

"A saloon open on a Sunday in this locality?" asked Seamus in mock surprise. He knew full well from his earlier observation that it had been open to at least one patron.

"But the saloon is not open at all, Colonel," said Mick as he knocked lightly on the door, "the establishment has been rented for the regular Sunday meeting of the Rip Van Winkle Nine Pins Bowling Association, and is closed to the general public."

The door opened and Mick and Seamus stepped into the cool dark of the saloon. As his eyes grew accustomed to the dim light, Seamus was able to determine immediately that the sport of nine pins had a vast following in Saugerties. At least a hundred men were crammed into the barroom and into the back room as well which was visible through a wide arch in the far wall.

As the two entered all conversation stopped and all heads turned in unison in their direction. Men stood two deep at the bar and lined the walls of the front and back rooms, each with glass in hand. They sat crowded at round tables tightly packed throughout each room some with drinks poised at their lips. Silence reigned until from beyond the back room came the thunderous crash of scattering bowling pins.

"What!" said Mick in a loud voice, "Is somebody actually bowling? Be gob, that's a first!"

A roar of laughter met this comment and when it had subsided, Mick, speaking in an even louder voice, introduced Seamus to the assemblage.

"Gentlemen! This is Colonel Seamus Delaney of the 69th. It was he and myself were together in the Wheatfield at Gettysburg when we took the stand of colors from the rebels and stopped their advance. Let him know that he is welcome here among us!"

The welcome took the form of an explosive roar from deep in the throat of every man in the room.

Mick gestured for quite and went on.

"It was the Colonel," he declaimed, "seized the Stars and Bars after he laid the rebel color sergeant low with an upper cut. I took the Carolina regimental flag and when we got back to our lines, the Colonel here turned and shook the rebels' own banner at them!"

Seamus recalled that last bit of bravado had nearly cost him his life. It was then that the rebel ball had creased his temple.

Mick paused and another roar was heard from the gathering. Here and there a Gaelic war cry ascended. Space was made at the end of the bar on the right side of the room and Seamus conducted to it amid pats on his back and hearty greetings. The white-haired, red-faced man in the apron whom Seamus had seen at the front door earlier in the day was behind the bar. He reached across the counter and shook Seamus hand.

"This," said Mick "is Terence Hurley, our host and landlord."

"*Failte.*" said the smiling Mr. Hurley. The purple veins stood out on his nose. "What can I get you, Colonel?" he asked.

Seamus hesitated. Better stay with the beer, he thought, much yet to do today.

"Beer, if you please," said Seamus, "and whatever you and the rest of the boys are having, sir." He put a twenty dollar gold piece on the bar.

"Your drink is on the house."

"Thank you, but I will stand the next round of drinks," said Seamus for all to hear.

Hurley smiled and nodded and another cheer went up.

As the landlord was getting him his beer, Seamus looked about at his surroundings. The bar was elegantly designed with the most up to date fixtures including a brass foot rail and a mahogany railing as an arm rest. Heavy, beveled and etched mirrors were set into the ornately carved back bar. Narrow columns of oak fashioned into delicate spirals flanked each mirror. At the center of the back bar was an engraved portrait of Robert Emmet and, to the left of it, one of General Thomas Francis Meagher. A small silk American flag stood next to the picture of the General and a green flag emblazoned with a golden harp next to that of the tragic Irish revolutionary. Above the portraits was a sign painted in green and gold stating *Cead Mille Failte*.

One Hundred Thousand Welcomes, Seamus translated in his mind.

Although the room was crowded, over-crowded really, and the outside temperature stifling, the air in the saloon was cool and fresh. Seamus looked up to see the cause of this miracle. A system of twin bladed fans rotated on cast iron stanchions suspended across the high, stamped-tin ceiling. The fans were linked together by long leather belts which transferred motive power from a heavy iron wheel, cast in a floral motif and situated near the floor by the archway to the back room. A belt attached to that wheel disappeared into a channel in the floor. Also at that end of the bar, stood the oily looking man Seamus had seen to enter the saloon before Mass. Next to him was a red -haired man who looked familiar, but from long ago.

"That's something isn't it, Colonel," said Mick tossing his head up toward the fans.

"It is, Mick."

"It's the latest thing. Runs by waterwheel fed from a cistern up on the roof."

Looking to the left, Seamus could see that in the season, heat could also be provided to the room by the more conventional means of a black marble fireplace. In front of the hearth now, however, stood four tall stools and silently seated on them a musical ensemble including a gray-bearded old man with a fiddle, a young man who appeared to be blind who held a set of Irish pipes in his lap, a lad with a wooden flute and a big man with a *bodrain* drum.

The landlord returned with Seamus pint of beer and one for Mick as well. When Mick got his drink he raised it high and in a loud voice announced; "Gentlemen, I give you Colonel Seamus Delaney, may his shadow never grow less!"

This was met with hearty cheering around the room and the lifting of glasses.

In response Seamus lifted his glass to all present.

"Gentlemen," he said, "I give you yourselves; the Irish in America. *Erin go Bragh!"*

More loud agreement, an isolated war whoop, and the musicians broke into the martial measures of the *Men of the West*. As the tune was played many sang along with the paean to the bravery of the men who fought in the Rising of 1798 and others engaged in conversation, talking louder and louder to get above the music. Amid the din, a very large man made his way toward Seamus, the crowd parting readily to his progress.

Seamus suddenly recognized the dark bearded giant as Cornelius Flanagan, former corporal in the 69th. He had gained some weight since they had last met. Flanagan reached out with his massive mitt and took Seamus hand.

"Colonel," he said with his accent that mixed Donegal and Brooklyn, "how grand it is to see you again."

Seamus was delighted to meet again with his old comrade and said so. Flanagan had been in the Wheatfield too.

The music concluded and Mick gestured for attention. He had finished his beer and Hurley, unbidden, had brought another.

"Gentlemen," said Mick raising his pint, "once more I give

you the Colonel, a true Irish warrior, he served not only in the late War of the Rebellion, but in the Crimea with the Dragoons."

Please, Mick, thought Seamus, give it a rest, but he noticed that the red-haired man at the end of the bar, who seemed the worse for drink taken, had looked up sharply at the mention of the Crimea. Seamus now knew for certain who the red-haired man was.

The man did not speak, but his oily companion did.

"The Dragoons was it," he said loudly, a sneer on his face, "Would those have been the same troop of dragoons as shot down the starving people in the streets of Dungarvan during the Famine?"

This was met with moans and groans throughout the front and back rooms.

"Oh Grogan, would you ever shut up!" said someone in tones of long suffering.

"Grogan, you bloody fool!" said another.

Flanagan, standing next to Seamus, said nothing but tensed like he would leap the length of the bar at Grogan. Seamus laid his hand on his friend's arm. He had heard the insult before; What have you done for Ireland? He stared straight into Grogan's pale, baggy and bloodshot eyes, and raised his own voice above the general murmur.

"No," he answered, "those were the First Royal Dragoons at Dungarvan, not my old regiment, but if you would like to discuss military history in more detail, at any time and at any place, I am at your service."

It was his stock rejoinder to the stock insult, but the insult always stung Seamus nonetheless. As usual the challenge was not taken up. Grogan just continued to sneer and took a taste of his whiskey.

Mick jumped into the breach.

"Aragh, it is no disgrace," said he, "for an Irishman to serve in the English Army. Many's the man has enlisted just to learn the arts of war so that a blow can be struck for Ireland."

"That's right," Grogan was quick, "and no disgrace to serve in the Confederate Army either like General Macy here did." He jerked his head in the direction of the red-haired man at his elbow, and went on.

"We struck a blow for Ireland in Canada last month, and before six months is out we will strike the Empire again, but this time it will be in Ireland! The invasion of Canada was a test, is what it was, and although we didn't capture any cities up there to hold for ransom against Ireland's independence and though the French Canadians didn't have a chance to rise with us in any big numbers, the action was still and all a success. Didn't we capture Fort Erie and hold it for a time? And when we met the enemy in battle, didn't we take the Queen's flag? And we lost only eight of our own brave lads killed and at the same time we killed twelve of those buggering bastards on the other side!"

A great victory, thought Seamus, we will now count the dead bodies to see who won.

"Watch your language, Grogan," said Terence Hurley, a hard edge in his voice.

Grogan, undeterred, took another swig of his whiskey and followed with a swallow of beer. Refreshed and emboldened, he continued.

"And we are only just beginning," he said, "the Brotherhood will be more and more under the command of battle proven veterans and the weakling politicians in our ranks are being pushed aside. Colonel Kelly, a Union veteran whose name you all know well, and Captain McCarthy, late of the Confederate States Army, will be crossing the Atlantic in the second week of January next year and Gordon Macy here, General of the Irish Republican Army, will be with them to take command of the troops around Cork and Limerick when the rising comes in the spring!"

Immediately, Gordon Macy broke into song, the band took it up, the drum pounding, and most of the crowd joined in with the new song and the refrain calling for all to make way for the bold Fenian men.

The lyrics described the squadrons of Fenians marching together to pay back the foreign invader.

More of the men joined in singing as the song recalled the rebels of old who had marched to their graves and to glory. All who loved foreign rule must clear the way for the bold Fenian men. The last refrain reverberated and echoed. The drum held a staccato role and stopped.

If, thought Seamus, poetry was tactics and if wars could be won on courage and spirit..., he left the thought unfinished. War was war, it was not poetry, it was just business. Deadly, brutal, efficient business or else it was just a pitiful waste.

"And that is not all!" Grogan was not finished. "Before next Easter, a ship, *Erin's Hope* will sail from New York harbor for Sligo with forty of our officers ready to take their commands in Ireland. The ship will be loaded with crates marked as pianos and sewing machines, but do you know what those crates will really hold?"

He paused, a sneering leer on his smug face, and took another sip of his whiskey.

"They will hold rifles!" he screamed, "Over five thousand of them, breech loaders and repeaters, the newest models, the best that money can buy, and with them, a million and a half rounds of ammunition. And the ship will be mounted with a three pounder cannon in case any of the bastards afloat in the English fleet should come nosing around!"

"Watch your language, Grogan," growled the landlord, "or I'll put you out."

The musicians launched into a rollicking medley of jig tunes, hornpipes and Kerry slides, the fiddler sawing away with abandon. One of those seated at a table near the band kept time rattling a pair of short, polished rib bones.

Someone had put a dram of whiskey before Seamus. He snatched it up in anger and drank it down. He grimaced and shook his head against the burn. His eyes watered.

God help me, he thought, has anyone ever told this fool Grogan that a secret society has to be secret. He is just after giving away the strategic timetable, logistics plan and movements and identities of the principal commanders of an entire campaign, and the "general" standing beside him there can think of nothing better to do then to sing a song! Did anyone ever tell him that military secrets were supposed to be secret? In a real army, the general would have Grogan shot.

Seamus mind raced on. Another whiskey appeared in front

of him and he drank it.

Did it ever occur to them, he thought, that there could just be an agent of the Crown in these rooms.

He picked up another whiskey and drank half of it. He shook his head.

What difference did it make, he asked himself. This same conversation, containing the same information, at the very least, was being carried on in crowded saloons and public houses on both sides of the Atlantic. If a Crown agent did not get the entire plan here and now, one or all of those numerous agents would get it complete sooner or later and another effort for Irish independence would end in disaster and become the stuff of poems. But as always there would be more than poems and songs. There would be dead young men, perhaps some of those in this very room now. Others would be maimed, captured, hanged, drawn and quartered, imprisoned, exiled to the other end of the bloody earth. There would be empty chairs at the dinner table, crying women and children. He finished his whiskey. Another appeared and he drank it.

He turned and looked at Mick who was chatting with Flanagan.

Men like Mick, Seamus thought, would lose everything because the lesson had not, in centuries of rebellion, been learned: Secrecy in military action was a matter of life and death. That was why spies were executed immediately upon discovery. Why informers or braggarts who gave away information, drunk or sober, met the same fate. It was simply too dangerous to let them live.

Mick and Flanagan's conversation began to come to Seamus through the storm of rage in his mind. Flanagan was speaking.

"After the battle of Ridgeway," he said, "we came back across the border into the States, and there we were met by the American Army; the Regulars. And didn't they treat us very kindly. They took away our guns, of course, but they gave us receipts for them. They had train tickets ready for us and each man was issued a ticket and taken to the cars and sent home. Once we were on the train and far from the border, the soldiers passed among us and gave us back our guns, unloaded to be sure, but none of he boys wanted to give the Americans any trouble anyhow. Many of us met old comrades from the war among the soldiers, and do you know who I met myself?" Flanagan's dark eyes danced, "Colonel Myles Keogh!"

Seamus recalled his old friend Keogh; Keogh the illustrious, of County Carlow, former soldier of fortune in Africa, former officer in Saint Patrick's Brigade in the Papal Army. Seamus pictured the man in the deep green Zouave uniform of the Irish who fought for Peter's Sede. Keogh who was decorated by the Pope himself. Keogh; a hero of the Civil War. Rather than abandon his general on the battlefield, he had allowed himself to be captured with his commander by the Confederates, when he could have easily gotten away. Myles Keogh; handsome, dark and wild.

"That's right," said Flanagan. "Myles Keogh. He gave me a drink from his flask. He is in the Regulars now, he told me, commissioned a Captain, but he was wearing civilian clothes on the train."

"Were not," asked Mick, "the Regulars under the command of General Meade?"

"They were," said Flanagan.

"Well, no surprise then that you were so well treated. Meade is of Irish extraction himself, and he must still appreciate the service the Irish Brigade did for him at Gettysburg where he beat Bobby Lee and won his fame."

Flanagan nodded vigorously and took a drink of his beer.

Seamus drank another whiskey and thought, but did not say, that George Meade was entirely a soldier and renowned for his acerbity. If so ordered, he would, Irish extraction or not, Irish Brigade or not, Gettysburg notwithstanding, have directed every Fenian he captured to be shot. But he had not been so ordered. His orders seemed to have been quite the opposite. Although he was grateful, for the sake of the lads, Seamus could not understand why the American government, having just survived a brutal rebellion itself, would exercise such extreme forbearance toward an armed force which had launched an invasion of a neighboring territory from United States soil. It was puzzling.

He looked back to the bar, picked up his beer and took a

taste of it. There were five more glasses of whiskey before him.

The musical medley ended and Terence Hurley raised his glass and announced: "Now boys, you're drinking on the Colonel here."

He turned toward Seamus and raised his small beer again.

"*Slainte*, Colonel," he said.

A chorus of toasts echoed from the crowd.

Seamus picked up another whiskey and raised it in salute to the multitude.

"*Slainte*, lads," he said, "good health to you, one and all!"

All drank and from the back room came a booming voice.

"Give us a song, Colonel!"

"Is that you, John Sullivan?" said Seamus. He recognized the voice that had once made itself heard to him above the thud of artillery and the peel of massed rifles.

"It is, Colonel!" A tall, rawboned man waved to him. "Give us *General Munroe* like you did in the old days!"

"Oh, not at all," Seamus feigned embarrassment. "I am no singer."

In fact, he was feeling precisely in the humor to sing a song and thought that if someone had not asked him, he would have started up on his own.

"Aragh, come on, Colonel," said someone in the front room, "give us a song."

"That's right," said another, "give us *General Munroe*."

Amid the barrage of encouragement, Seamus signaled for silence, took a great swallow of beer to wet his pipes, and took a deep breathe. He lifted his chin and began the long, intricate tale of General Munroe, a draper by trade, and a Protestant, as were many of the leaders of the United Irishmen. He had been an Ulsterman and fought in the Rising of 1798.

Seamus sang *acappela* and with eyes closed. The song was as much a test of memory as a musical performance.

The story came out in lilting stanzas of how the General had fought the English Army to a standstill at Ballinahinch and how, when he had retired for the night, he had been betrayed for money, surrounded by soldiers, arrested, jailed and hanged. In the charming style of the Empire, his dead body had been decapitated and his head mounted on a pike above the court house in Lisburne as a warning to others who would tempt England's might. The song ended with the suggestion that if all of Ireland's sons had been rebels, that country would have been free long years since.

The crowd hung on the very last quavering note and at the finish held silence for a beat and then broke into earnest cheering, again punctuated by war whoops.

Mick picked up the spirit.

"Three cheers and a tiger for the Colonel!" he yelled.

"HURRAH! . . . HURRAH! . . . HURRAH! . . . ," replied the crowd and then all gave a full throated.
"GRRRRAAAHHHRRR!"

Seamus grinned broadly; very happy with himself for having met the challenge of singing the entire saga without a hesitation or mistake. He drank off half a whiskey, and extracted a celebratory cigar from the case in his pocket. He took a match from the box of small lucifers on the bar. After a few unsuccessful strikes, the match ignited and, with some concentration, he found the end of the cigar and started it smoking. There now seemed to be about ten glasses of whiskey in front of him. He finished his half-glass and started another.

Mick spoke in his ear.

"Colonel," he said, "a lot of the boys want to buy you a whiskey, but you don't have to drink everyone they send you."

Seamus was shocked at Mick's impertinence and turned to tell him so when Grogan bellowed from the other end the bar.

"And why is it that Ireland's sons are not all rebels? Why is it that Irishmen, who were soldiers, and even Colonels in the Civil War, are not all volunteering their services for the cause of old Erin? Is it that they only fight for pay? Or is it that they used up all their courage fighting at the South and have now become just a bunch of cowardly bastards?"

Now it was Seamus turn to make as if to leap the length of the bar. Blind with rage he had a picture in his mind of his fist burying itself in Grogan's sneering face.

Mick and Flanagan restrained Seamus with some difficulty.

"Terrance!" Mick spat out, "would you ever shut that drunk

up!"

The landlord responded with alacrity.

"That's all the drink for you Grogan! I told you about your language three times. Now you put a quarter dollar in the cuss box for the good Sisters of Charity."

Mr. Hurley slammed the box down on the bar in front of Grogan. It was fashioned from an old wooden canteen and was indeed hand-lettered in black paint with the words; CUSS BOX.

Grogan balked.

"Go on Grogan," came a jeering voice from the crowd, "Sure, it's for a good cause."

This was met by laughter and cat-calls from around the rooms.

"What, Grogan," came another voice, "are you too mean to help the little Sisters?"

More laughter and Mr. Hurley's voice came even more threatening.

"I run a clean establishment here, Grogan," he said, "you know that. If you curse in here you pay the price. Now, put two bits in the box for the Sisters or I will bar you from the place entirely."

Grogan hesitated still.

"And," said the landlord, "I'll tell Father Power how you have been behaving yourself."

Grogan put a quarter in the box.

The crowd of men roared with laughter.

"Oh! That got him, Terrance!" said someone.

"He is petrified with the fear of Father Power!" said someone else.

The band took up the *Stack of Barley*, the fiddle fast and merry.

In the meantime, Seamus had thrown his cigar to the floor, and was still straining against the grip of his friends in his efforts to get at the man who had insulted him.

Mr. Hurley noticed and gave a wink and a nod of the head to Mick who relayed the message to Flanagan and the two started edging Seamus toward the door. Seamus was speechless with anger and literally unable to raise a protest.

"The Colonel," said Mick above the music, "bids you all a good day."

He scooped the change off the bar and put it in Seamus pocket and, as a round of good wishes ascended loudly from the assemblage, he and Flanagan muscled their struggling charge out the door and down the three steps to the pavement.

The sudden heat and glare of mid-afternoon gave Seamus pause and he brought his hands up against the grip of his escorts and shielded his eyes.

"Oh!" he moaned into his hands, "that dirty little bastard! Why wouldn't you let me have at him!"

"Ah, now, Colonel, that would never do," said Mick," you being an officer and all. Brawling in a saloon?"

Seamus dropped his now freed hands and made a sudden rush for the door. Flanagan had anticipated the move and snatched his former commander up in a bear hug, pinning his arms to his sides.

"Straighten up, Colonel, straighten up," Mick chided, "we are out in public now. You don't want to be making a disgrace of us and get Mr. Hurley into trouble as well, do you?"

Seamus shook his head and looking around noticed that a young fellow in a straw hat across the street was stepping along quite smartly, but at the same time was staring back at the trio before the saloon, until, while walking forward and looking backward, he walked into a lamppost.

"Alright, Alright." said Seamus.

Flanagan tentatively released him.

"Sure, Grogan isn't such a bad old skin," Mick was reasonable, "he just has a bit more taken today than he can handle is all, as can happen to any of us."

Seamus caught the edge in Mick's comment on the quantity of drink which one could safely consume.

"Grogan is just jealous of you, Colonel," said Flanagan, "Before you came in he was the center of attention, going on about the battle in Canada. When Mick introduced you to the boys, Grogan got pushed into the background. He figured he had to do something to get attention. He served in the Civil War too, and he is one of us, even if he is a bit of an eejet when he drinks.

And he is a good man to have on your side in a fight."

"Especially," added Mick, "if the fight is not going to be a very clean one."

"Anyhow," Mick continued, "you have much to do today, Colonel, or so you have been telling me, and time is marching on. We had better do the same. Now, I will walk with you to the stable."

Mick took Seamus by the arm and said good bye to Flanagan who reentered the saloon. They crossed the street and walked a half-block to the corner where they turned right on Jane Street, passing along behind storehouses and back yards.

"Colonel," said Mick after awhile, "why did you let Grogan get to you? You handled him well enough at first. You know better than to give a rise to a drunk."

Seamus stumbled on a seam between the flagstones of the footpath. Mick caught him when, in a few more steps, he stumbled again. Seamus had not noticed how uneven the stones were when he had passed this way earlier on his way to Mass.

"Ah, Mick," he said in a long sigh, "it was not just his insults that got me. It was his putting out the pay about the coming action in Ireland. That kind of talk gets people killed. I could tell you how during the war the bar talk at Willard's in Washington or at the Spotswood Hotel in Richmond, for that matter, would, the very next day, spell the doom of hundreds of troops at the front. And with much less information in detail than what Grogan just blabbed. I am not *with* the Brotherhood, but God knows I am not against Ireland or the boys either." He shook his head.

"But, we were all among friends, Colonel..."

"Were we Mick? Were we?" Seamus voice was thick. "When I knew 'General' Gordon Macy in the Crimea, he was a private using the name Patrick Conlon, and I do not remember him being particularly in favor of the cause of Irish freedom, quite the opposite actually."

Mick looked surprised.

"But," he said, "men find it necessary to change their names for many reasons, and, as you already know thanks to Grogan as you say; blabbing, Macy is one of the top men in the movement.

If he cannot be trusted, who can?"

Seamus walked along with his head down.

"I don't know," he said as much to himself as to Mick, "maybe no one."

"Oh, well," said Mick, "here we are."

Seamus looked up. Across the street was the stable. Daniel Patrick standing by the office door saw them and ducked into the barn. By the time they had crossed the street, he had led Sarge, who appeared well rested, out to the iron hitching post at the curb. The top of the post was cast in an effigy of a horse's head holding a large ring in its mouth.

"Hello, old Sarge," said Seamus, and he swung himself up into the saddle with such force that he nearly threw himself over the other side. Mick and Daniel were quick to steady him.

"Are you sure you are alright to make this trip, Colonel?" Mick asked.

"Of course, of course," Seamus replied.

Mick looked at him skeptically.

"Now, you have your maps," he said, "it is not that easy to find Phaestus' place. You go out the turnpike like you came in, but you turn to the right outside the town up the road to Katsbaan. Beyond Katsbaan you turn right on the road to High Falls...."

"I'll find it," Seamus interrupted, "I have a tremendous sense of direction."

Seamus made to depart and Daniel asked him to wait a moment. He hurried into the office and emerged in a second with Seamus' canteen.

"I refilled your canteen, sir," he said and hung it on Seamus saddle. "That cover on it is nifty." The boy ran his hand over the embroidered harp.

"Don't be talking slang." said his father.

"'Nifty' is it?" said Seamus.

He lifted the canteen off the saddle by the strap and draped it gently it across Daniel's shoulder.

"You keep it, lad," he said.

Mick and his son both protested, but Seamus silenced them.

"No," he said, "you keep it. You are the next generation,

Daniel Patrick and this is a part of your inheritance. It belonged to my cousin, Felim Duffy, Captain of the 69th. He died at Antietam." Seamus felt his throat tighten. He went on.

"You keep it, and your father will tell you all about Felim, won't you Michael."

"I have, and I will, Colonel," said Mick his eyes suddenly glistening.

"Farewell then," said Seamus.

"Farewell," said Mick.

Seamus spurred Sarge and, with a wave, he was off. He wheeled the horse about and headed straight for the door of the Congregational Church, a bit too fast. He corrected just before riding up onto the footpath and turned to the right in the middle of the cross street. He glanced back and waved again to the father and son and then grinned at the identical aspects of nervous apprehension each wore on his face. He spurred Sarge into a trot and headed directly up the street passing on each side houses, small shops and a number of brick buildings under construction. He reached another crossing street and looking to the right saw the now familiar entrance to Hurley's Saloon in the distance, about halfway down the block. It came to him that he had missed his turn and he stopped in the middle of the intersection. The thought occurred to him that he could ride down the block, enter Hurley's, and finish his business with Grogan and he sat his horse and pondered that course of action.

A lady and a gent in a buggy entered the intersection from behind him and each gave Seamus a querulous look as they were forced to make a wide circle around the barrier which he and Sarge were creating in the center of the thoroughfare. Sarge seemed embarrassed and stomped his foot.

Seamus shook his head and nodded silently to Sarge, appreciating the good sense implicit in the horse's impatience. He put thoughts of vengeance aside and retraced his path passing a small hotel and an old-fashioned tavern on the right side of the street. He recognized the next right turn he came to, looked up that street and saw the hardware store where he had gotten directions that morning. He followed the street to the edge of town where he discovered the beginning of the turnpike.

The heat pressed down on the open road and choking dust rose up at each step. Seamus' head began to ache. When he reached the rolling hills and fields where he had earlier envisioned the placement of troops and artillery or alternately the site of a musical concert, he found a road sign pointing north advising that Katsbaan was two miles distant. The odd sounding name seemed familiar. He took out his maps and fumbled with them as Sarge walked along. The writing on the maps looked to be blurred and proved difficult to read. The sweat ran down into his eyes so that he took off his hat and wiped his brow, the maps crunching in his grip. He smoothed out one of the maps but could not find Katsbaan on it and tried another. There he found the hamlet and reckoned that he was probably on the right road. He put the maps away and put his hat on. Smothering with the heat, he took off his coat and laid it across the saddle bow.

As he rode along, Seamus' thoughts went back to Grogan.

The impudent fool! he thought. Small wonder some consider the Irish to be, as a race, a laughingstock! So many of us sacrificing and giving our all, and a braggart like that disgracing us! No wonder people like Twilling the clerk look down on the Irish. Look down on me!

When I get back to the Mountain House, Seamus raged to himself, I will find Twilling before I do anything else and I will thrash him!

The picture of himself smashing Twilling in his punctilious face blotted out all other images. Twilling's face then became Booth's in Seamus mind; the arrogant, sneering face of the assassin.

Oh, how I would love to smash that face, he thought. Booth! Who by his cowardly act stole away the fullness of our victory. After years of pain and struggle we had won our battle honors dearly. Irishmen in America's service, we had marched up Pennsylvania Avenue, and later up Fifth Avenue in New York, line abreast, row upon row, the banners flying, red, white and blue, green and gold. The eagles on the flagstaffs hung with circlets of laurel cut from the banks of the Shenandoah. Fifes playing, drums beating out all the tunes of triumph, *The Mountains of Pomery, O'Donnell Abu, The Garryowen.*

But in Washington it was President Johnson who took the salute. It was not to the bosom of Abraham that we returned. The coward Booth had stolen him away, making for us a victory which would forever be ashes in our mouths.

Booth! thought Seamus, how I would love to kill Booth! If he were not already dead.

And with that last thought, Seamus came back to the present and realized that he was now climbing, on foot, a long and winding hill and leading Sarge behind him. He considered that he must have dismounted to give the horse a rest out of force of habit and without noticing his action while his thoughts were elsewhere. Now he remembered that he had passed at least two by-roads turning off to the right, one near an old stone house of the salt box style. He had traveled amid fields but was now flanked by woods. It occurred to him that he did not know where he was.

Tall trees shaded the road but he was nonetheless hot and thirsty. He reached up to Sarge's saddle only to find his canteen missing. He looked around the ground for it and was to the point of turning back to search for it when he recalled that he had given to Mick's son.

Good, he thought. He did not regret making the boy a gift of the vessel but wished that he had taken another container of water in replacement.

At the same time he was suffering from thirst, Seamus, paradoxically, found that he needed to relieve his bladder.

He came to the top of the hill and found a narrow road leading off through the trees to the right. The sign board read: HIGH FALLS 3 mi.

"There," he said, "you see, Mick. I have a tremendous sense of direction."

He also had the sense that he needed to get rid of the liquid he had imbibed and that, right away. He entered the road to High Falls and led Sarge to the side. He tried to tie the reins to the low thin branches of an oak sapling, but the thick leather would not stay in a knot. Finally, he let the reins drop and patted the horse on the neck.

"There, Sarge, you are a good boy, aren't you? Now don't

go away."

He stepped over a low stone fence into the woods and stumbled among the brush and fallen branches until he found a suitable tree behind which to stand.

After considerable fumbling he achieved his objective and made to return to the road by the way he had come. When he walked back what he judged to be the proper distance, the low stone fence, not to mention the road and Sarge seemed to have disappeared. All he could find was more woods. He tried again to retrace his steps, but the forest looked precisely the same no matter where he wandered. At last, he found a wide trunked tree and on one side of it, evidence that it was the very same tree which he had just used as an impromptu to privy. He stepped around to the dry side, slid down the rough bark of the trunk until he was sitting on the leaves, and with his back against the tree, he passed out.

# IX

## An Expert Opinion

Seamus awoke startled at the sight of a horse's muzzle within an inch of his face. The big pink tongue slavered his cheek, the breathe smelling of oats and grass. He pulled back and bumped his head on the root of the tree against which he had been propped. He was now flat on his back, the trees and the blue sky visible beyond the horse's face. He took the horse by the bridle and wondered dreamily where he was.

Suddenly the image came to him of Luther in his root cellar prison. Seamus bolted upright. His skull pounded with the leavings of the afternoon's whiskey.

Whiskey, he thought, people depending on me for their very lives, and I get drunk on whiskey.

He loathed himself. His stomach churned and he pictured himself murdering Emily's husband; Lt. Coltrane. His mouth was a fetid swamp. He despised himself.

And, he thought, I am going mad. Nightmares whilst I am awake.

Instantly he thought of his pistol and reached to his side.

Where is the damned pistol! End it all now, he screamed within himself, put a bullet in your brain!

No, he thought, no, he reasoned more calmly. Why did I let myself get drunk? Why? Why?

God help me, he thought.

"God help me," he said aloud.

He lifted himself up slowly, holding onto the bridle with one hand and the trunk of the tree with the other. When he was erect, he let go of the tree and put his hand to his brow. He bent to pick up his hat and a wave of nausea swept over him. He choked and gagged leaning again with one hand on the tree, a searing pain in his head. He took a few deep breathes and Sarge began to pull him along by the bridle. In a few steps he and the horse had returned to the road. There he found his coat lying in a dusty heap where it had fallen from the saddle over which he had draped it. He brushed at it absently and at his trousers and vest and wondered how long he had lain in the woods. Panic seized him.

The time! he thought. He must get to Phaestus' place and then up the mountain.

He took out his watch. The cheery notes of *The Garryowen* mocked him as the case popped open at his touch. It was after five o'clock.

God help me, he thought again. He did not even know for sure where he was or how far he had yet to go to find the gunsmith.

What if he is not at home? How long will it take to get from his house to the Mountain House?

How, he asked himself, can I expect to help anyone, if I cannot hold my liquor?

He shook his head and winced.

I go from a state of grace to a state of sodden stupidity in mere hours, he scolded himself.

But enough, he tried to calm himself, take some action.

He took a quick look at his maps again and reassured himself of the High Falls road sign. He put on his coat, checking the location of his pistol and mounted Sarge.

The horse as usual anticipated his rider's direction and began to trot along the primitive road.

The rutted and rocky track wound through the trees and meandered up and down hills. No farms, homesteads nor houses of any kind appeared and after a time, Seamus formed the conclusion that the road existed solely to connect the many blue stone quarries which he passed with the outside world. The path seemed to carry him and Sarge in a zigzagging course from one deep, square-cut hole in the ground, with accompanying pile of flat stones, to another.

His apprehension increased with the growing feeling that he was going absolutely nowhere and that rather quickly.

At length, horse and rider ascended a particularly steep hill and paused at the crest. From there the road descended into a hollow. A big red-tail hawk riding the humid air above the hollow caught Seamus' eye. The bird circled against the cloudless sky, halted in mid-glide, flared its wings and settled onto the topmost branches of a broad chestnut tree. It stood with its white front blazing in the declining light and behind it Seamus could see a thin wisp of smoke rising through the trees. He urged Sarge down the hill and presently on his right, in a small clearing in the forest appeared a long, low cabin built of logs. By the wall of the cabin was an open-sided shed and in it a brick forge where a banked coal fire glowed in the shadows. The smoke from the forge ascended into the still air.

Looking up, Seamus could see that the hawk was still perched at the top of the tree. It was now looking right back at him.

In front of the shed, at a table constructed of rough planks and saw horses, sat a lanky man with sandy hair going to gray. His head was down, and he was working intently at something on the table. A tool satchel rested on the table. No fence of any kind surrounded the property so Seamus simply rode off the road onto the greensward before the cabin.

The man worked away apparently oblivious of Seamus presence. A long haired, yellow colored retriever, who had been resting at the man's feet in the shade of the table, raised the alarm however, emerging into the light with two deep barks, bared teeth and a deep growl.

"Easy, Po," said the man looking up. He smiled, his lean, clean-shaven face twisting into an expression which contained at once humor and something more.

Irony, Seamus thought.

Crow's feet crinkled at the corners of the man's clear blue eyes.

"Easy Po, old boy," the man said again to the dog. "This fella don't look to be too dangerous."

Impertinent, thought Seamus.

"I beg your pardon," he said, "I am looking for the residence of Mr. Ishmael Phaestus."

"You've found it," said the man, the ironic smile steady.

"Mr. Phaestus . . . ," said Seamus, taking Mr. Beecher's letter from his coat pocket.

"Don't call me mister, I ain't *that* old, and don't call me Ishmael either. Nobody calls me that. My friends call me Cappy."

"Well then . . . Cappy, I am . . ."

"I know," Cappy interrupted, "you're Colonel Seamus Delaney. Don't need no letter. Sampson from the Mountain House came by a while ago. Told me to keep an eye peeled for you. He was surprised you hadn't been back up there yet. What happened; you get lost?"

"Um . . . yes."

"Sampson told me about what's going on with Luther, fine man Luther. Sampson said Constable Humphrey telegraphed Mr. Beecher and told him that the mob around the jail had just melted away about noon time. Humphrey was going along with one of the deputies back up to the Mountain House. They want you up there quick, but why don't you climb down off Sarge there and give him a rest for a little bit. Tie him off by the water trough over there." Cappy pointed to his left.

Seamus did as instructed and led Sarge to the end of the shed where a hitching post and an iron tub-shaped trough stood in the shade. A butternut mare was hitched behind the cabin. She looked at Seamus and Sarge and chewed a sheaf of hay.

Sarge looked back at her and availed himself immediately of the water.

"Come on back and have a seat here," said Cappy, "you look like you've had a rough day."

All the time Cappy spoke, he never rose from his seat as good manners would have dictated. This both added to and enhanced the over all impudent, mocking and rude attitude, it seemed to Seamus, Cappy was intent on displaying. Seamus was rapidly growing infuriated with this man.

A plain, straight backed, rush-seated chair had been pushed under the near end of the table. Seamus took the chair and seated himself. An arrant breeze brought the sulfurous odor of the coal fire in the forge to his nostrils and his stomach protested accordingly. He noted a number of shotgun barrels, in various stages of manufacture, stacked in the corners and hanging on the back walls of the shed.

He turned his eyes back to Cappy, who he perceived to be regarding him closely. He found this to be . . . unsettling.

"You look like you got into the whiskey today," said Cappy. The ironic smile seemed to be a permanent fixture.

This is too much! thought Seamus. He considered telling this . . . this . . . insolent . . . person that his drinking habits were no one's business but this own. He thought simply to leave. Instead, he said in a small voice:

"Is it that obvious?"

The smile left Cappy's face.

"It is, Seamus," he said, "to someone who knows. I had many days like that myself. But not any more."

The smile returned.

"Like the fella said; 'I done seen the light'. You could use some of Cappy's coffee, I think."

Cappy stood and Seamus saw that below the knee, the man's left leg had been replaced by a varnished and highly polished peg of wood. It appeared to Seamus to be teak wood.

Cappy loped in long strides to the forge and returned with a big tin plated coffee pot and two enameled tin cups. He poured out the coffee and placed the pot on the table.

Seamus took a sip and winced. Cappy was delighted at the reaction.

"Good strong coffee," he said, "strong enough you could float a horseshoe in it."

He placed an old three-legged milking stool next to his captain's chair, seated himself and propped is wooden leg on the stool. The peg was etched with ropes and anchors and crossed muskets all around. Near the knee, it was cut square and at the front, amid carved oak leaves, had been tacked a gleaming brass plaque embossed with an eagle, it's wings spread above a fouled anchor and the words *By Land and By Sea*. Seamus recognized the plaque as an old pattern cap badge of the Corps of United

States Marines.

He realized that he was staring at the prosthetic and quickly looked up.

Cappy was still regarding him.

"Not bad, eh?" said Cappy, "I did it myself."

Seamus eyes widened.

"No," Cappy laughed, "I didn't take the leg off myself, the rebels did that. At Hampton Roads. I was aboard the *Cumberland* when the *Merrimac* sunk us. First Sergeant and armorer of the Marine Detachment. While I was in hospital at Fortress Monroe some of my shipmates brought a few fragments of the spars from the wreck and I chose this one to make my new leg. Had plenty of time to work on it.

"I got the name Cappy while I was in the Marines too. Somebody found out that I had sailed on whaling ships out of the city of Hudson across the river where I was born. They started saying I'd been a whaler captain. Never had been, but they started calling me Cappy and the name stuck.

"I went to sea when I was twelve. Started drinking spirits then too. Wanted to see the world. And I did see a lot of it. Learned to forge harpoons and carve scrimshaw. At the end of the 40's though, I heard the story of the *Lawrence,* a whaler out of Poughkeepsie. I had known some of the crew. Heard how she fetched up off the coast of Japan. The Japanese rescued some of them, but kept them locked in a cage for a year. Japan is leery of foreigners. They don't want to end up like China where the English invaded the country to force the Chinese to buy opium.

"Well, I had no fear of death, but the idea of being locked up scared hell out of me. Figured if I wanted to continue touring the world, I had rather do it on armed vessels. Seemed the work of the Marines was easier on board ship then what the sailors had to do, so I joined the Corps. Got to go to Japan too. With Commodore Perry."

Cappy took a sip of his coffee. His dog came up under the table and lay his snout on Seamus knee looking up with soulful eyes. Seamus scratched the dog behind his floppy ears.

"Old Po likes you," said Cappy, "I named him for the

*Powhatten*, one of the ships of Perry's flotilla when we went into Edo Bay. I got to go ashore because, like a lot of the people here in the valley, I can speak Dutch and I could interpret. Many of the Japanese who are interested in the outside world learned Dutch since, for years, Holland was the only country they would trade with. They are a smart and disciplined people, the Japanese, and no less ambitious then us Americans. We'd be foolish to think less of them because they ain't white.

"Some of our crew at Edo weren't white either. Two of the biggest lads on board were a pair of black fellas. Giants they were and dauntless. I fitted each of them out with a brace of pistols, a dirk, a cutlass and a musket with bayonet fixed. They stood by the Commodore on the beach, one on each side of him and did they ever impress the shogun's samurai."

Cappy smiled at the memory.

He went on.

"So I stayed in the Corps and on Saturday, the 8th of March, in '62, the *Merrimac,* or *C.S.S. Virginia* if you prefer, took away my leg. I had feared only being caged and now I was a cripple. I wanted to be fancy free and foot loose, and now I had come to lose a foot clear up to the knee."

He laughed and suddenly his smile went like the sun passing behind a cloud.

"I was in a cage that I thought would never open. Wanted to die, but couldn't bring myself to squeeze the trigger. I had always used liquor and now, looking back on it, had gotten myself into trouble with it often. But after this," he patted the leg, "I crawled into the bottle and pulled the cork in after me. They returned me to Catskill and mustered me out as an invalid. I hung around the docks carrying luggage for the visitors or unloading wagons or just begging enough to get a drink.

"That's where Mr. Beecher found me. He knew me and my family from years back. He introduced me to the pastor of Katsbaan Dutch Church over yonder by the turnpike. The pastor has never been a drinker, but he hadn't always been a preacher either. He served in the war with the Ulster Guard and came out a leg lighter too. He understood. In time I was able to stop drinking and stay stopped. I know I can't take one drink. Like the Chinese say; 'The man takes a drink, then the drink takes a drink, and then the drink takes the man.'

"Mr. Beecher set me up in this gunsmith business and with the help of some of his people, Luther included, we built the cabin and the forge. I make high grade shotguns, mostly for Mr. Beecher's wealthy friends and associates."

Cappy picked up a piece of bone from the table.

"I practice my engraving on these. When I settle on a design, I decorate the guns I make."

Seamus looked at the carved flowers and leaves on the bone. They reminded him of the embellishments on the Japanese swords, bronze bells and lacquered boxes he had seen on display at the Smithsonian Institution.

"In the season," Cappy continued, "old Po and me take my customers bird hunting. This peg leg is not a cage. Barely slows me down. I have everything to be grateful for, and when I forget that, I saddle up my Missy back there and take a ride over to visit Pastor William and we talk. That's my story Seamus. What's yours?"

Seamus started up in his chair. How could he tell this man he had just met his life's story? But he did, completely and honestly. He held nothing back, including what had recently transpired at the Mountain House.

"And now, Cappy," he concluded, "I am haunted by the knowledge that I killed Emily's husband at Antietam."

Cappy paused not a moment.

"Then, Seamus," he said, "you will have to go back there and bring him back to life."

Seamus jaw dropped. Was this man to whom he had just bared his soul mad?

"I cannot do that, Cappy," he said," it is impossible."

"What?" said Cappy, "You can't go back to Antietam? It's still there ain't it?"

"Well, of course, but . . ."

"But, what? Is the Bloody Lane not there anymore?"

"I am sure that it is, but the battle is over. It is not the place that is gone, it is the day that is gone, and the man's life too."

"There it is," said Cappy and he said no more. He finished

his coffee, poured himself another, filled and lighted his corn cob pipe and smoked.

Seamus waited for him to go on. Cappy said nothing. The silence grew uncomfortable. Time passed. The hawk in the tree screamed and flew away.

"I cannot change the past," said Seamus at last.

"No power on earth can," said Cappy.

"But I must tell Emily."

"Why?"

"As I told you Cappy, I have feelings for her," said Seamus hesitantly, still embarrassed and surprised to admit his affection for the lady even to himself.

"Then why hurt her?"

"Should I not be honest with her?"

Cappy puffed out a puff of smoke and put down his pipe.

"Seamus, how many troops were engaged on both sides at the Bloody Lane? Thousands, right?"

Seamus nodded.

"From what you have told me, there is no way that you can be certain, *certain*, mind you, that it was your shot that killed the man. You were in the midst of the insanity of battle, wounded yourself, on the verge of fainting. It may not have even been Lieutenant Coltrane who you were shooting at and if it was him, maybe it was someone else's bullet that struck him. Believe me, they don't call liquor 'spirits' for nothing. The ghosts and demons you've been describing to me come directly from the bottle."

Seamus nodded again.

"And even if you could be certain that you had shot the Lieutenant, *and you never will be,*" Cappy paused and sipped his coffee, "what possible good could it do Miz Emily to know that fact? Leave the past in the past and drive on."

Seamus nodded yet again.

"Anyhow, we have spent enough time on you," said Cappy, the crooked smile was back. "Luther is the man with the real problem. Sampson told me you have a bullet for me to look at."

Seamus had been staring into the distance and now jumped in his chair.

The bullet! Please God, don't let me have lost it!

"Where have I put the bullet?"

He patted his trouser pockets and then gratefully extracted it from his vest pocket. He handed it over to Cappy.

The gunsmith took the gray cylinder of lead in his fingers and turned it over, cocking his head to the left and then to the right.

"And this is the round that killed the man?" he said.

"There seems to be little doubt, Cappy, we found it embedded in the ceiling of the porch, the blood spatters all around it."

"Well," said Cappy, "it may have killed your Mr. Clay, but it is not one of the bullets I made and gave to Mr. Beecher. It is an elongated ball, or conical bullet, or conoidal pistol ball or whatever you want to call it, but it was not molded by me. Matter of fact, I don't think it was made in this state or even in this part of the country, or at least the bullet mold for the machine it was made with wasn't. I think it was made south of the Mason-Dixon Line. If I was a betting man, I'd bet that it is a rebel bullet. In fact, allowing for the way it is deformed, it reminds me of the bullets that were made by the Richmond Laboratory."

"That was why the bullet seemed strange to me and yet familiar;" said Seamus, "it was made in Richmond! I used the products of the Laboratory myself on occasion. Why didn't I think of it?

"Yes," said Cappy sitting back in his chair, I would say this is probably a rebel bullet. What I can swear to is that I did not make it and it was not part of the ammunition I provided for Mr. Beecher along with the Colt's Dragoon pistol I sold him."

Seamus nodded.

"But," he said, "that does not mean that someone could not have loaded that pistol with ammunition other than that which you supplied."

"True." said Cappy. He picked up a brass caliper from the table and brought the jaws of the instrument together at the base of the bullet.

"This is a .44 caliber round," he said, "and rebel or Union, could have been fired from the Colt's Dragoon."

Seamus thought a moment.

"Could the pistol," he asked, "have been fired accurately at one hundred and fifty feet?"

"One hundred and fifty feet!" said Cappy, "Ten rods. That's some long shot for a pistol. The Dragoon was designed for cavalry work, close in. No pistol is made for long range, that's what rifles and carbines are for. Although it goes off with a bang, gun powder burns slow. The longer the barrel, the farther you can shoot and hit because the explosive force stays behind the projectile longer. Still, it is probably possible that an outstanding pistol shooter, using optimum powder loads, with no cross wind, might be able to shoot accurately at that range."

"To your knowledge," asked Seamus, sounding to himself like a lawyer, "is Luther such an outstanding shot with a pistol?"

"Not at all," said Cappy, "he was a trained and seasoned soldier, but, as an infantryman; the rifled musket was his weapon. He is known among us deer hunters hereabouts to be a good shot with the rifle, but when I had him and some of the other fellas from the Mountain House down here to practice loading and shooting the Dragoon, he told me he had never before that day had the occasion to shoot a revolver. After a while, I had Luther and all the lads shooting well enough, but only at eight yards range. We agreed that for their purposes, if someone chose to bushwhack them with a long arm at more than twenty-five feet there was little they could do but try to escape, if they were still alive after the first shot. The pistol was for the occasion when someone might jump out at them from the side of the trail. Luther was a good enough shot at close range, but we never even tried to shoot at one hundred and fifty feet."

Cappy thought a moment.

"Don't know as even I could hit a man-sized target at that range," he said with a shrug.

"Not man-sized," Seamus corrected, "the size of a man's head."

Cappy's eyes widened.

"Let's try it," he said, and he reached into the satchel before him and withdrew a massive Colt's Dragoon pistol, identical to that which Luther had possessed. He checked the hammer and the caps and laid the weapon on the table.

"I bought a whole consignment of these from the State Militia cavalry troop in Albany after they went over to the 1860 Model Colt's Army revolver. This one is loaded with the same measures of powder as the pistol Luther had. We'll see if we can hit the target at one hundred and fifty feet. You a good shot, on to it, Seamus?"

Cappy gave Seamus a narrow-eyed smile.

"It has been said that I am, on to it," replied Seamus.

Cappy laughed, a quick snort.

He rose and walked across the clearing and Seamus followed. They came to a small wood pile and Cappy paused.

"This is twenty-five feet from the table," he said as he picked up two round slabs of timber. The bark was still on them and they were about the diameter of a human head. Two planks of rough cut lumber rested against the wood pile. The center of each plank was full of bullet holes.

"These are the targets I had Luther and the others practice on," said Cappy, "Man-sized targets because I was teaching them to shoot for the widest part of the body, nothing fancy. So when I say they all learned to shoot pretty well, I mean up close and at a large target."

Seamus nodded.

They passed other wood piles about every twenty feet until they reached the last pile at the tree line at the edge of the clearing. Cappy propped the targets against the pile.

"That's one hundred and twenty five feet," he said, "we'll have to stand back behind the table and a little bit into the shed to make up the difference when we shoot."

They returned to the table and Cappy shooed Po out from under it and into the shed. He picked up the pistol and held it in both hands pointing the muzzle to the ground. He paced off the distance into the shed, Seamus pacing with him. He turned and pointed the pistol down range.

"There," he said, "that is just about the range. Now, we will figure that the murderer took a two handed grip to give himself the best advantage. Might he have been able to take a resting

stance?"

"Yes, he probably would have been able to steady his aim by leaning against the doorpost when he fired."

Cappy accordingly leaned his forearm against the upright which supported the roof of the shed.

"I'll take the right hand target," he said.

He cocked the pistol, sighted and slowly squeezed the trigger. The report thundered within the confined space of the shed and Seamus saw bark and wood fragments erupt from the wood pile to the right and about a foot above the target.

Cappy waited for the smoke to clear.

"How did I do?"

"Come left and down about twelve inches," said Seamus.

"Well, I would have been surprised to have hit it," said Cappy shaking his head.

He cocked, sighted again and fired. This time the strike of the bullet was about six inches under the target.

On his third attempt, Cappy hit slightly off the target near the upper right rim.

"Here," he said, "you try."

Seamus took the heavy pistol in both hands and leaned against the support. He cocked it and aimed carefully for the lower left hand corner of the target. He squeezed the trigger concentrating on the tip of the front sight. The pistol discharge came, as it should, as a surprise.

"Low," said Cappy, "off target about a half foot, I should say, to the left."

Seamus cocked and sighted again, this time holding high and to the right of the lower left hand quadrant. He squeezed and the pistol again surprised him as it jumped in his hand.

"You got it by jingo!" said Cappy with a slap to his thigh, "Good shooting!"

Seamus stepped forward, put the pistol on the table and together the two men walked to the wood pile.

Seamus' target had a .44 caliber hole at the very edge at the top and to the right of center.

Had the target, he thought, indeed been a human head, the wound thus produced might have been a grazing one and may not even have been mortal.

"So," asked Cappy, "have we proved that Luther did not kill the man?"

"No, would that we had. I know that neither of us believes that he did, but it is what can be proved in a court of law that counts. As we said before, we cannot prove that Luther did not use a bullet other than one of those which you supplied. And we would get nowhere trying to prove a negative; that Luther is *not* a good enough shot with the pistol to have killed at the range in question.

"Of course, the notion that Luther spent months practicing in secret with the pistol so that he could be ready, on the spur of the moment, to avenge on Saturday morning an insult which Clay had rendered him on Friday night, by shooting the man at one hundred and fifty feet, and hitting him in the head with one shot would be laughable. However, the implausibility of the notion does not constitute evidence."

Seamus looked at his watch. It was now after half-past six.

"I had better be going," he said.

They walked back to the watering trough and Seamus untied Sarge and mounted.

"If you go right up High Falls Road," said Cappy, "you can save time. When you get to Mountain Turnpike, go left and you can be at the Mountain House in under two hours without giving old Sarge here too much of a workout."

He extended his hand and Seamus took it. Cappy's grip was like a steel vise.

"You take care of yourself, Seamus."

"I will, Cappy, I will. Thank you . . . for everything. I would like to see you again."

"We'll meet again, God willing."

Seamus took the reins and rode across the lawn. He turned back to see Cappy waving. The ironic smile seemed warmer now.

He spurred Sarge into a canter and kept the pace for a time until they crossed a wide plank bridge before a waterfall below which stood an old mill built of stone. They slowed to cross the bridge. There was a small stone store house at the edge of the road and it appeared on both Sampson's map and the one which Mick had made. It was a relief to know that they were heading in the right direction.

"Although I wish I had a map to tell me who killed Clay," he said to Sarge.

Seamus considered all that he thought he knew and it seemed the more he learned, the more fog settled in his mind and the less he could picture the truth about the murder. One thing was for sure though; he knew that Leander Skhutt and his friends would be visiting the Mountain House tonight. Those who had left the street in front of the jail would reinforce the mountain top mob. Whenever the enemy withdrew unbeaten from one portion of a defensive line, they would be certain to strike at another and more critical point. Speed was therefore all the more of the essence.

Seamus and Sarge crossed the bridge, the horse's hoofs clomping on the planks. The warm closeness of the day lingered, but the searing heat was diminishing as the sun declined.

The road continued its meandering path up and down hills mostly through hardwood forests where a few small farm holdings were scattered in clearings. When the road intersected the Mountain Turnpike, Seamus turned west and spurred Sarge into a quick trot taking advantage of the superior road surface and the cooler temperature. The turnpike, in fairly short order, traversed the remainder of the plain of the valley.

They passed rich farm fields where corn and wheat stood in ranks and began to climb the lower ridges of the mountains. Seamus recognized the four corners where Bogart Road crossed the turnpike and he pressed on to the long hill before the last set of fields at the base of South Mountain. He dismounted to give Sarge a rest and climbed the curving hill leading the horse along behind him.

He was surprised to see a lone farmer working on a Sunday in a field of early ripening wheat. The man, attired in shirt sleeves, galluses and baggy trousers, attacked the new crop with a scythe. At the margin of the field lay the man's coat of Army blue, the brass buttons glittering in the sun. A canteen rested upon the coat. Had he not been in a hurry, Seamus would have stopped and chatted up his fellow veteran, but the man's back was turned and Seamus passed by without salute or comment.

At the top of the hill, he remounted and trotted along the flat between the low stone walls and tall oaks. The tollgate sat in the distance and the mountain brooded dark above the road, its black shadow stretching toward Seamus and eastward across the valley.

He rode up to the gate and greeted the keeper as the man rose from his chair.

"Well, sir," said the toll taker, "and there you are. I had almost nobody going by all day. Just Sampson come down and went back up a little later and Constable Wyncoop, he knows you, and his deputy, Willie Peters. They went up in the constable's buckboard. Say, you didn't see that fella who cut the tollgate this morning, did you? I told Humphrey about that."

"No, sir, I did not," said Seamus as he handed the man a dime for his toll, "you had no one else pass today, you say."

And he thought; that's good.

"Not a soul," replied the gatekeeper, putting the coin in his pouch, "course this is not the only road up the mountain, on to it, just the quickest and best kept between Catskill and the Mountain House. So if somebody else you know was going up, they might not have passed this way. The road through Palenville is the old route up the mountain. Follows the Kaaterskill Creek bed and goes the long way round. It comes out at Haine's Corners. Not as good for carriages, coaches and big wagons and such like though, hasn't been kept up proper since the turnpike here was built, but folks, if they ain't in a rush, can get to the mountain top that way. No toll either."

Seamus was dismayed. It had not occurred to him, although it should have, he thought, to inquire as to whether or not there was an alternative road between the towns of the valley and the Mountain House.

There is no time to waste, he thought. He bade the toll taker a good afternoon and trotted up the road. Again the man seemed disappointed that he did not pause longer to socialize.

Seamus regretted having to ask much more of Sarge but he

felt that he had no choice as he urged the horse on to make the best possible time. All the while he kept alert on the road for any sign of an imminent ambush.

He alternately rode and led Sarge up the steep road as quickly as possible. By the time they had reached the common before the stables both man and horse were near to being worn out. Seamus dismounted and gave Sarge a pat on the neck by way of saying thank you. He consulted his watch. It was twenty-five minutes after eight.

The time, he thought, the bloody time!

Young Frederick Douglass Van Bronc emerged at a run from the depths of the stable and took Sarge by the bridle.

"Colonel, they told me to be looking for you and I just stepped away. Mr. Beecher and Miz Emily and the constable and my father all have been asking for you," he said in a breath.

"Good man, Frederick, I will search them all out, but first I have to see Mr. Twilling. Now, if you please, give Sarge a good feed and drink and a rub down and let him rest a bit, but I need him to be ready again for me as soon as possible, the poor fellow."

Seamus turned toward the hotel.

"Colonel?" said Frederick.

Seamus turned back.

"Yes, Frederick."

"Is everything going to be alright, Colonel, you know, sir, with my father?"

Seamus put his hand on the lad's shoulder and looked down into his upturned face.

"Yes, Frederick," he said, "everything is going to be alright."

I pray to God, he thought.

He turned again and hurried toward the hotel. To the east beyond the roof top of the Mountain House, towering, convoluted clouds were painted scarlet by the setting sun. Above the clouds the clear sky ascended into a deepening blue. The great house itself glowed pink in the last reflected rays of the day. It seemed to him that every column, portico and cornice was etched as clearly as on an architect's rendering, each precise detail clear and highlighted.

On the small piazza above the back entrance a lady dressed in a bright green hoop skirted dress stood to one side. The deep cuffs on the sleeves of the dress, the collar and the belt at her waist were of yellow fabric and seemed to glow of their own inner fire in the gathering dusk.

As Seamus stepped onto the long flagstone walk between the lawns, he was struck by the hush, the solitary quiet of the grounds. It was as if only he and the lady were present on the property and abruptly she turned and disappeared through the French doors behind her.

Seamus strode briskly up the walk.

The time, he thought again.

A pair of ravens flew across the lawns from his right to his left. Their raucous croaking sounded, in an other-worldly way, nearly like human conversation. The shiny black wings glistened with orange sparks in the glancing light. Despite his haste, he could not help but stop and watch them pass. When he looked back to the hotel, the lady dressed in green and yellow came out the back entrance and walked quickly toward him.

It was Emily.

Seamus stood rooted, rather stupidly, he thought, to the spot. He was in a hurry, but he was simply taken by her . . . loveliness.

Yes, he thought, by her loveliness.

So, he just stood in the walkway until she came to him.

It was singular, he thought, how ladies in hoop skirts did not seem so much to walk, but rather, with their feet entirely hidden, to glide. It was a distinctly magical, and he felt mesmerizing effect and now that he did think of it, most likely was what the designers in Paris had in mind when they had invented the garment.

Clever fellows, those Frenchmen, he thought, and smiled.

Emily was upon him, she reached out her hands and he took them in his.

"Oh, Seamus, I am so happy to see you again. There have been comings and goings here and I was so worried about you. Everything seems to be so sinister, but you are here now. I asked Levi to have a cold supper ready for us in the private dinning room. I hope that was alright. I thought when it got to be later and later you might be hungry when you returned."

"That was very thoughtful of you, Emily, thank you."

Now that she had mentioned food, he *was* hungry. His sour stomach had fully recovered from the afternoon's excess.

They walked together toward the hotel.

"Comings and goings?" he asked.

"Yes. I did as you said today and stayed in the midst of the crowd. I spent my time on either the front piazza or, later in the day, when I was looking for you, on the back porch. I saw Mr. Beecher send Sampson down the road, and in a hurry too, and later I saw Sampson come back and talk to Mr. Beecher. The constable has returned along with another man. All were having hushed conversations and they all looked so grim that I was afraid that something had happened to you and that they would not tell me. If you had not returned before dark, I would have gone looking for you myself."

"No," said Seamus, "you should not think about doing something like that."

"Oh?" she said, looking him in the eye, "And why not?"

They entered the enclosed foyer allowing Seamus to dodge the question.

"I must speak to Mr. Twilling now," he said, " if you wish, I will join you in the dinning room directly after I go to my room and clean up a bit."

"Certainly, Seamus, then we can discuss why it is that you think you can tell me that I cannot go looking for you if I so choose."

She smiled brightly and turned and glided down the hall toward the dinning room.

He watched her all the way down the hall until she turned at the oval staircase.

Marvelous, he thought, she is marvelous.

He walked to the clerk's desk over which he found Mr. Twilling bent with his hat on and a newspaper under his arm, apparently in preparation of his leaving. Jacob stood by the desk ready to take on the duties of night clerk

"Mr. Twilling," said Seamus.

The man looked up suddenly from the register in which he

was writing. He appeared startled.

"I have need of your services as a telegrapher." said Seamus.

Twilling looked suddenly relieved.

He whined, notwithstanding.

"But, Mr. Delaney, as you can see I am just about to go home, and I had to work late, the records have gotten so far behind, this weekend has been so . . . so disrupted, I have closed the office for the evening and . . ."

"Twilling!"

Seamus interrupted the litany of excuses abruptly. He dropped any pretense of civility and dropped the cultured syntax which he usually employed when speaking with educated people. Having gained the clerk's attention, he continued.

"You see, Twilling, it's this way", he fixed the man with a flat stare, "you can send my message for me, or I will go in there and send it myself."

Twilling was aghast.

"Oh, no that would be highly irregular! Oh, no Mr. Delaney, I am responsible for that equipment . . ."

"Twilling, since we are such good friends, you can address me as Colonel Delaney."

Seamus winked at Jacob who quickly turned away and suppressed a laugh as he headed for the barroom.

"And, Twilling, you have just run out of time."

Seamus rounded the desk, stepped to the office door as the clerk literally jumped out of his way, and strode in with Twilling trailing after him.

"Mr. . . Colonel . . . please!"

Seamus flung open the telegraph cabinet with more force than was necessary. The batteries clinked and clattered together.

Twilling nearly swooned at the sound.

Seamus pulled out the swivel chair from under the desk and dropped into it. He slammed back the wooden cover on the key, threw the switch and adjusted an ivory knob.

"Please, Colonel, please!" Twilling implored placing his hand on the key.

Seamus stopped and looked up at him.

Twilling's eyes were wide, his tone conciliatory.

"Please, allow me." he said softly.

Seamus held the clerk pinned in his stony gaze a beat longer.

"Alright," he said and stood up.

Twilling gratefully took the chair, put down his newspaper and removed his hat. He slowly readjusted the ivory knob.

"Twilling, I am in a hurry."

"Yes, sir, . . . yes, now where is this to be sent."

Seamus handed him the paper which Mick had given to him that afternoon.

"The message is to be delivered to this address in Catskill. Tell Mr. Beecher's operator down there that it is to be taken to that address immediately, and by authority of Mr. Beecher."

"To *this* address?"

Seamus concluded that the man must almost always look aghast.

"Now, what did I just say?" he asked as of a particularly dull child.

Twilling nodded and began tapping at the telegraph key. Instantly, the operator at the other end of the wire, in Catskill, responded.

Thanks be to God, and to Mr. Morse, thought Seamus, and that, not for the first time in recent years.

"And the message, Colonel?"

"*Faughaballagh.*"

Twilling looked up from the key.

"I beg your pardon," he said.

"*Faughaballagh*, Twilling! *Faughaballagh!"* Seamus exhorted, forcing his features to register not even the hint of a smile.

"Yes, sir," said the clerk, "would you please spell that."

Seamus picked up a pencil and telegraph blank from the desk. On the back of the form he printed in big block letters; FAUGHABALLAGH, and held the paper in front of Twilling's nose.

"*Faughaballagh*, Twilling," he said, "spells just as it sounds."

Twilling taped out the letters in code.

"And?" Twilling asked.

"And what?"

"And what else do you want me to send, Colonel?"

"And nothing." said Seamus.

"That is all? Just . . . fowla . . . falla . . ."

"*Faughaballagh*, yes, that's all."

"Yes, sir."

Seamus leaned closer to the clerk.

"Twilling," he said quietly, "you're a good man. I think you should go home now."

"Yes, sir, thank you, sir."

Twilling confirmed that the message had been received as sent, closed the cabinet, took his hat and newspaper and, accompanied by Seamus, exited the office. He closed the door behind him, bade Seamus good evening, which was cordially returned, and left by the back entrance.

Seamus made to turn down the hall to the staircase when Jacob, Sampson, the constable, Dr, DuBoise and Mr. Beecher came out of the barroom and joined him.

"Colonel, it is good to see that you are back." said Mr. Beecher.

"It is good to be back, sir."

"Let us go into the reading room so that we can talk privately."

"Right, Mr. Beecher," said the constable, "time to wake Sylvester, on to it, anyway."

They walked down the hall, entered the cool dimness of the reading room and found it occupied by Humphrey's nephew *cum* deputy. He was asleep on a sofa by the window.

"Time to get up, Sylvester," said the constable in a booming voice, "you got to go out and relieve Willie Peters."

The youth stirred, sat up, stretched groggily and swung his feet to the floor.

"Aw, Uncle Hump, I just got to sleep," he drawled, rubbing his eyes.

"You been asleep since this afternoon when I got up here from Catskill with Willie. Now get up and get out to the root cellar. What do you think the county is paying you for? And don't call me Uncle Hump!"

"No, sir, I mean, yes, sir . . . I . . ."

"Don't *mean* nothing, Sylvester, just get out there!"

The constable guided the lad through the door.

When he had left, Seamus related Cappy's report that the bullet in question was not one of those which he had provided. Seamus did not reveal the conjecture that the projectile may have been of Confederate manufacture. Neither did he mention the speculation about whether or not Luther could have made the long range shot which took Clay's life.

The constable took the floor and told how, at about midday, a rider had come to the corner at the end of the street in front of the jail in Catskill and gestured at a man in the crowd to come closer. After a short conversation the man on foot returned to the main body of the mob. Clearly, the constable had seen, the word had been passed. Within half an hour the crowed had drifted away in ones and twos. It had seemed to Humphrey that the rider had been careful to stay at the far end of the street, and at such an angle to the front windows of the sheriff's office, so as to be almost out of sight. From what he could see of him however, the constable described a hefty man on a roan horse in gray trousers and tan jacket wearing a dark, wide-brimmed hat.

Reb Skhutt, Seamus knew.

Next, Mr. Beecher related his information.

He stated that his agents in Albany had confirmed by telegraph the embarkation of the judge and his party onboard the *Mary Powell.*

"I have," he said, “dispatched my own barouche to meet the steamer at the Catskill landing. With four horses pulling at all deliberate speed, and baring any unforeseen delays, there is a good chance that an inquest can be held here at the Mountain House by about midnight.”

Seamus hoped, prayed, that would be soon enough.

Sampson reported that the staff had continued to take every opportunity to surreptitiously search, and to search again in some cases, the rooms of the guests, but that nothing further in the way of firearms had been found. The search was ongoing. He mentioned that although the bar was officially closed on Sunday, Rolf had volunteered to stay at the hotel to help in any way he could.

Jacob stated that with regard to the security of the property during the night, all preparations that could be made were being made.

As Jacob finished speaking, a knock came to the door and in stepped a block of a man, short in stature but broad of shoulder. Even his head had a squarish look which was enhanced by the close cropped style in which he wore his straw colored hair. He had a ruddy complexion and a quick smile.

The constable introduced him to Seamus as Willie Peters.

"He is a veteran too," said Humphrey, "went into Mobile Bay with Farragut, and he served on the *Cairo*, before the rebels sunk her with a torpedo.  Willie and his brothers were the only ones I could find in Catskill with enough grit to back me up the last couple days".

When Willie reached out to grip Seamus hand, the man's jacket pulled to one side and the butt of a pistol could be seen protruding from his belt.

Look's like a Navy Colt, thought Seamus and he mentally added Willie to the list of effectives he now had on the mountain top with which to face Leander Skhutt's mob.

He ticked them off in his mind; the constable, Sylvester, Rolf, now Willie, Sampson, Jacob, a few other male staff members and the bandsmen, most or all of them unarmed, himself, Mr. Beecher to be sure, the doctor, although not as a combatant. It was a pitifully short list.

When all reports had been made, Seamus suggested that when the judge and his party arrived, the inquest should be held in the barroom.  He further suggested the names of all those who should be *invited* to attend and the constable, after licking the point of his stub pencil, wrote the names down in his note book.

Seamus turned to Dr. DuBoise.

"Doctor," he said, "I would appreciate your making yourself available for possible service tonight and keep, if you will, your bag of instruments with you."

"You feel it may come to casualties then?" said the doctor.

"We must assume that it will come to that, yes," replied Seamus.

Turning to Mr. Beecher, he added.

"In view of the fact that Mr. Twilling has gone home for the evening, sir, I suggest that someone who can operate the equipment stay on watch at the telegraph in case any messages come in regarding the progress of the judge and his associates."

"Yes, of course. Doctor, would you so oblige us since you are versed in the code?"

"Certainly," said Doctor DuBoise.

All were ponderously silent for a few moments.

Seamus broke the spell.

"Very well, gentlemen," he said, "there is nothing further that we can do but wait."

And, he thought, waiting is always the hardest thing to do.

All, save Sampson, left the room.

"Colonel," he said, "Luther has asked to see you."

Seamus said that he would visit Luther as soon as he had gone to his room, washed and changed his shirt. Sampson agreed to stop by the private dinning room and make Seamus' apologies to Emily for the delay.

Seamus went quickly to his room. He pitched his hat onto the hall tree as he entered and stripped to the waist. He washed, put on his last clean shirt and collar and stood before the mirror and adjusted his plain black silk cravat. The face in the mirror looked back at him, calm and resolute.

He donned his coat, put the last of his cigars into the leather case and hurried out the door, down the back stairs, through the central hall and out the rear entrance. He stepped out of the building into the cool of the evening. The stars were out and shinning so brightly and in such immense numbers, that they seemed to be near the earth and forming a low, overhanging ceiling just above the surrounding mountain ridges.

Now that all plans had been made, fear and foreboding had left Seamus entirely. His steps echoed along the flagstones as he nearly sprinted toward the root cellar. He felt courageous to the point of recklessness. He did not halt at the approach to the place of Luther's confinement as he usually did out of deference to Sylvester's shotgun. Instead, he hailed loudly.

"Hello, Sylvester, I am coming in."

And he cut through the trees, catching the deputy just rising from his chair. For once Sylvester had the weapon aimed at the ground and not at Seamus mid-section. The young fellow even seemed to have grown more adept at his act of juggling gun and key ring. He admitted Seamus to the root cellar and Luther rose in greeting.

They sat and Seamus offered a cigar, Luther accepted and lifted the lamp from its place on the upturned barrel so they could each take a light. The aromatic scent of tobacco replaced the damp smell of the cellar.

"They are coming tonight, Colonel."

Luther betrayed no emotion in making his statement. His coolness made Seamus uncomfortable.

"You are sure, of course," said Seamus.

"Certain, Colonel. Jubal got word to me through the scullery boys again. Reb is back on the mountain top and he brought most of the crowd from Catskill with him. Many are already at Brenner's, but some are congregating at a clearing in the woods between here and there so as not to attract too much attention. Not that it would make much difference. Who is there to stop them?"

Seamus said nothing. He puffed his cigar.

"More may still be arriving. Jubal believes that they may move at any time during the night, and that when they do there may be no fewer than one hundred of them. Not many of them have horses, most of the mountain top locals arrived on foot. Skhutt brought the Catskill mob up by way of the old road in a pair of char-a-bancs which he must have hired at the dockside in the town. Of course, neither those vehicles nor their drivers will have anything to do with tonight's action. They simply deposited their passengers at Brenner's and departed immediately for Catskill. I do not know that the lack of horses will impede them though, mounted or on foot, there are more than enough of them to accomplish their objective."

Luther paused. Seamus said nothing.

"By the way," Luther continued, "Jubal finished his report

by volunteering to come here and help with the defense. I sent back word that under no circumstances was he to come here tonight. No matter what happens in the next few hours, in the future Skhutt or people like him will have to be dealt with. Jubal is more valuable in his present position. We need a spy for the future more than we need an extra hand this evening."

Seamus nodded. They each smoked quietly for few moments and then Luther went on.

"Which brings me, Colonel, to the question of tonight and what I am to do."

Luther fixed Seamus with his eye. The haze of cigar smoke was amber in the lamp light.

"Colonel, I am not going to be the object of sport for this mob. I have no fear of death, but I have an absolute right to fight, if not for my life, then to insure that I not be taken alive. In the war it was always my intention to fight unto death rather than to be taken and either enslaved or hanged at my captors leisure, which as you know was the stated Confederate policy for black Union soldiers who surrendered. I always intended to put up such a fight as to make it impossible for anyone to take me without forfeiture of his own life. I wish to have that same freedom of action now, but without a weapon . . . "

Luther turned his face toward the door of the cell and then turned back to Seamus.

Seamus stood and turned his back to the door. He reached into his coat pocket, took his pistol out, spun it around on its trigger guard and offered, handle first to Luther.

Luther hesitated, astonished.

"Take it!" said Seamus in a tight, dry whisper.

Luther complied and quickly hid the weapon beneath a sack by his side.

"Your word of honor, Luther, that you will not use it against Sylvester," said Seamus in a low voice.

"You have my word, Colonel," said Luther, his strong jaw still slack with amazement, "but what about yourself, what if you need to defend yourself?"

"Luther, if it comes to that, I will borrow what I need from someone. Now, I must go."

"As the Spaniards say, Colonel, go with God." said Luther rising and offering his hand.

Seamus took the firm hand in his.

"Amen." he said.

He called for Sylvester, the lad undid the lock, and with a wink to Luther, Seamus was up the steps two at a time, out of the root cellar and cutting across the grove of trees. When he had gained the walkway, he looked up at the stars arching overhead.

*Alia jacta est,* he thought as he pressed toward the hotel, as old Caesar said, the die is well and truly cast, the Rubicon crossed, the bridges burnt, no turning back. I have given a firearm to a man being held in felony incarceration, charged with murder. What happened to the disciplined soldier I used to be? Follow all orders, obey all rules.

The answer is, he told himself, that sometimes orders and laws don't count. President Lincoln knew that when he so correctly suspended the right of *Habeas corpus* at the outbreak of the war and when he positioned artillery so as to encourage the elected officials of Maryland to refrain from taking that state into the secessionist rebellion.

I should have known that too, he thought, at the President's second inaugural and I should have shot Booth and then Lincoln would still be President and the country headed in the right direction instead of God knows where, as it is now. What could they have done to me? Court-martialed me? Hanged me? What of it? Was I not willing to lay down my life for the country, for the President all through the war?

Cappy's voice came to him; no power on earth can change the past.

Well, let the past go then, Seamus answered Cappy in his mind, but I cannot guarantee that the mob will not overwhelm us tonight. Luther has every right to defend himself from the type of death they would have in store for him. It might even do some good; it is ever the character of *terroristes* to prefer their victims un-armed and docile. If Luther can respond to a few of them in kind it may scare off the others at least for a moment or two.

Not very likely, he told himself, but I have placed myself outside the law and so be it. Besides, why should I be concerned about breaking the law? There is a fairly good chance that I will be killed myself tonight.

He laughed quietly.

"Ever the optimist," he said to the stars above.

He entered the brightly lighted hall and did not slow his pace until he turned at the spiral staircase and stood before the door to the private dining room. He knocked and the door opened. Emily was seated at the table facing him. She smiled as he entered. Levi, holding the door open, smiled too.

"Are we ready then, Colonel?" he asked.

"If you please, Levi," said Seamus taking his seat.

"How is Luther?" Emily asked.

Levi, now at the sideboard, paused before carving the cold roast beef and awaited Seamus reply.

"He is in very good spirits and looks forward, as do we all, to an early resolution of this situation."

Levi commenced his carving.

"And how was your day, Emily?" Seamus asked in a deliberate effort to change the subject.

"As I said, I spent a good deal of the day on the front piazza and on the back porch, as well. I did some embroidery and I read a bit. *Harper's* had a story about the *S.S. Great Eastern* and the recovery and repair of the Atlantic cable."

"I remember," said Seamus, "touring that ship when it came to New York before the war. It was well worth the twenty-five cents fee we paid. She is a magnificent vessel, incredibly big, a mechanical wonder and an architectural masterpiece."

"And," Emily continued, "I also read in the *Nation* about the new rules for croquet. Simply fascinating!" This was said with a mock ardor which made them both laugh.

Levi served them each with a plate of sliced meats with greens and potato salad. Corn relish, piccalilli, chutney, wedges of lemon and horseradish sauce were served on separate plates as were thick slices of buttered wheat bread.

Levi filled Emily's stem glass with chilled Rhine wine, and Seamus placed his hand over his glass to prevent the man doing the same for him.

"Just the ice water tonight I think, Levi," he said.

"Yes, Colonel," said Levi and he put the bottle into a silver ice bucket on a stand by the edge of the table. He filled a cut crystal goblet with water from a pewter pitcher and placed it before Seamus.

"I will return shortly to see if there is anything else you need," he said and stepped out of the room.

Emily took a sip of her wine and they ate silently for a few moments.

"I also read an article," she said at length, "in a back number of the *New York Tribune* about the indictments that were issued in May against President . . . I mean *Mister* Davis and General Lee, John C. Breckinridge and Judah P. Benjamin charging them with treason. Do you think that if Mr. Lincoln had lived, he would have caused or permitted those men to be so charged, Seamus?"

"Certainly not," said Seamus, "I am sure that he would not have done anything of the kind, Emily." He wondered if the sound of her name spoken on his lips was so endearing to her as was the sound of his name on her lips to him.

"Poor Mr. Davis; languishing in Fortress Monroe in a casemated cell. They say that his health is failing and that Secretary Stanton insists on his being held in irons. Mrs. Davis; . . . Varina, . . . I met her when we were both volunteers at Chimborazo Hospital in Richmond, . . . is petitioning all in power to have some relief for her poor husband. It is said that she may even soon meet with President Johnson. I feel that all this hatred stems not from the war itself, but from the assassination of Mr. Lincoln. I cannot believe that Mr. Davis had anything to do with the murder of the President. Even Mr. Stevens, the most radical Republican in the Congress, though avowing his personal hatred for Mr. Davis and all the Southern leaders, said he knew Mr. Davis to be a gentleman and incapable of countenancing assassination."

Seamus knew, at first hand, far more about the subject of the assassination than did Emily, or for that matter than almost anyone else in the country, and he was not nearly so certain as she as to who was and who was not involved in the conspiracy.

Emily went on.

"Mr. Davis may be held responsible for starting the war but he is a man of old- fashioned honor and would never have stooped to murder."

"Emily," said Seamus, "who do *you* think was responsible for the war?"

"Many in the North and South made foolish decisions," she said, "even Mr. Davis, in his actions, can be seen to have been misled."

God protect us, thought Seamus, from leaders who are misled.

"However," Emily went on, "I think the war was simply a disaster which was bound to happen. I blame no one for the war, nor for the damage done, not even for the losses I have suffered myself. The war killed my Robbie and my father. The war itself. It became a force unto itself. Some of the men who were in a position to stop it before it started did not have the wit to do so and so can be held responsible to that extent, but I think the war had to come because what else would have ended slavery? One great brutality wiped out the other. There is no point in assigning blame. What is done is done and we had best look to the future."

They sat for a time in silence. It occurred to Seamus that most of the decent acts committed by the human race were committed by the decent females of the species. He thought of Emily laboring among the wounded Confederate soldiers at Chimborazo. Maybe Susan B. Anthony was right. If women had a say in the matter, would not the wars that consumed their sons, fathers, brothers, husbands and indeed themselves be outlawed?

"So," he said, "you bear no bitterness about . . . your . . . loss?"

Do you blame me? he thought.

"No, none at all. Sadness but no bitterness. I blame no one. There is too much to do today to carry around the past. I can see that now. We should spend our time making today and tomorrow better, rather than waste our time dwelling in the past."

She took another sip of her wine and continued.

"Another part of my day was passed in the company of Mrs.

Van Wyck. She and her husband have received some very distressing news. It was my turn today to comfort her as she had comforted me on the day Fenton was . . . on the day he died."

Emily paused. After a moment she went on.

"And that reminds me. Why is it that you think that you can tell me that I cannot go looking for you if I fear you may be in danger? Did you not rescue me twice in as many days? And did you not tell me that you would be there to rescue me again, should the need arise? Do you think you are the only one capable of rescue? Do you think that I am not capable of such service? Am I a helpless child in your eyes?"

Both her color and voice had risen. Her gaze was relentless.

She waited for Seamus' answer.

"No, not a child, no not at all . . . ," he fumbled, he wished she had not been reminded of the issue.

"Not a child, only a woman," sarcasm dripped from Emily's voice.

"But it is just that there could be great danger . . . ," Seamus struggled.

"Do you think," she sprang like a cat, "that there are many women in the South who have *not* faced great danger and hardship and that on a daily basis, year in and year out? But you have not answered my question. Why do you think that I should be forbidden from coming to your assistance?"

When he did not answer, she prodded.

"Well, Seamus?"

"Because," he blurted, "I care a great deal for you. More than any lady I have ever met and I do not want to . . . to lose you."

Emily smiled, her eyes danced in the lamplight.

Seamus could feel his face registering a look of bewilderment.

A knock on the door and Levi entered with Sampson.

"Excuse me, Colonel," said Sampson, "but we need to go to Mr. Beecher's office right away." He gave a look that conveyed the gravity of the situation.

"Of course," said Seamus vaguely, "of course."

He looked back at Emily. She was still smiling.

"If you will excuse me . . . ," he said.

"Yes, I promised Mrs. Van Wyck that I would join her in the lounge this evening." said Emily rising.

Seamus stood and together they stepped into the hall. Samson lingered with Levi while Emily and Seamus walked to the staircase. She took his hand in both of hers and looked into his eyes.

"And so a brief adieu, Seamus until we meet again." She was still smiling merrily.

He could say nothing and so just nodded dumbly. She walked to the lounge, opened the door and entered. Seamus stood watching the place where she had vanished and Sampson came up behind him.

"Colonel," he said, and Seamus jumped back into the present moment.

"Colonel, it was necessary to interrupt your supper because I must tell you that our continued investigation of the guest's rooms has turned up another firearm."

Sampson paused.

"And this," he went on, "in a room which had been previously searched and found to be empty of weapons. The gun was discovered by Sally, one of our chambermaids. She made a sketch and a rubbing of. . . . "

Seamus interrupted.

"Where is the sketch?"

"In Mr. Beecher's office . . ."

Seamus was vaulting up the stairs his mind racing.

Did the person who removed the gun from the room at first anticipate a search yesterday and have something to hide? Had they since returned the weapon to their own room because they had further use for it, or was it all just happenstance and coincidence?

On reaching the third floor Seamus turned into the hallway and fairly raced to the door of Mr. Beecher's suite. He stopped short and knocked. Mr. Beecher himself let him in. Sampson caught up and entered behind him.

Sarah Van Bronc stood by her employer's desk with a petite young lady dressed in the uniform of a chambermaid. She looked to be about sixteen years of age. She had round face and big brown eyes which now seemed to be full of apprehension. She held a small packet of papers clutched to her throat.

"Thank you for coming so quickly, Colonel," said Mr. Beecher, "I am sorry that we had to take you away from your supper."

"I am at your service, sir," was Seamus reply. He was careful not to let his wild yearning to see the new intelligence intrude upon the courtly manner which his host maintained at all times.

"I understand that some new information has been obtained," he said in what passed for nonchalance.

"Yes," said Mr. Beecher, "Sarah, if you please . . . "

"Thank you, Mr. Beecher. Colonel, this is Sally."

Seamus' smile seemed to put the young lady more at ease.

Sarah continued.

"Today Sally was, as usual, making up the rooms and, as instructed, continuing to search for firearms. She has been covering again rooms that were already searched yesterday on the floor were she is normally assigned and she discovered a weapon in one of those rooms. Sally, please give the Colonel your sketch."

Sally handed the paper to Seamus and he slowly, carefully unfolded it.

Before him was a very neat and fairly well detailed rendering of what looked to be a double-barreled shotgun. A double-barreled shotgun having the barrels one above the other instead of side by side with each other as was more common; unusual but not unheard of.

A hollowness grew within Seamus, but he was alert not to show his disappointment. Fenton Clay had certainly not been murdered with a shotgun of any description.

Sally spoke.

"I found the gun in the back corner of the wardrobe behind the clothes and it was not there yesterday when I looked, I'm sure of it, Colonel."

"This is a very good sketch, Sally," said Seamus. He thought, but did not say, however, this is not the murder weapon.

"Why, thank you, sir," said Sally brightening, "Miz Sarah says I am the best student in her drawing class."

Sarah smiled and so did Seamus.

"Um, Sally," he said, "what is this line here?" He pointed.

"There is an iron ring," Sally indicated a part of the sketch depicting the grip of the stock, "it folds over and it's attached to the wood with screws. Tied to the ring is a long loop of leather bootlace."

Seamus looked at the corner of the sketch and saw that Sally had pressed one of the muzzles into the paper and traced the outline.

Strange, he thought, a very small gauge shotgun.

"Sally," he asked pointing to the muzzle impression, "was the other barrel just as big around as this or was it smaller or bigger yet?"

"Other barrel, Colonel?" she replied looking to Sampson, "The barrel is the part the bullet comes out of, isn't that right?"

Sampson looked to Seamus.

"We gave all the staff who had no experience with them a quick course on firearms when we gave them there assignments yesterday so that they would have an idea of what to look for." He turned to Sally.

"That's right, Sally, the barrel is the part the bullet comes out of."

She looked perplexed still.

"Well, Colonel, that gun had only one barrel," she said.

"One barrel," Seamus repeated, "then what is this?" He pointed at the upper part of the gun in the sketch.

"That's a glass, Colonel."

"A glass?"

"Yes, Colonel, a glass, like you look through to make things come closer, a spy glass."

A telescope sight! Seamus could feel the blood pounding in his temple. He tried to sound calm.

"Sally," he said, "how long would you say this gun is.?"

She held her hands at the height of her shoulders, spread them, looked at them each and spread them again.

"That's the funny thing about that gun, Colonel," she said,

"It's longer than what Sampson told us was a pistol, but not so long as what he said was a rifle."

She again pointed to the sketch.

"This part here?" she said pointing to the area of the gun above the trigger.

"Yes," said Seamus.

"This part looks like the part of a pistol Sampson said was the cyl . . . cyl . . . "

"The cylinder?" said Seamus. Both of his temples were now throbbing.

"That's right, sir! The cylinder. This part looks like the cylinder that's shaped like a can and were the bullets go before they come out the barrel and every time you shoot, it goes around!"

Seamus nodded slowly.

"That gun," she said "it looked to me like it was a pistol *and* a little rifle with a spy glass on top."

Seamus closed his eyes. A Colt's Carbine, not a shotgun, a Colt's Carbine. A short, repeating rifle developed by the late Samuel Colt from his revolver design especially for cavalry. Hundreds had been purchased by the Southern militia units between the time the first states seceded and the actual firing on Fort Sumter. The U.S. Sharpshooters had first been armed with the same weapon, but in full rifle length. And with a telescope; a sharpshooter's weapon indeed.

Seamus opened his eyes and looked again at the muzzle impression on the corner of the paper. There was no doubt in his mind; .44 caliber.

Sally spoke again.

"There was writing on the barrel part of the gun," she said, "but I heard someone coming down the hall and I didn't have time to copy it. I know I saw the word *Hartford*. . I did have time to take my pencil and rub the writing on this part of the gun," she pointed to an oval depicted on the stock of her drawing, "onto this paper here. I thought this writing was more important. It was written all pretty in swirls and the metal it was carved on; I think it was real silver."

She handed the slip of paper to Seamus. On it was a rubbing of an ornately engraved plaque bearing the words:

presented to: The Patriot,
CAPT. BRUTUS LEJEUNE, CSA
by his comrades,
the officers and men of the
MARYLAND PARTIZAN ZOUAVES

Brutus Lejeune! Brutus Lejeune! Seamus was staggered; his mind instantly recalled the file in the Secretary's office: Brutus Lejeune; guerrilla and bushwhacker of the border between Maryland and Virginia. Implicated in the hanging of Union officers he captured *in* Federal uniform. Brutus Lejeune who emulated the depredations of Quantrill and Bloody Bill Anderson of the western battlefronts. Brutus Lejeune who, with his band had stopped a train in southern Maryland in 1864 and found that some of the passengers were unarmed Union soldiers going home on furlough. The soldiers were lined up along the track and all twenty seven of them gunned down. Brutus Lejeune; warrants for murder were still outstanding. Where was he? No one knew. What did he look like? No one knew, he was never photographed, never sketched. Well, someone knew, but no one was telling. Was he here now, in this building? Or was this weapon just a war souvenir now belonging to someone else? Who?

Seamus suddenly realized that the silence was heavy in the room.

"Sally," he said and his voice cracked. He cleared his throat and started again.

"Sally, can you tell me in which room you found the gun."

Sally handed him the last piece of paper which she had been holding. It was a portion of the list Mr. Beecher had made of all the rented rooms with the names of the guests noted. Sally pointed to a room number which had been underlined. A name was neatly printed next to it.

Seamus silently read the name and walked to the window with the paper in his hand. He stood looking out into the night. There was little to see, just the few lights of scattered farm houses and, to the south, the grid of street lamps in Saugerties.

If it were not a Sunday, he thought, the gaslights in front of Hurley's would be flaming now adding their brilliance to the distant glitter of the town. His memory went back to his afternoon at the saloon and it became clear to him why Clay had been shot and who had shot him and how the murderer had done the shooting.

Seamus put the papers in his vest pocket and took out his watch. The jaunty chiming of *The Garryowen* did not cheer him.

The time, he thought, the bloody, stinking time!

He turned and told all present what they must do in the next few hours in order to save Luther's life. Then, feeling an overwhelming need for fresh air, he excused himself and left the room. He walked quickly down the hall to the stairs and descended one flight to the second floor and thence onto the upper piazza. He turned left and at the far end of the porch, he flung himself into a wicker arm chair. He put his feet on a footstool and stared into the sky above the Hudson. A shooting star blazed across the diamond studded heavens.

Seamus took from his pocket the bent silver spoon he had retrieved from the south courtyard the previous morning and rolled it over and over in his fingers without looking at it. Far down the side of the mountain an owl intoned a sepulchral WHO! . . . WHO! . . WHO! . . . WHOOOO!"

"I know who," said Seamus to the night.

# X

## An Inquest

Felim looked first rate and was in fine form. He took another deep draught from his mug of ale and set the drink on the table next to his forage cap. He wiped his lips with the back of his hand. He was in uniform and the gaslight twinkled on the brass buttons and gold shoulder straps. The light sparkled wildly on the brazen numeral *69* on his cap. They were sitting in the back room of McSorley's and it was warm and exceptionally bright. A log blazed in the fireplace where mugs of ale were lined up, heating on the hod. The Stars and Stripes hung in a gilt frame behind Felim.

Seamus was so happy to be seeing Felim again, and Felim seemed so happy to be here that Seamus thought it would be wrong for him to mention to his cousin that he was dead.

There was a glad murmur of voices at the bar in the front room. An old man sat by the stove tapping out a Kerry slide on a pair of polished rib bones to the accompaniment of a concertina. Jokes were passed and friendly jibes flew. A greeting was shouted as another old comrade came through the door in a whirl of snowflakes. Laughter blended with catches of song.

Seamus noticed that many of his old friends at the bar and at the other tables in the back room were dressed in soldier's blue, as was Felim, and that they were also dead. And again he knew that it would never do for him to call anyone's attention to the fact.

"Seamus," said Felim, "finish your drink and we'll have another."

Seamus looked at the mug before him on the table. It was

full, had not been touched. He did not wish to drink. He just wanted to keep looking at Felim. It was so good to see him again.

"I don't think I'll take any drink tonight, Felim," he said.

Felim looked serious for a moment.

"No," he said, "maybe you'd be better off if you didn't. You might rather be keeping your wits about you." The smile came back to his face.

"Well," he said, "here's to temperance." It was one of his favorite toasts.

He finished his ale, stood and put on his cap. He adjusted it to a rakish angle and looked down at his cousin.

"I must be off," he said, "I'll see you in a bit, Seamus."

"See you in a bit, Felim."

Felim walked out through the front room to a chorus of farewells.

"Goodnight, Felim, see you again lad."

"Goodnight, boys, goodnight," was Felim's reply to one and all. When he reached the door he turned and gave Seamus an off-hand salute and a dazzling smile. Then he was out the door and into the snowy night.

Seamus sat looking after him.

"Colonel, Colonel," said an insistent voice at his side.

"Colonel, Colonel, they are coming."

He turned to his right. It was Sampson. Sampson was crouched down close to him. Sampson; here in McSorley's.

"Colonel," Sampson said again, "they are coming."

Seamus awoke. He was one the piazza of the Mountain House, sitting in a wicker arm chair, a woolen blanket thrown over him.

"They are coming, Colonel," Sampson said yet again.

Seamus rubbed his eyes.

"Who are coming, Sampson?"

"The judge and his party. Jacob is up on the roof and he just called down to me that he can hear the sound of Mr. Beecher's barouche coming up the mountain road. I stationed Jacob up there as you said and I thought it wise to load Mr. Beecher's Pennsylvania rifle and give it to him. Jacob is a very good shot with that rifle, he has taken many a deer with it."

"Good, Sampson. What time is it anyway? How long have I been sleeping?"

"It is about a quarter to one, I found you sleeping, Colonel, about an hour ago when I came out after I stationed Jacob. There seemed no reason to wake you."

Seamus stood and laid the blanket on the chair. Now they could both hear the sound of the four horses beating steadily up the road, the wheels of the carriage crunching on the road bed.

"Any sign of the mob?" he asked.

"None yet, Colonel," was the reply.

How much longer before Reb Skhutt and his gang gets here, Seamus wondered. Not much longer, he knew.

The two men leaned out over the porch rail, straining toward the sound of the carriage down in the dark of the woods where the road lay invisible in the night. Presently, the headlamps of the barouche flickered into view, disappearing and reappearing amid the trees.

"They are on the Long Level," said Sampson, "they will be here in about twenty minutes."

"Very well," said Seamus, "we had better have the staff set about gathering up the guests whose presence is to be required at the inquest. All else is in readiness?"

"Yes, Colonel."

They walked to the second floor entrance where a shaft of lamplight illuminated a patch of the piazza floor. Seamus took Sampson by the hand.

"Whatever else happens tonight," he said, "I want to commend and to thank you for the work you have done." He smiled and added. "If ever I need a lawyer, you will be the man, Sampson,"

Sampson laughed, his spectacles flashed in the light from the doorway.

"Yes, Colonel, I will be." he said.

Seamus asked Sampson to request Mr. Beecher to meet him in the barroom and then turned quickly for the backstairs. He went to his room and entered with his usual caution. He opened his trunk and lifted out the rebel officer's jacket. In the inside pocket he found what he was looking for and he transferred it to the inside pocket of his coat. He closed the trunk, left the room, went down the backstairs and proceeded through the central hallway.

He found Rolf dozing behind the front desk. He laid his hand on the man's shoulder.

"Time to open the barroom, Rolf," he said, "the judge will be here in a few minutes."

Rolf arose, rubbing his eyes.

"I was just sitting in for Jacob as night porter," he said.

"We will have no need for a night porter now," said Seamus, and he raised his voice, "nor for a night telegraph watch for the rest of the evening. Doctor, if you will kindly join us."

The doctor emerged from the clerk's office carrying his black bag.

"Quite so," he said, "quite so."

The three crossed the hall to the barroom and Rolf unlocked and opened the door.

"Did the missing keys ever turn up, Rolf," asked Seamus as he passed through the doorway.

"No, they did not, Colonel."

"If you please," said Seamus, "unlock also the door to the casino."

Rolf complied and Seamus stepped behind the bar, squinting in the darkness. Rolf returned to the end of the bar and struck a match and lit a taper. He went to the middle of the counter and reached up and lighted the two lamps which hung from the ceiling together on the same brass rod, then he turned and lighted the lamp on the back bar.

Now that he could see where he was going, Seamus walked to the hatch to the casino and determined that the stout oaken panel was securely locked and could not swing outward as it did when in normal use.

"Do you want me to unlock the hatch, Colonel?" asked Rolf.

"No thank you, Rolf," said Seamus, "quite to the contrary."

He walked to the end of the bar by the hall door and stood in what he now realized was his usual spot.

Habit, he thought.

Rolf went about lighting the other lamps in the room and the doctor sat himself at a table against the wall beyond the piano. When Rolf had finished with the lamps, the doctor spoke.

"It has been a long . . . and dry . . . watch on the telegraph machine tonight, Rolf old boy," he said peering at the barman through his *pince-nez*. "Now, I know that the bar is officially closed, but do you think that a short brandy, and a discreet one at that, since this room is about to become a court of law, might not be out of the way?"

"Say no more, Doctor," was Rolf's reply and he went behind the counter and took a fresh bottle of Hennessy's Five Star from the back bar. As he was uncorking the brandy, Mr. Tompkins walked in and stood next to Seamus.

He was snappily attired in black trousers, and a black, gray-stripped frock coat with a velvet collar and silk trimmed lapels. His waistcoat was mauve in color and embroidered with tiny flowers. His cravat was lavender and was held in place with a gold stick-pin depicting in profile the wreathed head of Caesar. He yawned demonstratively.

"Good evening," he said to all present, "or is it good morning?"

Seamus smiled.

"Either way you like it," he said.

Rolf stole a quick glance at Tompkins, took a heavy brown ceramic coffee mug from beneath the bar and poured a none too short brandy into it. He returned the bottle to the back bar and walked around the bar to deliver the drink to the doctor. As he passed the end of the bar, Tompkins winked at Seamus.

"So that is the game," said Tompkins, "I will have one of those 'coffees', Rolf."

He took a silver half-dollar from his vest pocket and with a sly smile, held it up for Seamus inspection. Tompkins' right thumb, Seamus could see, had, at some time in his life, been flattened in what must have been a very painful mishap. A puckered, red patch of scarred skin on the back of the hand seemed to testify to a serious burn in the not too distant past.

As he put the brandy on the doctor's table, Rolf looked back over his shoulder.

"Well, sir," he said, "the bar is officially closed, but . . ."

He got no more out before Tompkins had slapped the fifty cent piece on the mahogany and stepped behind the bar and headed for the brandy bottle. He fished under the bar for another mug and when he found it, gave a boyish whoop. He took the bottle from the back bar and carried it with him to the counter at the end of the bar by the hatch. He poured himself a large drink and lifted it in toast to the others.

"Who knows when we will get another drink tonight or this morning or whatever it is." he said with a laugh.

The others remained silent and Rolf's color rose at this effrontery. One simply did not invade the barman's domain; very bad form.

Tompkins quaffed deeply and treated the others to a wide grin. He leaned back with his elbows on the counter of the hatch behind him looking very pleased with himself the mug still in his hand.

Rolf returned to his station behind the bar.

"Can *I* get *you* anything, Colonel?" he said with more than a trace of irritation in his voice.

Tompkins gave no indication of reacting to the not too indirect barb. He kept grinning and took another deep swallow from his mug.

"Not at the moment, thank you, Rolf," said Seamus, "I had better step outside and see if I can find Mr. Beecher."

Seamus left the bar and found Mr. Beecher immediately. He was standing with Sampson in the foyer by the entrance. More lights had been lighted by the back entrance and presently the constable and Willie Peters came hurrying in the door.

"The carriage is just now coming up the drive," said Humphrey puffing slightly from his exertions. "We left Sylvester at the root cellar, I guess we should go back and bring Luther over."

"If you would oblige me, Constable," said Seamus, "I think it would be best if Luther stayed where he is for just a while longer."

The constable looked to Mr. Beecher who nodded his agreement.

"Alright, Colonel, if that's what you and Mr. Beecher think is best," said Humphrey, "but Luther has a right to be present to hear the charges against him, and to confront witnesses and such like, on to it."

"Constable," said Seamus, "you know that we all have Luther's best interests at heart. His rights will be respected at all times."

Humphrey nodded.

"Good," said Seamus, "Constable, when we all go into the barroom I think you should place yourself close to the judge, Sampson I want you to stand inside the door to the hallway and Mr. Peters . . ."

"Aw, just call me Willie." said Willie.

"Willie, I want you to stay by the door to the casino. No matter what happens, no one should leave the room without permission once the hearing gets under way."

All signified their understanding.

With that the bright yellow barouche pulled up in the portico. Small flames burned behind the cut glass lenses of the lamps at the four corners of the vehicle. The footman, dressed in Mountain House livery, jumped down from the box and opened the little door of the open carriage. A heavy man, with white *mustachios*, dressed in a plain brown suit and a big, white, western-style sombrero, stepped down and turned to assist an old gentleman in a tall hat to descend. Under that man's arm was a folio and in his left hand he carried a golden headed walking stick.

"Judge Livingston, my dear friend," said Mr. Beecher taking the judge by the hand, "I hope your trip was not too arduous."

"It was indeed rapid, Charles," said the judge, "but thanks to you, sir, it was made in first class comfort". A smile creased the judge's slim and leathery face disclosing a row of large, tobacco stained teeth.

The judge and Mr. Beecher stepped into the foyer arm in arm, with the man in the sombrero following. Seamus noticed that the third member of the party was left to descend the steps of the barouche without the help of the man in the white hat.

That gentleman was middle-aged and also wore a tall silk

hat. From beneath the brim of the hat sprouted straight, lifeless looking, sand colored hair which nearly covered his ears. His frame was thin to the point of being cadaverous, an impression enhanced by the pallid complexion of his spare face. He carried a small writing box.

When they had entered the hall, Mr. Beecher made introductions all around. In addition to the judge, he presented the sombrero-wearing sheriff, John Cass, who wore a silver six-pointed star on his breast, and the county coroner, Ezra Saulpaugh, whose handshake Seamus found to be cold, clammy and flaccid.

"Mr. Saulpaugh will also be acting as the recorder for this hearing," said the judge.

Seamus asked if he might address a few words to the court of inquiry by way of background prior to the actual commencement of the hearing.

The judge looked at Mr. Beecher who returned to him a single nod of the head.

The judge agreed and suggested that they get ready for the hearing.

Mr. Beecher directed the party into the barroom and Seamus looked up the hall to see several of his fellow guests being shepherded toward him by Levi, Sarah Van Bronc and Sally.

Seamus turned to the constable and Willie.

"You had better take up your positions," he said, and the two officers of the law entered the barroom.

The first of the guests to reach the entrance to the bar was McCain, attired as always in black frock coat and tall hat.

"Mr. Beecher," he said in greeting to his host, and he allowed his icy glance to slide briefly across Seamus face as he passed through the door.

Next came Major Savage with Scipio at his side. The major looked at Seamus absently, a dreamy expression on his face.

Laudanum, thought Seamus.

Scipio directed the major toward the door and went to take up his usual position in the hall.

Seamus spoke to Sarah.

"Would you please act as interpreter and ask Scipio to attend the major in the barroom?"

Sarah agreed and spoke to Scipio in the exotic tones of the Gulla language, which sounded even stranger to Seamus' ear for the occasional utterance of an oddly pronounced word of English or French.

Scipio's usual emotionless and self-contained mien changed suddenly. A widening of his eyes seemed to register surprise at the request that he be present at the hearing. Just as quickly his features recomposed themselves to their accustomed expression of regal detachment. He accompanied Sarah through the door.

Shortly, the Reverend and Mrs. Van Wyck and Emily came down the hall. The dominie acknowledged Mr. Beecher and Seamus with bowed head and averted eye and ducked into the door.

Mrs. Van Wyck and Emily, walking with arms linked, hesitated before entering the barroom. The older lady's cheeks were streaked with tears and she held a lace handkerchief to her nose. Emily looked to Seamus. Her eyes too were red. Nonetheless she had a small, brave smile for him as she bade him and Mr. Beecher, good evening.

Seamus for his part could not easily take his eyes off her as she and Mrs. Van Wyck passed through the door. He marked the fact that she had changed into the blue and gray plaid dress she had worn when he had first seen her.

As all who had been requested to come to the hearing were now in attendance, Seamus held the door open for Mr. Beecher and entered behind him. As he did so, he turned to Levi and Sally and gestured with his thumb over his shoulder. The two hurried away.

He stood in the doorway and quickly scanned the room. His gaze fell first upon Tompkins, who stood at the moment with his back to the assembly by the closed hatch. His elbows were raised and Seamus guessed that he was replenishing his coffee mug. Tompkins turned, and seeing Seamus looking in his direction, raised his cup slightly, winked and grinned.

Seamus smiled back and, looking away, saw that Rolf was at the near end of the bar by the ice water crock. Sampson was standing next to Rolf and was closer yet to the hall door. The

Major, with Scipio standing behind him, was in his usual chair at the table to the right of the door. Standing by Scipio was Sarah and closer to the door on Seamus right was McCain who did not return Seamus gaze, but who instead directed his attention at the judge and the coroner who were seated side by side along with Mr. Beecher at the table beyond that of the major. The judge was leaning on the piano and using it as a makeshift desk. He had spread upon it some packets of papers bound in red ribbons and was jotting on the cover of one of the packets. At his left, the coroner had set out his small silver ink well, his pens, seals and a bar of red wax. He was squinting in the lamp light at the tip of a pencil which he was sharpening with a small knife. A pad of paper lay on the table before him.

The sheriff and the constable stood behind the judge. Out of deference to the ladies, they and the rest of the men in the room had doffed their hats.

At the table beyond the piano, the Reverend and Mrs. Van Wyck and Emily had joined the doctor where he still sat sipping, occasionally, from his coffee mug.

No others were in the room, save Willie Peters, who, as Seamus had requested, had stationed himself against the wall by the door to the casino, next to the doctor's table.

The old Dutch clock behind the bar struck half past one.

We might make it yet, thought Seamus.

Mr. Beecher looked to Seamus, who gave the slightest nod of his head. The proprietor nodded to the judge and the judge turned to the sheriff.

The sheriff cleared his throat. When he spoke, his deep voice resonated through the room.

"Oh, Yez! Oh Yez! All ye who have business with this Court, come close and give heed, for the Honorable Court, in and for the County of Greene, is now in session!"

"Thank you, Sheriff," said the judge over his shoulder. He surveyed the assembly, paused and then spoke.

"This," he said, "is a hearing to determine the circumstances of the death of one Fenton Clay at this hotel at about five o'clock in the morning on Saturday last. This proceeding will be an informal hearing in order to discover certain facts in preparation for a coroner's inquest and possible arraignment to follow. Although the proceedings will be, as I say, informal, they will be recorded stenographically." He inclined his head toward the coroner who had been writing away assiduously since the judge had first spoken.

Judge Livingston continued.

"All discourse will be recorded whether sworn or not, so as to guard the rights of the accused; Luther Van Bronc. Colonel Delaney has asked to address a few words to the court before Mr. Van Bronc is produced. We have assented to his doing so because it is our understanding that he has, at the request of Mr. Beecher, been assisting the duly constituted agents of the law in gathering information regarding the matter."

The judge paused to allow Mr. Saulpaugh to catch up. When the scribbling hand stopped, the judge turned to Seamus.

"Colonel?" he said.

"Thank you, your Honor," said Seamus. He looked around the room and began.

"On Saturday morning, I witnessed the murder of Fenton Clay. At the time of the murder, I was in attendance at the sunrise services on the piazza and was standing next to, save one person, the deceased. Only the victim's wife was standing closer to him than was I. She was standing on his right. Mr. Clay was standing in the doorway and was shot from behind. His associate, Mr. McCain was standing to the left of Mr. Clay when the fatal shot was fired."

Seamus looked at McCain who stared directly back, his eyes glacial. Seamus went on.

"After I passed Mrs. Clay over to Mrs. Van Wyck, who had been standing on my right, I carefully looked around the door and saw a man, a black man, standing at the far end of the hall, in the back entrance of the building. That man proved to be Luther Van Bronc and I became his unwilling accuser as he was shortly found to be holding a pistol which, upon inspection, was seen to have been recently fired.

"Luther's explanation was that he had fired earlier that morning to frighten away a bear which had hindered him while he was driving the meat wagon up the mountain. He said that he had just pulled the wagon up by the scullery entrance when he had heard the shot at the back door. He had come around to the door while holding the pistol in reaction to what he thought might be a situation where he would have to use force. In essence, Luther was claiming that he happened to be in the wrong place at the wrong time. An alibi not uncommonly used by those who truly are guilty of criminal acts."

The law officers and the judge nodded in unison

"However," said Seamus, "I believed Luther's story almost from the start for a number of reasons not the least of which was that I, myself, and apparently I alone, had actually heard the shot which Luther had fired over the bear on the side of the mountain.

"But, suspicion also pointed to Luther because he and the deceased had exchanged bitter . . . very bitter . . . words on the evening previous to the shooting.

"Indeed," Seamus looked to the constable, "I was briefly suspected of having shot Mr. Clay myself, since I also had . . . an altercation. . . .with the man on that same Friday night before the murder. I, however, had a perfect alibi as I was standing on the piazza amid the worshippers when the victim was shot. I, if you will, was in the right place at the right time. Luther, on the other hand, was standing on the spot from which the shot had apparently been fired, standing, in fact, in the midst of the gun smoke which had issued forth from the murder weapon."

Seamus stepped to the judge's table and continued.

"And so," he said, "as the morning wore on, and in very short order, more evidence was found which seemed to point to Luther as the murderer. The doctor here determined that Clay was likely shot with a conical bullet of the type with which the pistol Luther had was loaded."

Seamus reached into his pocket and took out the bullet and held it up.

"This bullet," he said, "was found in the back wall of the stair case as witnessed by the doctor and others. It will, I am sure, be shown to be the round which passed through Clay's head."

Out of the corner of his eye, Seamus saw Emily start at this brutal description.

Sorry, Emily, he thought but this is necessary. He noticed no reaction from any of the others.

"And," he continued, "I submit it to the court to be entered into evidence."

The judge nodded and Seamus gave the bullet to Ezra Saulpaugh, who examined it minutely, set down his pencil, picked up a tag and wrote upon it in ink. He tied the tag to the deformed lead cylinder with a bit of string and placed it on the table. Seamus went on.

"As I have said, despite the evidence mounting against Luther, much of which I myself had discovered, I continued to believe in his innocence. This belief came partly from my head and partly, I must confess, from my heart. The more I came to know Luther and the more I learned of him from others, the more I was convinced that he was not one who would shoot an unarmed man from behind regardless of what words had passed between them. Further, when I stood by the barroom door that morning and looked down the hall, and looked behind me yet another distance to the spot from which the shot had been fired, it occurred to me that unless Luther was an outstanding pistol shot, it would have been virtually impossible for him to have killed Clay with a single shot to the head at such a range. I deduced this simply by putting myself in the murderer's place and concluding that I would have been very hard pressed to have duplicated that feat. And I, not to brag, but as a matter of fact, won the 69th Regiment's Annual St. Patrick's Day Officers Pistol Shooting Contest every single year that the regiment was in the field. I have the honor to be the undefeated regimental champion and yesterday, when I tried a shot at the same range in practice, I was indeed unable to hit the target on the first try.

"Further, I again that morning looked at the question of motive and could not picture a brave, intelligent, upstanding, sober, reliable family man like Luther sacrificing everything he has worked for in order to take revenge for bigoted and ignorant remarks of the type which he no doubt has stoically endured for most of his life."

Seamus paused and looked around the room. His eyes rested for a moment on Sarah Van Bronc. Her face glowed, her eyes shined. A tear ran down her cheek. She did not brush it away.

"So," he continued, "I pondered this question of motive. I even wondered for a time whether or not Clay was really the intended victim. Was it possible, I wondered, that someone else on the piazza had been the actual target of the murderer and that the bullet had struck Clay by accident."

His eyes found Emily's.

"But my heart told me that Clay's murder had been no accident."

Seamus paused and then, still looking Emily full in the eyes he went on.

"It was clear that others had motive to take Clay's life"

Emily's regard was steadfast.

Seamus turned toward Major Savage. The man's aspect remained vacant.

"For," said Seamus, "not just one, nor just two, but three of us had disputes with the murdered Mr. Clay on the night before his death. Major Savage had challenged him to a duel."

At this the major smiled in an uncharacteristically agreeable way and even let go a short chuckle.

"Why," said Seamus, "even the victim's associate, Mr. McCain, here, had been angry with Mr. Clay's . . . untoward . . . behavior and had become short with his . . . friend."

"What of it!" McCain rasped. Standing by the door he wore an expression on his face which by itself seemed capable of killing.

"What of it indeed," said Seamus.

Looking back to the major he thought to himself, McCain would dearly love to murder *me*, God help us!

"So, I thought of the possibility of the major having acted on his vehement demand, of the night before, for Clay's life. The major, after all had no alibi whatsoever except to say that he was asleep when the murder was committed. Further, by his own admission, he possesses a pistol which it seems was capable of causing the fatal wound."

The major's face had gone back to being a blank.

"Still," said Seamus, "I kept coming back to the evidence of my own eyes. The shot had been fired, I had looked back around the door way and there I had seen *Luther* standing. Not the major, but *Luther*. However, the more I thought about it the more it seemed to me that I was adding in an error in my calculations. The shot had been fired and I *had* looked back through the doorway. But not immediately. I, after all, did not survive the late war by immediately sticking my head up from cover every time I heard a shot fired."

Seamus laughed at his own small witticism. He noticed that only those in the room whom he knew to be veterans, the major included, joined him in laughter. McCain, though, did not laugh.

"There was," said Seamus, "an interval between the firing of the shot and my looking back. In retrospect it was difficult to estimate how much time had elapsed, but I recalled that after I had placed Mrs. Clay out of the line of fire and waited some moments, only then did I steal a glimpse around the door post. In fact, I remembered that I had peeked around the doorway three separate times. At first I had seen a man in the back entrance. When next I looked I could discern that the man in the back door was a black man. The third time I looked I recognized Luther.

In my mind I looked again at the scene which I had beheld when first I looked around the door way. I had seen a man. On the second look I had seen a black man."

Seamus turned to face Scipio standing behind the major with Sarah by his side.

At that moment the door to the casino opened and Levi entered. He carried on his shoulder what appeared to be the longest and widest tray of which the kitchens of the Mountain House could boast. Willie Peters held the door for him and Levi proceeded to the center of the bar where, with a muffled clatter of crockery, he set down his linen covered burden.

"Beg your pardon, your Honor," said Levi, "with the compliments of Mr. Beecher. He thought some refreshments might be in order."

"Thank you, Levi," said the judge. He nodded his appreciation to his host.

The aroma of fresh coffee filled the room as Levi returned

by the way he had come. Willie Peters closed the door and took up his position before it, his brawny arms folded across his broad chest.

Seamus walked to the middle of the bar and lifted the corner of the covering linen slightly and bent and savored the fragrance of the coffee.

"Hmmm!" he intoned, straightening up, "Now where was I? Oh, yes."

He turned again to Scipio.

"I had seen a black man standing on the spot from which the shot had almost certainly been fired. A black man standing in the very cloud of smoke which had been created by that shot. But was the black man Luther? There were many other black men on the property that morning. Did any of them have a motive to take Clay's life? Did the noble and loyal Scipio take it upon himself to avenge the honor of his friend, Major Savage? Did he, at the behest of the major, carry out this act of revenge and then disappear from the doorway to be quickly replaced by the unwitting Luther in the space of time between my having glimpsed around the doorway the second and third times?"

Sarah was whispering rapidly in Scipio's ear, translating. When she stopped Scipio continued to look at Seamus in his detached and regal way. No reaction of any kind did he show.

"But again," said Seamus, "both my heart and my head came into play as I pondered the possibilities. It was the major himself who had so clearly indicated to us both before and after the murder that he had wanted to take Clay's life. Was he capable of murder? He had told us that he was."

The major, slouching back in his chair, smiled another dreamy smile. Seamus blanched inwardly and went on.

"But would the major have prevailed upon Scipio to carry out the deed for him? If asked by his friend, would Scipio have obliged? Would he have done it on his own? I had no way of knowing for sure, but on the face of it I could not believe that a man of such apparently noble character as Scipio was capable of such an act any more than was Luther. And finally, if the major or Scipio had in fact killed Clay would either or both of them then have been willing to let Luther take the blame?"

Seamus paused and Sarah whispered a few more words of Gullah to Scipio and stopped. Still no reaction from Scipio could be seen. Seamus continued.

"It is one thing," he said, "to commit murder. It is something else entirely to stand by and to let someone else be hanged for the crime."

Seamus paused again while Sarah translated.

"Colonel," said the judge, "The court finds your ruminations to be of interest but..."

"Beg your pardon, your Honor," Seamus interjected, "but if I have a point, would I please get to it, right?"

"Precisely." said the judge, not without equanimity.

"I will, sir and shortly," said Seamus, "To continue then, I found myself thinking not only about the kind of person who could commit murder; almost anyone, in my experience, but also about the kind of person who could commit murder and let another pay for it with their one and only life. A particularly cold type of person, I thought. While I did not entirely put aside the notion that the person I had seen at the back door could have been Scipio, the idea brought me to another point. If someone other than Luther had fired the deadly round and then had stepped away from the door to leave Luther to 'stand in' for him as it were, where could the actual murderer have gone without Luther seeing that person as he departed the back entrance.

"If the killer had run away across the open lawns in the direction of the stables, Luther could hardly have missed him. If the killer had run along the back of the building to the south, he would not have come to a window to duck into until he had reached the corner of the wing as the windowless trunk room runs behind that wall. Luther would certainly have seen anyone who would have tried to run the distance to the south corner and enter one of those rooms through a window. If the killer had run along the north wall, he would have run into Luther's arms immediately."

Seamus stopped and looked around the room at those present.

"No," he said, "the killer sought refuge *in* the building after he had fired by rushing into the central hallway. If I or someone else on the piazza had, at the instant of hearing the shot and witnessing Clay collapse, turned and looked back up the hall, the culprit would have been seen running toward us through the cloud of gun smoke. But no one was looking up the hall during the scant seconds between the time when the actual killer was occupying the space and when he had disappeared from view and before Luther had placed himself in the back entrance. No one was looking up the hall before I had peeked around the door post on the piazza. And where had the murderer disappeared to?

"There are only three possibilities; he could have turned to his left and entered the barroom here, but the barroom was supposed to be locked at that hour. He could have vaulted the clerk's desk on the right and hid there, the office behind the desk also being locked at that time. Those locked doors, by the way, may not have posed that much of a problem for our murderous friend, but neither of those courses would have put the killer where he wanted to be immediately after he had fired the shot. No, you see he wanted more than just to murder Clay; he wanted to get away with the murder.

"He wanted to have a perfect alibi just like the one I had. He wanted to be on the piazza at the time Clay was killed. Only the Almighty can be in two places at once but our man wanted to give the impression that he was standing near Clay on the porch when Clay died. So, the instant he fired the shot, he was off and sprinting down the hall toward the body of the man he had just killed. As soon as he had passed the front desk, he turned sharp right into the corridor that runs south passing the telegraph office and the trunk room. On the left of that corridor are the windows which let on to the south court yard. At the end of the hall is the intersection with the corridor which provides access to the rooms with low numbers; eight through thirty-one, which make up the ground floor accommodations in the south wing. If the murderer had a room in the south wing, he could have turned right and found refuge there, but as I have said, he did not want to hide he wanted to be seen. So, he instead could have turned left and passed along that corridor to the intersection with the front hall which eventually leads to the central staircase and, indeed, to the doorway where the victim was standing when he was shot. The murderer would hardly have wanted to emerge onto the piazza from that doorway, however, but he did not have to. The front hall passes the entrance to the lounge and the lounge, in turn, has a door which lets on to the piazza to the right of where the unfortunate Mr. Clay was standing at the time of his death."

The judge spoke.

"Colonel, I have a reputation among my colleagues for permitting no nonsense in my court. Now, I realize that this is an informal hearing and I in no way wish to demean the efforts you have made, but I fear this is verging on the nonsense which I do not permit. I am asking you to get to your point, and soon, or I will have the accused brought in and commence the formal inquest and arraignment. Please, Colonel, it has been a long day . . . a long several days for us."

The judge's face bore an expression combining weariness and growing irritation.

"Your Honor," Seamus used his most conciliatory tones, "I will give the court, in a very few minuets, information which I believe will make it unnecessary for the accused to appear at all."

"Very well then, but *very* shortly if you please."

"Thank you, your Honor. The real killer entered the piazza from the lounge. I *saw* the killer on the piazza scant moments after Clay collapsed."

There was a collective sucking in of breathe around the room at this news and Seamus paused and then went on.

"I did not know at the time, of course, that the person I saw was in fact the murderer. His plan, you see, was working. He was being seen at the place where the bullet he launched had concluded its flight, rather than at the place from where the round had been fired. The killer had certainly not planned for Luther to be standing at the entrance when I looked back. That was just a matter of luck, as matters of life or death often appear to be. Just a matter of luck; extremely good luck for the killer, extremely bad luck for Luther."

Seamus eyes again found those of Sarah.

"So," he said looking back to the judge, "the killer had rushed from his firing point to the piazza, but not by the long route of circumnavigating the south court yard via the corridors, but rather by the shortest possible route. The shortest distance between two points, as the venerable Euclid knew, is a straight line. The shortest way to get from the back entrance to the piazza is by way of the central hall. That route was obviously out of the question for our killer. The right turn into the south corridor followed by two left turns and another right turn would get him to the piazza by way of the lounge but was, by my calculations, to time consuming. The more nearly straight line, and that which our killer chose to take in this well planned crime, was for him to take the right turn into the south corridor, but to then immediately turn left and enter the south court yard by way of the door across from the telegraph office. The killer then hurried through the yard eschewing the gravel path which did not lead to where he wanted to go. Where he wanted to go was to the window of room number four. The door of that room is opposite that of the lounge. When the killer walked through the grass of the yard, his feet became wet with the morning dew. Later, I quite accidentally found that the carpet between the door of room number four and the door of the lounge was still damp from the passing earlier of the sodden shoes of the killer. Later still in the day a search of the room revealed a dead ant on the floor beneath the window. By it self the ant meant nothing, but since the rooms of this hotel are kept scrupulously clean, the discovery set me to wondering. Perhaps the flattened insect had been either carried into the room on the shoe of the killer, or if the creature had already been in the room, had been trodden upon when the killer climbed in through the window. In any case, it came to me that our murderer had been able, by taking the shortest possible route, to simulate omnipresence and to almost be in two places at the same time. He entered the piazza from the lounge behind the crowd of those who were now directing all their panicked attention to the fallen Mr. Clay.

"It mattered not to the killer that both the inside and outside doors to the lounge were usually locked at that hour, nor that the door to the unoccupied room number four as well as the window to that room were usually locked and latched. Locked doors were no obstacle to our murderer, he was, you see, and doubtless still is, in possession of a missing ring of keys. The keys which were usually given to Rolf each evening and which the killer stole on the night before the murder. With them he created a pathway of unlocked doors and an unlatched window for himself as he quietly roamed the building on the night before the murder when all were asleep and he was making all necessary preparations for the crime which he had to commit. Once he had entered room number four from the courtyard, he locked the window behind him and locked the room door too when he exited."

All eyes in the room followed Seamus as he edged closer to the bar. The judge, he noticed, was no longer inclined to hasten him but now hung on his every word.

Seamus stood by the tray on the bar and again lifted the linen covering.

"But," he said, "perhaps we are moving too quickly here. Maybe we should pause for some coffee and sweet rolls."

"Colonel!" the judge bellowed in exasperation.

Seamus pulled the linen towel entirely from the tray and draped in on the edge of the bar.

"What have we here?" he asked in mock astonishment, "Why, it is the murder weapon."

From amid the silver pots and china cups and saucers on the tray, he lifted the Colt's Carbine and held it up for all to see. The light from the twin lamps hanging over the bar glowed in the polished gun stock and glinted off the silver presentation plaque inletted into the wood. Highlights played off the telescope tube, the barrel and the cylinder. The brass of the trigger guard and butt plate shown like burnished gold. This firearm had been lovingly cared for.

"Yes, your Honor," said Seamus, "this is the weapon which was used to murder Fenton Clay at this hotel on Saturday morning last. I am sure that it will be found to be loaded with .44 caliber bullets which are the mates to the one which I have presented into evidence; elongated, conoidal or conical pistol balls, which, I have it on expert authority were very likely manufactured in the former Confederacy. Rebel ammunition. Not surprising since this gun belongs to a former rebel officer and a rather notorious one at that. It was brought here just now from the room of that man, the man who murdered Fenton Clay."

Seamus turned to Tompkins who still stood in front of the bottle of brandy on the counter of the hatchway.

"This is your carbine, Mr. Tompkins, it was found in your room."

Tompkins gave a start and then laughed. He said nothing.

"Or," said Seamus, "Should I address you, sir, as Captain Brutus Lejeune, for that is who you are. The man to whom this weapon was presented by his command; the Maryland Partizan Zouaves."

The man behind the bar laughed again and looked around the room with an expression of incredulity upon his face.

"Colonel," he said finally, "you are joking, or, if you are in earnest, then it must be that you have again been addressing yourself to your flask. I, Brutus Lejeune? The idea is ludicrous. No one in the whole world is less like that dashing scoundrel than am I, sir. I am a keeper of books, a trader in goods a very ordinary businessman."

"You are a veteran of the late war, sir," said Seamus, "when I made my little joke earlier about not sticking out my head from cover when I heard a shot, only we veterans in the room laughed, you Captain, and the rest of us who have been under fire. Civilian citizens do not understand our humor."

"I was simply being polite," came the reply, "but if my laughing out of courtesy at your wit has condemned me in your eyes as a murderer, than I must throw myself on the mercy of the court."

The whiskey drummer laughed, winking at the judge.

"Colonel," said the judge, "May I assume that you have some actual evidence to support this most serious allegation?"

"Yes, your honor," said Seamus turning to the judge, "the court shall hear exactly how Captain Lejeune here murdered Clay and tried to cover his guilt and leave Luther to hang for the crime."

Seamus had taken his eye off his quarry for only a moment and now he turned back to him.

"The night before the murder you determined that you must kill Clay and you immediately set about planning the crime and putting your plan into motion," he said to the man, who, for his part was beginning to show signs of irritation although he still wore a smile. He moved closer to the center of the bar and stood across the counter from Seamus.

"On that night," said Seamus, "you were at the end of the bar, by the hall door there and while the attention of all in the room was focused on the altercation I was having with Clay in the casino, you took the keys from the bar where Luther had laid them. Later, when all were asleep, you used the keys, as I have said, to make a trail of unlocked doors for you to follow to the piazza. You also used the keys to gain entry to the silver case from which you stole this . . ."

Seamus took the bent spoon from his waistcoat pocket with his left hand, still holding the carbine in his right.

"You used this spoon, or rather intended to use it, to hook onto the inside waistband of your trousers thus . . ."

Seamus demonstrated hooking the now S-shaped utensil into his own waistband.

" . . . then suspending the weapon from this bootlace tied to the saddle ring on the side of the stock and secreting the firearm down inside the leg of your trousers like so . . . "

Seamus slid the carbine down into the leg of his trousers from his waistband and held up both of his hands. The weapon was completely concealed.

"I say you *intended* to use the spoon in this manner, and I suspect that after killing Clay you planned to transfer the weapon from your hand to your trouser leg once you had gained the privacy of room number four. That was your intention, but you were momentarily impeded. You dropped the spoon as you were climbing in the window, and that is where I found it later in the morning, in the grass of the courtyard beneath that window. If you knew you had dropped it, would you have simply reached out the window for it? Perhaps. After all, by my calculations you still had plenty of time to make your appearance on the piazza. So, I think you did not realize where the spoon had fallen. But, seasoned agent, and, may I say it, bushwhacker that you are . . . "

"No! You may not say it, sir!" came the heated response

which was quickly and incongruously followed by a smile and a laugh.

"Well, as you wish," said Seamus, "your *experience* then has taught you to be resourceful, so you pressed on regardless, simply sliding the carbine down your trouser leg but now being careful to keep a grip on it either with your hand under your coat, or even with your elbow, thus . . . "

Seamus demonstrated by holding his elbow into his side.

"The muzzle, of course, reaches bellow the knee and so you had to walk with your leg stiff, and when I looked back the third and final time from the door post on the piazza on the morning of the murder, by my calculations, about one and one half minutes after Clay was shot, I looked down to see you half-kneeling as if to offer assistance to the man you had just murdered. I noted then that your leg was sticking out as stiff as a crutch. By the way, it was only after I became sure that you are the murderer that I realized that your presence on the piazza fit amply into the time elapsed between the shot and your appearance. Your supposed crippled leg did not slow your progress."

The man behind the bar opened his mouth to speak, but Seamus cut him off.

"Yes, we know Captain, you suffered a riding accident as a youth which kept you out of the war, and which causes you still to limp. But as I saw on the first night I met you, sir, in this very room, it is your left leg which is somewhat stiff and as you kneeled by Clay's body it was your right leg which was sticking out, because it was down your right trouser leg you had thrust the carbine, ready to use again if need be. Later, when you feigned illness and absented yourself from carrying the body into the lounge you where seen dragging your leg up the central staircase and clutching your side. You were not sick, the sight of the blood of people you have killed does not bother you, does it? No, you were just being careful not to let the weapon fall. Perhaps you really do suffer from a game leg, but I do not believe it kept you out of the war. I believe it may be the result of a wound incurred during the war. In any case, your limp is usually not so pronounced as the doctor described to me after he saw you going up the steps that morning. You went up and hid the weapon in an unoccupied room, again using the stolen keys. A very wise tactic. As you surmised, if the rooms were to be searched at all, occupied rooms would be searched first. Later the weapon was returned to your room."

Seamus kept his target fixed in his view as the man behind the bar turned to the judge.

"Your Honor, am I to be accused in such a way without being able to speak? This is still the United States, is it not?"

Seamus found the reference to the United States ironic.

"Sir," said the judge, "you may indeed speak for yourself or you may remain mute. No charges have been brought."

"Thank you, your Honor. Aside from the fact that all of what Colonel Delaney has been saying regarding me is preposterous, which it is, what possible reason would I have for murdering Mr. Clay, a man I had never had any dispute with, and a man to whom I had never been introduced and whom I never even had seen until I came to this hotel?"

Seamus responded instantly.

"Your reason for killing Clay was because, far from being a stranger to you, he was your associate, or underling really, in a secret and violent force which operated before, during, and after the war and which apparently is still in operation to the present day."

Seamus pulled the weapon from his trouser leg, placed the spoon on the bar and read the plaque on the stock of the carbine aloud. When he finished reading, he looked again to the man behind the bar.

"This weapon was presented to you, Captain, by your comrades of the Maryland Partizan Zouaves, an elite contingent of guerrillas founded early in the war to carry out secret and destructionist operations particularly along the border of Maryland and Virginia. Did Clay work for you then? Not as a soldier to be sure, he did not seem the type, but perhaps as a smuggler of blockaded goods? As a spy as well no doubt. And now your operations continue in coordination with the secret society, or rather societies, which Clay mentioned drunkenly on the night before his death. He divulged the information for all to hear after I knocked him down in the casino. But most of us just dismissed as incoherent ramblings his references to an 'invisible empire'; the Order of American Knights, and an 'unbroken circle', the Knights of the Golden Circle, of course, and the 'blooming camellia'; the Order of the White Camellia. All majestic and pretty words for murder gangs and the slaughter of the defenseless. But even before that you had determined to kill Clay and to silence him forever. Is that not right, Captain?"

The man remained silent and smiling, but Seamus did not wait for an answer.

"You decided to kill Clay when you and I were standing at the end of the bar that night and he addressed you, you who were supposed to be unknown to him, as that which you were; his captain. Clay had said something about southern honor and the fight not being over yet and then he said, ' . . . isn't that right, captain.' Clay was looking in our direction when he spoke and I thought he was speaking to me, but he was not, he was speaking to you. And that would never do, would it? A secret is not a secret if a drunk is blabbing it all over a barroom, is it? For whatever reason you had been tolerating Clay up to that point, he had crossed the line when he publicly called you by your proper title, and his fate was sealed from that moment. He had to die and soon. He was too dangerous to let live. You began to lay your plans there and then and carried out your intention the next morning when you shot him with this carbine," Seamus shook the gun at the still smiling drummer, "as the sun was rising and your victim stood outlined in the door to the piazza. A difficult shot with a pistol, an easy shot for one of your experience with this weapon."

"Is that all?" asked the man who now stood accused. "Is that all?" he repeated.

He did not wait for a response.

"If this is your 'evidence'," he said, "then I have to say that I am not Captain Brutus Lejeune and that I have never seen that gun before in my life. If it was found in my room, I have no idea how it got there. As you have pointed out Colonel, locked doors do not seem to be much of a barrier in this establishment since someone, not I, but someone, has supposedly stolen a set of keys."

He smiled and chuckled at his own humor. But his complexion blazed scarlet. He drained his mug and set it down on the counter.

The judge spoke.

"Colonel, this is all very circumstantial, and then there is the question of search and the seizure of evidence . . ."

"If your Honor please," said Seamus, "there is more."

He set the carbine on the bar reached into his pocket and came forth with a packet of paper which he unfolded and held up over his head. There were lines of writing on the page and signatures and red wax seals at the bottom.

"I have here," he said, turning to the man behind the bar, "a document which I will offer into evidence. It is the sworn statement, Captain, of your associate, Leander Skhutt, now in custody, in which he attests that when you fired the fatal shot, he was standing by your side!"

"The liar! He was miles away when I . . . "

"When you what, Captain?" asked Seamus.

The man who had been known as Tompkins was silent. His color was high but his expression was blank. And then he began to smile. As Seamus watched, although the man never ceased to smile, his face took on a mask of cruelty and hatred.

No, thought Seamus, it is not as though he is putting on a mask, rather as though the mask that was the innocuous Tompkins is falling away and the true face of Brutus Lejeune is being shown to us for the first time.

"When you what?" Seamus goaded.

Lejeune continued to smile, his eyes like the black muzzles of two pistols leveled at Seamus face. The reflected flames of the overhead lamps danced in each iris.

"When," he said, at last, "I killed that hopeless fool, Clay."

A silent instant passed and then Lejeune spoke again.

"Well, Colonel, you have found your Lucifer . . . "

He grabbed the carbine from the bar and swung it up and smashed the chandelier.

A shower of burning oil cascaded onto the counter engulfing the sleeve of Seamus coat.

"Now!" shrieked Lejeune, "Burn!"

With a laugh like a howl, he smashed the butt of the weapon into Seamus' face. Seamus stumbled backward and fell among the tables and chairs, swatting furiously at his burning arm with the sealed document. The fabric of his coat blazed up and the paper caught fire. He threw it to the floor.

"Burn!" Lejeune screamed again. He reached behind him, snatched another lamp from the back bar and threw it half the length of the mahogany to where it smashed in front of Rolf. Flames exploded both before and behind the bar.

"Burn! Burn! Burn!" Lejeune dashed to the hatchway, took the bottle of brandy from the counter there and rocketed it into the blaze at the center of the bar. The flames jumped to the ceiling.

Seamus, flat on his back and beating at his burning arm, saw Lejeune leap through the hatchway, and turning saw Willie Peters, pistol in hand, push through the door to the casino in pursuit. Before the brave fellow had cleared the doorway, a muffled blast catapulted him back into the barroom amid a cloud of smoke. He crashed alongside Seamus, his face blackened on one side and a great gout of blood spurting over the short blonde hair of his head.

"Oh God," moaned Seamus. Above the screams and the roaring of the flames, he could hear the tinkling smash of the disintegrating French doors in the casino.

Lejeune, Seamus knew, was away.

# XI

# Engagement and Pursuit

Lejeune was away and Seamus lay on the floor choking on the blood running down his throat. He rolled over on his left side and smothered the flaming sleeve of his coat. He gagged and spit blood on the floor in front of his face.

Emily was at his side.

"Seamus," was all she said.

He struggled to his feet.

"Lie still," she said, "you are hurt."

"No," he managed to say, "No, see if you can help poor Willie there. I am all right, just a bloody nose." And a broken nose . . . again, he thought.

The butt of Lejeune's carbine had caught the bridge of his nose. There was no pain yet, just the familiar feeling of pressure between the eyes.

Emily peered through the smoke and saw the form of Willie Peters, his feet still stuck through the half open door to the casino.

"Oh, my," she said, "Doctor, please come and help!"

The doctor turned from his occupation of the moment. He and the Reverend Van Wyck were beating out the flames by the bar with their coats. He took his black bag from the table, gave his coat to Seamus and knelt with Emily by Willie's inert form.

Seamus replaced the doctor fighting the fire and, shoulder to shoulder with the dominie, succeeded in putting out the fire at the center of the bar. Rolf had taken the crock of ice water from its stand and was judiciously splashing the contents on the flames which snapped behind the bar. Presently, that fire too was extinguished.

The sheriff had been beating at the flames with his sombrero and now stood for a moment looking wistfully at the scorched remnant of his once proud headdress. With an expression of resolution, he put it on his head.

The major seemed to be the only person in the room who had not taken some part in the firefighting effort. He continued to sit in his usual spot a look of unfocused amusement on his face.

"Well, Reverend," he asked loudly, "has this been a preview of the Hell to which you have told me I am headed? I find it rather more stimulating than the one to which I was consigned at Andersonville. There the agony was prolonged and not nearly so bracing. I feel I will much prefer the fires of Gehena."

The reverend wiped his brow, his face dark. He swabbed with his handkerchief at the oily grime around his eyes. He looked away and said nothing in reply.

The major laughed. He laughed and laughed, choked and coughed. When he caught his breathe, he laughed again.

Seamus spoke.

"Scipio, why don't you take the major to his room."

Sarah translated and the two of them lifted the now wheezing man and took him out the door.

"Sampson," said Seamus, a sudden catch in his voice, "where is Sampson?"

"Here."

The voice was that of Mr. Beecher. He rose from behind the corner of the bar along with the constable. The grimacing and bent over Sampson was supported between them.

"I am alright," said Sampson. But he gasped with pain and held his midsection. He took a breath of the smoky air and hacked it out again. Seamus stepped over the broken glass in front of the bar and came closer to Sampson who, with a will, straightened himself up and spoke.

"I am sorry, Colonel, I had stationed myself next to McCain just as you said I should, but he was too fast for me. At the very second that Mr. Tompkins, or I guess really Captain Lejeune, shattered the lamps above the bar, McCain whirled around and punched me in the breadbasket.  All the wind went out of me. I went down and could not get up again and he was out the hall door. I expect I underestimated him. I am sorry."

Seamus put his hand on the man's shoulder.

"It is not your fault, Sampson," he said "it is mine.  I am the one who underestimated the whole situation here and I have no excuse since I should have known better considering the type of people we are dealing with.  No time for regrets now though. Sampson are you up to pursuing these two?"

"I am, Colonel," came the response. Sampson's eyes flashed with a fierce vengeance.

"Good," said Seamus, "Sheriff, Constable, we had best be after them."

The two lawmen already had their guns out.

Seamus turned to the judge who, along with the coroner, was gathering his singed legal papers from the floor.

"Your Honor, will you order the release of Luther Van Bronc?"

The judge coughed and cleared his throat.

"So ordered," he rasped.

The coroner squinted with watery eyes and recorded the court's order on a partly charred slip of paper.

"Thank you, sir," said Seamus as he headed for the casino door. He paused and looked down at Emily and the doctor kneeling on each side of the prostrate Willie. One of the intact lamps had been set on the floor by his head.  His wound was awful to behold.

The doctor and Emily looked up.

"You're bleeding, Seamus." said Emily.

The doctor reached into his bag and handed Seamus a tuft of lint which he wadded and pressed into his nostril. He wiped his face with his handkerchief.

"Willie?" he asked.

"He is still breathing at least." the doctor replied and he bent again to his work.

Emily still looked up at Seamus, her eyes fearful.

No time for this, Seamus thought and he turned to the door.

He carefully pushed the door open and let it swing shut

again. He glanced at the men behind him, gestured for them to stand fast, faced front and rushed though the door.

He ran across the darkened casino looking toward the French doors and took cover behind a table. Nothing happened. Lejeune had not tarried to ambush him. But from now on I will have to be more careful with these men; studied murderers that they are, he thought.

He looked at the broken frames of the French doors, the remaining shards of glass hung at odd angles.

Lejeune, he considered, did pause to shoot poor Willie, but had not paused to unlock, with the stolen keys, the flimsy doors which were more glass than wood. No need to. During the inquest, he had however used the appropriate key to unlock the stout hatch while he had his back to the rest of those in the barroom, and while he was incidentally replenishing his mug with brandy.

"Hadn't thought of that had you, my lad?" Seamus whispered to himself in the darkness. The starlight filtered in through the broken panes in the doors.

"Right!" he then said in a loud voice.

Sampson and the two lawmen came in from the barroom. Sampson now also had a revolver in hand.

"Miz Emily just gave me this," he said, "it belongs to Willie."

"Good," said Seamus, "let us hope that you will be able to return it to him later today."

"Amen," said Sampson.

They approached the French doors carefully. One of them hung open, the small lock broken. Seamus stuck his head out the door and then stepped back quickly. Nothing disturbed the silence of the early morning mountain wilderness. The stars shown clearly in a sky like black lacquer.

Seamus and his companions stepped gingerly out onto the grass and then onto the curving driveway. The gravel crunched under their feet. The constable spoke in a low voice.

"No telling where they're gone. So, McCain was in on it too."

"Yes," said Seamus, "Lejeune and McCain meet on the

backstairs the night before the murder. I had heard them behind the wall of my room as I was falling asleep but, of course, I did not know it was them at the time. I had forgotten about it until I began to put the information together. Lejeune must have instructed McCain to force Clay to come to the sunrise service and to center him in the doorway so that there would be a clear shot. When I was making my accusations before the judge, I did not want to implicate McCain yet. I thought it better to deal with them one at a time. No good did I do with that idea, they are smart and were ready for any eventuality. In any case, I had to concentrate on Lejeune and get a rise out of him. I even laid the carbine before him in hopes that he would make a play for it. I was foolishly sure that we would be able to overpower him before he could get off a shot. Who would have thought that he would set the place on fire?"

Seamus shook his head ruefully and went on.

"I should have thought of it, that's who. But I had to make him react in some way as I had no other means of proving him guilty of murder."

"You had not?" asked the constable, "What about Skhutt's deposition?"

"It was a lie, I had no such deposition. But it worked."

Seamus smiled, winked at the constable, and immediately winced in pain.

His broken nose started to throb and the burned palm of his right hand was sore. His left arm was also starting to feel hot and raw.

"It was a lie?" the sheriff repeated, "Then what was that paper you showed the court, Colonel?"

"That," answered Seamus, "was a safe conduct and pass to cross Confederate lines at Chancellorsville, bearing the signature; I might add, of none other than General Thomas Jackson, CSA, himself.

"Oh," said the sheriff, duly impressed, "I saw that paper burn in the fire back their when you were trying to knock out the flames on your arm. Too bad. I'll bet someday people will be willing to pay a pretty penny for old Stonewall's signature. That document would have become valuable."

"It would," said Seamus, "had it not been a forgery. I wrote it out, signed it and sealed it myself on the night of the battle of Chancellorsville back in '63."

When, he thought, but did not say, our defeat appeared to be as total as it does now with the escape of Lejeune and McCain.

"Oh," said the sheriff again, "Well, since Skhutt is in custody, we can probably get some kind of a statement out of him, if he is approached in the right way."

The sheriff made a strangling motion with his two beefy hands.

"Uh, whose custody is he in anyhow?"

"No one's that I am aware of, Sheriff," said Seamus offhandedly as they walked along.

"But, Colonel," the constable put in, "you said that Skhutt was in custody."

"Another lie, I must confess, in my effort to get Lejeune to tip his hand. But regardless, convicting evidence is not much good to us if we do not hold the murderer."

Suddenly from beyond the lake came the insistent call of a bugle, the notes muted by the distance.

"*Officers Call*," said Sampson, "Professor Smith demonstrated for us some of the bugle calls they used in the war. I remember that one, that's the *Officers Call*."

Seamus peered into the night.

"Right you are, Sampson," he said, "that *is* the *Officers Call*. It tells me that Mr. Leander Skhutt and his friends are coming to pay us a visit. Let us go down and greet them as they come. Perhaps we can ask old Reb about making that statement for us."

They picked their way across the dark lawn as quickly as they could and presently came near to the place of Luther's imprisonment. A small lantern glowed amid the trees.

"Sylvester!" the constable called out to his deputy, "If you are awake, don't shoot us, and let Luther out of the root cellar."

"A course I'm awake, Uncle Hump," the nasal high pitch of Sylvester's voice came back.

"Be damned if he isn't awake," said the constable to his companions, "that boy is getting better."

"Uncle Hump," Sylvester keened again, "are you sure I

should let Luther out?"

"Aw, dammit, Sylvester, here I am just bragging to these gentlemen how you're finally showing some sense and you go and mess it up by giving me an argument.  Judge Livingston has just ordered Luther released.  Now do you want to violate a court order and then I have to put my own nephew in jail.  And don't call me Uncle Hump."

The constable finished his speech and convulsed in suppressed laughter.

"No, no," Sylvester's nervous voice came back, "no need to get mad, Unc...I mean Constable. I just wanted to be sure is all."

The clink and jingle of the lad's key ring were heard through the pines and presently the working of the lock and the groan of the door.

The sounds of freedom, thought Seamus.

"Come on down here, Sylvester and bring your lantern with you." the constable barked out his orders.

The deputy and Luther joined the group at the edge of the grove and the constable took his former prisoner by the hand.

"We heard a shot . . . ," said Sylvester.

"We'll tell you all about it later," the constable cut him off, "Congratulations, Luther. The Colonel here got you cleared of the charge.  Sorry to have locked you up, on to it, but I sure am glad to see you free."

"Thank you, Constable, Colonel," said Luther, "but do you know who did murder Mr. Clay?"

"Tompkins," said the constable.

"Tompkins?" Luther repeated, "Mr. Tompkins the whiskey drummer?"

Astonishment echoed in Luther's voice.

"Surprised all of us. Colonel here figured it out."

"In truth," said Seamus, "Sally is the one who broke the case.  As the constable said; we will explain it all later."  If there is a later, he thought.  He went on, urgency in his voice.

"Tompkins and McCain, his accomplice, managed to escape, only for the moment I hope, but your innocence is of no account to Reb and his friends. They are on their way here right now, and nothing has changed as far as their intentions toward you,

Luther."

Seamus crouched down beneath the cedar bows and peered into the night.

"Look," he said, "you can just make out their torches through the trees."

All bent down and looked at the place across South Lake where Seamus was pointing.

A long strand of individual orange flames lead by a tight knot of flames was streaming inexorably through the darkness along the north shore. The flames were mirrored perfectly in the still waters making the approaching mob seem less like a crowd of men and more like some mythological night beast with gapping jaw.

As Seamus watched; the fiery dragon flexed around the inward curve of land heading toward the isthmus between the two lakes.

Seamus straightened up and spoke to Luther.

"There is no sense in you staying here now; if they cannot reach you they cannot harm you. One man more or one man less will make no difference to our side. They will be here very soon now. I suggest you at least go back to the Mountain House, and if need be, make your escape from there."

Luther put on the forage cap he held in his hands, and stretched the strap into place below his powerful jaw. The numerals '54' flashed in the light of Sylvester's lantern.

"As you say, Colonel," he said quietly, "nothing has changed; I will make my stand here."

Seamus had received the reply he had expected.

"We will go down then to the common and meet them," he said to the small band of defenders, "but Luther, if you please, at least stand behind me so that you will not be shot the moment you are seen."

"I will, Colonel, but I expect that they do not have such a quick end in mind for me."

Luther, Seamus knew, was all too right. He put the thought from his mind and led his little detachment to the edge of the common and halted them. He arranged them in a line with the constable, Sylvester, the sheriff and Sampson on his left and

Luther, who towered over him, to his rear. Seamus himself formed the right flank of the line.

Beneath the overarching dome of stars all was silent. The stables stood dark and still off to the left. No signs of life could be seen. An owl screeched above in the woods beyond North Lake and suddenly hushed, the call echoing and fading across the water.

The approaching sound of a lone man jogging up the road from the lakes was now heard. All eyes turned in that direction to see Professor Otis Smith, his bugle tucked under his arm, come puffing into the circle of lantern light.

"Colonel," he said stopping at Seamus right hand. He paused and gasped for breath.

"Colonel," he began again, "you heard my call. I sounded *Officers Call*, as you said I should, from my post by the old charcoal pit when I first saw them coming along the lake. They heard me too, I am sure, but did not see me go. I left there just now as they came close to the pit. They are just behind me by a minute or two. As best I could see they are mostly armed and all or most have torches. Only one is mounted, a big fellow on a big roan. He looks to be the leader."

Leander Skhutt, Seamus knew. The professor continued.

"They have a little four wheeled, one horse farm wagon with a few of them riding in it. As I said, all the rest of them are on foot, but Colonel," the Professor looked wide-eyed around at the small body of defenders, "there are a lot of them, no less then one hundred, I would say.

"My first coronet, Mr. von Jung, has the watch on the road to the Falls by the cliff called Pudding Stone Hall. Mr. Carlin, our second coronet and fiddler, has the watch on the mountain road. All the posts have been kept by my bandsmen in rotating watch after dark as you directed on Saturday night. I have heard nothing from von Jung or Carlin tonight either one way or the other, so I think it is safe to assume that this is the only force we face. But Colonel there *are* a lot of them."

"Very well," said Seamus, "very well."

The sound of another set of footsteps now came from beyond the stables. A man emerged from the woods at the end of the small field there, and trotted up to them, quick and ghostly in the starlight.

"Mr. von Jung," said the Professor.

"Colonel, Professor," the man replied in breathless, fairly fluent English, "I am just coming down from my post where I was having a very good view of the whole area around the lakes. After I hear the Professor's call and I see the torches across the water, I come down to see if I maybe help here because I see no other movement on the road from the Falls."

He stopped, took a few deep breaths, and went on.

"One strange thing though. A while ago, just after I think I hear sound like a shot back at the hotel, I hear and then I could just see two or maybe three people running along the road, going *to* the Falls. I don't sound *Officers Call* because my instructions are to raise the alarm at any approach along the road, coming *from* the Falls. I hope I did right."

"You did fine Mr. von Jung," said Seamus, "thank you." Lejeune and McCain, he thought, and maybe another, heading in the direction of the Falls. Seamus had not been entirely unprepared for such a circumstance and he was hard pressed to keep himself from going off in pursuit of them at that moment.

One battle at a time, he thought.

In the next instant the sound of many rough shod feet hurrying up the shale road bed from the lakes drove all ideas of chasing Lejeune and McCain from his mind.

Torches could be seen bobbing behind the intervening screen of trees and now angry and slurred voices were heard. The menacing buzz of voices increased and blended into an animal growl, low and guttural.

"Professor Smith," said Seamus, "if you will stand behind me please, on my right. Yes, that's correct, thank you. Mr. von Jung do you have a firearm? You do not. Very well, if you will stand behind Sylvester there, thank you."

Professor Smith cleared his throat and spoke.

"By now, Colonel, as you directed, some of my other bandsmen are guarding the doors of the hotel with the few shotguns Mr. Beecher was able to supply us from his gun cabinet."

"Very good, Professor, let us pray that they will not be called upon. Sylvester, extinguish your lantern if you will." No need to target ourselves, thought Seamus.

The light went out and they stood in the dark.

The massed torches came into view to the right front. Seamus immediately picked out the man he knew to be Leander Skhutt astride the big roan, a long firearm resting across the pommel of his saddle. The weapon looked to be a Henry Repeating Rifle, the flat brass receiver gleaming amid the flames.

A knot of armed men surrounded Skhutt as he wheeled into the common. The small spring wagon crunched and squeaked behind them. The driver and another man, both armed, sat in the seat and three gunmen now rose up in the body of the wagon behind them.

The rest of the column followed as Skhutt slowly walked his horse toward the center of Seamus abbreviated line, and fanned out to fill almost the entire common.

Seamus could now see that each and every man, Skhutt included, wore a white hood over his head with two eye holes cut out. The hoods looked to be fashioned from cotton sacks such as those used to contain flour or salt.

Seamus, accustomed to facing bands of brave men who boldly turned their, naked reddened faces to their enemy, felt that he now confronted a horde of goblins, . . . pookahs, . . . non-men. A shiver went through him.

"Halt!" he barked in his best drill master style.

To his mild surprise the mob indeed halted.

Seamus estimated the distance to Skutt's chest at about two rods. There are no bad shots at ten yards range; he mentally repeated the old bushwhacker's credo. Of course, that wisdom worked both ways in face to face encounters, he knew.

"Mr. Leander Skhutt, good morning to you, sir," said Seamus in a loud and cheery voice.

A murmur went through the mob. Seamus guessed that some of the brave lads were taken aback by the fact that the hood did not guarantee anonymity.

All was quiet for a long moment.

A harsh voice came from behind the hood of the mounted man.

"You know so much, mister", he said, "then you know why we're here. We're here for justice!"

The mob roared its agreement.

"For justice!" Skhutt bellowed again "We are here to take Luther Van Bronc, who murdered a white man here on Saturday!"

The mob erupted again, profanities this time spicing the outburst.

When they quieted some, Seamus spoke in a voice for all to hear.

"Justice, is it?" said Seamus, "Well then, your services are no longer required. Justice has been served with regard to Luther. He has been cleared of all charges this very night by Judge Livingston, who arrived here a few hours ago. The murderer, you see Mr. Skhutt, is your associate; Mr. Tompkins, or is he your captain, Captain Brutus Lejeune. Either way, you know who I mean."

"Lies!" screamed the mounted man, "Lies are not going to save you Luther, I see you there."

Luther immediately pushed through from behind Seamus and stood to the front of the line.

"If you want me Reb, here I am," he said evenly.

Seamus spoke out of the corner of his mouth.

"Professor, sound *Assembly.*" he said. God help us, he thought, I hope this works.

"Sir!" came the reply. The professor put his burnished bugle to his lips and let forth with the call. He did not miss a single note.

A loud crack was heard from the roof of the Mountain House and the common was filled with the electric blue-white blaze of the huge searchlight. Skhutt's horse shied sideways and he jerked his hand up to cover the eye holes in his hood. Half the mob did the same while others dropped their heads to avoid the searing beam. Immediately, the double-quick cadence of marching feet was heard on the right and the left. A file of men ran up the trail from the mountain road and another from the woods behind the stables. The limelight glinted on the slanted barrels of their muskets, and here and there a bayonet flashed. The two files formed on the flanks of the line of defenders and, at a word from their leader, faced sharply toward the foe. The leader was Michael Dolan.

"Good morning, Colonel," he said as he positioned himself on Seamus' right, in front of the professor.

"Good morning, Michael," said Seamus, and then to the professor, "Professor if you will, the *Cavalry Charge*."

"The *Cavalry Charge,*" repeated the professor.

As he put his bugle to his lips, Seamus spoke again to Mick Dolan.

"Pre-sent", he said.

"Pre-SENT!" repeated Mick at full voice.

The rumble of at least fifty rifles being snapped to shoulders was nearly drowned by the simultaneous cry of; *"Faughaballagh*!"

The sound of rifle hammers cocking into the ready fire position reached the faces behind the hoods just as the notes of the *Cavalry Charge* echoed across the common.

The thundering hooves of scores of horses rose up from the pines on either side of the mob. Troops of mounted men poured into the common. They hemmed and crowded Skhutt's minions in on each flank. Pistols, carbines and shotguns sparkled in the hands of the riders. Horses whinnied and stomped, leather creaked, accouterments jingled, hammers clicked.

"ANYONE WHO MOVES WILL BE SHOT!" Seamus bellowed. Without taking his eyes off Skhutt, he spoke again in a loud voice.

"Sheriff, to make any shooting we may have to do legal, would you be so kind as to deputized these . . .um . . . volunteers?"

"Done!" said the sheriff.

"Very good," said Seamus in a voice just as certain to be heard by all, "now, you are all under arrest for; . . ."

"Riot, inciting to riot, unlawful assembly and conspiracy to commit murder," announced the sheriff in a deep and resonant voice.

"Thank you, sir. You will all ground your weapons now and your torches as well or I will give the order to open fire without any further warning. Weapons down. Now!"

The thump of a few guns hitting the ground was heard promptly and in another heartbeat more weapons were dropped and then more and then the torches.

Skhutt still held his rifle. He peered around him for a long moment.

"Bastards!" he screamed and drove his spurs into the ribs of his horse. He hauled the reins around violently, and the roan bolted for the trail to the mountain road.

"Sergeant!" said Seamus.

"Colonel!" replied Mick Dolan, his Spencer rifle coming up to his cheek as smooth as silk. The weapon discharged in flame and smoke, Skhutt's horse reared, and he fell backward from the saddle with a high pitched scream, his rifle clattering to the ground beside him. The horse raced away into the night. The report of the shot redounded off the ridges across the lakes. Skhutt, sprawled on the gravel, grunted and moaned. A white cloud of gun smoke hung like an apparition in the illuminated air.

*Click-click* and *click-click*, Mick levered another cartridge into the breach of his repeater and cocked the hammer.

"Good shot, Michael!" said Seamus.

"No better than the shot I made on that rider by Chancellorsville, and the night dark as sin." replied Mick, never taking his sights from his now prostrate target.

Seamus put his finger to his lips.

"Hush, the less said about that one, the better."

Mick uttered a grim little laugh.

"Aye, but this time I only winged him like you said, Colonel." The former sergeant sounded deeply satisfied.

Seamus spoke loudly to the mob.

"Now, there you have it. Someone moved and he was shot, just as I said he would be. Are there any more who want to be shot?"

Seamus waited for a reply. None came.

"Very well then," he went on, "hearing none, we will proceed in a democratic fashion. Those who do not wish to be shot, signify so by raising both hands directly over your heads and keeping them there until further instructed."

A forest of upraised hands appeared before the defenders.

"You!" growled Seamus, "In the wagon, dis-MOUNT!"

The driver and his passengers scrambled down.

"Keeping your hands in the air, those in front of the wagon step back and those behind step forward and form a line at the back of the wagon. Any ONE of you tries anything, and EACH of you pays with his life. Slow and easy . . . MOVE!"

The mob, stumbling and bumping, followed instructions and formed into a ragged line at the back of the wagon.

Skhutt's moans rose and articulated into whining words.

"For gawdsakes will you help me! . . . I think my shoulder's broke . . . I'm bleeding to death . . . Aaaggghhh . . .!"

"Professor, Mick," said Seamus, "See to him, will you. Be sure to take his rifle first, though."

Mick advanced slowly, his Spencer still sighted on Skhutt, Professor Smith following behind.

A tall stocky man with a brush mustache approached Seamus from the right of the line and saluted. A man holding a copper and brass six-keyed trumpet came with him and saluted also. The tall man spoke.

"Colonel, good morning, sir, I am Frank Treacy, former sergeant US Army Regulars, and the owner of the Exchange Saloon in Catskill."

And the Fenian Centre for Greene County, Seamus guessed, but did not say.

"Pleased to meet you," he did say instead while returning the salute, "More pleased than I can express at your timely arrival at our little gathering here this morning."

"Everything went like clockwork, Colonel," said Frank Treacy, smiling broadly, "We waited in the afternoon at my saloon with Mick Dolan and his boys after they came up from Saugerties. When we received the telegram which you had forwarded to us from here in the evening, we headed out. Mick had brought most of the horses for our 'cavalry' from among those he had boarding at his stable. The owners probably won't mind, in fact they probably won't even know about it. One of my boys has a cartage business at the Catskill docks, and he supplied a couple of spring wagons so the 'infantry' could ride in good style.

"Well, sir, I had cavalry scouts riding out in front and before we had gotten to Kiskatom, they came back and told me that we were following the judge and his party in Mr. Beecher's carriage, so we just kept it that way. We were escorting them from a distance and they didn't even know it."

Frank smiled and went on.

"We left our wagons at the base of the Mountain Road so as to proceed more quietly. We got to the top of Long Level and there I had my scouts and skirmishers whistling *The Rising of the Moon*, just as instructed, so that your *vidette,* Mr. Carlin here, would know that we were friends and not the mob. We brought Mr. Carlin in with us and took our positions just as quiet as you please, sir, and waited."

"You did a grand job," said Seamus, "and you have my undying thanks."

He shook hands with each man in turn.

"Now, sergeant, if you would please detail some of your men to collect the weapons which are lying about and put them behind our defensive line here and also some men too to assist with the prisoners at the back of the wagon."

"Sir!" said Frank Treacy and he was off and Mr. Carlin with him.

Seamus walked over to where the lawmen were standing with Luther and Sampson.

"Gentlemen," he said, "I suggest we get these people identified, charged and locked up as soon as possible. We can have our friends on horse-back herd them, I suppose, to your stable Constable."

"Yes, Colonel, that would be best, at least until this afternoon when we can start transporting them down to the jail. Sylvester light your lantern. Sheriff, let's go over to the wagon and start taking names."

The sheriff pulled a notebook and pencil from his coat pocket and the three crossed the common which had so nearly become a killing ground. Torches still burned where they had been dropped. Groups of volunteers moved about cradling there own weapons in their arms, stooping here and there to pick up the guns which had been so readily discarded.

Luther and Sampson stood before Seamus.

"Suppose," said Seamus, "we go and have a word or two with old Reb."

Sampson smiled. Luther did not. He nodded slowly, almost imperceptibly, the blue haze of the searchlight behind him, the flames of the grounded torches reflected in his dark eyes.

The three walked to the spot where Skhutt lay. Professor Smith, his bugle slung from its cord across his shoulder, carried Skhutt's Henry Rifle. He walked back toward the wounded man carrying two of the torches and stuck them in the ground on either side of the recumbent figure. Skhutt's hood had been removed and was rolled up under his head. He moaned.

"Help me, would you, I'm bleeding to death."

Seamus stooped down and looked into the man's eyes. Luther stooped down too, his face next to Seamus' face.

Skhutt recognized Luther and the whites of his eyes bulged around their dark centers.

Luther spoke.

"Hey, Reb, how you feeling?" His voice was like a dagger of ice.

"Oh, Luther it's you," Skhutt's voice trembled, "You gotta help me. You know me and the boys were just looking to scare you is all, on to it. We didn't mean you no harm, honest."

"Is that so, Reb?" said Luther softly.

"Owooooo! Dammit! You don't gotta tear my head off! Ouch! Owooooo!" a voice by the wagon protested in pain.

Seamus called out toward the wagon.

"What is that?"

"All is well, Colonel," the voice of Frank Treacy came back to him, "Private Grogan here is just helping some of Reb's boys get their hoods off."

So, thought Seamus, it's Grogan.

As Seamus watched, another prisoner stepped up to the back of the wagon. Grogan stood with a short barreled shotgun in his left hand and swung his right at his victim. He hit the man on the top of his head, knocked him to the side, and at the same time took full grip of the hood and yanked it off on the backswing.

"OWWW!"

Grogan shook out the hood.

"Got some hair with that one too!" he shouted with glee. "I always knew I should have been a mountain man. Scalping is just the thing for me. And look who we have here. Why if it isn't Clyde Vedder. I always figured you for a secret Know-Nothing. Not so secret anymore, are you Clyde?"

The sheriff wrote the man's name in his book. Grogan threw the hood into the wagon and shoved Clyde toward the burly Flanagan and the giant Sullivan, who quickly searched the man's clothes and pushed him into line alongside the vehicle.

Grogan turned on the next prisoner. The hood was jerked off.

"OOOWWW! Take it easy would you, Grogan." said the man in a pitiable voice.

"What?" yelled Grogan in reply, "Houlihan! Larry Houlihan! An Irishman all hooded up with this bunch. You bloody *amadan*! What were you thinking of, man?"

"Oh, Grogan, I don't know. I had a few drinks with Reb and the next thing I know this sounded like a good idea."

"Tsk, tsk," Grogan sucked his teeth, "Tsk, tsk, Larry, but you know what they say; 'Lie down with dogs . . . ', Only this time you could have got up dead and not just itchy."

Grogan laughed at his own humor.

"Well my lad," he said, shoving Houlihan along, "you will have plenty of time to mull it over in Sing Sing."

He turned to put the hood in the back of the wagon and suddenly started and grinned.

"Hello there," he said and turned and shouted to the recumbent Skhutt, "Hey Reb, this must be yours."

Grogan took up from the bed of the wagon a coil of rope from which dangled a noose. Holding the trophy high he slung his shotgun over his shoulder and scurried across the common to the place were Skhutt lie. He stood over the man the tips of his boots nearly touching his head.

"Here, Reb," he said and crouched down and, none too gently, raised the man's head from the ground enough to slip the noose around his neck. Skhutt moaned and Grogan tightened the knot up to his neck. He fussed with the rope, straightening it on the man's chest, patted it roughly and stood up.

"There now, that will make a lovely cravat for you, Reb," he said looking down into wild inverted eyes, "Very becoming, especially as someone took the time to make a genuine hangman's knot in it."

Grogan looked at Seamus and smiled. The sneer was still there, built into the smile it seemed.

"Morning, Colonel," said Grogan, "Maybe we can save the executioner some trouble . . ."

Skhutt screamed. Howling up to the stars like a wounded dog.

"That will be all . . . for now, Grogan," said Seamus. "Why don't you go back to doing what you were doing."

Grogan sneer-smiled again.

"My duty is my pleasure, Colonel," he quoted, "See you later, Reb." and he was off.

Skhutt screamed again and started to whimper.

"Please, please," he said, "My arm is bleeding, I can feel it."

Seamus and Luther crouched down again. The sleeve of Skhutt's jacket was soaked in blood from shoulder to elbow. Seamus took his flat German knife from his pocket and opened it. The long blade flashed in the torchlight as Seamus passed it across Skutt's face.

"Here, Luther," he said and Luther took the knife. He held it still closer to Skhutt's face. The man's eyes crossed focusing on the cutting edge. Drool formed at the corners of his mouth and dribbled onto the scruffy whiskers of his chin.

"Suppose," said Seamus to Luther, "you . . . slit . . . Reb's . . . sleeve, so we can see what the damage might be."

Luther, with far more delicacy than Seamus thought appropriate, slowly cut away the fabric of the jacket and that of the shirt beneath.

Skhutt moaned.

"Colonel," came a voice from behind. A man was approaching from the direction of the hotel. "Are you and Luther now taking up the practice of my profession?"

Doctor Duboise came across the common to where the two ministers of mercy huddled, stopped and looked down.

"I heard that shot before," he said, "and now all this screaming, and I thought it best that I come and see if someone needed my services. Bring the light, if you please."

Mick Dolan took one of the torches and held it next to Skhutt's head.

The doctor stooped and Luther and Seamus made room for him.

"Oh, Doc; Doc Duboise, you got to help me! I was shot off my horse, I'm bleeding to death!"

"Leander," said the doctor, "I am the physician. I will tell you if you are bleeding to death. Now, shut up."

The doctor opened the cut in the sleeve.

"Doctor," said Seamus, Willie Peters is he . . ."

"The young Mr. Peters will, I believe, make a full recovery, although it is difficult to tell with head injuries. I have left him, for the moment, in the able care of Miz Emily, who, by the bye, is quite a fine nurse. He is still unconscious, but he is breathing regularly and his pulse is strong. Most importantly the cranial case is intact.

"When Willie burst through the door to the casino, his assailant must have pressed the muzzle of the gun directly to the lad's temple. Our young man flinched in the instant, or turned slightly, but either way, the bullet when fired then passed along the right side of his head instead of going through it. Willie has a bad gash and will have a permanent powder burn tattooed, as it were, on the side of his face. His right ear was mostly blown away, which is of no great account since he will likely be deaf in that ear for the rest of what, I hope, will be his long life. I found that the bullet had apparently gone on to penetrate the door of the butler's pantry.

"Willie was fortunate," the doctor concluded, "You were

too, Leander, somebody only just winged you."

Seamus looked up to Mick holding the torch. Mick gave him a very smug grin.

The doctor brought the light closer to the wound. The big Spencer bullet had gouged a deep furrow through the flesh on the outside of the upper arm. The blood was oozing steadily.

"But my shoulder's broke," moaned Skhutt.

The doctor pushed aside the hangman's noose, gave a Seamus look, and pulled open the shirt. He poked and prodded at the discolored skin on Reb's chest and the man screamed. He lifted the injured joint and Skhutt screamed again.

"I would dare say," the doctor was judicious, "that your shoulder may not be broken, but that it is certainly dislocated. Your collar bone however *is* broken, but not from the shot. The joint and bone injuries are the result of your fall, I take it, from a horse. But we do not have arterial bleeding here, so you are not bleeding to death, not yet anyway. I will just clean the wound and apply a bit of lint . . ."

The doctor opened his bag and Seamus stayed his hand.

"Doctor," said Seamus, "I would certainly not tell you your business, but I am sure you have read in the latest medical journals that if, during the war, the surgeons had allowed gunshot wounds to . . . ah . . . to . . . 'bleed out' . . . yes, that's it . . . to 'bleed out' . . . instead of bandaging them prematurely, why then inflammation, sepsis and gangrene would have been avoided in more cases, and fewer amputations would have been necessary. We would not want old Reb here to loose his arm now would we?"

The doctor's head shot up, he looked Seamus in the eye and his response was heated.

"Bleed out!?! Bleed out!?! That is the most ridicule . . ."

"Doctor," Seamus was mild, "Surely a man of your learning has read the articles of which I speak. Luther and I have some questions to ask Mr. Skhutt here and during that time perhaps we can allow his wound to 'bleed out' and cleanse itself while you go back to the bar and both check on Willie and see perhaps if Rolf can provide you with some refreshment. Later, when you come back, in an hour or two, you can bandage the wound. If there is a crisis here sooner than that, we could send for you, sir."

The doctor started again to protest, but then his eyes narrowed.

"Oh yes," he said," 'bleed out', quite so, quite so. Yes, as you say, Colonel, I have read those articles. Yes, I will return in a few hours to see how the ... 'bleeding out' ... is progressing." And the doctor rose and walked away.

"Noooooo!" Skhutt screamed, "Nooooo, doc, you gotta come back, you gotta help me!"

Seamus bent low into Skhutt's face.

"Shut your mouth!" he rasped.

Skhutt was silent.

"It's this way, Skhutt, your are going to answer my questions and tell Luther whatever he wants to know, or you *will* bleed to death."

Skhutt was silent still.

"Or maybe," Seamus went on, "you would like me to let Grogan play with you."

Skhutt made no answer. Seamus looked up.

"Private Grogan!"

Grogan's head snapped around, his lips parted and teeth gleaming in the searchlight's glare.

"Colonel?" he smiled and sneered.

"No," Skhutt moaned, "No, I'll talk, anything ... anything."

"As you were, Private Grogan," Seamus called out still looking into Skhutt's face.

"Why did you try to kill Mrs. Clay at the dock in Catskill and later here on this property?"

"No! No I didn't ..."

"Alright you can talk to Grogan ..."

"No! No, I ... mean I didn't do it on my own. Clay wanted her dead so that he could inherit her company. As her husband, he was her only heir."

"I figured that Skhutt what else?"

"The captain; Captain Lejeune and Mr. McCain had me help Clay because they all belong to the Order and they would have had a share of the profits for the Order and they wanted an import-export company so that they could use it as a cover for the workings of the Order all around the world."

"The purpose of the Order being the persecution of Freedmen at the South and the undermining of the United States, no doubt," said Seamus.

"I guess," said Skhutt, "They made me do it. It had to look like an accident or the inheritance wouldn't go through. The marshal in Georgetown was suspicious of what happened to Mrs. Clay's aunt."

"You murdered that poor woman, Mrs. Clay's only blood kin and only heir besides Clay. You pushed her into the canal, didn't you!"

Skutt answered in even greater panic.

"No! I didn't do that! Clay did it himself! He hated the old lady; *he* pushed her into the canal, not me!"

I doubt it, thought Seamus. Whether he hated her or not, why would Clay do his own dirty work when he had this creature to do it for him. If that were the case, Clay would have murdered Emily himself for he surely hated her too. But, that would be a matter for another time. At the moment, he only wanted to ask Skutt one more question.

"Lejeune and McCain escaped down the Falls Road, where are they headed?"

Skhutt had started gasping for air, he did not respond.

"The longer you take to answer," said Seamus in a matter of fact way, "the closer you get to being dead."

"I hid the horses for them at the abandoned tannery beyond the Kaaterskill Falls, in case anything went wrong tonight. The trail leads to the left of the Falls across from The Laurels. You go down the bank of the creek and then below the next falls, that's Bastion Falls, the trail curves around the side of the mountain going south down into the gorge. That's where the tannery is, under the trees by the side of the creek. Now, please, the doctor . . ."

"To be sure, Reb, to be sure. Just as soon as you answer the questions Luther is going to ask you."

Skhutt moaned.

Seamus stood and Luther with him. He told Luther the questions he wanted him to put to Skhutt, turned and took off running at top speed across the common toward the stables.

"Colonel! Colonel!" Luther called after him, "Wait!"

Seamus ran and ran until he reached the shed on the far side of the horse barn. Sarge was saddled and tethered just where young Frederick Douglass Van Bronc had left him. Seamus swung up into the saddle and pulled the reins around. Horse and rider shot across the common to the trail head. A volunteer sent up a Gaelic yell and jumped to one side to clear the way. The eastern sky was brightening to the color of a gun barrel, the Mountain House silhouetted black, the searchlight shinning like a great morning star at the roof line.

"Colonel, wait! Come back!" Luther's voice was fading in the distance as Sarge and Seamus charged down the trail to the Falls Road. The road bed was just visible in the flat light, but Sarge galloped on instinct with Seamus, blood up, wind in his face, reckless, providing little direction. The dark forest sped by on either side, and the road to the boat house was quickly gained and passed. The South Lake shown in the early morning glow like a vast pool of quicksilver, a layer of mist hanging above the surface. The thud of the hooves rang out hollow in the empty woods. Seamus' unspoken thoughts kept time with the beat as he pictured Lejeune in his mind; He can't get away, He can't get away . . .

The road curved away from the lake to follow the creek toward the Falls. As Seamus came near the place where Skhutt had planted the snake and Emily's horse had run away, a pair of deer stood in the road. They held their ground a moment, turned toward the Falls, reconsidered and leaped into the woods to the right, their white tails up. Seamus turned his head for an instant to watch them springing among the trees along the game trail he had followed on Friday afternoon in his search for Skhutt. It seemed like a year had passed since then.

Pounding on, pounding on, he can't get away, he can't get away . . .

The dawn came on steadily. They neared the bridge Emily's buckboard had by-passed, and Seamus rose up, looking for the sharp right. He reined Sarge in, just slowing now for the turn. White smoke billowed out from the tree line across the creek, the hum of a bullet coming in, the blast of a powder charge and Seamus heard and felt a thump in front of his chest. Sarge fell away from under him.

Seamus cleared the saddle flying through the air. He tucked his chin, landed on the right side of the road and rolled into the trunk of a tree. There was the iron taste of blood in his mouth and he put his hand to his face as he lay by the tree. When he took his hand away he saw his palm full of gore. He felt his jaw, his neck, his chest. He pulled out his shirt tail and looked at the pale skin of his belly. He could find no wound.

A bullet slammed into the tree at his back, the report thundering through the forest. He spun over and lay on his stomach, and buried his head at the base of the trunk. The smell of the damp morning soil was in his nostrils and with it, the sharp scent of his own blood. He turned his head carefully to the left and looked back. His breath caught in his throat.

Sarge lay in the middle of the trail, his head flat on the road bed. A tinny trickle of blood ran down from the hole in the center of the white blaze on his face. His eyes were wide open and starting to loose their light.

Poor Sarge, thought Seamus, poor lad. What have I brought you to? You took the round meant for me.

He raged in himself, and anger seized him. He wanted only to close with his enemy at whatever cost. He reached into his coat pocket for his pistol and came up only with his extra cylinder.

The pistol, he puzzled, where did I leave . . . ? He remembered; I gave it to Luther. Remembered too the sound of Luther's voice just now at the common calling to him to come back, come back. He reached for his knife and recalled that he had given that to Luther as well.

Regardless, he thought, I have to see where the shooter is.

He peeked around the trunk and quickly pulled his head back. He had seen nothing.

He started to look around again and a bullet smashed into the tree in front of is face and sent a shower of bark chips into his eyes.

He rolled on his back and took a deep breathe and then

another. The rage drained away.

This will never do, he thought, if I let him kill me, he will get away. Stop and think . . . think. He took out his handkerchief and cleared his eyes, blinking and rubbing lightly. He now realized that the blood on his face was from the bloody nose which had been restarted by his fall from Sarge's back.

No major injury there, he thought.

He took from his nose the sodden piece of lint which the doctor had given him and replaced it with a corner he ripped from the handkerchief. All the time he kept in his right hand the spare cylinder from his missing pistol. He could not imagine why.

Useless, he thought, regarding the cylinder.

He noticed that blisters had formed on his hand from the fire in the barroom and he was sure that his left arm had been blistered too, but he did not wish to explore under the charred fabric of his coat. His fine Brooks Brothers suit was *hors de combat*. He took further stock of his condition and noted that his left shoulder ached a bit where he had crashed into the tree, but altogether he felt fit enough to fight. He waited and waited, and considered his tactics.

Lejeune is not coming back after me, he concluded, after a few minutes. He would never expect that I was foolish enough to chase after him unarmed. Why should he risk closing with me if he thinks I am armed? Neither would Lejeune think that I would be foolish, no, stupid, enough to come after him alone. No, when he heard the hoof beats coming, he hung back to pick off the lead rider to slow down the pursuit, just as he hung back in the casino to shoot Willie Peters. When he saw it was me, which he undoubtedly did through his telescope sight, he stayed a little longer and tried two more shots. But he is the one who is in a hurry, he wants to get to those horses and out of this neighborhood and fast. So *I* have the advantage.

The absurdity of that notion, made Seamus snort through his nose at himself and then to wince in pain. His eyes filed with tears and he wiped them away.

I have the advantage, he told himself again, and Lejeune is gone now.

He stuck his head around the trunk and pulled it back in. He repeated the exercise two more times and then dashed from behind the tree and down into the bed of the creek. He ran splashing through the shallow stream and up the far bank where he found another broad tree to hide behind. He was now on the same side of the creek as the shooter and had drawn no more fire. He started to feel more confident and reminded himself to be cautious for a change. He peeked around the trunk and pulled back, looked around again for a little longer time and could see no movement in the woods. He pulled his head back.

The sky was turning salmon pink and shafts of orange light glanced among the trees. Seamus considered that he could make use of the growing brightness. He searched in his pockets for his spy glass and remembered that he had given it to Emily on the night before.

I have come well equipped on this campaign, he thought, I shall have a word with the quartermaster about the lack of supply.

He peered around the tree trunk again and then ran to the next tree along the bank, and then to the next. He continued the process until he saw that he was approaching the Laurels. He paused and scanned the woods to his front. All was still.

As still as the first day of creation, he thought. He ran crouching to the next tree, a towering pine.

A single raven croaked in the top of the tree and flew off towards the Falls. Seamus watched it fly and with his finger traced a cross three times over his heart in response to the ill omen of the lone dark bird.

Ahead, the woods opened onto the hotel grounds. He tarried longer behind his tree. He could make one more dash to a tree and then he would be without cover. The wide sky above the gorge of the Kaaterskill Falls glowed coral, the vivid color deepening to purple near the ridge of the mountains.

I shall have to go down into the bed of the creek to get cover, he thought. That will give Lejeune, if he is still lingering about, the advantage of the high ground, but I have no choice. Better poor cover than no cover at all, and I have to cross over the creek here in any event to follow the trail that leads down below the Falls and to the tannery.

He ran in a crouch to the next and last tree along the bank. It barely concealed his body and that only if he stood sideways. He slowly looked around at the hotel and its grounds, giving particular attention to the porches and balconies where early morning shadows clung. He examined the gazebo and saw no movement behind the latticed screens of its railings.

He looked across the stream. No signs of life appeared among the hemlocks which grew thick on the steep, high flank of the mountain, but the sun had not yet begun to infiltrate the dark abode of the evergreens.

A troop of cavalry and a battery of artillery could hide in there, he thought, and I would not be able to see them at this hour.

He hesitated a bit longer and looked down to the brink of the Falls. He thought it remarkable that although the Kaaterskill Falls was higher than Niagara, the cliff at its top was no wider than perhaps one rod. This time of year, with the water low, he thought, a man could easily hop across the narrow channel at the center of the cliff through which the creek flowed to become the Falls itself. One step to the right of that channel, however, began the singular glory of the Falls as it plunged nearly two hundred feet. dispersing into a long white veil of water. Clouds of thin vapor now rose from the gorge and turned pink in the morning light.

On the far side of the cliff, a tremendous blocky boulder stood. It was the size, at least of the gazebo on the near side which in a sense it seemed to balance, with the channel of the Falls as the fulcrum.

Seamus resolved to duck down the bank and run parallel to it to cross the stream at the cliff, vaulting the channel and not stopping until he reached the cover of the great boulder on the far side.

He looked about once more, took a deep breath, let it out, took another, and ran for the bank. He dropped down to the edge of the creek, sprinted to the cliff, turned sharp left onto the flat and ran for the channel. He looked down to hop the channel and was struck a violent blow on the left side of his head. He fell on his back into the knee deep water above the channel, while a peel like thunder boomed and echoed. Blood ran into his left eye stinging and blinding. His head pounded with pain. He rolled over on all fours and struggled to rise. He gained his feet, the world swimming, and struggled to rise. He turned his good eye toward the end of the cliff. A small cloud of smoke hung before the boulder. A man stepped from behind the massive rock.

It was McCain. He spoke not a word, but raised his pistol in his right hand, his left hand in his pocket, as if he were at a shooting gallery.

Seamus rose up on his feet, still double over, knees bent, legs shuddering. He half turned and looked straight into McCain's frozen blue eyes.

*Click.*

McCain's pistol misfired. He cocked it again without hesitation.

Seamus was already whipping around his right hand out from his side. He put his whole body into it and let fly with the fully loaded spare pistol cylinder. It hit McCain square in the face. Blood spurted and McCain's hands jerked convulsively upward. The pistol flew from his grip and arced and tumbled through the sunlit air sparkling gold, like a meteor. It landed with a splash in the pool upstream of the cliff.

The force of his throw put Seamus off balance and he fought to stay upright. His heels found the slippery moss of the flat creek bed before the channel and he fell on his back in the water. His head went under; he breathed water and came up coughing and spitting. He struggled to keep his head above the surface, but felt himself weakening.

He watched immobile as McCain thrashed in the pool for his lost weapon. McCain tore at the water coming up with long green streamers of slimy moss. He searched and searched and then abruptly stopped. He looked over to Seamus and bent down again with his hands in the water. This time he came up with a big round stone, and started slogging across the creek toward his prey.

Seamus propped on his elbows, just barely keeping his nose and mouth above water. He clung to consciousness, but otherwise could no longer move. In a detached way, he considered how much McCain's stone resembled a thirty-six pound cannon ball. McCain came closer, holding the stone to his chest, the blood running down his face onto his white shirt. He stood over Seamus, blotting out the pink and blue sky. Silently, he raised the stone above his head with both hands.

Seamus felt himself going . . . going, the light fading. McCain straightened his elbows the stone directly over his head.

This, thought Seamus, is a real killer. No wasted words. He isn't even angry. Just going about his business.

McCain took one step forward and his feet went up in the air. He fell back into the channel.

Seamus followed with his eyes and saw the man's two boots, one with a clump of bright green moss stuck to the heel, tip heavenward as McCain went over the falls on his back, head down-most. Never a sound escaped from his lips.

Heartened, Seamus found the strength to make one more effort to right himself. He succeeded only in rolling onto his stomach before his arms gave out entirely. His face now underwater, his head clouded and throbbing, the light current pushed him toward the channel. He felt himself again paralyzed, unable to move. He held his breath as long as he could. He knew it made no difference. He could feel death coming closer and closer, hooves pounding.

Is it the death coach approaching, he wondered, the Coach naMbhan? Is it death on horseback?

He could hear the hoof beats quite clearly now.

And behold, he thought, a pale horse.

His lungs screaming, he drifted toward the brink.

Confetior Deo, he thought, Oh my God, I am heartily sorry. .

Against his best efforts to stop it, his breath came slowly out his mouth in bubbles. The water tasted earthy. He opened his eyes under the water. All was green. The moss shrouded his face.

He closed his eyes.

# XII

# An Awakening

Seamus Delaney awoke in hell. Hell was green, he was surprised to see. Not dark either, but bright and sunny and green. Hell was Antietam at the Bloody Lane with the green September fields of Maryland rolling before and behind the rebel line.

As always, he was lying on his belly before the Sunken Road. Another volley erupted from the road, blue-white clouds of smoke and orange fire dancing along the rail fence. The muzzles of a thousand muskets flamed. Bullets hummed, and shot and shell screamed and whistled above. Explosions of artillery pounded and pounded inside his head, sucking the breath from his lungs. Oppressive heat, he sweltered parched.

So, he thought, this is hell. Is it hell for every sinner or is it just for me?

He looked to his left. Something was different. Felim was not lying there with dead eyes open to the sky.

No, of course not, he thought, Felim; good man that he was, is not here. He is in heaven.

He looked around some more and saw no one that he knew, saw no faces, just shadows rushing here and there huddled about in clumps.

This is hell for me, he thought, the same over and over, for ever and ever.

As always, Seamus looked to the front. At the center of the line of gray clad shadows the rebel officer raised his arm, sword in hand. The gold glittered on his sleeve and Seamus, as always, raised his pistol, braced it, took steady careful aim.

Hell for murderers, is it? he wondered. Condemned to kill the same victim again and again into eternity, murder mounting on murder, guilt upon guilt, the debt of retribution compounding without end.

He peered along the barrel of his .44 Remington, put the tip of the front sight blade below the left eye of the gaunt face. The breeze blew the thin, fair beard and moustache of the handsome young officer.

I must kill Emily's husband, or whoever this is, over and over . . .

He squinted and the face beneath the gold trimmed cap changed. Gone were the blonde beard and hollow cheeks. Emily's sweet face looked back at him, pert and charming in the stiff uniform, the collar far too high for her.

This is hell, he raged in himself. Throughout eternity, I must kill the kind, gentle lady I . . . I love. He closed his eyes.

He dropped the pistol from his hand and rolled on his back.

"No," he said aloud, "I will not...I will not."

He put his hand to his aching head. Rested his palm on his forehead.

"No," he said and opened his eyes. Emily was crouching over him. The gold trim on her cap bright in the clear afternoon sunlight, she looked down into his eyes. He raised his voice.

"No!" he yelled, "I love you. I will not kill you . . . I will not . . . I love you!"

"Of course you will not kill me," she said with a nervous little laugh, "hush now."

As he looked up at her, she changed. She wore no cap, but had a yellow ribbon in her hair. She was not wearing a uniform, but her green dress with the high yellow collar. Her cool hand was on his forehead.

"Hush," she said again, blushing. She looked across Seamus as he lay on the bed.

"Well, well," said a voice filled with mirth, "the dead arose and showed themselves to the living."

Seamus turned his head to the left. Doctor Duboise returned his glance, peering at him through his pince-nez. He smiled broadly, but his eyes were flat, serious. Seamus rolled his head back. It felt as though his skull had been infused with liquid pain. He looked up and saw not the blue Maryland sky, but a textured tin ceiling. Two tall windows stood beyond the foot of the bed in which he lay and the sun shone brightly. He was covered up to his chin by a heavy quilt and he was uncomfortably warm.

"Water . . . please," he said. His voice was hoarse. Emily brought a cup to his lips. The water was cool and sweet.

He was in a room of the Mountain House he was sure. Although it seemed familiar, he was certain he had never been in the room before. It was a large room and several other people were in it with him.

His eyes focused at the foot of the bed. Mr. Beecher stood there.

"Mr. Beecher," said Seamus. He could think of nothing else to say.

"Oh! My boy!" said Mr. Beecher, "Colonel, thank God you have recovered. We have been so concerned all this time that you . . . that you might not regain consciousness.

"Thank God!" he said again.

Seamus looked to Mr. Beecher's right. The Reverend and Mrs. Van Wyck stood side by side, both smiling.

"Our prayers have been answered," said the good preacher.

Next to the Van Wycks stood the Van Broncs. Seamus thought that this was an appropriate arrangement; the two Vans together. It occurred to him that this last thought was rather nonsensical and he wondered if he were now awake or dreaming. His head ached as he rolled it on the pillow to focus on Mr. and Mrs. Van Bronc. He decided that he was probably not dreaming.

"Luther, Sarah," he said.

Sarah smiled, tears in her eyes.

"Colonel," she choked.

Something was different about Luther. He was smiling broadly. Seamus had never seen that before. Luther had a fine, strong, open smile.

"Good afternoon, Colonel," said Luther, "It surly is good to talk to you again."

"Afternoon?" said Seamus, "It is afternoon?"

"Yes, Seamus," said Emily.

How I love hear her say my name, he thought.

"It is afternoon," she continued, "and you are in Mr.

Beecher's bedroom in his suite in the Mountain House."

"Yes," said Seamus. He was filled with a sudden transcending emotion of relief and joy, an emotion he had felt before; after the other battles he had survived.

Well, he thought this is fine! Sparred again! Still alive! As the black folks say; Thank you, Jesus! Sparred yet again. This time to renew the hunt for Lejeune.

He pushed the quilt down to his waist and started to sit up. The doctor stayed his hands and pressed him down gently.

"Slow and easy, Colonel," he said, "Easy and slow, not too much all at once."

Seamus turned to the doctor. His head hurt not nearly so much now, it seemed to him.

Standing next to the doctor's chair was Michael Dolan. He was dressed in his uniform and Seamus appraised him quickly with the eye of an inspecting officer.

Mick wore his original 69th Regiment jacket, neatly mended and brushed. The dark blue blouse was highlighted by the collar, up-pointed cuffs and down-pointed sergeant's stripes, all rendered in bright green. His scarlet sash was wound about his waist, the shining black leather belt hooked about it. The trousers were sky blue replacements for the old gray ones. He was nicely turned out, his brass buttons and belt plate gleaming. He wore the Medal of Honor over his heart. The bronze inverted star fairly glowed, the red, white and blue ribbon stood out in cheerful contrast to the dark of the soldier's blouse.

For an instant, Seamus thought that he had lapsed again in to the Land of Dreams.

No, Michael was real. Seamus felt his thoughts coming clear now. The pain which had filled his head was, he was sure, now subsiding and being replaced by questions, many of them.

"Sergeant," said Seamus, "Do you have a report for me?"

Mick started and then smiled.

"Colonel," he said, "it is plain to see that you are getting back to your old self again."

He stiffened to the position of attention.

"Sir!" he said, "Beg to report!"

"Report!" said Seamus

"Sir, immediately you left the common, we finished collecting the arms and put them in the little farm wagon. Then we started the prisoners toward the constable's stable with most of our cavalry escorting them. By now they have been taken down the mountain to Catskill, where they have been crammed into the jail. The judge said that their cases should keep the bench and bar of Greene County busy for some time to come."

Seamus was amazed that the prisoner transport to Catskill had been accomplished so quickly. The sergeant went on.

"When Luther here was finished questioning Skhutt, Sampson went and brought the doctor back and Miz Emily came with him to help. Just as the doctor was getting started with Skhutt and I was getting some of the remaining mounted fellows together to follow you down the Falls Road, we heard a shot and then two more.

Miz Emily ran up to me, Colonel, and asked me where you were and I told her you had gone after Lejeune. Without another word, the lady, hoop skirt and all, jumped up into the little wagon, took the reigns and the whip, and off she went down the Falls Road like blazes!"

Seamus turned to Emily. She averted her eyes and the color again rose up her cheeks.

"Well, sir," Mick was saying, "in no time she was out of sight and I took one of the horses and went after her and a few of the boys coming along after me.

"Miz Emily was not hard to follow, leaving a trail like she was of firearms tumbling out of the wagon behind her. We never did catch up to her though, until we came to poor old Sarge lying in the road . . ."

A chill went over Seamus at the mention of Sarge. He pictured the horse in his mind; the wide open eyes, the lolling pink tongue, the blood . . .

Mick continued, "Miz Emily had stopped where Sarge was lying and she was standing up in the wagon, looking around her into the woods and calling your name, sir."

Seamus again looked back to Emily. This time she returned his glance, looking very directly into his eyes. She took his hand in hers.

"As soon," said Mick, "as we came up behind the wagon, we heard another shot by the Falls. Miz Emily took her seat, lashed the horse and was off again heading for the bridge, it being just there, and we were off again in her trail. But, sir, she never slowed for the bridge, she did not even take the turn, she just slipped past the bridge railing and down the bank and into the creek bed!"

The consternation was still ringing in Mick's voice and flashed in the look he gave her.

Emily replied in a low and reasonable voice.

"I do not know why I did that," she said, "except that I had done it before and perhaps thought that it would be quicker than taking the road."

She smiled a small smile.

"I could not believe what Miz Emily was doing," said Mick, "even as I watched her do it, but for some reason, I jumped the bridge right behind her and down the bank and into the creek I followed with some of the boys as unwise as myself coming in too. The more educated lads took the road and raced along behind us up on the farther bank.

"We crashed and dashed through the creek bed, Miz Emily up ahead at full tilt. When the top of the Falls came into view and Miz Emily showed no sign of slowing, I just started to say my prayers. But then, in the last little pool before the Falls, she pulled the horse sharp around to where it stumbled and the wagon skidded sideways, and she jumped out and into the water, hoop skirt and all . . ."

"That dress is now ruined, I am afraid," Emily interjected.

Mick gave her an incredulous look and continued.

"Miz Emily hit the water running, in a manner of speaking. I didn't know what to think with her charging straight at the brink of the Falls, but then I saw where she was going. There you were, Colonel, face down in the water. I thought it was all over for you."

Mick paused, cleared his throat, and went on.

"But Miz Emily, she pulled your head up out of the water just as you were half drifted into the channel into the Falls. Then I jumped down off my horse and we got you over to the bank.

The boys got one of the rain barrels from the Laurels and we rolled you on your stomach over it and got the water out of you. And then we put you on your back and Miz Emily put her lips to yours and . . ."

"It's the new artificial respiration . . . ," Emily interjected.

" . . . and she breathed life into you, sir, while I pressed your chest and pumped your arms. Between us we got you breathing again. We put you in the back of the wagon with Miz Emily. She ripped off the hem of her skirt and held it up to your head to staunch the bleeding. We got you back here and Doc Duboise commenced to work on you. And here we are. In the end I guess it was a good thing that Miz Emily skipped the road and went right down the stream, in another instant you would have been over the Falls like McCain. She really saved you, Colonel."

Seamus again rolled his head on his pillow toward Emily.

"Turn about is fair play, is it not Colonel?" she said smiling.

At length Seamus replied.

"It is indeed," he said, "thank you for saving my life."

The room was silent a long moment. Outside a mourning dove cooed; long slow notes hanging in the air below the windows.

Mick broke the silence.

"Speaking of McCain, Colonel, we have all been wondering how he came to be at the bottom of the Falls, where we found him and you at the top with a gunshot wound to your head and half drowned."

Seamus recounted his movements after he left the common. He spoke in fits and starts as the memory of the morning came back to him. He did not mention why exactly he did not have his pistol with him at the time.

As the story unfolded, Mick got redder and redder in the face. When Seamus was finished, Mick spoke. It was clear that he was working hard to remain civil.

"Colonel," he said, "would you ever in the future not put yourself into situations where you have only the slimmest chance of coming out at the other end alive? You did the same thing in the war, and if you keep it up, sooner or later you will find that your… ."

"Mick," Seamus spoke soothingly.

". . . that your nine lives have expired . . ."

"Mick," Seamus tried to speak above his friend. Mick spoke the louder.

". . . each and every one, and that you are dead. And then it will be too late for anybody to do anything to help you, and, and . . ."

"Mick, Mick," Seamus mollified, as the sergeant sputtered to a stop. "Mick I promise to be more careful from now on. But to finish your report, please tell me what success you may have had in picking up Lejeune's trail below the Falls."

The sergeant paused a few beats to indicate that he was aware of the ploy to change the subject from that of Seamus' recklessness.

"Right," he said finally, "once we got you back here and under the care of the doctor, we joined up with Luther and Sampson and headed back down to the Falls. Oh, that reminds me . . ."

He reached under his blouse, pulled out a big, sleek revolver and held it with the muzzle pointed to the floor. He turned it sideways in his hand for Seamus' inspection.

It had a slim, gracefully curving handle with finely checkered blond wood grips. The finish was of darkly blued steel carved intaglio overall with floral rosettes, vines and leaves and the engraving inlaid with gold. There was no lever under the barrel, but instead a plunger device for clearing the fired chambers of the spent metallic shells. Seamus knew that he had seen the revolver, however briefly, before.

"This must be the pistol McCain shot you with," said Mick, "When we went back and crossed the pool above the Falls on horseback, I spotted it under the water just on the edge of some drifting moss. The sun was higher then and happened to be shinning right on it. It was easy to see from up on a horse, sparkling away there under the water, and a beautiful piece it is. It's a Le Faucheux, .12 millimeter made in France and it's a pin fire with copper cartridges. One chamber had been fired and the hammer was resting on another cartridge. The primer on that cartridge was dented, but the round had not gone off, thank God.

I turned the cylinder back to rest on the empty shell for safety."

Mick laid the gun on the washstand by the bed.

"That goes to prove my point, does it not Mick," said Seamus, "that these metal cartridges are not reliable enough yet to the trusted."

He could not resist prodding his friend. The debate between them concerning the benefits of metallic cartridges versus individually loaded cap and ball charges went back to their earliest days together in the war.

"Colonel, for a young man you are awfully old-fashioned. You know as well as I that during the war many of the boys would swear by metal cartridges, particularly pin fire rounds. Sure, they have been in use all over the world for years and are constantly being improved. My Spencer has never failed me. That this round didn't go off only proves that, as usual, you have had more luck than you deserve and that your guardian angel has again been worn out trying to keep you alive."

Mick sighed.

"But to continue," he said, "I picked up the revolver, Luther and Sampson guided us down the trail to the east side of the Falls and we saw where McCain had landed," Mick frowned and shook his head, "in due course we found the tracks of one man on foot. We followed the tracks down below Bastion Falls and down the side of the mountain to the edge of the creek, where the ruins of the old tannery are.

"Just as Skhutt had said, two horses had been there, plenty of sign of that. But by the time we got there the horses were gone. The hoof prints lead into the creek. Lejeune is a real fox. We thought he might have followed the creek down stream for a bit. That made sense, it was quicker than going up hill, and we figured he would want to get toward the river valley, to the better and faster roads as quick as he could rather than go up stream into the wilderness. There was very little sign to follow, of course, as long as he stayed in the stream, but there was some. After a while the tracks went onto the old creek road and that is where we found that we were following the trail of only one horse. He must have led the spare horse, the one meant for McCain, behind him as he went down the stream and then whacked it on the rump and sent it trotting down the old road towards Palenville. After that we figured he must have doubled back up the stream and stayed in the creek bed back by the old tannery and followed the other branch of the creek back up past Haines Falls. By the time we had worked that out, the trail was growing cold. We found his tracks just once, when he diverted through the woods on a deer trail to get around the Haines Falls gorge, but then he was back in the creek and we lost him for good. We later heard that a lone rider fitting Lejeune's description was seen by a bark cutter crossing through Stony Clove Pass near the standing rock they call the Devil's Tombstone."

Very good, thought Seamus, we know what direction he is headed. We will have to start right away while there is still light. Seamus was reasonably sure that he felt up to the pursuit. Something was puzzling him however.

"Mick," he said, "you look grand in your uniform," he smiled at the sergeant, "but would you mind telling me why you are wearing it?"

"I put it on for the parade, Colonel, we all did, all the boys who are veterans wore their uniforms. I just now came up from marching in the parade . . ."

"Parade?" said Seamus, "What parade might that be?"

"Why, the Fourth of July Parade in Saugerties, Colonel."

"The Fourth of July," said Seamus weakly. "You mean that it is not now Monday afternoon?"

"No, sir it is not. It is Wednesday, July Fourth."

Mick took Seamus' watch from his own waistcoat pocket and opened it. *The Garryowen* tinkled thinly in the big room. Mick read the watch.

"Wednesday," he repeated, and handed the open watch to Seamus, "at half-past three in the afternoon. Your watch had stopped, got wet when you were in the creek. I took it to the watchmaker in Saugerties. It's all fixed now."

Seamus looked at the face, closed the cover and held the watch to his chest. He closed his eyes.

"Where would the road through the Stony Clove lead," he asked, "into the wilderness you said?"

"Yes, sir," Mick replied, "but before long to Phoenicia and then south to Kingston…"

"And from there to a river steamer," Seamus interrupted, "and thence to any place in the wide world. And Lejeune has been gone since early Monday morning and this is Wednesday afternoon."

"Yes, sir," said Mick.

"He is gone and he has gotten away." said Seamus.

"Yes, sir, he has."

The doctor put his hand on Seamus brow.

"Of course," he said, "you could not have known how long you were unconscious. You took an awful blow to the head; the bullet grazed you very closely. Miz Emily and I were just now changing your dressing when you started to show signs of coming back among us, so we sent for all here present in the room to come and bid you welcome."

Doctor Duboise took a closer look at Seamus' left temple. He patted the wound with a feathery touch of his fingertips.

"Yes," he said, "you are healing nicely, little inflammation, the stitches are holding . . . "

He looked across his patient to Emily.

"Lovely work, Miz Emily," he said, "lovely work."

He spoke again to Seamus.

"You are more in this lady's debt than you know, Colonel."

He held up his crippled right hand.

"With my souvenir of Gettysburg here, I had to rely on her hands to do the actual stitching on your wound while I provided some guidance. She did not need much guidance. So your new scar will match very nearly the one on he other side of your head; *your* souvenir of Gettysburg. That wound as you recall, was half closed by myself and in my own inimitable style. Although it was Miz Emily's fine hand which closed this new wound, that too has been done very much in my style, albeit, even at my best, I doubt that I could have come near to matching the delicate stitch which the young lady produced."

Emily spoke.

"I grew up with needle point samplers and embroidery. This was really just a simple straight line. In my days and nights at

Chimoborazo, I became acquainted with wounds of all kinds."

"The doctor is right," said Seamus, "I am deeply in your debt."

"No, Seamus, you are not," Emily replied in an instant, her eyes fixed on his, "there can be no debt between us. All is freely given and all freely received."

The mourning dove again cooed outside the window.

This time the doctor broke the spell.

"To complete my medical report of our action of the other night, I will inform you Colonel that Willie Peters is doing very well indeed. He regained consciousness rather more quickly than you did, and has been staying here at the Mountain House as a guest of Mr. Beecher in another room on this floor. He will be delighted to hear of your awakening. In fact, as soon as we finish changing your dressing, Willie is to have his changed as well and Miz Emily and I will be off to tend to that task. We will bring him the good news.

"Oh, yes, the burns to your left forearm and right hand, although they resulted in some blistering, are healing very well, and we are no longer dressing them, but leaving them open to the air."

Emily placed a small bowl on Seamus chest and the doctor dipped a cloth into it and dabbed the stitches. The faint, familiar scent of dilute carbolic acid drifted in the room. He took a dry cloth and pressed it lightly to the side of Seamus' head.

As he worked, he spoke again.

"I tended to Skhutt, and he is on the mend now down at the jailhouse in Catskill. We want his arms to be in good condition for his next career which will be at Sing Sing breaking rocks with a sledge. Unless, that is, his career is brought up short by the outcome of the legal proceedings which are about to commence against him in Georgetown."

The doctor pressed a cold, damp pad against the stitches and continued.

"It seems," he said, "that Sheriff Cass telegraphed the city marshal there and that worthy gentleman has had lingering suspicions. He was very interested in learning what role Skhutt may have played in the tragedy of Miz Emily's aunt. He is reopening the investigation."

A shadow of pain passed over Emily's face at the mention of her aunt's death, and she spoke as she passed a strip of clean cotton to the doctor.

"After Luther told me that Skhutt was the drunken man in Catskill who caused the stampede, and the one who put the snake in the road, and after I got a close look at him, I realized that I had seen him in the company of Fenton and McCain in Georgetown. I told Sheriff Cass that now I recall seeing him in the crowd of onlookers on that terrible morning when my poor aunt's body was recovered from the canal. There had always been a question as to why she had even been in that quarter of the town. And too, I remembered that it had been Fenton who suggested that I go for a drive on Friday afternoon. He said he would be busy talking business with McCain. He knew that I love to drive, and he ordered the buckboard from the stable for me when I told him I wanted to go and see the Falls."

Emily stood and held up Seamus' head with one hand, while with the other she wrapped a bandage around it. She smelled to Seamus like roses.

"There we are," said the doctor.

"Finally," he went on, "I had yet another patient Monday after the smoke cleared as it were.

"On that morning Major Savage made an excellent effort at drinking himself to death. As it turned out, that package he had sent the innocent young Terwilliger to pick up for him at Brenner's contained a stoneware jug of applejack, the brandy which they distill up here in the mountains from hard cider. It appears that Scipio had grown very concerned about Savage's condition and his increasingly maniacal behavior and was trying to limit the man's access to spirits. Few are wilier than the drunkard in his pursuit of his heart's desire. The major clearly was able to obtain the jug without Scipio's knowledge.

"Whether he drank the entire contents of the vessel simply because he could not stop, or because he had lost track of what he had consumed, or whether he wanted, as it were, to get rid of the evidence before Scipio discovered him or whether he was just tired of living, I cannot say for certain. I am inclined, however, to believe the latter was his motive.

"In any case, he must have drunk the entire jug at one sitting in his room before noon on Monday, when he was thought to be sleeping. When Scipio found him, he was very near death with a weak and thready pulse. But, as I once before observed, the major must have the constitution of an ox because he is still alive. I had him admitted to the sanitarium in Saugerties and he is there yet. The last I checked, he had not yet regained consciousness, but I will look in on him tomorrow afternoon. The constant Scipio is, of course, there with him, by his side at every hour. I do not know if that man ever sleeps."

The Reverend Mr. Van Wyck spoke.

"Indeed," said the dominie, "I cannot imagine how one could be blessed with a more loyal friend than a man such as Scipio. He is certainly not simply a servant to the major or he would have just done the major's bidding without any thought of the consequences, but his friend's best interests are ever uppermost Scipio's heart. And here the poor man was unable to communicate, in any deep sense, with virtually any person at this establishment.

"When, through Sarah, Scipio found that Mrs. Van Wyck and I are fluent in his language, he sought us, and poured out his fears for the major's welfare. You see, early in the war, my wife and I were among the first to travel to Beaufort and to Hilton Head in South Carolina, to continue the work of Abolition after the Army, the Navy and the Marines had cleared the rebels from the coastal plantations there. We set about God's work of educating the liberated slaves to thereby hasten their entry into full membership in the American community.

"We found, however, that our first task was to educate ourselves in the Gulla language so that we could converse with them. And this we did. How well I remember the day when the privilege fell to me of reading to our assembled students the Emancipation Proclamation in their own language, in the shade of a great live oak in the summer of '63; the Spanish moss wafting in the light breeze . . ."

The dominie was lost in the reverie of his reminiscences. His wife brought him back.

"Schyler, dear," she said, "you digress."

His face reddened.

"Yes, my dear, I digress. Ahem, to the point at hand, when Scipio came to us, as we walked along the drive on Saturday, and asked if we could help in some way, I agreed to speak to the major. Scipio had tried his best to keep his friend away from ardent spirits, but to no avail. So, I went to the lounge that afternoon along with Mrs. Van Wyck and . . . well . . . well you yourself, Colonel, were in the doorway when I departed from the interview. I tried to bring the word of God to the major to get him to repent of his destructive and wicked ways and he became so . . . so aggravating in his responses . . . mocking me, mocking the Lord Himself . . . well I . . . I . . ."

"You lost your temper, dear," Mrs. Van Wyck assisted her husband in his account.

"Yes," he said, "I lost my temper and that in front of others. You, Colonel, and Mr. McCain as well, who fled the lounge as I became more heated in my discourse. I must confess I became embarrassed and then even melancholy about the incident and my whole calling . . . I questioned myself; was I being grandiose and self-righteous in my ministry? That was never my intent when I started on my vocation. Have I become used, perhaps, to dealing with those who wanted to be saved or who had already been saved? Had I been, as it is said, 'Preaching to the choir'? Was there depth to my own faith if, when confronted by resistance to my efforts, I immediately began damming and cursing the recalcitrant man.? He is after all just a poor suffering sinner in need of my prayers and not my curses.

"Then on Sunday we received a telegram with the horrid news that . . . that. . ."

Tears filled the minister's eyes and he choked. Mrs. Van Wyck finished her husband's sentence.

"That the wife of our parish sexton and one of his dear little daughters had succumbed to the cholera which grips New York City and is now infecting, as well, the City of Brooklyn where we live."

The dominie recovered himself and continued.

"When I heard the news, it was revealed to me that I had

come up here to the healthful mountains with the intention of staying all summer, not because I deserved a vacation, as I told myself, but because I feared the pestilence of the city and wanted to shield myself and my wife from it."

"Dear," said his wife, "you do not have to . . . "

"Yes, my dear, I must. I must confess to you all that while preaching the word of God, I was like unto the whitened sepulchers, which indeed appear beautiful outwardly, but are within full of dead men's bones and all uncleanness.

"My place was with that poor gentle woman and her dear family, and not hiding in the very lap of luxury here at the Mountain House. And God showed this so clearly to me again and again; a man shot down before me at a service I was conducting, and all the sacrifice and danger the Colonel and all here have put themselves to in order to help each other. Then while the court was in session the other night, the madman; Lejeune burning the place, shots fired that night. What was I hiding from? There is no safe place this side of eternity. I did not start out such a coward. I used to rush to the forefront in all Abolition work in years gone by, no fear to go against the Fugitive Slave Law, and then to the battlefront itself.

"It came to me that I had grown spiritually fat as the pastor of a well established church in civilized Brooklyn, but when those of my flock were in need;, I had deserted them. As long as this plague rages I should be with them to help them in their physical distress and in their spiritual need as they pass out of this life. Therefore, tomorrow, I return to my parish, come what may. I thank you all. The pluck and courage you have displayed has brought me back to my senses. Luther's life, Miz Emily's life, the Colonel's life and my very soul have all been saved this past weekend by the Power of the Eternal through the agency of those in this room."

Mrs. Van Wyck took her husband's arm.

"I thank you for your honesty, reverend," said Seamus, "none of us are perfect.

"You have just reminded me that before McCain appeared in the lounge that afternoon, I saw him coming down the stairs. I did not realize it at the time, of course, but he must have had

Lejeune's carbine hidden beneath the coat he had draped across his arm. Lejeune had not gone to his own room on the ground floor after he feigned illness and begged off helping to carry Clay's body. No, the doctor, saw him going upstairs. He hid the weapon, using the stolen keys in the empty room next door to McCain's room. Later, after the occupied rooms had been searched, McCain returned the gun to Lejeune's room."

Mr. Beecher spoke.

"And I must thank you as well Mr. Van Wyck," he said, "for volunteering to officiate, on such short notice, at the joint burial of the late Mr. Clay and the late Mr. McCain in the graveyard behind the Methodist Church in Haines Corners Monday afternoon. Your ministrations uplifted and assuaged the pain which has oppressed many of us these last days. I am sure that I can speak for Miz Emily as well as for myself in attesting to the fact that your thoughtful words helped to rest our hearts and minds as we stood with you at the graveside"

Three people at a funeral for two dead men, Seamus thought to himself, and one of them the preacher. He could not help but feel that it was a larger turnout by three than the decedents deserved. He fought to put such un-Christian thoughts from his mind. He was only partly successful. An urgent thought came suddenly to him. He turned toward Luther.

"Luther," he said, "were you able to ask Skhutt the questions we had discussed?"

"I was, Colonel, and before I report, I wish to say that I believe his answers were as truthful as we may expect to receive from a man such as he. He got more cooperative the longer I questioned him. First, he said that he had no idea of where Lejeune and McCain planned to go beyond the old tannery. They had given him no information about any planned escape route they may have had. Second, he admitted, as you said he would, that it was he who galloped down the mountain ahead of you on Sunday morning and that it was he who later in the day approached the mob in front of the jailhouse and had them disperse to reform on the mountain top that night to come and take me.

"By the way, the jailhouse action was, as you guessed, a

diversion to keep the lawmen engaged. Skhutt knew that Mr. Beecher had been able to contact the judge and his party, and that they were returning in order to hold an inquest into Clay's death. Once he heard that, he raced down the mountain to redeploy his troops, so to speak."

Seamus spoke.

"The next question was; *how* did Skhutt know that the judge had been contacted and was returning?"

"Here is the answer to that question, Colonel," said Luther.

He took a flat, oval shaped box out of his pocket and passed it over to Emily, who, with a curious look, handed it to Seamus.

"This!" Seamus started, "I am a . . . "

I am a bloody fool! he completed the thought unspoken out of deference to the ladies.

He knew what the object he now held in his hands was the moment Luther had taken it from his pocket.

"We found it," said Luther, "in the saddle bag on Skhutt's horse. Sampson discovered the roan drinking from the lake."

Seamus examined the box. The lid was made of hard, brown gutta percha, molded with cross-hatchings like the checkering on a firearm, to ensure grip. In the center of the lid was an oval stamp with the words; 'Invention of Dr. Samuel F.B. Morse, Patented.' Seamus flipped open the lid.

Inside, and attached to the wooden base of the box, was a cylindrical brass battery lying on its side with ivory knobs at each end. Attached to the brass posts upon which the knobs sat was a coiled length of fine copper wire. Set across the length of the box was a miniature telegraph key also with an ivory knob.

What Seamus held in his hands was a device for listening in on the telegraphic messages of others or for sending one's own messages over lines owned by another. He was very familiar with the device and still had the one which had been issued to him in the name of the Secretary. He had used it many times at the South during the war and more recently, in Canada. In point of fact, his own little telegraph machine, very much like this one, a bit larger perhaps, was just now resting in his carpetbag, in his room.

For that reason, Seamus now wished that he was in a

position to literally kick himself.

"Confession," he said to the room at large, "is, as the Reverend here has demonstrated, very good for the soul. I must confess, therefore, that when I was jogging around the lakes Sunday morning I must almost have come upon Skhutt listening in on the telegraph from the Mountain House. When he heard me coming, he evidently took off so fast that he left this," Seamus uncoiled a bit of wire and held it up, "hanging from the telegraph pole. A clear image of what had happened jumped into my head but I, like a; . . I foolishly suppressed it. I expect that I rather arrogantly refused to believe that we were dealing with so sophisticated a foe. The sight of the wire hanging from the pole should have told me that they were listening in on our communications. Instead, I offhandedly assumed that the dangling wire had been left when the pole was installed.

"After I passed, Skhutt must have come back from where he was watching after galloping a short distance down the slope and retrieved the wire and headed out for Catskill and the jail because he knew that the judge would be returning. When I passed by on my way down the mountain and the wire was gone, I paused again and I could see by the signs around the telegraph pole that someone had waited there. Again I should have realized what was happening, but I simply would not listen to my own instincts."

Mr. Beecher spoke.

"In the event, however, Colonel, all worked out for the best because, although Skhutt must, as you say, have heard our messages regarding the return of the judge's party, he did not know that when I included in the telegraphic message to the constable the instruction 'proceed as planned' that meant for him to get the *Mary Powell* underway."

"That is right, Mr. Beecher," said Luther, "Skhutt, when I was questioning him, could not believe that the judge's party had returned so quickly from the Adirondacks. At first, he really thought that we were lying when we told him the inquest had been concluded before he had arrived with his mob. But then he had seen the sheriff with his own eyes and believed. Skhutt and the rest of them had no idea that the judge would be back so soon. They thought they had plenty of time. So, even though the party got here later than we thought they would, if you remember we were hoping for a midnight arrival, they still came long before our enemies expected."

"Then," said Seamus, "what we know of a certainty is that McCain and Tompkins, or Lejeune, and Clay conspired first with Skhutt to kill Miz Emily in order for Clay to gain control of her company. From what she has told me, I suspect that an attempt was made to poison Miz Emily while she lived at the South. That plot was thwarted by her moving in with her aunt, who herself, poor woman, may have suspected the source of Emily's illness was in fact poison. Emily's aunt was murdered in Georgetown I am sure, possibly because of the lady's suspicion, but surely because as an heir and partner, she stood in the way of Clay and his associates gaining control of the company. Two further attempts were made on Emily's life after she came north; the one at Catskill where Skhutt caused the cattle stampede, and the one on Friday afternoon when he put the snake in her path.

"As we have seen, the cabal of Lejeune, McCain, Clay and Skhutt was willing to try only the most subtle means, so as to raise no further suspicions. If they failed in one attempt, they could always try another. Emily was innocent of their motives and actions and was in no way on guard against them and her demise needed to look like nothing but an accident.

"But then, Clay by his drunken rantings made himself a danger to Lejeune and McCain and the secret workings of their *terroriste* brotherhood. They resolved to murder Clay and that they did. To their great fortune, Luther was immediately and erroneously accused, thereby providing them with a cover and, as we have seen, they went on to attempt to arrange for the lynching of the mistakenly accused Luther, thus ending any further investigation of Clay's murder which could result from an actual inquest. They assumed that little effort would be expended to clear the name of a hanged man, and they did not want Luther around to defend himself.

"But, my question is and has been; why did they go to that effort? Why did Lejeune and McCain not simply leave the Mountain House after Clay had been killed? They made no further attempts on Miz Emily's life, for the simple reason, we know now, that neither of then could benefit by her death. The cold blooded devils, after they had killed Clay, could not profit from her death. So, why did they stay on?

"McCain and Lejeune had been asked by the constable to stay as had most of the other guests at the sunrise service, but they could have left as had many others. Why did they run the risk of staying? Why did they go to all the trouble of getting their mob organized and moving to lynch Luther? No one was pointing the finger at them. In Lejeune's case, he was not even supposed to be acquainted with Clay. That is my question; the most puzzling question I asked Luther to put to Skhutt when I left the common in pursuit of Lejeune on Monday morning. And what was his answer, Luther?"

"Colonel, he said that he did not know why they did not just leave when they had the chance. As I said before, I believe him. He told me that Lejeune and McCain never gave him any more information than what he needed to know to carry out their orders to him. He said he wondered himself why they stayed after they had killed Clay, especially since they had no more chance of taking over the company and since circumstances had provided a scapegoat for the crime. Skhutt said that he never broached the question with them, because he never questioned them about anything. He said that he had found to do so could be dangerous. He feared both Lejeune and McCain, but McCain particularly. They would brook no inquiry, Skhutt told me, least of all from him. So, Colonel, I have no answer to the question of why they did not just depart after killing Clay."

Mr. Beecher spoke.

"I believe," he said, "that . . ."

And he stopped. It seemed to Seamus that the old gentleman had checked himself in what he was about to say. He then went on.

". . . that we all must get ready for the memorial service which will take place at five o'clock behind the stables."

"Memorial service?" said Seamus,

"Oh, yes, Colonel, I keep forgetting that you have, so to speak, not been 'with us' for the last few days. It is our tradition to have a memorial service on the Fourth of July to remember all who have sacrificed for the Republic over the years. The service is followed by a picnic on the great lawn and, in the evening, by dancing in the ballroom and illuminations launched out over the valley from the ledge in front of the piazza. This year, we will again, as we did last year, remember and honor particularly the veterans of the late war and I have invited your friends, the volunteers who saved us from the mob, to be my special guests. They have, most of them, already arrived and are assembling by the stables even now. It is a pity, Colonel, that your medical condition will preclude your attending . . ."

Seamus interrupted.

"Mr. Beecher . . . sir, I *will* attend."

Mr. Beecher looked to the doctor, who, in turn, opened his mouth to speak.

"It makes no difference what the doctor says," Seamus continued, "I will attend because I wish to render honor as you have described, and because I came up here to the mountains for relaxation and have, as yet, seen but little of that commodity and because to day, sir, I wish to celebrate, as it is my birthday."

"Happy Birthday, Seamus," said Emily.

"Thank you, Emily," said Seamus.

Mr. Beecher looked again to the doctor.

"Ah," said the doctor in exasperation, "what is the difference. He should stay resting in bed, but we cannot force him to do so. I will be in attendance myself and will be able to render any medical assistance as may be needed. If the Colonel collapses, we can carry him to bed."

"Sure, we have done that before," said Mick.

"We have," the doctor agreed, "and if he dies, we can bury him."

"Sure, we can do that too," Mick smiled.

"Doctor! Mr. Dolan!" Emily cried.

"Tut, Miz Emily," Dr. Duboise laughed, "tut, soldier's humor is all, just rough soldier's humor."

Seamus laughed too, and started to get out of bed. The doctor pressed him down yet again.

"You will need some clothes, Colonel," he said quietly.

Seamus became aware that he was dressed in a garment he had never seen before; an elegant but rather antique linen nightshirt having puffed sleeves gathered at the wrists with bands of lace and lace worked around the neck.

"Your attire, which Mr. Beecher was kind enough to loan to you, is," said the doctor, "very becoming I, am certain, but probably not appropriate for the patriotic convocation which you are so insistent upon attending."

Mick Dolan spoke.

"I will go to your room and bring back what you need, Colonel," he said, and was out the door.

"We must depart as well," said the Reverend Mr. Van Wyck, "we look forward to seeing you at the service, Colonel."

The dominie and his wife left and the doctor stood.

"Miz Emily, we should go and change Willie's dressing before the ceremony begins," he said.

Emily softly stroked the back of Seamus' hand twice, rose, and left with the doctor. Seamus eyes followed her to the door.

Mr. Beecher spoke.

"Colonel, if there is anything you find yourself in want of, just send for it and we will do the best we can to accommodate you. Again let me express the joy which we all feel at your recovery."

Mr. Beecher left and Luther and Sarah also said their good-byes and followed their employer out the door.

Luther turned back and quickly stepped to the washstand at the side of the bed. He looked back to the empty doorway, turned to Seamus and reached under his jacket. He took Seamus' Police Revolver from his belt and laid it on the stand next to the pistol which had been McCain's.

"Much obliged, Colonel," he said.

"Ever at your service, Luther," said Seamus with a smile.

Luther responded with a quick and dazzling smile himself and turned to leave. He stopped and took from his pocket Seamus long, flat German clasp knife and moved to put that on the washstand also.

"Luther," said Seamus, "if you please, I would appreciate it if you would pass that on to young Frederick Douglass with my compliments; that is if you approve of him having such an implement."

Luther's brows knit.

"Oh, he is old enough to have a knife, Colonel, and he would be delighted I am sure, but Sarah and I are raising him not to take what he has not earned. We want him to be proud of doing for himself."

"Luther, it is not a gift. It is an award for duty well performed. I had asked him to quietly saddle Sarge for me and to place him discreetly behind the barn Sunday night. When I needed Sarge, there he was comfortably tethered, nickering away at his oats. Frederick did a good job for me. He earned his reward."

"In that case, I will accept this with thanks on my son's behalf. I can just see his face when he receives it."

Luther smiled again and left.

Alone, Seamus closed his eyes and offered a prayer of thanksgiving and, while he was at it, a prayer asking God to bless his continued hunt for Captain Brutus Lejeune. A hunt which was, he assured the Almighty, by no means over.

The mourning dove cooed again.

# XIII

# In Memoriam

Mick returned in a few minutes, his arms filled with Seamus' property. He hung the uniform coat on the hall tree in the corner and set the carpet bag on the chair by the washstand. The revolvers resting there caught his eye and he commented dryly.

"Well, Colonel, today you have two weapons, where on Monday morning you were 'armed' only with your spare cylinder. I have known you to be reckless in the past, but I never before knew you to go to a gunfight without at least bringing along a gun. How did you come to be without a revolver when you went after Lejeune, may I ask?"

"No, Michael, you may not ask. Here, give us a hand."

Seamus swung his feet to the floor, paused, rubbed his brow and stood with Mick holding him by the elbow. He tested his balance, tried a step and stumbled against his friend.

"Colonel," said Mick, "would you ever reconsider and spend the day in bed."

"No, Michael, I will not."

"No," quoted Mick, "no, of course not, that would make too much sense."

"What, Mick, would you have me spend my birthday in bed, and you and the boys right outside my door celebrating on my behalf?"

"I suppose not," said Mick, considering briefly the argument. "I never knew you were born on the Fourth of July."

"I may have been," Seamus replied, "you know that we didn't pay much attention to birthdays in the old country, but before I came over, Felim wrote and told me that the Americans put great stock in written notice that one has actually been born.

I was able to get my baptismal certificate from the chapel in Ballyhaunis. I found that I was baptized on the 31st day of July 1838. The same day that the Irish Poor Law Act, which had been passed by the English parliament, became law. I discovered that bit of information, by the way, in the Jesuit school library in Georgetown, long after I came over.

"Those of us who know Ireland's history, know that legislation became the death warrant for a host of our friends and relations during the Famine. The pitifully mean 'relief' it authorized assured slow and fatal starvation for the poor."

Mick nodded, his face grim.

"Well, after I came over, got into the army, applied for citizenship and such like, I needed a birth date to put on the documents. I could have used the date of my baptism, but it seemed such an ill-omened one, and since I was becoming an American, I chose the birthday of my new homeland for my own."

"A good choice, I would say," Mick agreed, "by the accounting of the last several years, it seems to me that July Fourth is a fairly-omened date of birth. The country appears that it will go on for awhile longer, and you as well, if you would only be a bit more careful . . ."

"God help us!" Seamus was aghast at what he saw when he faced the mirror. Looking back at him from the glass above the washstand was a face with two black eyes, or rather a face which had had two black eyes. The color was now fading back to normal, but he still looked as though he had gotten the worse of it in a boxing match.

Also, his nose appeared to have grown larger during his long nap. He touched it and pulled his hand away. It still hurt, was still swollen.

"It's too bad that you are not an actor, Colonel, you could reach into your kit and find a cosmetic to make your shiners disappear. But don't be feeling sorry for yourself, you look not near as bad today as you did yesterday. Although you still do resemble one of those 'typical' Irish saloon brawlers, the ones Nast is so fond of drawing in *Harper's*, the ones you are always telling me, when you are sober, that you do not wish to be like.

“But on Sunday afternoon, you may recall, that is just what you wanted to be like. Didn't it take Flanagan and myself to remind you that you always wish to appear as an officer and a gentleman, do you remember?"

Seamus turned to Mick.

"You are right, Mick, we both know that, and I thank you."

Mick was serious.

"I think, Colonel, if you would just not start with the whiskey . . ."

"No, Mick, it is not the whiskey alone. I cannot take ardent drink of any description, cannot drink at all; never could really. But you needn't worry, I will not be embarrassing the Irish nation at the picnic today."

"Neither will anyone else," Mick replied, "Father Power is here today. He gave all the boys the word on the behavior question and he saw to the mixing of the punch himself. Mr. Beecher donated some of Tompkins', or Lejeune's whiskey for the punch that he had in his warehouse in Catskill. He said that it is forfeit since the man departed without paying his hotel bill. But Father Power made sure that it was well 'baptized', as he put it, with water. He put a special ban on Grogan in particular and I myself put that lad under the care and protection of Flanagan and Sullivan. They will not leave his side for the whole of the festivities. No one will disgrace us in front of the gentry; the boys will be fine. Mr. Beecher, wise man that he is, invited the wives and sweethearts as well, so all will be exhibiting their best demeanor."

"As will I," said Seamus, "I will stick with the lemonade. If I forget, remind me."

"That I will, Colonel, that I will, but we better be getting you ready for inspection, in a manner of speaking. Here let me help you out of that elegant regalia you are wearing. You look like the fella in the nightshirt and cap who got a visit from St. Nick."

Seamus shed the borrowed sleeping gear, getting a painful reminder when he raised his left arm of where he had landed when Sarge was shot. He washed while Mick stood by and caught him the few times he started to keel over trying to stand on one foot. He shaved and found his hand to be steady, but noticed that when he looked down he became dizzy, so Mick held up the bowl of hot water for him. He toweled off, applied witch hazel to his face and donned clean drawers, and a fresh shirt and collar, which articles, Mick informed him, he had donated himself.

While Seamus sat on the edge of the bed and put on stockings which Mick had also donated, the former sergeant buffed his dress shoes which had managed to survive their dunking in the creek.

Seamus stood and pulled on his old militia pattern trousers of light blue fabric with dark blue stripes down the seams. Seamus had inherited them from Felim's paternal cousin, who had also died at Antietam. By the end of the war, they were the only presentable pair of uniform trousers Seamus owned.

Mick helped him to attach the galluses to the trousers and then helped him knot the simple bow tie of black silk around his collar. He then addressed himself to Seamus' uniform coat. He brushed the dark blue material and used a corn cob to brighten first brass buttons and then the gold and silver of the shoulder boards and finally the badges and medals on the left breast. He finished his work with a few swipes of a cotton cloth until they all glistened like liquid. Mick regarded them as he helped Seamus on with the coat.

At the top was the badge of Sheridan's Corps; a tiny model, in German silver, of a Sharp's carbine with a guidon hanging down suspended by a fine little chain. Crossed sabers were imprinted onto the guidon. Next to that was the badge of Hancock's Corps, a gold star burst also with crossed sabers at the center. Below the badges was pined a rectangular ribbon of sky blue silk with yellow strips at each end. Next to that were two medals; one with a dark blue ribbon suspending a silver cross and crown pendant and the other with a pink ribbon with dark green stripes bearing crossed scimitars and a round silver pendent inscribed with an exotic cipher in a strange and flowing script.

"Colonel, I have seen you wearing these in the days gone by and I recognize the badges alright but these others look foreign. I always wanted to ask you where are they from."

"They are from the Crimean War, Mick. The ribbon from England, the others from the Allies; the cross from Sardinia and Piedmont, the one with the odd writing from the Ottoman Turks."

"And," said Mick are you not going to wear the one they gave you for taking the stand of rebel colors at Gettysburg?"

"I will Mick, I keep it in its box there in the carpet bag."

Mick poked in the bag and came up with two long slim black boxes tied together with a scrap of string. He undid the string and opened one box.

"Oh," he said, "this is not it." The medal; in the box had a ribbon with the colors of the one on the coat, blue and yellow from which hung a round silver pendent with the portrait of a crowned Queen Victoria.

"That," said Seamus, "is the Queen's Crimea Medal. I wear the ribbon in memory of the lads I served with. They were good lads, Mick and many of them never saw home again, but I do not wear the medal. I do not care to display the image of a ruler who would let people she claimed as subjects starve to death year after year in Ireland, perishing by the side of the road with the green mouth from eating grass in their ghastly frenzy to stay alive."

Mick nodded and closed the box.

"We cannot, of course, forget," said Mick, in mock reverence, "that she gave two thousand pounds of her own fortune to Irish Famine Relief."

"No," said Seamus, a grim smile showing his teeth, "nor must we forget just how far that pittance went to keep the millions of wretches from slow death.

"As for the medal, I could not bring myself to just throw it away, it means much to me. Not for the war, that was an abomination. All for greed; throwing shot and shell into the streets, houses and churches of Sebastopol, for what? To save the Ottoman Empire! And at the same time our commanders ordered a cease fire on a more tactically important target when it was found that one of our Allied nations had financial investments in the neighborhood. I kept the medal, not for the war, but *In Memoriam.* It does mean much to me. It is a reminder of the lads and of the lad I was myself."

Seamus had an idea.

"Let me have that, if you please, Mick"

Mick handed him the boxed medal and Seamus put into his inside coat pocket.

Mick opened the other box. The inside of the lid was a cushion of white satin imprinted with the trademark of "William Wilson and Son, Manufacturers of Silver Ware, Philada. Penn." He took out the Medal of Honor from the box and pinned it to Seamus' blouse, at the left of the others. He straightened the medal to his satisfaction and stood back.

"That was some day in the Wheatfield was it not, Colonel."

Seamus felt the hair on the back of his neck stand up.

"It was, Mick, it was," he said clearing his throat, "the boy's performed splendidly, just as your boys performed on Sunday night and Monday morning against that mob."

"That they did and they did it all for you, Colonel. They would do anything for you. Many of us know Luther and would do all we could to help him. But, to be honest, some of the lads, as you know, have no love for black folk. Still, they all heeded your call at once. Father Power giving them General Absolution at Tracey's place on Sunday didn't hurt either."

Seamus was silent.

Mick went on.

"When I think back on the war and the wonders we did on the battlefield for America, I cannot help but remember what many a lad would say, and him all grimy with powder at the battle's end; 'What harm' he would say, 'if it were for the poor *ould dart*!' How would it be, Colonel, if we did what we did for poor old Ireland?"

"True enough, Mick, that day may come yet, but in the mean time, our cause must be the cause of justice for everyone. Didn't Patrick O'Connell, the Great Liberator himself, see that when he met with Frederick Douglass in Ireland and wrote that the Irish in America should join with the Abolitionists to end slavery? Freedom is for everyone, and no, Mick, I will not join the Fenian Brotherhood. It need not be said that neither would I ever betray them."

Mick put a look of surprise on his face.

"And why, Colonel *alanna*, would you think that I would be recruiting for those fellas in the Brotherhood, sure, my relations with them are entirely social."

Mick took the maroon, tasseled officer's sash from the hall tree and wound it around Seamus waist. As he worked, he spoke.

"Still and all, Colonel, I do recall that during the war you attended quite regularly, when we were in camp, at the meetings of the Fenian Officer's Circle on the first Sunday of every month."

Seamus, his hands held up over his head as Mick wound the sash, his shoulder aching, replied with some exasperation.

"Mick, I attended each meeting after the political session was over, and after it was opened to non-members, only to sample the whiskey punch and to listen to Surgeon Reynolds declaim the ancient poems. I remember crawling back to my tent from one of those meetings on my hands and knees."

"I recall that one," said Mick, "you didn't make it all the way. Flanagan and I found you face down in the company street, picked you up and carried you the rest of he way."

"Were you the ones who did that? I am much obliged."

"Not at all, Colonel, happy to be of assistance at any time."

"In any case, Mick, I was not then, nor am I now ready to swear myself to the Fenians."

"To be sure," said Mick and muttered, "still there's always hope."

"Here," he said, "is your belt. Should we detach the holster? You don't have your Army revolver, do you?"

"No, I left the Remington at the Armory; this was *supposed* to be a vacation. Let us leave the holster on though, it will give me someplace to put McCain's revolver. I don't wish to leave it lying around. Metal cartridges or not, I doubt if it would go off after the soaking it got in the creek, but it is safer if I keep it with me. And I'll put my Colt in my hip pocket."

Mick gave the big square, eagle embossed waist plate a quick scrubbing with the corn cob and buffed it with the cloth. He put the LaFaucheaux revolver in the holster closing the flap over it and buckled the belt about the sash at Seamus' waist. He handed the Colt to Seamus who pocketed the weapon, and took a kepi from the carpet bag and placed it on Seamus' head. The numerals '69' were embroidered in gold at the front of the cap amid a wreath of shamrocks. The cap covered pretty nearly the bandage around Seamus' head.

Mick took his own forage cap from the hall tree and put it on his head. A patch, in the form of a red trefoil was sown to the crown; the insignia of the 2nd Corps. It was, Seamus remembered, the very cap Mick had worn at the Wheatfield. Mick adjusted his cap to a jaunty angle and saluted. Seamus adjusted his kepi likewise and returned the salute. They both laughed and Mick led the way out of the room.

They went through the door into Mr. Beecher's office. They found the room empty and Seamus pointed out the idealized print of Lee's surrender at Appomattox with the comment:

"Ain't the way I remember it, Mick."

Mick cast a jaundiced eye upon the engraving.

"No, it doesn't look like the Appomattox I was at either. Maybe there was a different Appomattox, Colonel, one that we missed and that the *artiste* attended."

They both laughed again,

The door to the hall opened and Sampson entered, latch key in hand. He too was well turned out in black frock coat, collar and tie.

"Sampson," said Seamus, "it is good to see you again. You look like you are already a lawyer and a prosperous one at that."

Sampson clasped Seamus hand.

"You are looking very well, Colonel. I am glad to see you recovering so quickly."

"You and Jacob did excellent well in suggesting we move the searchlight to the back of the roof. It was aimed perfectly at the common, blinded the mob and made them perfect targets for us. Jacob's timing was right on the bugle call, I must thank him."

"He is at the memorial service along with everyone else. I stayed back to guard the door here. Mr. Beecher feels we still must be careful with Lejeune at large."

Seamus thought, but did not say, that he would love nothing

better than for Lejeune to come back. Would give an arm, left or right, if the murderer would return. He was certain, however, that the man was no fool and that by now he was far, far away, probably to the south, possibly out of the state if not out of the country.

The three men left Mr. Beecher's office and followed the hall to the central staircase. Descending the stairs proved to be something of a challenge for Seamus. He leaned heavily on the banister and was grateful for Mick's support at his elbow. His eyes focused only with difficulty on the stairs as he took each step slowly and individually.

When they reached the bottom of the stairs, Sampson excused himself.

"I will go ahead, Colonel and let them know that you are on your way so that they can get ready to start the ceremony."

"I trust they are not waiting for me," said Seamus.

"In fact," said Sampson, "they are."

"They needn't do that, Sampson." Seamus was embarrassed to learn that he had been holding up the afternoon's activities.

Sampson smiled and hurried off through the corridor and out the rear entrance.

Seamus and Mick followed at a statelier pace. It occurred to Seamus that he probably *should* have stayed in bed, but that he would take his chances. He felt the need for both the reflection and the celebration which he anticipated that the memorial service and the picnic would provide. The sun shown invitingly through the back entrance at the end of the hall.

"So," he said, as he picked his way toward that goal, each bump and wrinkle in the carpet like a small ridge either to be surmounted or tripped over, "Father Power gave the boys General Absolution before our . . . um . . . engagement."

"He did," said Mick, "and that's not all. It was himself who told me I should 'encourage' the boys to organize and help you fight off, if necessary, Skhutt's mob, in defense of Luther's life and the Mountain House. He gave me the word on Sunday in front of the church right after Mass and just before he gave you and me his blessing. You remember he and I spoke privately for a moment?"

Seamus remembered.

"He said," Mick went on, "that it would be an appropriate penance for those who had participated in the raid on Canada, which, as you know, he viewed to be of 'questionable moral standing.' The good father told me the boys could hardly put their arms to a better cause than helping you to help Luther and Mr. Beecher."

Seamus was speechless.

"So, Colonel, Father Power was the prime mover behind me writing Frank Treacy's name and the name of his saloon in Catskill on that piece of paper I gave you and telling you to telegraph; *'faughaballagh'* when you needed help and wanted us to come up the mountain."

"I must express my gratitude to Father," said Seamus finding his voice.

"If it's all the same, I would appreciate it if you don't let on to Father that I told you that getting the boys together was his idea. He would not be happy if he knew that I told you. Nor, if he knew that I told you that on the night of our engagement with the mob, he was here on the property, watching, just out of sight behind the root cellar. You see, he would not only give the boys a General Absolution and send them into battle and leave it at that, anymore than did Father Corby at Gettysburg. Father Power trailed us from a distance and followed us up the mountain to be near just as Father Corby had stayed near us should the worst happen and any of the lads need his comfort as they went on to the next world.

"Once the matter had been settled in our favor the other night, he rode back down the mountain quietly. Myself, and now your good self, Colonel, are the only ones who know that he had anything, apart from the General Absolution, to do with organizing the defense. Father feels that it would be unseemly for it to be generally known that a priest was involved in this kind of business. So, mum is the word, Colonel, and mum it will have to stay."

Seamus nodded his agreement.

They reached the back door and crossed the circular drive and walked along the flagstones toward the common. The sky was clear and bright above the trees by the stables where the assemblage had gathered. A tall pole had been erected in the paddock for the occasion and from it a huge garrison flag swung majestically in the light breeze. As they passed the grove on their right the same breeze wafted the aroma of chicken broiling over a charcoal fire. Seamus looked in the direction of the enticing scent and saw that a pit had been dug just before the trees and flocks of split chickens had been left to cook themselves on grilles elevated on iron stakes over the coals. Long rows of tables had been set up in the shade and the tables were heaped with delicacies.

Seamus was ravenous but, with a will, he put aside thoughts of food and continued his cautious progress along the flagstones which seemed as determined to trip him as had the carpet in the hall. He and Mick entered the common, where dozens of buggies, gigs and buckboards were parked, and crossed to the stable area. The afternoon was warm, as befitted a Fourth of July, but the air was fresh, light and not at all close. Behind the stables, the broad green paddock stretched back to the evergreen woods where the left wing of the volunteers had concealed themselves on Sunday night. Now the flat grassy space was filled with a veritable concourse of humanity. At the back of the paddock, within the shade of the pines, a small stage had been built next to the flagpole. The stage was bedecked in bunting, and along the left side of the clearing stood rank upon rank of blue clad veterans. To their front and center, the National Standard and the green flag bearing the gold harp and sunburst of the Irish Brigade rode on the summer air. The ladies and the children of the Brigade stood in groups on the flanks of the company. Across and facing inward also were the assembled members of the Mountain House staff and their children. Some wore the livery of the hotel and some were dressed in their finery. In the center of the paddock, and facing the stage were the remnant of the guests of the hotel who had not been driven off by the occurrences of the last several days. They were all richly, but informally dressed. Here and there a pastel parasol bloomed above a lady vacationer.

"Colonel," said Mick, as they slowly approached the rear of

the crowd of guests, "we have here what looks to be a parliament of all the world's people."

"It is America, Mick," said Seamus quietly, "I was a day in the bar of Willard's back in '63 in the good company of Myles Keogh and the noble Luigi Palma di Cesnola, who later was awarded the Medal of Honor. And it struck me as singular that here was Colonel Cesnola who had been born an Italian count, and Myles, from a well off family in County Carlow, who had each served in Italy, but not on the same side, and myself who had nearly perished of famine. The Count and I had served on the same side in the Crimea, not that we had met there, and here were we all in America and fighting in this great cause. We were none of us mercenaries nor presently soldiers of fortune either; America had brought us together. Mick it *is* a union, not just of states, but of people."

"It is that," Mick agreed.

They had reached the back of the crowd of guests, where Seamus felt he would be quite content to stay. It was not, however, to be.

From the podium, Mr. Beecher spoke in a clear and strong voice.

"Oh!" said he, "I see that Colonel Delaney has joined us. Please, let us welcome him. Come forward, Colonel."

Professor Smith's Coronet Band, standing at the left of the stage, struck up *The Garryowen*, the people in front of Seamus turned and parted while applauding vigorously and Frank Treacy bellowed:

"THREE CHEERS FOR THE COLONEL!"

"HURRAH! HURRAH! HURRAH!" rumbled forth deeply from the leathered throats of the veterans.

Seamus felt chilled and dizzy and his face burned with embarrassment. He did not care to be the center of attention. Nonetheless, he stiffened to attention and marched, with Mick at his side, to the podium. On his right he saw Luther and Sarah standing at the forefront. Luther was resplendent in his uniform, buttons gleaming, bright sergeant's chevrons slashing down the arms, creases sharp, cap squared above his brow, the numerals '54' burnished still more brightly than usual.

Beside him stood Sarah, radiant in a dark blue dress trimmed with lace so black as to shine like the raven's wing. In her hair, two combs of Spanish silver flashed in the sunlight.

Seamus caught the eye of Luther, who, without the hint of a smile, and while gravely frozen at the position of attention, winked.

Next to Sarah stood Emily in her green and yellow dress, and next to her, Mrs. Van Wyck in a dress of white and blue. Emily was smiling; Seamus was sure, at his unease.

He marched across the paddock where, in front of the stage, lay the mounded earth of a freshly covered grave. A wide oaken plank, cut to the shape of a tombstone and painted dark green stood at the head of the grave. At the top, the deeply carved and gilded letters had been arranged in an arch. 'The Roland of Horses', they read. A rendering of a galloping horse, surrounded by vines and floral rosettes, had been etched below the dedication and beneath that, the name 'SARGE' in large block letters. Seamus eyes, filling and burning as they were, followed the lines of the inscription:

> "'SARGE' A veteran of the *War for the Union*, killed in action, July 2, 1866. His tread never faltered. Faithful unto death."

A wreath of laurel leaves bound by red, white and blue ribbons rested upon the grave.

Seamus raised his hand in salute and Mick did the same.

After a moment, they cut away their salutes sharply and Seamus started to walk toward Emily. He was brought up sharply.

"Colonel, please join us on the dais," said Mr. Beecher.

The old gentleman smiled down from behind the railing of the platform where now hung the framed portrait of Abraham Lincoln from his office.

There was nothing for it and so Seamus resignedly climbed the few short steps while Mick followed, ready to catch him should he stumble.

Willie Peters stood at the top of the stairs. His flat, round sailor's hat did not conceal the broad bandage wrapped around his head. He smiled winced in pain and smiled again. Cappy Phaestus stood next to him. Next to Cappy stood a tall man whom Seamus did not know, but who resembled a younger, handsomer and slightly less angular version of the late President whose likeness was nestled amid the bunting at the front of the stage. The resemblance ran to the dark beard, free of a moustache, and the thick hair combed in a wave from the lofty forehead. This man however, dressed as he was in a black suit of clothes, differed from the President in that he rested some of his weight on a crutch, his left trouser leg pinned up; empty.

Cappy extended a helping hand as Seamus tripped on the top step. He flashed his crooked, ironic smile.

"Are we a little groggy today, Colonel?" he half whispered. A blue kepi was perched on his head; a brass French horn infantry insignia enclosing the letter "M" on a red field was pinned above the brim.

Seamus took the powerful, callused hand and shook it. He was delighted to see Cappy again.

"This," said Cappy, "is Pastor Williams of the Katsbaan Church."

The pastor's hazel eyes, deep-set like Lincoln's, appeared filled with compassion. He extended a firm handshake.

Mr. Beecher beckoned Seamus to stand by his side. The other clergy assembled on the dais included the Reverend Mr. Van Wyck, the stalwart Levi, who stood straight and distinguished in a long black frock coat, the Good Book in his hand clasped to his breast and to his right, Father Power, dressed, as was his custom, in plain citizen's attire. The breeze tousled the mound of curly red hair on the priest's head as he gave Seamus a smile. Doctor Duboise stood next the Father Power. He wore a blue kepi with the numeral and insignia of the Ulster Guard on the crown. He squinted at Seamus through his pince-nez, a smile on his lips.

Mr. Beecher stood to the front of the stage and leaned his hands on the railing. Professor Smith gave the down beat and the band struck up the *Star Spangled Banner* in a slow yet bounding time. The color guard popped the Flag straight up and smartly, while the Green Banner was slowly lowered almost to the ground. Each flagstaff bore at its top a wreath of fresh laurel leaves. All in uniform saluted, while all in civilian dress held their hands over their hearts, the men doffing their hats. When the last strains of music died away, Frank Treacy gave the order "Ready...to!" and "Rest", and the flags resumed their positions at the bearer's sides.

Mr. Beecher invited Reverend Mr. Van Wyck to give the convocational prayer, and he did so.

"Dearly beloved," he said, "our late and revered President when dedicating the cemetery at Gettysburg taught us that brevity is not only the soul of wit, a subject with which he was well acquainted, but also the soul of piety, a subject with which he was no less familiar. And this most especially in the matter of memorializing those who have been lost in the struggles which have wracked and, as we have lately seen, still trouble our country. It is enough for us to remember those who have gone and to remember them with love and warmth. They have, as the late President said, not died in vain. Their sacrifices were wholly true and just. Nothing more need be said except for us to call upon God in the words of Paul." He bowed his head as all present did the same, and read:

"Blessed be God, even the Father of our Lord Jesus Christ, the Father of mercies, and the God of all comfort, Who comforts us in all our tribulation, that we may be able to comfort them which are in any trouble, by the comfort wherewith we ourselves are comforted of God . . . Amen."

"Amen," came the response from the congregation.

Mr. Beecher stepped to the fore again.

"Ladies and Gentlemen," he said, "it is usual for an Independence Day observance such as we are conducting to have as its centerpiece, as it were, a patriotic speaker, often an elected or appointed government official or perhaps a figure of historic or military note. I had planned to have just such a person present here today to fulfill that aspect of our ceremony, however it would appear that that gentleman, a dear friend of mine for many a year, has been delayed. I therefore will be so bold as to call upon another to address a few thoughts to us on this anniversary of the founding of our country. He is a military man whose gallantry and dash is well known to all of us."

Mr. Beecher turned.

"Colonel Delaney, if you will."

Seamus looked around quickly at the others on the podium. They were all smiling, rather wickedly, he thought, even and especially Father Power. They had all known, Seamus could see, that Mr. Beecher had intended to have him speak in replacement of the delayed keynote orator.

Seamus felt his face growing more and more scarlet. He would literally have preferred to face Kershaw's Brigade of fierce South Carolinians once more than to stand before this or any other group and make a speech. Again, however, there was nothing for it, he knew, so he stood to the railing and mumbled thanks to Mr. Beecher and looked to the audience. He noticed immediately that Luther, Sarah, Mrs. Van Wyck and Emily, most of all, wore bright smiles. They too, had known.

Why, he wondered, do people, and particularly my friends, take such delight in seeing me discomfited? He began:

"Reverend clergy, Mr. Beecher, friends, comrades, ladies and gentlemen," I will keep this short and sweet, he thought, "the memory of those who went before us in the Revolution and since that time and in the war so recently concluded will never fade as long as this nation lasts. As many of you know, although I am an American, I was not born here as, indeed, many of you were not, but it is not just those who were born here, or even those of us who immigrated here who turn their eyes toward the principles expounded on that first Independence Day.

"In those principles and in this nation are embodied the yearning of the oppressed and dispossessed throughout the world. We cannot let this country fail therefore. It must last and continually improve itself as a beacon unto humankind. The War for the Union was the combined effort of peoples and of groups who none would have thought had a common interest; the native born, the immigrant, the enslaved, the freeman of color, the Indian, the rich, the poor, the country man, the city dweller, the farmer, the mechanic, men, women, Jewish, Catholic and Protestant; all united in the just cause. Now that the war is over, that unity must prevail if we are to observe Independence Days in the future.

"Many of you know of the events of the last days here on the mountain top," and those of you who don't know all that transpired, I am not going to tell you, he thought, "in many ways that struggle was like the War for the Union; a combined effort in which all took part for the cause of justice. Like the Civil War, and for that matter, like the Revolution, all gave some, and some, like old Sarge here," Seamus indicated the grave before him, "gave all. But one person in particular performed a service which provided the key to the entire affair. I see that young lady standing there among you," Seamus pointed to Sally standing with Sarah, "and I ask her to come up here."

The girl's eyes went wide, and with considerable coaxing, she joined Seamus on the podium.

Seamus took the Queen's Crimea Medal from his pocket and removed it from its box. He held it up for all to see.

"This medal was awarded to me long ago and far away for enduring arduous and dangerous duty. I am here and now awarding it to Sally for the same reasons. Without her work, the happy outcome of the recent affair would simply not have been achieved."

Seamus pinned the medal to Sally's light blue shawl. As he did so, he whispered an inquiry if she would care to say a few words. She vigorously shook her head in the negative. He smiled and they both laughed. He turned Sally to face the audience. The sun glinted off the silvery image of Victoria Regina as off a mirror.

"Three cheers and a tiger for Sally!" Frank Treacy barked.

The veterans responded as the crowd applauded.

"HURRAH! . . . HURRAH! . . . HURRAH! . . . Grrrrrrrrrr!"

"Thank you," said Sally and Seamus together, and they both withdrew.

Mr. Beecher stepped forward again.

"Thank you, Colonel and thank you Sally," he said, "our thanks also to Mr. Ishmael Phaestus, who, on very short notice, was kind enough to fashion the fine marker for the gave of

Sarge, which we will now dedicate."

The audience applauded and Cappy rendered a casual and offhand salute. Mr. Beecher called upon Pastor Williams and Father Power and the two clergymen stepped forward. The priest, draping the violet ribbon that was his ecclesiastical stole around his neck, raised his hand and recited St. Francis' Blessing for Animals. The minister responded by commending Sarge to the honored memory of all those present.

Seamus noted that the pastor differed from Lincoln in that his voice was deep and melodious, not high and nasal as had been that of the late president.

At the conclusion of the dedication of the monument, the staff of the Mountain House, singing as a choir under the direction of Levi, who lead them from the stage, intoned the spiritual; *Swing Low, Sweet Chariot*. The powerful, haunting refrain resonated above the trees on the brow of the mountain. Sally stepped forward and sang the last verse in a lovely voice, displaying her talent for singing as well as she had previously for drawing and for secret service.

At the conclusion of the hymn, Mr. Beecher called upon Levi to pronounce the benediction:

"Brothers and Sisters," said Levi, "Let us pray . . . ", and all lowered their heads, "in *Jesus* name that we may all go on from victory to victory in justice and righteousness", he prayed earnestly, the beads of perspiration standing out on his forehead. Individual responses sprung forth quietly from those in the choir, "Yes, sir!", "Yes, Lord", and "Lord, bless."

Seamus had always marveled at and admired the way the African congregations harmonized so with their ministers in the give and take of their liturgy. He found the custom at once exotic and engaging.

Levi went on, building in vehemence and feeling.

"For in the words of that great old prophet; Isaiah" and he raised above his head for a moment the Book, but did not open it. With eyes tightly closed he quoted from memory:

'First the Lord degraded the land of Zebulon and the land of Naphtali, but in the end he has glorified the seaward road, the

land of the Jordan, the District of the Gentiles.
Anguish has taken wing, dispelled is darkness:
for there is no gloom where but now there was distress.
The people who walked in darkness
have seen a great light;
Upon those who dwelt in the land of gloom a Light has been shown.
You have brought them abundant joy
and great rejoicing,
As they rejoice before you as at the harvest,
as men make merry when dividing spoils.
For the yoke that burdened them,
the pole on their shoulder
And the *rod* of their *taskmaster*
you have *smashed*, as on the day of Midian!'

"Amen," said Levi, and the choir began to sing, *acapella,* the *Battle Hymn of the Republic.*

Toward the end of the song, Sally stepped forth again and sang solo. After the last solemn notes had faded up into the blue sky, Mr. Beecher thanked all who had participated and invited everyone to partake in the picnic on the lawn.

Professor Smith and the band took up the tune of the battle hymn as the veterans withdrew the colors and dismissed and the audience dispersed. All on the dais descended and Seamus made his way as quickly as he could to Emily's side while Mick, Cappy and Pastor Williams followed. Seamus had an overpowering desire to take Emily in his arms, but propriety won out and instead he said as he approached her where she stood with the Van Broncs and the dominie's wife; "My friends . . . " He said it an exaggerated and mocking way.

Emily was quick with a retort.

"You were very eloquent, and it did you no harm to say a few words."

Sarah joined in the assault.

"Indeed not, Colonel, but poor Sally, when you called her up there, I thought the child would swoon, but she is very appreciative and you have made a friend for life,"
Sarah looked around her, "I wonder where she has disappeared

to?"

The crowd strolled toward the lawn. Some of the staff hurried ahead of them to the grove where the picnic dinner had been laid. Mick and his family joined Seamus and the others. Introductions were made where necessary as all progressed to the tables which fairly groaned with their burden of food.

The staff set to with alacrity and in no time the lines of guests were being served from the platters of cold ham, beef and turkey. Baskets filled with broiled chicken were passed to the diners along with greens, salads, collations of potatoes and yams baked in the coals of the fire.

Seamus noted that many of those dressed in blue uniform had lined up at the adjacent beverage table rather then at those which dispensed food. There, a full sized keg stood on end, the letters 'XXX' stenciled on the side in black paint. Rolf was filling half-pint tankards from the spigot and handing them out while young Terwilliger, at the other end of the table, took dripping ceramic bottles of beer from a tub of ice water. They were snatched up as quickly as he could set them down.

While edging forward on the food line, Seamus kept looking over his shoulder at the flashing and clinking tan and brown bottles sliding across the table. They bore the names and marks of Schindler's Brilliant Brewery, Albany, of Stoll Brewing of Hudson, NY, with an embossed picture of an American eagle surmounting a beer barrel and of the F&M Schaeffer Co. of New York City and Brooklyn, branded with a circular seal depicting a friendly handshake. Welz and Zerwick Brewers of Brooklyn were also represented, as were a number of other beer and ale concerns.

Seamus could not take his eyes from the icy wet bottles. He watched as one veteran, laughing and joking, popped the porcelain and rubber stopper from one, lifted the foaming brew to his lips and drank deeply.

"Would you like a nice cold beer?" came a voice in Seamus' ear. He started; it was Cappy standing at his elbow.

"No," said Seamus, ". . . well, to be honest, yes."

"Alright, then, take one."

Seamus turned to look Cappy full in the face.

Cappy's eyes crinkled, his lip curled into the old ironic smile.

"But," he said, the smile suddenly gone, "when you take it, you will have to take all that goes with it."

"Right," said Seamus looking at his shoes, "right." He did not want all that went with the drink, not any more.

When he looked back up Cappy's smile had returned, he smiled too and turned back toward the food.

While he had been distracted, he had reached the table and Emily had been filling his plate for him as well as her own.

"Help yourself to the lemonade," she said.

Seamus dipped a stoneware mug into the big glass bowl where chunks of ice and lemons floated and followed Emily and the Van Broncs across the lawn to the tree line below the slope of the mountain. Mick and Kathleen and their children followed along. Daniel Patrick carried little Suzy on his shoulders while she whooped and hollered in her tiny voice.

They crossed the circular drive and took their ease on blankets which had been spread on the grass. Prof. Smith and his band stationed themselves beneath a lofty old sugar maple near the center of the walk way. They began a serenade of sweet and soothing tunes. The music commenced with *Come Where My Love Lies Dreaming*, and slipped in to *Annie Laurie*.

Sarah and Kathleen knew each other well and chatted away, while Emily seemed content to listen to the music and watch Seamus with an amused mien while he tried manfully to maintain some semblance of decorum and good manners as he pitched ravenously into the chicken. He found it to be delicious; roasted over the open fire to a turn, and basted with what tasted like a combination of honey, lemon juice, butter and herbs; sage, thyme and a wisp of garlic being the highlights.

He surveyed the scene as he ate. He noticed that most of the veterans and their wives had arranged themselves on the far side of the lawn nearer the tables of viands and beverages. Many blue uniforms, in fact, were clustered in front of the table where Rolf and his young assistant strove to stem the tide and keep the glasses full.

The staff, for the most part, occupied the near side of the

lawn, clustering at the west end. The adult hotel guests centered themselves on the lawn closer to the rear entrance. There, a croquet match was being organized; the ladies in white, blue and red, a man in a straw hat, on his knees among them, measuring out the distances.

The children of all, however, seemed delighted in fresh acquaintance and commingled joyfully in the center of the lawn. Some of the boys rolled hoops along the walkway, the girls already were forming themselves into games of Grand Mufti, French and English and Blind Man's Wand.

Despite the activity of the children, the accompaniment of the band, and the general hum of conversation, Seamus marveled that there seemed to be a silence, peaceful and profound, hanging above this ledge upon which the hotel sat, and above the forest and the lakes, which muted all sounds. It was no wonder that people returned, time and again to this serene place.

The band played *Home Sweet Home*.

Yes, he thought, one could make a home here and a sweet one.

He turned to Emily. She had been watching him the whole time and now she smiled.

"Would you like me to get you another plate?" she asked.

He looked down and realized that in the short time while he had been observing the scene, he had devoured enough food for two, possibly three, people.

"Oh . . . uh . . . no," he stuttered and then, "well, yes actually, but I will get it."

Mick rose too.

"Just one more sample of the punch," he said.

Kathleen shot him a glance of her sharp green eyes.

"Just one," Mick said reasonably to his wife, and he followed along with Seamus, sidestepping around his daughter Mary who played at the edge of the blanket with little Suzy, who in turn chewed absently on a bit of an apple. Daniel Patrick watched while Luther showed his son how to safely handle his new knife in whittling on a stick.

Mick spoke as they walked to the far side of the lawn.

"On a day like this, Colonel, you would think that there had never been a war or even the slightest disturbance among people in the entire history of the world."

"My feelings exactly, Michael."

"Aaahh," said Mick, "if peace would only reign supreme at all times."

He paused, changing subjects.

"The old punch is not so bad, Colonel. It is the same recipe that we used in camp; whiskey, condensed milk, nutmeg, lemons and water, but this has a lot more than a little water. It hasn't the smack of the genuine article, but the mellow flavor is there."

Seamus reminded himself that he had never cared for the flavor of whiskey punch. It was not for the flavor that he had imbibed the concoction in the past, but for the effect, an effect he did not want today.

He refilled his mug at the lemonade bowl and reached the food table as Levi was directing what amounted to a changing of the guard. Many of the staff who had been picnicking replaced those who had been serving, and the erstwhile servers came around the tables and began filling their own plates.

Luther joined Mick and Seamus.

"Part of the tradition," he said as he took a slice of thickly buttered wheat bread for his plate.

"Mr. Beecher has always had the staff share in the Independence Day festivities, and this way some work while some rest and altogether everyone has a good time."

"But what of Levi?" asked Seamus, "I have not noticed him resting at all."

"Levi," answered Luther, "as you have seen, is our preacher and he says that hospitality is part of his ministry. He takes his joy, he says, in seeing others jubilant. Also," Luther smiled and lowered his voice, "he likes to be in charge. It is his pride, and he is a master at his work. As it says in the Good Book, whatever it is we set our hand to, we should do it with all our might."

"Right you are Luther," said Father Power placing his empty mug next to the lemonade bowl. Luther tipped his cap to the priest as did Seamus and Mick.

The priest turned to look Seamus squarely in the eyes.

"We must," he said, "take the talents which God has given

us and use them to the fullest for the glory of God in heaven and the cause of justice here on earth. We must not hide our light under a bushel, but let it shine. We must carry on the work to which the Creator has fit and fashioned us. We must, Colonel, be about our Father's business."

Unsmiling, the priest held Seamus gaze a moment longer and then smiled and went on.

"I, too, must be about my Father's business as must Pastor Williams and Mr. Phaestus, I will be joining them in their trip down the mountain. Colonel, I trust we will met again, I bid you adieu. Good day Luther, Michael; I will remember you and your families in my prayers." He was off, walking at a brisk pace to join Pastor Williams heading toward the common. Cappy came over with a quick good-bye.

"Stop by the forge anytime you're in the neighborhood, Seamus, the coffee will always be on the boil."

He shook hands all around and was off after the clergymen, closing the gap with them at amazing speed, his highly polished leg sparkling in the sun and not slowing him at all.

When the three had disappeared among the vehicles in the common Luther spoke.

"Before the war," he said, "Father Power's business included that of his being a 'station master' on the Underground Railroad. The 'station' was a secret tunnel under St. Mary's Church."

Jacob replaced Rolf and young Terwilliger behind the beverage table. The demand for liquid refreshment had slowed.

Seamus took the opportunity to thank Jacob for the work he had done with the searchlight on Sunday evening, and replenished his plate at the food table.

The three men then returned to the ladies who were now all chatting away. They sat on their blankets and in short order, Seamus had again devoured the contents of his plate. He still craved more, but determined not to embarrass himself and appear a glutton, any more than he already had.

The Coronet Band continued the serenade, the deep swells of *Shenendoah* rolling out, as the shadows stretched across the lawn. Slowly, the western sky went from deep yellow, to orange, to crimson.

"Ah, sure, the Irish in America," Kathleen Dolan, was saying, "some of them, think that they are so grand, better than others, better than black folk. If they knew their own history, they would know that they themselves have been no better than slaves lo, these hundreds of years in Ireland. In the olden times, when the forces of the Crown and Cromwell would lay waste to the country, didn't the invaders gather up the poor starving children from the roadsides and ditches after they had slaughtered their parents and sell the little ones into slavery in the West Indies and Georgia and the Carolinas?"

"I know that they did." said Emily quietly.

"If the Irish in this country want to persecute the black people today," Kathleen went on, "then they might want to be careful that they wouldn't be going against some of their own distant relations.

"But it was the Famine that caused the trouble between the Irish and black people in this country. So many of us came here in destitute hordes and put the Africans, who were here before us, out of their jobs. That started it, and the cheap politicians have always been ready to take advantage of bad feeling, setting the poor against the poor. Instead, we should all be working against the common enemy, the exploiters and the oppressors. But no, so many Irishmen stand ready to listen to any agitator who will lead then in the wrong direction. That is how those disgraceful riots were started in New York City during the war. The rebel agents, who were sent to the City from Richmond to foment chaos in the Union rear, had an easy enough task among the Irish that summer. And now, how many Irishmen are still opposed to granting suffrage to Freedmen? When we women get the vote, we will not be swayed by some fat man in a high hat, smoking a big cigar and standing on a barrel of whiskey. We will use our power with decency, charity and for the good of all."

"Brava!" said Emily, and she and Sarah clapped their hands.

Kathleen's discourse was interrupted by the approach of Flanagan. The big man lumbered up and stood over Mick.

"Grogan is ready to go," he said and thrust a thumb over his shoulder.

Seamus looked across the lawn and saw Grogan standing

near the keg of punch with the giant John Sullivan. Despite the fact that Sullivan clasped him about the shoulders with his long and powerful arm, Grogan swayed like a willow in the wind.

"What!" said Mick, "Didn't I ask you to keep him limited to a few beers and away from the whiskey?"

"We did Michael," said Flanagan, looking hurt. "We did the best we could, but who would have thought that he'd bring his own jar of *potcheen* with him. He must have drunk it in a swallow the minute our backs were turned."

Flanagan looked back toward the undulating Grogan, who was, at the moment, a living testimony to the potency of homemade moonshine.

"He waited though," said the big man with a laugh, "until after Father had left."

Mick laughed too.

"Oh, he would that! He would that!" said Mick, "He is scarred to death of Father Power."

Seamus spoke.

"Is he that frightened of having his name read out from the altar at Mass then?"

"Oh, I doubt it," Mick answered, "I don't know that Grogan much cares for priest nor Pope when it comes to it. But once, he gave Father a surly response to a civil question about the state of his immortal soul and added words to the effect that if Father were not a priest, he would invite him to have it out with his fists. The good Father told Grogan not to worry about that and proceeded to give the lad an unforgettable boxing lesson."

"Father thrashed him cracker-jack well." Flanagan put in with undisguised glee.

"Of course," said Seamus.

"Anyway, Mick we will be off," said Flanagan, "good luck to you, Colonel, Luther, ladies." He turned and crossed the lawn to join Sullivan in sandwiching Grogan and escorting him toward the common. At times, the feet of their charge could be seen to leave the ground, as the two big men supported him by the elbows. The band was now playing *After the Fox*, and to Seamus' eye, Grogan's pedaling feet seemed almost to dance in the air with the accompaniment of the jig-time tune.

Grogan and his keepers halted at the common to allow Mr. Beecher's barouche to pass. Despite the fine weather, the black leather top of the vehicle was up, obscuring from view any who might be seated in the rear. The matched horses, pulling with measured hoof beats, turned into the circular drive and the bright yellow sides of the conveyance were set blazing by the declining sun as it jingled and crunched past Seamus and his companions. It came to a stop by the back entrance to be greeted by Mr. Beecher himself. He extended his hand to a man in a tall hat and black coat who descended. Another man, of larger stature, similarly dressed, also stepped down and all three entered the Mountain House. Seamus could not get a good look at the two who had arrived, but something seemed familiar to him about each of them.

A porter removed a couple of small valises from the rack between the rear wheels and the barouche pulled away. Seamus followed with his gaze as the driver completed the circle of the lawns and headed for the barns. He looked back to the rear entrance and pictured again the two men and tried to parse out what it was about them that had sparked his memory.

The building was tinted a soft pink in the setting sun. As he watched, Sally came out the door and crossed the lawn toward him. He rose as she approached. She held in her hands a sheet of parchment and the medal he had given her was a blazing orange meteor on her shawl when she stopped before him.

"Colonel," she said, "I made this for myself, but now I want you to have it, if that is all right."

She looked to Sarah, who nodded.

"Yes, child," said Sarah.

Sally turned over the paper and revealed sketched upon it a neatly finished portrait in pencil of Seamus himself.

Sarah spoke.

"Colonel, Sally would come up every afternoon to the room while you were unconscious and draw studies of your face for our evening drawing class."

"Yes, Colonel," said Sally, I had your face done and today I added the rest. After you gave me this medal, I wanted you to have something from me."

"It is a fine piece of work, Sally, thank you," said Seamus, "I have never had a real portrait done of me, just a few tintypes."

Seamus took the picture in his hands and looked at it. It was a good likeness, but far more handsome and heroic looking than he thought realistic. It depicted him from the chest up, the medals and badges portrayed in excellent detail. He wore his kepi and an expression, at once distant and defiant; the chin upturned, the eyes, yes, rather cold, looking into some far away place.

"Sally, will you be an artist or a concert singer?" he asked.

"Can I not be both?"

"Yes," said Sarah with a smile, "yes you can."

"Then I will be both. Colonel, I will go and have this put in your room."

Seamus thanked Sally again and she departed. As she entered the back of the hotel, Sampson came hurrying out. He strode down the walk and joined the professor and his musicians under the tree. They were playing *The Angel Band*, and when Sampson spoke a few words to him, the professor brought the tune to a quick conclusion, raised his coronet to his lips and played the short notes of the *Call to Attention.*

Sampson's deep voice resounded.

"Ladies and Gentlemen," he said, "Mr. Beecher asks that one and all join him in the Grand Ballroom for the remainder of the evening's entertainments which will include cake, coffee and tea and dancing to the music of Professor Smith's Coronet Band. For the children, we will have sweets and buttermilk in the casino and games and the singing of songs, as well as magic lantern slides. Young and old will be welcome to assemble on the piazza later for the illuminations. Now, if you will all please follow along with the Professor . . ."

Professor Smith struck up the band and they marched up the walk to the back entrance to the tune of *When Johnny Comes Marching Home*.

Emily took Seamus' arm and joined in the concourse of guests, staff and veterans, many singing the words of the popular song as they went with a light and cheery step into the hotel.

# XIV

# Illuminations

The beat of the drums and the impassioned call of the horns resonated through the central hall of the Mountain House and the standard bearers carried the colors immediately behind the band as the Professor led the way to the staircase. The children were diverted by Sally, Frederick Douglass Van Bronc, and young Terwilliger into the casino.

The adults followed the band which marched, never missing a note, up and around the turning stairs to the first floor. Seamus caught a glimpse out the door to the lower piazza of the peaceful evening creeping across the Valley of the Hudson, the distant Berkshires deep purple against a violet sky.

The band and the color bearers marched into the ballroom and to the far end of the long and captious chamber, arranging themselves, while playing steadily, around the music stands before the French windows. The flags were hung, with their staffs crossed, behind the musicians. The last rays of the setting sun shown through the glass of the doors and lighted from behind the two banners.

The celebrants filling the room deposited there hats and parasols on the tables at either side of the entry. Seamus noted that an interesting variety of military headgear was represented as he put his own cap on the table to the left were Sampson stood.

"Sampson," said Seamus softly, "is there a safe place I can put this," he touched his holster, "for now."

Sampson replied in a voice even softer.

"Colonel, I believe Mr. Beecher would prefer you to keep

your pistol on your person tonight."

"Certainly, Sampson," replied Seamus, and he thought; What, now?!?

The Dolans, the Van Broncs, Seamus and Emily stood together near the entrance.

A rich aroma of coffee filled the room and tables along the right of the dance floor had been laid with cakes and china pots of hot drinks. The staff seemed hard pressed to keep up with the sudden demand for desserts and Sarah and Luther excused themselves to go and help out.

After they departed, Seamus spoke quietly to Emily.

"Those silver hair combs look very becoming on Sarah."

"They do," Emily replied, "she wanted to return them to me, but I insisted that she keep them as a token of our friendship. She took a great deal of convincing. I told her it was by no means a diminishment of her pride; friends have a right to give each other gifts. And, I said that nothing had changed; I still want her to remember me, even though I may not be in the next world but nonetheless far away."

Seamus did not like the idea of Emily being far away, not from himself anyhow.

He changed the subject.

"Mick," he said indicating the flags, "how did you acquire that fine stand of colors."

"Grand aren't they, Colonel." Mick replied. As the last of the guests arrived the band finished their playing with a flourish and Mick lead the way to take a closer view of the banners.

"Major Donovan," he said, "is now in the Veteran Reserve Corps and he has designated us; the veterans of the Irish Brigade of Ulster and Greene counties, that is, as official keepers of these retired colors of the 1st Battalion of the 69th. You remember the Major don't you?"

"Indeed I do." said Seamus. He recalled to his mind the vision of the spare and sprightly John H. Donovan, a halo of wild and curly hair around his head. The high cheek bones, the thin mustache, a razor of a man. He resembled a buccaneer of olden times with a black patch covering the socket of the eye he had lost at Malvern Hill four years ago now, almost to the day.

"These are the very flags then that we took to the Peninsula, Mick?"

"That they are, Colonel *macushla*, that they are. Lately," Mick lowered his voice, "the Green Flag went to Canada, as well."

Intrigued, Seamus stepped closer. He could see now that the biggest rents in the flags had been carefully mended. Some bullet holes in the Green Flag had been left. Or were they new ones?

The National Standard hung to the left, the gold stars in the big, light blue canton rippling in the draft from the window. The broad red and white stripes bore faint gunpowder stains. Below the canton he read the letters sown on in scarlet fabric; *69th Regt. N.Y. Vols. 1st Bat.*

On the Green Banner, the heroic harp stood out, rendered in gold silk, the sun burst and descending rays floated above the names of the twenty three campaigns for which battle honors had been conferred upon the regiment. Seamus read to himself; Bull Run, Peninsula, Antietam, Fredricksburg. He thought of how fortunate he had been to be wounded at Antietam so that he had missed the carnage of Burnside's blunder before Marye's Heights.

Had Seamus Delaney been with the Brigade at Fredricksburg, would he have survived, he wondered again as he often had before.

He read on; Chancelorsville, Gettysburg . . . another lucky shot that had put him out of action for the unrelenting hell of the next three campaigns; Wilderness, Spotsylvania and Cold Harbor; the redoubtable Grant's mistake. All in God's hands, he thought, spared again and again.

"Beautiful laurel wreaths there at the tops of the flagstaffs," he said, coming back to the present.

"Miz Emily made them," said Mick, "made the one for poor Sarge's grave too."

Seamus turned to Emily.

"You all earned your laurels over and over again these past days," she said, "and dear Sarge, as well. And I had to have something to keep my hands busy while we waited for you to return to us after you were wounded on Monday."

"Every time I came to your bedside," said Mick, "there would be her ladyship, sitting by and working away at the wreaths."

Seamus could not stop looking down into the calm blue lakes that were Emily's eyes.

"Sally helped me to gather the laurel leaves along the cliff path," she said, "it was no trouble . . . ," her voice trailed off. She stood looking up into Seamus' eyes.

Mick broke the spell.

"We should be getting some of the treats, before they're all gone." he said.

Seamus reluctantly took his eyes from Emily's. He looked toward the tables and saw Levi in the middle of the room supervising the lighting of one of the three great Waterford chandeliers which were spaced the length of the lofty ceiling.

He took one more look at the Green Banner and beyond it saw a man standing at the far French door looking out toward the stables. He recognized the man immediately. It was General Thorne.

What in the world, Seamus wondered, is he doing at the Mountain House.

The General continued looking out the window and Emily tugged at Seamus sleeve.

"I am sure," she said "that they will not run out, but let us have some cake before the dancing starts, because I expect to have many, many requests for dances and will need to eat to keep up my strength."

General Thorne, Seamus was thinking, still staring at the man, and then he thought; many requests for dances?

His head snapped around.

"Many requests for dances?" he said.

"Yes," said Emily, smiling brightly, "many." And she hustled him to the center table where wedges of cake with red, white and blue frosting were set on little china plates. The rush having abated, the Van Broncs rejoined them. Each took a plate of cake and a cup from the table. Seamus noticed Rolf pouring out the coffee, and saw Doctor Duboise hand him his cup. With a deft movement, Rolf lowered the cup beneath the level of the table. He looked about quickly and took a brown glass flask from his pocket. In a trice, the flask had been upended, returned to Rolf's pocket and the cup, with a dash of coffee added in, had been returned to the doctor.

"Good man, Rolf," said the doctor, with a broad smile, "thank you kindly."

"My pleasure, Doctor."

The doctor turned and greeted Seamus.

"My favorite patient," he said, "and how are you holding up so far?"

"Tolerably well, Doctor," Seamus lied. He had just now started to feel dizzy and his head throbbed, but he was determined to see the celebrations through.

The physician did not appear to be convinced by this optimistic report.

"Oh really?" he said, and he greeted the others and asked if he might join their party.

All agreed that he was most welcome and they crossed the room and seated themselves on the sofas before the windows of the south courtyard.

"Mrs. Dolan," said Doctor Duboise, "I trust little Suzie's tummy has improved since I last saw her."

"Oh, it has, Doctor," said Kathleen, "the paregoric that you prescribed was just the thing. She is fine now, thank God and your good self."

Seamus allowed his gaze to wander about the room. He saw that General Thorne now stood in the far corner, beyond the band, carefully surveying and scrutinizing every face in the room. At one point he looked directly at Seamus and held his eyes unblinking and steady upon his face for several seconds. Notwithstanding the fact that they were well acquainted with one another, the General showed not the slightest flicker of recognition, much less acknowledgment.

Does he not know me, wondered Seamus. Do I look that much different? It has not been so long since we last met.

For an instant, Seamus questioned his own identification of the man.

Maybe it is not Thorne, he thought . . . no, it's him alright, the same high forehead, the same cold and tired eyes, the same down turned mustache. Well, the man has always been nothing, if not phlegmatic.

The General stood with his arms crossed on his chest. Seamus noted that his right hand was under his left arm, but inside his coat.

Most of the celebrants having been served dessert and having found their seats, the Professor struck up the band with the *Cape May Polka.* A number of couples immediately took to the dance floor. Seamus, still watching General Thorne, absently tapped his foot in time with the lively tune.

"Well, that, at least, is a start," said the doctor taking a pull from his cup.

The comment brought Seamus back to his present company. He noted then that all in his party were staring at him, rather expectantly, he thought.

"A start?" he asked the doctor.

"Yes," came the reply, "Your tapping of your foot is a start toward dancing."

"Dancing? Me?" he looked quickly to Emily, felt his face going red. Emily was smiling a small smile.

"Um," he said, "dancing. Yes . . . I fear I am not very good. "

Emily interrupted.

"Did you know, Colonel, that while you were unconscious, Mr. Dolan and I had a long talk about the subject of dancing? And that Mr. Dolan told me that during the war, General Meagher insisted that, if they were to be called gentlemen, all his officers must learn the art of dancing, and that your regimental dancing master always pointed to you as being his most talented student? Did you know that, Colonel?"

"No, I mean, yes . . . I . . .," Seamus looked at Mick. The former sergeant said nothing; his eyes sparkled in the light from the chandelier above. Nothing for it, Seamus thought. He turned again to Emily. He stood and bowed at the waist.

"Miz Emily, would you do me the honor of . . ."

"Why, it would be my great pleasure, Colonel," said Emily in what to Seamus sounded like more, both in quality and quantity, than her usual Southern accent, "how kind of you to ask."

She rose and in an instant was in his arms and whirling about the floor.

In short order, Seamus began to feel in his head the effects of this vigorous twirling and the entire room seemed to start rotating counter to the direction in which he and Emily were dancing. Then, however, the band slipped into the rather more sedate *Palmyra Schottische* and he regained his equilibrium. He began to appreciate the delight of being encompassed by Emily's fragrant arms, and his dancing felt to him to be effortless. No conversation passed between them. They held each others gaze as the room, its windows, the crystal shinning lights, the furnishings, golden draperies, the doors, the red, white and blue and the green of the banners and the other dancers passed 'round and 'round about them.

In no time at all, it seemed the music ended and the dancers stopped of a sudden.

Odd, thought Seamus, only two tunes and the band has completed the medley.

As they all stood on the dance floor, Professor Smith sounded *Attention* on his coronet and Mr. Beecher walked from the doorway toward the bandstand. The crowd parted at his passing and those who were seated stood to see what was happening.

On reaching his goal, the old gentleman spoke a few words to Professor Smith, turned and, smiling, greeted the assembled guests.

"My friends," he said, "I beg your indulgence for my interruption, but I am certain that you will forgive me when you hear what I have to tell you."

He paused and looked about the room.

"Firstly," he continued, "allow me to most fervently offer my heartfelt thanks to you men of the Irish Brigade and to your ladies as well, for they also shared in the sacrifice. I thank you for the action by which you came, once again, as you did in the late war, to the rescue of the just from the clutches of the unjust."

He led the audience in applauding the veterans in the room.

"Further, I wish to publicly thank my staff for the extraordinary service they have rendered in bringing about the happy outcome of the last several days."

He paused again and led the applause, the veterans this time joining in with great gusto.

"Finally, I am happy to announce that the speaker for whom Colonel Delaney so kindly substituted this afternoon has arrived and will address us with a few remarks. His address will be, of necessity, brief because, like many of you here gathered, he too served his country in the War of the Rebellion and, though his leadership was exercised not at the battlefront, but at the very centers of power within the Union, his position proved no less perilous than had he been in the trenches and fields at the South. He too became a casualty of the war and could have very nearly been, but for the eternal mercy of a loving Providence, one of its last fatalities. He suffered wounds of the most severe kind in his struggle for the Republic and is even now still recovering his health and strength. Nonetheless, this stalwart and constant patriot would not allow an Independence Day to pass without all the traditional ceremonies being properly observed.

"With service to his fellow Americans always foremost in his heart and in his actions, this truly great man has earned the admiration of the nation which he yet serves. All here present know this gentleman by his words and by his deeds and so permit me, rather than to *introduce* him, to *present* him to you."

Mr. Beecher raised his hand indicating the entrance at the other end of the room.

"Ladies and Gentlemen, the Right Honorable . . ."

Seamus turned his head toward the empty doorway. A man appeared. He walked into the light of the ballroom, slow of step, below average height, bent.

My good God! thought Seamus, it's . . . it's . . .

"Mr. William Henry Seward . . . ," said Mr. Beecher.

It was the Secretary.

" . . . the Secretary of State of the United States."

Mr. Beecher's voice and, indeed, the band's fanfare, were drowned in the wildest cheering and applause.

The Secretary proceeded through the crowd which again parted like the waters of the Red Sea before Moses and the Children of Israel. Holding his left hand on the silken lapel of his fine black coat, with his right hand he waved to each side in acknowledgment of the ovation. His stiff white collar stood up next to his lean cheek and, ever the dandy, he wore a broad cravat of bright red, white and blue stripes. The striking necktie, it seemed to Seamus, was like a forlorn flourish of the colors, made by the maimed standard bearer of an all but defeated regiment. The Secretary had suffered greatly since the days when Seamus had first been summoned to his service. He was now deeply scarred in his body and in his soul. The hollowness of his cheeks made his large nose even more prominent. The hair, cut like that of a noble old Roman, seemed to be even grayer than when they had last met, only weeks before. And yet, Seamus saw no sign of surrender in this bloodied but valiant campaigner.

The Secretary approached nearer in his halting, bow-legged gait, and paused before Seamus. He quickly turned his head and his bushy eyebrows arched. He twisted his scarred mouth into a smile.

"Colonel," he murmured through tight jaws.

"S-sir," Seamus stammered, still astounded at the man's presence here.

To Emily, the Secretary inclined his head courteously.

"Ma'am," he said.

Emily curtsied most gracefully.

"Mr. Secretary," she said.

With a bow to Emily, the Secretary's bright, expressive, deep-set eyes again flitted to Seamus' face. He seemed amused at the look of amazement he saw there. He nodded and resumed his progress toward the bandstand amid the unceasing roar of admiration.

All present knew how this man had stood by President Lincoln throughout the war, and how on the night of the assassination, Mr. Seward himself had been attacked in his sick bed, his face slashed, in his home near the White House. How he had very nearly been killed himself by one of Booth's agents.

Mr. Seward was known to all as one of the true heroes of the war. In his years in the employ of the Secretary, Seamus had come to learn of many other ways in which the man's heroism and devotion to the nation had come into play, but in secret.

The Irish in the audience knew that the Secretary's steadfast insistence on the fair treatment of Catholics and his absolute refusal to compromise, in any way, with the Know-Nothings had been one of the two major factors which has cost him the Republican presidential nomination. He, and not Lincoln, might have been president, and the Irish Catholics in the audience were letting him know that they appreciated his sacrifice.

The other big block to the nomination had been the Secretary's long record of opposition to slavery, his unashamed affiliation with Abolitionists, and his long battle against the Fugitive Slave Act. In his way, Mr. Seward had been more anti-slavery than had Lincoln.

The black people in the audience knew all this, and they too were thanking him for his sacrifice on their behalf.

So, on and on the cheering went. All the Americans; the African, the Irish, the old Yankee and Dutch descendants, clapped and hurrahed, expressing gratitude for the country as a whole and for their individual portions of it.

At length, the din in the room began to abate and the Secretary could be heard, albeit faintly.

"Thank you . . . thank you, my friends . . . thank you . . ."

When all were silent, he spoke, projecting his words as loudly as he could given the limited movement he had regained in his injured jaw.

"Thank you, Mr. Beecher, thank you one and all. I am reminded of a July Fourth address which I made forty-one years ago this very night. Back then, our present century was only in it's mid-twenties, as, indeed was I myself, and perhaps that is the reason why, in my youthful innocence, I then attempted in that speech to look down the years yet to come and divine the future. I predicted that there would never be a civil war between the North and the South."

He chuckled, and winced slightly.

"Let that be a lesson to soothsayers, especially youthful

ones."

The audience joined in his laughter, and the Secretary shook his head ruefully and continued.

"In that speech, I remember that I said that the Missouri Compromise had settled the question of slavery and that all would now be at peace because none in this nation would ever be aroused to tear the Union asunder over any single issue, be it slavery or states rights. But, perhaps it was not just my youth, for as late as 1850, I still felt my premise to be correct and said so in public.

"Well, my friends, I do not have to tell you that I was wrong. History has told you that. I was wrong about slavery; no compromise would settle that issue, only the total abolition of the hideous institution. As it turned out, only the war would bring about abolition. I had underestimated the power which greedy and small minded men could exercise toward inflaming a whole section of the populous to enter a war which they could not win, and which, had they looked at the issue clearly and logically, as I had in my youth, would have known that they could not win. But people do not enter into war with clear eyes but, rather, with eyes already clouded by blood.

"Later, when the war was beginning, many doubted the North's ability to pursue the matter successfully and I myself had my doubts. But I see now that I and the other doubters had again committed the sin of underestimation.

"I had underestimated the resolve and courage of a President who came to be my friend."

The Secretary was halted in his discourse by more wild cheering occasioned by his reference to Mr. Lincoln. When the applause stopped, he resumed.

"And, I underestimated the vast extent to which the heroic virtues of that truly great man would be reflected and magnified in the hearts of a great people. How you," he raised his hands in an embracing gesture, “would put aside individual concerns and pursuits, and petty differences to unite into an indomitable force for justice to prosecute the war to its just and Providentially blessed end.

"In the course of that struggle you, the American people,

endured hardship, dangers and horrors which I, and the contemporaries of the youth I was, when I made my speech some forty Independence Days ago, could never have conceived in the very darkest of our nightmares.

"This nation will never again know the innocence of the 1820's and so we must not try to *see into* the future, but must instead *see to it*, with vigor and optimism, but always with a discerning and watchful eye.

"And so, in conclusion, for what you have done, and for what you are still doing, to protect and preserve this Union for yet another Fourth of July, allow me please, as an old New York State Militiaman, to salute you."

Mr. Seward straightened himself to a stiff position of attention and, with his head held high, raised his trembling hand to his brow. The audience burst once more into wild applause, and closed in around the Secretary still clapping their hands. Seamus was drawn forward as well. The central question as to why the Secretary was here at the Mountain House was now joining and melding with other questions which raced through his mind. Questions, he expected, only Mr. Seward could answer.

The crowd had the Secretary fair surrounded now and Seamus could see that General Thorne had advanced from the corner he had occupied during the speech. He was stretching his neck and even hopping up to look over the heads of the audience. The general's eyes seemed to Seamus to be straining to glimpse the back of the Secretary's head. He seemed also to be making a vain effort to get closer to Mr. Seward, but he was getting washed, like an unsuccessful salmon, further back by the torrent of well-wishers which now engulfed the Secretary. Soon, Seamus found himself, and Emily beside him, in the forefront of the circle around Mr. Seward.

Luther and Sarah stood to Seamus right. The Secretary bowed to Sarah.

"The charming Mrs. Van Bronc," he said, "and Mr. Van Bronc, and how is the namesake of the worthy Frederick Douglass."

"He is fine, Mr. Secretary, fine, he is just downstairs with the other young people," replied Sarah, her smile radiant.

The Secretary shook hands with Luther, and then with Frank Treacy, who stood within the circle.

"Captain Treacy," he said quietly to the big Irishman.

Captain? wondered Seamus. Frank Tracey's sergeant stripes were plain to see on his uniform sleeve.

"I am very happy," Mr. Seward continued, "to see that you returned safely, and have come through this more recent action here unscathed."

"Most of our friends have come back in safety, sir," Frank replied in a low tone, still clasping the Secretary's hand. Bending down, he talked almost into the man's ear. "I speak for all when I say thanks to you, sir. We are, Mr. Secretary, always ready and at your service."

The Secretary smiled discreetly and nodded.

Seamus was beginning to understand, or, then again, he thought, maybe not.

"Colonel," said Mr. Seward, to Seamus, "would you care to join me on the piazza, I feel the need for some fresh air in which to smoke a cigar."

"Yes, sir."

The Secretary raised his voice and addressed all present.

"I had no intent of disrupting the festivities. Please, do resume your dancing."

Mr. Beecher signaled the Professor who struck up the band and the crowd melted away some to the sidelines and others to become dancing couples, as the strains of the Irish tune; *Skibereen,* played in waltz time, filled the ballroom.

Seamus turned to Emily as the doctor nimbly interposed himself between them. The doctor bowed deeply to Emily.

"If I may have the honor of this dance, ma'am," he said, "I feel I may demonstrate that the Colonel, pride though he may be of his regimental dancing master, cannot hold a candle to me, when it comes to the waltz."

Emily curtsied and joined the doctor in the dance.

The Secretary and Seamus made their way out to the piazza, and stood by the railing on the darkened porch, a pool of light from the open door behind them spread on the floor. The stars shown brilliantly above the quiet valley below.

The older man withdrew a large black leather cigar case from his inner pocket, offered a fine, slim, habana cheroot to Seamus and took one himself. He struck a match and lighted Seamus cigar and then his own. The faces of the two were illuminated briefly and then could be distinguished only by the burring embers on the tips of their smokes. The music came out to them through the door.

The Secretary spoke.

"*Skibereen,*" he said," a lament for the dead of the Great Famine in the land of your birth, as you know, Colonel, and already it has become a tune for dancing. We humans are a strange species, how quickly we scab over our hurts, heal and make light of our wounds. Sometimes, though, the scars are festering beneath."

He said no more, but smoked quietly.

Seamus burned to ask his questions, but one did not pose questions to one's superior. Most certainly not in the business in which he and the Secretary were usually engaged. One was told what one needed to know, no more, no less; it was hoped no less, at any rate.

The Secretary savored his cheroot.

"My last remaining vice," he said, taking the cigar from his mouth and regarding the tip, "along with the occasional glass of port," he added.

He put the cigar back between his lips, left it there, and spoke, as was his custom, with it bobbing up and down.

"You were surprised to see me here, Colonel."

"I was, sir, but now I take it that I am here because you were coming here. This is not a coincidence."

"Very good," said the Secretary. They had often played this game; Seamus trying to determine facts not known to him, but known to his chief. Mr. Seward encouraged the development of deductive reasoning as well as of minute observation in the members of his 'irregular staff.'

"I also take it, sir, that you knew you were coming here to the Mountain House, although I did not, and that Mr. Beecher knew that I work for you, and that is why I am his 'special guest' and why he was aware of my talents with regard to investigations even though I had never met the gentleman before my arrival here."

"Excellent," said the Secretary.

"And so, you dispatched me here, sir, as . . . as . . . what? . . . an advanced scout?"

"If you like, Colonel," the Secretary smiled mildly behind his cigar.

"You know what has transpired here lately, sir, do you not."

"Quite, Mr. Beecher has given me a full report."

"But you could not have known when you sent me here that Luther was to be falsely accused."

"The reason I sent you," said the Secretary, "had nothing to do with Luther, although you did splendidly in helping him to clear his name and in preventing his lynching. But it is not fair for me to keep you guessing.

"I had planned for some time to come to the Mountain House. I had, and still have business to the north and incidentally wished to visit my old friends here in New York State. Certain persons, who wish never to see that business completed, became aware of my planned itinerary and laid their own plans to interrupt, permanently, my travels. To put it simply, Colonel, they meant to kill me. Through particular channels, I learned of their plot, but only in rather general terms. I could not cancel my trip; my business, the nation's business, in this case, cannot wait, and as you know, if I cancelled a trip every time I heard someone wanted me dead, I would never go anywhere. I cannot allow myself, nor our government, to be paralyzed by fear. I therefore kept to my schedule and sent you ahead. Since a hotel is filled constantly with strangers, it seemed to me a likely spot for our enemies to assemble an assassination team. As it turned out, I was right."

"Sir, you mean to say that Lejeune, McCain . . ."

"And Clay too, Colonel."

"And Clay too, had come here to lie in wait for you."

"Precisely, and as you deduced, when Clay became a liability, Lejeune disposed of him."

"And that, sir, is why Lejeune and McCain did not leave

after they murdered Clay."

"Correct again, Colonel. Once they had gotten rid of Clay, and had enjoyed the devil's own luck in having Luther for a scapegoat, they had no reason to abandon their plan. They had simply to continue their intrigues with Skhutt to ensure that Luther would be lynched before a proper investigation and inquest could be completed.

"I am sure they had no idea that you worked for me. If they had, I expect they may have tried to dispose of you as well. As it was, they were clearly aware of your efforts on behalf of Luther, but probably considered you to be just an amateur detective, whose murder would have caused yet more attention still to be directed at the Mountain House, thereby placing their mission in even more jeopardy. As it was, they felt that Luther would surely be dispatched and that they only need wait until I arrived.

"Incidentally, Mr. Beecher pointed out to me the fact that Lejeune had chosen to stay in room number twenty-eight, on the inside corner of the rear south wing; one of the least desirable rooms, but one which commands an excellent view of the rear entrance and the perfect place to observe the comings and goings of the coaches. Perhaps he intended to shoot me as soon as I arrived and was disembarking from my coach. His operatives at the boat dock in Catskill could have alerted him to my arrival there, giving him plenty of time to lay an *ambuscade*. Failing that, he could have shot me at any time I was passing the back door. He certainly had the right weapon for the job and since number twenty-eight is a corner room, he could have shot me from the inward facing window and escaped through the other window in his room, that which faces west. In a matter of seconds, he could have been within the cover of the woods behind the stables."

The Secretary pondered silently for a few moments and then went on.

"When one has been the target of assassination plots as often as have I, one begins to think as do the assassins.

"In any case, I thank you Colonel and I apologize for using you, so to speak, without your knowledge as my forward picket or *vidette*. I could not be sure that the attempt would come here or that it would come at all. My first stop in New York had been at the town where I was born, Florida, in Orange County. There, I was among friends and relations and it is a small town where everyone knows all about everyone else. Strangers in that town would have been remarked. From Florida, my itinerary took me to Newburgh where I boarded the steamer to Catskill and thence to here . . ."

The mention of the town of Newburgh opened a 'file', as it were, in Seamus' brain. The assassin Booth had maintained contacts in the town and had been seen there shortly before he murdered the President. A veritable den of Copperheads during the war, Newburgh was a place Union soldiers had been advised to avoid while on leave, least they be set upon by Sesech plug-uglies.

The Secretary was still talking.

"After I leave here, my schedule takes me north, to Auburn where I will be with my family; again not a likely place for a murder attempt either. I have planned no public appearances, tonight being impromptu, so this hotel seemed the most likely site for an attack. But I honestly sent you here to have a rest, and despite the events as they occurred you seem to me to have benefited. You are looking well, your bandage and bruises notwithstanding."

Seamus still felt vertigo in his head.

"Any how," his chief continued, "I was sure that if anything was afoot, you would discover it or, at the least, be in place as a reserve, available to me upon my arrival. Had there been no plotters about, you could have enjoyed a pleasant vacation in lovely surroundings, and I would have surprised you for a Fourth of July celebration. I could not tell you of my suspicions because the fewer who know that I have a source within the secret body which directs these assassins, the better. I tell you now because you have seen for yourself their handiwork, and because you will have to learn more about them in the future.

"By the bye, with regard to the man known as McCain, you may have rendered, in some measure, a stroke of vengeance in the matter of the Great Famine in Ireland."

Seamus felt his mouth fall open.

"Tell me, Colonel, where you able to closely observe the man, did you see on McCain any tattoos?"

"I did, sir. On the edge of his right hand was a tattoo in blue ink: a jagged line or two . . ."

"Old Blue Lightening," said the Secretary speaking in a sigh out into the night above the valley, "it *was* he after all."

"Sir?"

"McCain; it is as good a name as any to call him by. It may even have been his true name. He has used dozens. He came from the land of your birth, Colonel. We are sure of that and the fact that he was late of the Royal Inniskilling Dragoons. He worked for powers within the English Empire for many years. He operated all over the world but most especially in North America and he traveled often between Canada and the United States, as well as those states which were in rebellion during these last years. He did his bit to incite the draft riots in New York City in '63, calling himself Edward Nelson and posing as a dentist back then. But, he concentrated his efforts on inciting the Indian tribes against the Union . . ."

"Sir," Seamus could not help himself from interrupting, " I think our own government has done a great deal itself to incite the Indians, particularly through it's own Indian agents, some of them, and their evil and corrupt treatment of the people they were supposed to be helping. And still, many tribes sided with the Union during the war."

"True enough, true enough, but McCain was always there to exacerbate a bad situation. He had become a member of one of the tribes in the north, not that he truly loved them, he despised them, as he did most people. But, he wanted to use them and so ingratiated himself and stirred up risings that he knew could only end in failure in order to bring as much pressure on the Union as he could. That tattoo on his hand was a lightening sign, a symbol that he had been initiated into the tribe. The Indians gave him the name Old Blue Lightening. He sometimes used that *nomme de guerre* on cipher communication which we have intercepted.

"It was McCain who fomented the rising of the Lakota on the Great Lakes frontier during the war . . ."

"The fact that the Indians were starving," Seamus interrupted again, "may have had something to do with their rising up." He never before spoke to the Secretary in such a sarcastic fashion, but the subject of famine was a sore one with him, and despite his affection and respect for his chief, he found that the man, like many of his contemporaries, had a blind spot when it came to the Indians.

"Too true," the Secretary continued, "Sad to say, their United States Indian Agent told the tribes that if they were hungry, they could eat grass. This, after their government issue of provisions had disappeared before ever reaching them, and after their crops had failed."

"Was not," asked Seamus, "that same agent, one of the first to be killed in the rising, and his body later found with grass stuffed into his mouth?"

"He was," the Secretary replied.

"Poetry," said Seamus.

"The point is," said Mr. Seward, "the Indians' crops failed due to a previously unknown disease, just as the potatoes in Ireland failed from a blight previously unknown in Ireland, but known elsewhere, notably in Nova Scotia, Canada. Do you remember the report I showed you to the effect that diseased potatoes had been imported into Ireland and had spread the blight there?"

"I do, sir."

"Well, Colonel, the spread of crop-damaging disease, as well as the distribution of disease infested clothing and bedding among civilians, as was sometimes done by rebel destructionists, was McCain's specialty. Do you remember the English gave pox laden blankets to the Indians in Pontiac's War in the last century, and how we suspected the rebel agent; Dr. Blackbourne of attempting to send the clothing of Yellow Fever victims from Bermuda to Union cities? Well, McCain also carried on the technique of spreading pestilence. If the potato blight was deliberately introduced into Ireland, he was the agent who did it."

Seamus was silent in the darkness. His cigar tip glowed as he inhaled.

"I see," he said at length, "but I did not strike a blow for revenge, sir, McCain destroyed himself in his effort to destroy me. He wreaked vengeance upon himself."

"Quite," said the Secretary, "that is often the case with men like that. It is a pity that they do not always destroy themselves *before* they inflict so much suffering on humanity. And that is why we must never stop in our efforts to root them out before they do all the damage they are capable of doing, and to hunt them so that do not get away with their depredations, but instead are brought to the bar of justice. That, Colonel, brings me to a subject which I have intended to broach when I met you here, whether or not the assassination plot this time proved to be real ."

"Sir," Seamus again could not help but interrupt. The word *assassination* had again brought a question to his mind which he could not forbear asking.

"Sir, Brutus Lejuene; . . . is he . . ."

A flash of white light from below and BOOOMMM!

In an instant, another flash from above and BOOOMMM!

Seamus felt the reverberation in his chest and flinched. The Secretary ducked his head.

Rapid footsteps from behind. Seamus spun around, faced a silhouetted figure rushing from the open hallway door. A man darted toward them. The pistol in his hand sparkled in the light from the door.

Nickel-plated revolver, Seamus thought.

He stepped in front of the Secretary shielding his chief's body with his own. Reached for the pin-fire pistol in his holster, hesitated, thought of the drowned cartridges. Too late. The man was upon them. It was General Thorne.

"Gentlemen! Please!" the Secretary shouted, "Please! Before someone is hurt, put up your gun, General! Stand easy, Colonel! There is no danger, see . . . it is the fireworks."

He pointed down at the ledge below the piazza. A man stood there, barely visible in the dark. An orange point of fire smoldered in his hand. He stooped. Another explosion. In the flash, Seamus could see that the man was Jacob. He had just fired a bomb from the small coehorn mortar which squatted smoking by his foot. By its burning fuse the projectile could be seen arching out over the valley. Presently, the paper bomb exploded in the sky with another flash and a boom and a shower of gold and silver sparks rained down.

The general spoke.

"Your pardon, Mr. Secretary, but what with Mr. Beecher has told us about the goings on here, and the crowd around you before, I confess to some nerves. We have no way of knowing whether or not Lejeune is still lurking about, and the sudden explosion; I . . . I am afraid I thought the worst, sir."

As he spoke, he returned his pistol; a nickel-plated Colt's Sheriff's model, Seamus could now see, to the shoulder holster under his coat.

"I doubt Lejeune is within a hundred miles of here now, General, but I do appreciate your concern. You are of course acquainted with Colonel Delaney."

The Secretary knew of a certainty that Seamus and the General were acquainted, as he had employed the both of them at various times during the last several years in the same capacity, that is when Thorne was not occupied in his other duties of providing General Grant with information about the enemy.

"Delaney." said General Thorne by way of greeting.

"General Thorne." Seamus replied, matching the man's cordiality.

"Actually," said Mr. Seward, "the General is no longer a General, save in the Veteran Reserve Corps. He is now a detective in the Department of State. The exigency fund, which I carefully husbanded since the war's end, and out of which I was able to pay you gentlemen through your military paymasters, has expired. However, there is much yet to be done and I have been authorized to hire a number of detectives. That is one of the things I wish to discuss with you, Colonel Delaney. But, that will have to wait."

The Secretary gestured, cigar in hand, toward the doorway through which the guests, summoned by the explosions, were now streaming to view the illuminations.

Emily came to Seamus, and linked arms, moving him to a place by the railing. As she did so, she smiled at the Secretary.

"May I have Colonel Delaney back now, sir?" she asked.

"You may," he responded, quite charmed, and with a chuckle in his throat, "and I am sure, ma'am, it will be most agreeable for the Colonel."

Seamus felt his face burning and was glad of the dark. The closeness of Emily he found to be very agreeable indeed.

Flash, BOOM! Another aerial bomb detonated over the valley.

Jacob leaned with his match to a row of rockets arrayed along the cliff edge. WHOOSH! WHOOSH! WHOOSH!

The rockets rose up, red tails glaring behind them against the night sky. One, two three, the rockets blossomed into flowers of flame out over the side of the mountain. The muffled reports came back; PUFF . . . PUFF . . . PUFF. . .

More rockets were launched and the mortar blasted again. The bright flashes, the streamers of brazen sparks were greeted by reserved murmurs of *oow* and *aah* from the upper piazza where the adults stood, and by high pitched cheers from the lower piazza where the children, less confined by the strictures of convention, gave vent to their excitement in a more demonstrative way.

Seamus always found fireworks to be both mesmerizing and disquieting. Still, the tingle he felt in his stomach at the wild display was not unpleasant. He felt suddenly light-headed and leaned carefully against the rail.

The illuminations went on and on, ending finally in a veritable crescendo as Jacob fired off a barrage of rockets and mortar bombs. As the last echoes of the fireworks faded across the valley from the Catskills to the Berkshires, far to the right more flashes could be seen as tiny sparks in the southeastern sky.

"Poughkeepsie," someone said, "There are Poughkeepsie's illuminations."

Next a cloud of sparks billowed up into night even closer still.

"There is Kingston," the voice said.

The rain of gold and silver was followed by a rumble like distant thunder.

One by one the towns along the river, from the south to the north sent up their salutes to Independence Day. Saugerties and

Catskill lighted the sky and across the river; Hudson. To the north, Athens and Coxsackie added their fiery testament to freedom and dimly the flashes could be seen over Albany.

In the midst of these displays a boat on the river sent up rocket after rocket and her steam calliope could be heard much louder than any of the ship's bands on the previous evenings.

"It is the *Armenia,*" said the all knowing voice, "on her July 4th excursion from Newburgh."

A cheer went up from the young people below as the vessel caught the Mountain House in her searchlight. From the roof, the hotel's powerful light responded in kind, and the calliope rendered a jaunty version of *Isn't He a Darling, Bould Soger Boy*.

Many of those present, including, to Seamus surprise, Emily, sang along. She leaned close to his ear and sang the comic song to him. In the glow of the searchlight, he could see her smiling brightly, her eyes twinkling.

The *Armenia* turned in the middle of the river and headed to the south as the illuminations diminished across the valley. Her calliope rang forth yet with *The Battle Cry of Freedom*, and again many sang along. Seamus and Emily remained silent, looking into each others eyes until the searchlights were extinguished and the music hushed on the dark river.

With almost no interruption, however, the coronet band made itself heard from within taking up the serenade with the *Port Royal Gallop*, thus enticing the assembly to return to the dance.

As most of the crowd moved back into the ball room, the Secretary turned to Seamus and Emily.

"I will take this opportunity," he said with a bow, "to make good my escape to my room. I am very tired and so I will say, good evening. I will meet with you tomorrow, Colonel, if you please. Perhaps about noontime here on the piazza, if that suits you."

"I am your servant, sir," said Seamus. But not for much longer, he thought.

They followed the crowd entering the hotel and parted by the staircase.

The Secretary and the general started to mount the stairs.

"Mr. Beecher," said the Secretary, "has been good enough to give me the use of his suite during my stay here. He is really too kind. Once again; good evening to you."

Thorne nodded and they were off.

As Emily and Seamus entered the ballroom, she took him in her arms and they were again circling the floor among the dancers.

The band swung without halting into the *Nightingale Waltz* and then into the *Storm Gallop*. At the conclusion of the later, all present let forth with three generous hurrahs.

Finally, the band played *The Garryowen* in waltz time and then the traditional going home song; *Kathleen Mavourneen.* Everyone stood on the dance floor and sang along. Many a voice cracked with emotion and Seamus dared not to look at Emily as he felt his own eyes filing. At the end of the song, the room was filled with applause for the Professor and his musicians and the leave taking began with the band's lively recessional; *We Shall Meet, But We Shall Miss Him.*

Seamus bid farewell to the Dolans, and Frank Treacy and the others among the veterans as he and Emily stood near the sofas on the south side of the room. After most had passed out of the room, a black curtain came down over Seamus' eyes and after a little while he found himself no longer standing, but now sitting on the sofa which had been directly behind him. Emily was kneeling at his left and the doctor at his right. He looked from one to the other. Emily was rubbing his hand and the doctor was taking his pulse and squinting at his watch. Luther and Sarah were crouched in front of him and Luther spoke.

"Looks like you fainted for a moment there, Colonel." he said.

"Oh?" said Seamus. He sounded rather stupid to himself.

"Yes," said the doctor, "Good thing you had the sofa to sit on, or you would be lying on your back right now. Told you to stay in bed, did I not? But the patient always knows best, especially you Irishmen, always so reasonable. No damage, I think, but you will go to bed now, will you not, Colonel?"

It was not the end to the evening which Seamus had

envisioned. A stroll on the piazza with Emily would have been infinitely more to his liking. Indeed, he would have protested now, except that he felt he could not stand at the moment without help. He looked to Emily piteously. She clearly read his mute plea.

"Would you care to join me for breakfast tomorrow, Colonel?" she said. It was plain that she stood on little or no ceremony and was not at all shy about making such an invitation.

"I would be delighted," said Seamus brightly.

"We will meet by the private dining room at seven then."

He would have preferred an even earlier meeting but refrained from saying so in front of the others.

"Fine," Doctor Duboise interposed, "Now that's all settled, we had better get you to your room. You need sleep; I believe you are more exhausted than anything else."

Seamus made to rise, but was able to do so only with the aid of Luther and the doctor. They helped him to his room with the ladies following. The men entered and after they had gotten Seamus undressed and under the covers in bed, the ladies entered.

The doctor changed Seamus dressing, replacing the bandage with a small plaster. He then announced that he had an appointment to meet with Rolf in the barroom, where he would be for a while if needed, and left.

Seamus thought it amusing that even though he had taken no drink this day, he still needed someone to put him to bed.

Emily saw Sally's portrait of Seamus standing on the chiffonier and took it in her hands.

"Would you make me a gift of this picture?" she asked Seamus.

He said that he would and she put her cool hand on his forehead.

"Goodnight," she said, "until breakfast, then," and she left.

Luther told Sarah he would stay in the room for a time and would join her directly. She said good night and departed.

Seamus felt himself already falling asleep.

Tomorrow will be another day, he thought and he thanked God for this one.

His last thoughts were that tomorrow he would ask Emily to marry him, she would say yes, and he would bid *adieu* to this soldier's life. He would decline, with gratitude, the Secretary's offer of employment as a detective and settle down to a real life like Sarah and Luther and Mick and Kathleen had. Tomorrow would be different.

# XV

# A Parting

The orange sun sent a shaft into Seamus window, filled the room with light, and his eyes opened. Squinting at first, he rolled out of bed and put his feet upon the floor. Sampson was dozing in the chair and awoke as Seamus rose and went to the window.

"Good morning, Colonel," he said also squinting, "are you alright?"

Seamus smiled at the rising sun and then at Sampson.

"Sampson, my friend, I am more than alright, much more than alright."

He had slept a dreamless sleep for the first time in many a year, and felt refreshed and strong. He flung up the sash to the chill air and took in great deep breaths.

"I spelled Luther this last watch until sunrise in case you needed any help during the night."

"Thank you Sampson. I think I am fully recovered. I do not know when I have felt so well. But, I have a breakfast engagement."

He looked at his watch and confirmed his estimate of the sun's elevation; he was past his time. It was already half-past six o'clock. He would not keep Emily waiting this morning.

"I am running late," he said. Nonetheless, he paused caught by the sight of the glistening ball of fire just clearing the wine dark ridge of the Berkshires. From the horizon up, the sky was cloudless, changing in tone from coral to turquoise to violet. Below, the Hudson reflected flame as a mirrored blade slashing, north to south, through the dark blue-green of the valley. Thin clouds of mist now rose up the mountain taking on a more vivid hue of scarlet, like rivulets of blood flowing from the wounded land below.

Little by little, one precinct and then another was plunged into the brightness of the day. Here a wheat field would explode in a blast of sunlight; there a tree line would erupt into a conflagration of vermilion. Individual houses and the little hamlets would suddenly ignite in crimson. And so the dawn came in small and intricate flanking movements across the Valley of the Hudson, as in a well laid plan of battle.

Seamus pulled himself away from his observations. He washed and shaved himself. All the while, he calculated that now he had no other presentable clothes but his uniform. With Sampson's help, he quickly removed his medals and badges, and the ribbon from the Crimea from his blue coat and stored them away in his carpet bag. He reckoned he would feel odd enough walking about in the civilian world in uniform, without the added show of the decorations.

He dressed hurriedly and Sampson assisted him with his gun belt, the pin-fire still resting in the holster. He decided to carry both guns again for safety sake, rather then to leave then lying about. And too, while he agreed with the Secretary that Lejeune was likely long gone, he knew of a certainty that it was better to *have* a defense and not need it, than to need it and *not* have it. He put the Police Model in his inside coat pocket and reminded himself to reach for it first should the need arise, while he devoutly prayed that no such contingency would come to pass. Looking again out the window at the sunrise, he wished nothing more than peace now, deep and long-lasting.

He looked back to the mirror, put on his kepi, adjusted it at the rakish angle to which his present ebullient spirit moved him and winked at his reflection.

Well now, my lad, he thought and grinned at himself in the glass.

"Very elegant, Colonel," said Sampson with a broad smile, "very elegant indeed."

"Thank you, Sampson."

Seamus consulted his watch again and the two men were out

the door and striding down the hall.

As he walked along, Seamus felt neither the weakness nor vertigo of the day before. He felt first rate and felt like running around the lakes at top speed, but more than that, he felt like taking Emily in his arms.

They reached the central staircase and Sampson left to ascend and, as he stated, to wait upon the Secretary and General Thorne as per Mr. Beecher's instructions.

Seamus descended while taking another quick glimpse at his watch. It was four minutes until seven o'clock. He was not late, but there was Emily standing by the private dinning room door.

She was dressed in a close-fitting crocheted jacket of dark blue with long sleeves, high collar and fabric covered buttons down the front. Her wide hoop skirt was of sky blue and she held crocheted purse of the same color in her hand. On her head she wore the small round straw hat with the black velvet band she had worn on the first day he had seen her.

She watched him come down the last few steps, a bright smile on her lips.

"Our colors match," she said.

"I am afraid my wardrobe has been severely reduced," he replied," I hope you will not mind being seen with me in this garb."

"Of course not, Seamus," she said moving closer to him and smiling up into his face, "the uniform suites you perfectly."

He thought to tell her that once they were married he would put it away and never wear it again. But, talk of marriage would keep unit they were in the seclusion of the private dinning room.

"Are you hungry?" she asked.

"I am," he said, "breakfast has always been my favorite meal and it occurs to me that, with one thing and another, I have not had a real breakfast since I arrived here."

He started toward the dinning room door, but she stopped him, taking him by the arm.

"If you do not mind being hungry a little longer," she said, "I thought we might have a sort of picnic breakfast."

She turned him toward the central hall and together they walked to the back entrance and out to the drive where the younger Van Bronc stood holding the bridle of the same mare, hitched to the same buckboard, with which Emily had nearly gone over the Kaaterskill Falls on the Friday before. They boarded the little vehicle, Emily took the reigns and they bade Frederick Douglass farewell and circled the drive. They passed the ice house which had served as Clay's temporary crypt and passed the root cellar which had been Luther's jail. They crossed the commons, where Skhutt had been shot from his saddle, and took the road to the Falls.

Seamus rode in silence. He tried to think of ways to propose marriage to Emily. Tried to think of the right time to make the proposal. The peacefulness of the grounds and now of the woods belied the landmarks of the violence and near tragedy of the last few days; the ice house, the root cellar and now they passed the place where Skhutt had planted the snake, and then the place where Sarge had died and where Lejeune had pinned Seamus down with deadly carbine fire. All was hushed and as peaceful as Eden. Beyond the bridge, a glade filled with low ferns was occupied by a doe and two spotted fawns. They looked on placidly as the buckboard passed.

It is like the battlefields, Seamus thought. All is again as God made it. Man came and played his bloody comedy on the stage, is now departed and peace has returned; the cattle graze by the Rapahannock, the corn ripens along the banks of the Antietam, all is quite along the Kaaterskill.

They were across the creek and pulling up in front of the gazebo by the Laurels before Seamus realized that he had not spoken a word to Emily during the entire trip. Had not taken advantage of their privacy in any way, had not asked her to marry him.

He helped her down from the buckboard and they entered the gazebo. She showed him to a seat in a white wicker chair at the same table they had occupied before, and addressed herself to the basket on the wire connected to the hotel kitchen. She wrote upon the order card and sent the message on its way with a pull of the bell cord. Almost immediately it returned with a silver coffee pot and china service.

Emily unloaded the cargo and returned the basket. She

poured the coffee and the comforting aroma floated in the still air. She took her seat across the table.

"Do you like my idea of a breakfast taken *al fresco*? It seems to me that we spend altogether too much of our time indoors, when God's creation calls to us."

"Yes, I like it very much," said Seamus. Will you marry me? he thought but did not say.

He looked away for fear that he would blurt his sentiments without a proper framing of the question. The grounds seemed deserted. Most of the guests, he suspected, had departed after the July Fourth holiday. If the Mountain House did little business during the week this early in the summer, the Laurels would presumably do that much less.

He sipped his coffee. It was delicious. He rested his elbow on the railing, cup in hand, and looked at the Falls tumbling down into the dark gorge. The morning light glanced through the woods above the tall and narrow column of water, catching and turning to pink the mist and spray rising up from the blackness below.

Seamus pictured McCain silently mingling with the cascade, head down-most, falling, falling with the water . . .

He took his eyes from the Falls, looked all about again. He thought of many things he knew how to do, and to do well; to ride and to shoot, to command, to direct artillery fire, to see without being seen. He knew the intricacies of the electrical telegraph and of the photographer's art and how to detect a masked enemy battery in a grove of trees by looking up to see the sunlight reflected from the brass barrels of the cannons among the leaves overhead. And he knew other things, many other things, none of which knowledge was of any avail to him whatever in the task presently at hand.

How, he wondered, does one ask a lady to marry? How is that done?

Start by telling her you love her, he responded to himself, then ask for her hand in marriage.

Yes, that seemed to be the right order; love then marriage.

But, what if she says no?

He looked around to his left. They were not entirely alone.

Behind them, behind the hotel, on a small promontory jutting above the gorge of the Falls, on the same side as they, sat an old man on a camp stool beneath a white umbrella. He wore a linen duster and a wide brimmed straw farmer's hat. An easel was set up before him. It was the elderly artist whom Seamus had seen from Mr. Beecher's window on the morning Clay was killed. He was not more than two rods distant and seemed to be looking right into the gazebo, but Seamus assumed that he must be looking beyond them, rendering the Falls on his canvas.

The artist worked slowly. He would turn his head and make some strokes with his brush, turn back and study his subject . . . make some more strokes.

Is he within hearing distance? Seamus wondered.

What of it, he told himself with irritation, drive on regardless!

"Emily . . . ," he said softly.

The bell by the kitchen window rang and the basket came singing along the wire.

"Oh! The rest of our breakfast." she said with a cheery smile.

She rose, and Seamus with her, and together they laid out their meal on the table. There were coddled eggs in porcelain coddlers with silver tops and green leafy designs matching their coffee cups. There was a rack of toast and a tub of butter, slices of country ham, and potatoes with bacon, strawberries and cream and sweet roles still warm from the oven.

He allowed himself to be distracted from his amorous intentions as the inner-man demanded food. They ate in silence, speaking to each other only with their eyes. At last, as they were sharing the strawberries, Seamus thought the timing perfect and, disregarding the old artist, he spoke.

"I love you, Emily."

"I know, Seamus."

"I love you, and I want . . . you *know*!?"

"Yes," said Emily with her littlest smile, "I know."

"You know," he said. Presumptuous, he thought. "*How* do you know?"

"I know because you said so. I know, and so does everyone

else who was in the room when you awoke yesterday afternoon. I know, and so do Mr. Beecher and Mr. Dolan, and the Van Wycks and the Van Broncs and the doctor, of course, they all know you love me. When you were coming out of your long sleep, you must still have been dreaming. 'No!' you shouted ever so loudly."

Emily put a fierce look upon her face and deepened her voice theatrically.

"'No! I will not kill you, I love you, Emily!'" she smiled, "So, you see, Seamus, everyone knows."

He felt his face burning once again in the cool morning air.

It is singular, he thought, the effect she has on me.

"But I will not hold you to it," she said with seeming seriousness, "you are hardly responsible for your words if you were dreaming."

"No," said Seamus quickly, "I mean, yes . . . yes do hold me to it. That is to say, I do love you. I say it now, in my right mind, or as close as I may get to that state whenever I am with you."

"Well then, I love you too, Seamus." She reached across the table and took his hand.

"Splendid!" he said, "This is splendid!"

He felt that he had never been so happy. The rising sun was sending its rays deeper into the gorge. The Falls sparkled like nuggets of gold dropped from heaven. A pair of cardinals flashed crimson across the brink, blazing and flickering in the broken shafts of light among the trees. First the lady bird and then the male behind her, they flew right past the gazebo singing to one another.

Press on, Seamus thought, press on to the objective and do not hesitate.

"Then, Emily, will you do me the great honor of consenting to be my wife?"

Her grip on his hand tightened.

"I will, Seamus . . ."

"You will? You will! Oh, this is, is . . ."

The warmth rose in his chest, swelling so that he could not speak.

"I will, Seamus, if . . ."

A cloud crossed the sun, the light around them faded.

". . . if I am ever to marry again."

A fist of ice crushed his heart. He could feel the color drain from his face. He spoke in desolation.

"But if we are in love, why should we not marry?"

She held his hand the tighter.

"When I was in despair, Seamus, you asked me to give you time until you worked out what was happening here on the mountain top. Now I must ask you to give me time to work out what is happening in my life. I do not need to say that my marriage to Fenton was much more than a mistake. I am not foolish, but in that time I let my feelings about my loss of Robbie interfere with my thinking. Now, I must have time. Marriage is the most serious of considerations. I have just come back from the very edge. I know that I must not make another ill considered leap. You are a very good man, the man I will marry if in God's time I am shown that marriage is His will for me.

"We can still be in love, but I have responsibilities. I must see to my father's company; my company now. But not only mine, it belongs too, to the many employees and farmers at the South who must depend upon it now more than ever for their salaries and to market their produce. Since it is incorporated in Washington, it is one of the few such concerns in the South which are still in operation. There are a great many people depending upon the company's continued functioning and increase and I am the last living person who is fully knowledgeable in its workings. I must go to New York City to meet with Mr. Isaiah Ezeikial, one of my father's oldest friends. He is also a small stock holder in our company and together we must develop a plan to restore and expand the business. This will be an important step toward rebuilding the South and the whole country. Love you though I do Seamus, I cannot put my own desires ahead of the needs of the many.

"The Van Wycks are returning to Brooklyn, as you know, and they have asked me to join them."

"Brooklyn and New York City," he said suddenly going from despairing to anxious, "but the cholera is there."

"Another of the responsibilities I mentioned," she said, "I am a trained and experienced nurse. I intend to stay at the Van Wycks' home and help them with their suffering parishioners and any others who may need my help. I have no choice but to offer what I can of the talents God has given me."

"Emily," he said, his voice low and thick, "I fear for you, . . . the cholera, it killed, along with the other illnesses, more soldiers during the war than did bayonet, saber or ball. In fact, I would be less fearful if you told me you were going to war, where one can duck and dodge, and at least fight back. There is no defense against the cholera; no bombproof, no refuge."

"And there is no safe place, Seamus, this side of eternity, as the dominie said."

To this there was no reply, and he sat in silence until, at length she spoke.

"You are not angry with me, Seamus, are you?"

"No," he responded quickly, "I can never be angry with you."

She reached into her purse and took out his spy glass.

"I forgot to return this."

"Please keep it," he said, and made himself smile, "perhaps someday you will look through it and see me coming to you."

Perhaps, he thought, but did not say, I will go to Brooklyn too, and then he remembered that he had not been invited. It was true; all that she had said. True though it was; it was no less painful.

He looked away, his gaze coming to rest upon the old artist who was just folding his easel. He furled his umbrella, stooped and collapsed his camp stool. He flung it across his shoulder and rested his easel and umbrella on the other shoulder and came directly to the gazebo. He stood by Emily and tipped his hat. A light breeze rose from the gorge and stirred his long white locks.

"Your pardon," he said, "I am Asher Durand. Please be so kind as to accept this small token."

He handed Emily a card which she took and showed to Seamus. Upon it had been sketched, in water colors, a study of the Falls, the wild mountain side behind it, and in the foreground, the gazebo and within it the forms of the two of them holding hands across the table. All appeared bathed in the warmth of dawning light. It looked to Seamus to be the very gem of illustration.

"You will please forgive my intrusion into your privacy, but I am afraid that I simply could not resist drawing you as you portrayed to me the purest expression of romance and civilization amid the wilderness, rendering the surroundings both sublime and picturesque. Please accept this sketch as partial recompense for my intrusion."

They thanked the old gentleman and protested that this was hardly an intrusion. He tipped his hat again, his actions having that dreamy quality which the actions of artists, it seems, so often do have, and he was off wandering slowly into the woods beyond the hotel.

They watched him depart and it became apparent that they too must leave.

They cleared the table and Emily insisted upon paying the bill, saying that it was her idea to dine at the gazebo. She put a greenback into the basket, they boarded their vehicle and in a few moments they were back across the creek and on the road to the Mountain House.

Seamus could think of nothing to say. He thought to ask Emily when she would be leaving for Brooklyn and New York, but feared it would be very soon, and decided that he would rather not know.

When they reached the spot where Emily's horse had bolted not quite a week before, she pulled up and turned to him, she took his hand and put her face close to his. He circled his arm about her shoulders and kissed her full on her soft lips. He kissed her again and again and stopped and looked into her eyes and kissed her again on the lips and then on the neck. He spoke into her ear.

"I love you, Emily," he murmured.

He looked her in the eyes again.

"I love you."

She took his hand and kissed it.

"I love you, Seamus."

They held each other in the silence of the forest for long, warm moments, and then he kissed her hand and her eyes told him they must part now. Her eyes told him everything.

She turned back to the road, and started up the mare again. They drove on and passed near the South Lake. A dozen Canada geese exploded from the reeds where the lake flowed into the creek. They formed hastily into a tight echelon, trim as cadets in their gray, black and white plumage, and were away, beating along the tree-lined shore and then out over the open water.

As always, the sight of these travelers made Seamus think of the Wild Geese of Ireland, the old Celtic nobility driven by the English from their homeland two hundred years since. They and their children wandering the wide world, fighting for Spain, for France, for Russia and now for America; fighting every fight but Ireland's fight. Was this, he wondered, to be his life, to be one of the rootless Wild Geese?

He watched the flock climb into the blue sky, cross the yellow disk of the sun and turn out above the thin mist rising from the valley, their calling hollow, distant, mournful.

Presently, the buckboard came to the common, crossed it and entered the circular drive. A bright red stage coach with yellow wheels stood at the back entrance of the great house. Emily pulled up behind it and Frederick Douglass Van Bronc took the mare by the bridle. Sampson called down from the coachman's box.

"Your luggage is all on board, Miz Emily and we are ready when you are, ma'am."

Seamus descended and helped Emily down from the buckboard. Mr. Beecher, the Van Broncs and the doctor stood by the coach and made their farewells; Sarah and Emily embracing. Seamus took off his kepi and stood by Emily's side. The Van Wycks, already seated within the coach, bade Seamus good-bye. Emily took his hand in hers and held it to her cheek.

"Forgive me," she said, "I could not bear to make a long leave-taking."

Tears came into her eyes.

"Remember, Seamus, we are parting just for a time, not forever."

He could not speak.

"Yes, Emily," he said finally, "just for a time, not forever."

He prayed this were true as he helped her into the coach. She passed to him from the window Asher Durand's picture of them together and he put it into his tunic. They held each other's gaze as Sampson roused the team and the coach circled the drive. Then the vehicle turned right into the common at the end of the grove of trees by the root cellar and they lost sight of one another. The coach disappeared down the trail to the mountain road. The others went into the hotel and Seamus remained yet awhile bareheaded in the drive, watching the place where she had gone from view.

With hat in hand, he turned and walked slowly into the Mountain House. The door to the bar was open and a strong, astringent scent of alcohol issued forth from within. He stepped into the cool, dim room and, as his eyes adjusted to the dark, he found himself standing next to Doctor Duboise at the end of the bar.

Rolf was just adding the *royale* to the doctor's mug of coffee. He corked the bottle of Hennessey's and set it on the bar.

The sharp alcohol aroma, however, did not come from the brandy. Across the room Jacob, assisted by young Terwiliger, was kneeling by the piano applying shellac to the corner of the instrument where it had been damaged by the fire of Sunday evening. The corner of the bar where Seamus stood had also been burned and now appeared to have been repaired to as good as new condition.

"Your pleasure, Colonel?" said Rolf.

Seamus considered a moment.

Upon hearing Rolf address Seamus, Jacob turned from his work.

"Colonel," he said, "Mr. Seward said that if I saw you, sir, I should let you know that he is waiting upon you on the upper piazza."

"Thank you, Jacob, I shall join him directly."

Seamus made up his mind. He took the flask from his inside pocket.

"Rolf, would you give me the full of this of Hennessy's Cognac," he said. And remembered how the Hennessy family was making brandy in France on the land given to them by the

King whom their ancestor, one of the Wild Geese, had served.

The barman took the flask and took up the desired bottle.

Seamus turned to the doctor.

"Sir," he said, "you have rendered me your professional services, it seems, almost exclusively and very nearly daily since I arrived here, in one way or another. It occurs to me that I owe you for your fee."

"Not at all," the doctor replied, "not at all. Consider my efforts in your behalf as service to the Republic. I did not join the Ulster Guard to make my fortune. If I can see my way to clear to do so in the future, I intend to continue my policy of never charging a veteran for my doctoring. I will accept no fee from you, Colonel, and that is an end to it."

He took a deep draught from his mug by way of emphasis to his pronouncement.

"I thought not," said Seamus taking the filled flask from Rolf and pressing a silver dollar into the barman's palm. "In that case you will, will you not, do me the honor, sir, of accepting this token of my appreciation for saving my life?"

"I did not save your life, God spared you, but yes, Colonel, I will accept your gracious gift and with many thanks."

The doctor lifted his mug in salute, as Seamus put the flask before him on the bar.

"Good," said Seamus, "and now I had better keep my appointment above."

He made his good-byes and left the barroom.

Luther and Sarah busied themselves by the clerk's desk with a trunk and a pile of men's clothes.

"Lejeune's property, Colonel," said Luther, "he left without packing."

Seamus brightened. Clues, he thought.

Sarah read his mind.

"We searched the room at length, Colonel," she said, "and very carefully. We found nothing but these clothes and Mr. Beecher suggests that we pass them along to those in the community who can most use them."

The clothing was of high quality. Seamus picked up a long gabardine overcoat with a collar of Persian lamb's wool. He went through the pockets of the coat and found them empty. He picked up a frock coat with a velvet collar, while Sarah examined another coat and Luther a pair of trousers.

From the inside pocket of the frock coat in his hand, Seamus extracted a lady's handkerchief with a small silver hair clip attached. He unfolded the handkerchief and found it to be bordered with fine lace and embroidered white on white with the word "Asia", in severe Old English calligraphy. He held the square of linen to his nose. It bore the fragrance of patchouli.

Sarah opened the trunk. It contained three shirts, three collars and two pairs of shoes.

"I did not see this before." she said.

Pushing aside the shoes she came up with a pocket-sized case fashioned of tortoise shell. She opened it and a fine pink powder spilled forth. It contained powders and paints of various hues and small bushes. A little looking glass was concealed in the lid.

"It is a case for lady's face-paints," she said and handed it to Seamus.

He looked at the case in his one hand and the lace and linen square in the other.

Souvenirs of Lejeune's feminine conquests, he thought. And then he thought again.

No! Something else! His mind screamed within. Suddenly it became clear to him. The shock of revelation left him staring; mouth agape.

"Colonel," said Luther, "Are you alright?"

"Yes," said Seamus, "Yes," and he departed without another word, leaving the Van Broncs looking quizzically at each other.

He slowly walked the central hall, his thoughts far away, and climbed the stairs to the next floor, where he stepped out onto the piazza. The aroma of cigar smoke directed him to the Secretary who sat in a wicker arm chair in the far north corner. He gave Seamus a cheery wave, and Seamus looked to his right where he was not surprised to see Thorne sitting in the far south corner, trying to look unobtrusive. The detective gave Seamus a quick glance and went back to pretending to read his newspaper.

Seamus joined the Secretary, taking a seat in the other arm

chair which had been pulled up to a small white painted table near the railing. A tea service of blue and red floral patterned china was set upon the table.

"Will you take a cup of tea with me, Colonel?" said Mr. Seward, as he poured a cup without waiting for a response.

"Tea," he said, passing the cup to Seamus, "the cup which cheers but which does not inebriate. Those of my generation, such as Mr. Beecher, grew up rather more with tea than with coffee, as I expect you may have, Colonel, in your native land. And how are you feeling this morning, sir? I must say you are looking well. I should opine that you are in full recovery from the wound which you suffered at the beginning of this week. Did you enjoy Independence Day this year?"

Seamus did not know which question to answer first, so he simply said:

"Yes, sir."

He was used to his chief's rapid fire inquiries. The man was a lawyer first and always, and one of brilliant intellect. These were attributes which Seamus found, sometimes, to be daunting.

"Yes, a much better Fourth then we had last year," the Secretary went on, "when we were all awaiting the grim ceremonies surrounding the execution of those who conspired to assassinate the President and of poor Mrs. Surratt. It seemed sure that she was to be pardoned at the last moment.

"I remember General Hancock, to whom, as you yourself remember, had fallen the unenviable duty of carrying out the executions. He suffered the tortures of the damned as he waited and waited for the word of reprieve which never came. It was a difficult time for my Catholic friends. The bigots in our society were only too ready to see a Roman plot in what was nothing but an unfortunate circumstance. A coincidence that Mrs. Surratt, a Catholic and Southern sympathizer that she was, happened to own the home where the conspirators sometimes met. Albeit, her son *was* an agent of the rebel government and was certainly involved, I doubt if she had any direct knowledge of the plan to kill the President. She may have known of the plot only to abduct him. Many thought that her death sentence had been only a ploy to get her son to return from Canada and surrender himself. He apparently thought so himself, as he did not return. He seems to have been convinced that his mother would not die."

The Secretary passed one of his cigars to Seamus.

"What a dangerous game it is," he concluded, "to hold the life of an innocent hostage."

Seamus was surprised that the Secretary had brought up the subject of the assassination. It had been an episode of such devastating pain to him that Mr. Seward almost never spoke of it in informal conversation, normally referring to it only in official discourse.

But was this an informal conversation, Seamus wondered. He had his answer immediately.

"I mention this, Colonel, because, as I said last night, I am shortly to take into the employ of the Department of State a number of detectives and I earnestly hope that you will consent to be one of them."

The Secretary paused and, apparently reading the ambivalence on Seamus' face, went on with vehemence.

"You cannot say no, sir, because the country, and soon your co-religionists will be in dire need of your continued service. What I am about to tell you, I tell you only because I have the utmost faith in your loyalty and probity. I trust you with my life, and what is more by far, with the security of our nation. I know that you will not repeat this outside of our company within the Department. I have received from Europe an intelligence which will this Fall become public knowledge; John Harrison Surratt is presently serving under an assumed name in the Papal Zouaves."

Seamus was stunned to speechlessness.

"I will need you, as a distinguished veteran, and as a Catholic to help do what must be done to bring him to justice and to offset, here in America, the wave of anti-Catholic bigotry which will sweep the country when the news is made known to all. You cannot turn down my request that you join our detective force in the Department of State."

Seamus could not think of an answer, so he thought to change the subject. He had been puzzling as to how to broach the matter, but since Mr. Seward had brought up the assassination . . .

"Sir," he said, "Brutus Lejeune is John Wilkes Booth."

"What!? What is this nonsense you are saying!?" the Secretary's voice rose in anger, his face colored, the scar on his chin went livid.

"Booth is *dead!"* he said and looked away.

Still looking out over the valley, he went on more quietly, his tone still testy.

"*You* were present at Booth's death, Colonel Delaney, I read *your* report! Here I am making a serious proposal to you, and you respond with this absurdity!"

"Sir," Seamus went on in a low and unhurried voice, forcing the Secretary to listen to his calm and reasoned words, "when I first met the man, then known as Tompkins in the bar at this hotel on Friday night, I thought instantly that he was Booth. And then I convinced myself that he was not. I thought why would Booth, if he were still alive, walk about the world looking like Booth? Now I have come to realize that he had no fear to do so, since all the world thinks Booth dead. Why should a man of Booth's vanity not choose to look like himself? None are searching for him. He is an actor; he was playing the role of Tompkins until I confronted him in the barroom on the night of the inquest when he stepped out of his role. Now I know that the man we saw, once the mask had dropped, was Lejeune *and* Booth.

"During the war, when Booth was not, 'playing himself', if you will, he was the notorious Captain Lejeune. And that goes to explain the many reports we received of Booth having been present in Stonewall Jackson's camp and in the company of Major Mosby at various times. Booth took part in the war both as actor/rebel agent and as the shadowy guerrilla raider. We only kept track of him when he was in the capital. Who knew where he went when he left the city?"

Mr. Seward affected an expression of nonchalance, but his eyes betrayed an intense concentration upon what he was hearing. Seamus continued.

"The man I first knew as Tompkins walked with a slight limp, favoring his left leg. Booth fractured his left leg, we know, jumping from the box in Ford's theater after he murdered the

President. On the night of the inquest, I noticed that the so-called Tompkins had a crushed right thumb, also fitting the description of Booth."

The Secretary interrupted, impatience edging his barely controlled voice.

"I reiterate, Colonel, you witnessed Booth's death and in the wake of the late war, there are literally legions of men, and for that matter, many women and children, bearing the marks of injuries of all kinds. Scars are no rarity in our land in this year 1866."

He absently rubbed the ridge of flesh on his chin.

"Granted, sir, which may be why I did not more quickly come to see what I now know to be the truth; that Booth is alive and committed murder here at the Mountain House on Saturday, and that he is was lying in wait here to kill you too."

The Secretary opened his mouth to speak. Seamus cut him off.

"Sir," he said, "when the supposed Booth was dragged from the burning barn on Garrett's farm, none of us present at first recognized him as Booth. The man who had been shot in the barn had reddish, sandy colored hair, not the jet black hair all knew Booth to have. Further, he had freckles all over his face, blemishes which Booth did not have. We all then imagined that Booth, the actor, had thus disguised himself with face paint and hair dye, as well as having shaved off his moustache. But, sir, Davey Herold, whom we captured just before the barn was fired, said that man inside was not Booth. Later, he changed his story. When we got the body to the monitor *Montauck*, the doctor from Washington examined the body and at first did not recognize it as that of Booth, although he himself had removed a tumor from Booth's neck in life, just a short time before.

"Eventually, they based their identification of the body as Booth's from the tumor scar beneath the hair at the nape of the neck, though it looked more like a burn than the result of surgery, and from the tattoo 'JWB' on the back of the right hand. But, sir, scars can be made on anyone, and tattoos can be put on or burned off.

"The man I confronted in the barroom on the night of the

inquest had a burn scar on the back of his right hand and I now believe that scar erased the tattoo of John Wilkes Booth's initials."

The Secretary was clearly bursting to speak. Seamus gave him no opportunity and pressed on.

"I know, sir that you read the *post mortem* report on Booth where it says that Booth died from the perforation of his spinal cord by a conoidal *pistol* ball, fired at the distance of a few yards. We both know that Sergeant Corbett, who was believed to have shot Booth in the barn, was not armed with a pistol, but with a carbine of over .50 caliber on the night in question. And we both know that Secretary Stanton later decided to issue the weird little Sergeant with a pistol and to make him a hero rather than to court-martial him for disobeying orders. I myself thought it possible that, if Corbett had shot, he had missed and that Booth had actually shot himself in the neck in a botched attempt at suicide, but I always wondered; where were the powder burns? The man in the barn had been shot at close range; a few yards, but not with the pistol pressed to within inches of the neck, as would be the case in a suicide.

"Now I believe there were three men in the barn; Davey Herold, whom Booth allowed to surrender, and another whom Booth had induced to be his double. That man had been partially prepared for that role, probably to lay a false trail, by the application of the tattoo and the counterfeit tumor scar, and then Booth murdered him in order to make good his escape and then did in fact escape through the collapsed rear wall of the burning barn."

"And when, Colonel," the Secretary asked in a voice dripping sarcasm, "did you come to this startling conclusion?"

"Just now, sir, when I had the opportunity to examine the clothing which Lejeune, or Booth, left in his room. These items were discovered among his clothes."

Seamus placed the tortoise shell case and the handkerchief and hairclip on the table.

"This case contains paints and powders as used by ladies and actors to change their appearance, to improve upon nature. I was reminded of this yesterday when Sergeant Dolan joked that if I had such powders, I could conceal my black eye.

"I now recall that the man who called himself Tompkins had particularly dark eyebrows. Though he may have felt safe looking like a man everyone is sure is dead, he nonetheless, I feel, was being prudent enough to cover the scarred right eyebrow which was also included in the official description of Booth. Or it may have just been vanity, which in itself also describes Booth. The man in the room rented in the name of Tompkins, known to be a Marylander as is Booth, possessed this case for the purpose of disguising himself. Then, sir, there is this."

Seamus picked up the handkerchief, undid the clip and spread it on the table.

"It is, as you can see, sir, embroidered; 'Asia'."

"So?" said the Secretary, "The man; . . . Lejeune . . . , perhaps has a collection of ladies handkerchiefs bearing the names of the continents; Asia, Africa, Europe, and he may have a collection named for the seven seas."

Mr. Seward blew a smoke ring. His eyes still betrayed agitation.

"Asia, sir, as you well know, is the name of John Wilkes Booth's sister; Asia Booth Sleeper Clarke of Bel Air, Maryland and Philadelphia. They were . . . are . . . devoted to one another. Here we have Booth, the knight errant, as he fancies himself, still at war, bearing the favor of his lady. Very chivalrous."

"Colonel, are you through?"

Without waiting for an answer, the Secretary went on.

"Booth is dead, dead, dead. He need not still be alive for me to yet be the target of assassins. Even before the war, I was given the distinction of being the foremost among anti-slavery politicians in the North by some of the slave-owning 'gentlemen;' of the South. They conferred that honor upon me by putting a price of $50,000 on my head. The assassins of lesser lights than I would receive only a $25,000 bounty. For all I know, that offer may still be outstanding. But more than that, there are those abroad who would wish me dead today, not because of what I have done before, but to prevent me from doing what I am about to do."

He was silent for a moment, his eyes boring into Seamus.

"But, really Colonel," he went on, "you are worse than the newspapers in your concoction of fictitious plots and counter-plots. Now, the scribblers are writing that I. . . I!", . . .his chin glowed scarlet again and he sputtered in anger . . . "acquiesced in the attempt upon *my* life on the night of the President's murder, so the office would fall to me as Mr. Johnson was simultaneously murdered. That I had plotted to allow Booth's henchman; Paine with an 'i', or Payne with a 'y' or Powell . . . ,"

"Who, in his testimony, always referred to Booth as 'captain'", Seamus interjected and immediately regretted as his chief's face grew crimson.

" . . . OR WHATEVER! . . . his true name may have been, to enter my home and slash me in my sick bed and stab my soldier nurse, and my son, . . . and . . . and all this before the innocent eyes, . . . and in reach of my poor . . . poor young daughter, Fanny . . . my poor, darling child . . ., " the Secretary choked, paused a moment, . . . "*That* is what the papers are writing."

Seamus' regrets at pressing so hard mounted. He spoke softly.

"How is Fanny doing, sir?"

The Secretary looked up, his eyes desolate.

"Not well, I am afraid, Colonel, thank you for your solicitude. You have always been one of her favorites among our staff. She has nightmares still. She has waking nightmares. She is distant, . . . melancholic . . . she will not eat, . . . becomes thinner and thinner . . . the poor child . . . my last born child, my only daughter, the delight of my old age . . .," he covered his eyes with his hand, leaned on the table, . . ."she has never been the same since that night . . ."

All was silent on the piazza. One muffled sob came from deep within William H. Seward's throat.

Presently, the Secretary steeled himself and recovered. Seamus thought of how the man had thrown himself into his work immediately after that tragic night in April of 1865. How he had ordered soldiers to carry him to his office in a chair; his only balm and healing medicine his single-minded, even ruthless, service to the Republic.

"Forgive me, Colonel, we have given much for our country. I fear to think how long it may be before Fanny becomes yet another fatality on the causality list of that night. You know my dear wife's death shortly after was a direct result of Paine's attack. Neither could she recover from the shock, and now the press writes this nonsense."

He paused again took a deep shuddering breath and then spoke with the voice of authority, looking straight at Seamus through reddened eyes.

"Booth is dead, Colonel Delaney. That is the official report and the official position of the government of which I am a member, and that is all I have to say on the subject."

So that is it, thought Seamus, the 'official report', the 'official position of the government'. The Secretary would say nothing contrary while he still served President Johnson, despite what he might know or surmise. Wartime security still prevails. Indeed, Seamus reminded himself, the war was not yet legally finished, although he had heard the President would so announce in the next month.

"We have pressing issues with which to deal, Colonel, and I beseech you to assist me, to assist your country, in these matters, and to cease and desist from squandering your special talents upon this assassination plot humbug. Leave that to the ink-stained wretches of the cheap press. We must deal with the real and actual world, which is frightening enough."

"Yes, sir," said Seamus, and added, he hoped not too archly, "and you feel that my 'special talents', as both you and Mr. Beecher, termed them . . ."

The Secretary interrupted with irritation.

"Precisely, Colonel, your *special talents*, which are yours ONLY so that you may share them with the cause that is just. And you will be able to make a decent salary, although that is the least consideration. Mr. Beecher, now that you mention him, has been placing himself in the service of justice and of his country for many a year and without remuneration and in fact at the risk of his livelihood as well as of his life.

"Back in 1836, the Caroline Affair occurred; you would not

remember that . . ."

Hardly, thought Seamus, since I had not yet been born.

"At that time, some of the freedom loving people of Canada rose in rebellion against England. Some others, on this side of the border, sought to help them and fitted up a ship, the *Caroline*, to be a privateer on the Niagara River. One night persons from Canada, who were later, by their own admission, proven to be English agents, on Her Majesty's Service, crossed the border into New York, fired the ship and sent it over the Falls. They did not bother to awaken the crew before they did the deed. We nearly went to war once again with England, in fact, the Empire was eager for such an opportunity to regain its 'lost colonies.'

"Winfield Scott himself was dispatched to the border and was able to settle the affair peacefully, but he would never have gotten there in time, if it were not for Mr. Beecher. Our host, and his father, controlled the stage transport in the Hudson Valley, but to no avail, since the winter of '36-'37 was incredibly harsh, and all the roads were buried in snow. Mr. Beecher, with great ingenuity, provided a coach with a feather bed, quilts and rugs. Skids were placed on the wheels, and relays of horses sped the coach 150 miles up the center the frozen Hudson River from the Bowery in Manhattan to Albany, while the redoubtable Scott slept within through the long winter night. He was awakened at Albany with the coach drawn up in front of his hotel with the words; 'General, your breakfast is served', music to his ears I am sure, you remember what a *gourmand* our old friend was."

Seamus smiled and nodded.

"My point is that people like you and Mr. Beecher make this Republic what it is, Colonel, and insure its survival amid a world of strife."

The Secretary flicked a cigar ash over the railing it emphasize his point.

"By the way," he went on, "at the time Her Majesty's government claimed no responsibility for the destruction of the *Caroline*, saying that her destroyers where private individuals acting on their own. Later, one of them in an unguarded moment of boasting said that he had acted as a secret English agent. Unfortunately for him, he made that boast on this side of the border and was promptly arrested for murder and arson. I had the honor of serving as Governor of this great state during that time and came under tremendous pressure from our own federal government to simply let the man go. Apparently, Lord Palmerston's threats to wage a 'war of retaliation and vengeance' against us, if the man they now admitted was one of their agents, was not released, had the administration in Washington cowed. I insisted that the man be tried, and he was. He was acquitted on a technicality."

The Secretary smoked quietly, savoring the reminiscence.

"So," said Seamus, "if the United States were to turn a blind eye to a group of American citizens invading Canada, the Fenians, for example . . ."

The Secretary looked around sharply at Seamus.

"... it would," Seamus continued, "simply be a matter of returning the favor of a visit, as it were."

A sly smile briefly crossed the Secretary face.

"Very good, Colonel, very good."

"I could not help but notice last night sir, that you are acquainted with Mr. Frank Treacy; former *Sergeant* Treacy."

"I am," said Mr. Seward, his face a portrait of innocence, "he was an early supporter of my Whig, and later of my Republican candidacies here in Greene County. I have no association with him in any military capacity."

"You addressed him as 'captain', sir," said Seamus, guessing that was probably Frank's title in the military wing of the Fenian Brotherhood.

"Did I?"

"You did, sir."

The Secretary puffed his cigar, gazed out over the valley. At length he spoke.

"The great purpose of the late war, Colonel, was Emancipation, but the great danger of the war was not that Emancipation would not occur. That was bound to happen sooner or later. It is a matter of historical evolution. Slavery would go one way or the other. It could not go *too* soon, especially for those in bondage, but as an institution, 'peculiar' or otherwise, it was doomed. Those enslaved themselves would rise successfully, or the South would go bankrupt. There was never any chance of slavery's survival in the long view.

"No, the great danger of the war was that this country would be destroyed by forces both within *and* without. The empire building nations of Europe were perched like so many vultures watching the death throes of the majestic eagle which is this Republic. They watched and they waited and extended their influence to hasten the demise of this country so that they could pick her bones. Imagine what would have been in store had secession succeeded; further disintegration of the Confederacy into a gaggle of petty states feuding among themselves. The whole continent but a theater for European intrigues, the weakened United States virtually defenseless, alliances, counter-alliances, one regional war after another; horrific.

"There was not a great European country during the war that did not work and hope for the dissolution of the Union and the demise of the American nation unless it was Russia. It was from Russia that we secretly learned that France had proposed to England that the two act in concert in their dealings with Mr. Lincoln's government, and that was to be the first step toward their joint imposition of peace by armed intervention on behalf of the rebels. Indeed, the 'courtesy tour' upon which Russia sent her magnificent fleet to visit our harbors on both coasts early in the war, was in effect the Czar 'loaning' his navy to us until we could build up our own naval squadrons to protect our own shores from both foreign and domestic enemies.

"It has long been the desire of many in the ruling class of England to reverse the American Revolution both for the pure greed of regaining the vast wealth of our nation and to prove that a republic cannot work and thereby give credence to their oligarchic philosophy. It would not do for the working classes to see that there may be a place in the world where the common man might rule himself.

"With the outbreak of our Civil War, the Europeans moved with alacrity; first the English to supply guns, ships and other diverse military goods to the rebels and later the French to establish themselves in Mexico; an incursion with which we have yet to fully deal, although I trust we may now be able to do so diplomatically. And diplomacy may now succeed only because I illustrated to France immediately after Appomattox that our back was no longer turned. As you recall, I did so by requesting the immediate dispatch of your old commander; General Sheridan to the Rio Grande and with such speed that he was not able to participate in the Grand Victory Parade in Washington; an honor he most richly deserved. But I had to deprive him of the celebration because I could think of none other who could strike such fear into the hearts of the French interlopers. So I caused to have sent that whirlwind of battle who was Phil Sheridan to the border to carry the diplomatic message to Napoleon, as General Joshua Lawrence Chamberlain put it; that a French army cannot force an Austrian Emperor on the Mexican Republic. The French knew, as did I, that; given the word, General Sheridan would have his cavalry and horse artillery in Mexico City in a week.

"England also established bases of operations for the rebels both in the Caribbean and in Canada, the latter launching the raid on St. Albans, Vermont and many other assaults against the Union, both overt and covert.

"England is our permanent concern. British America; Canada will not simply go away. At the time of the Trent Affair, when our navy had taken rebel emissaries off an English ship on the high seas, as you remember, English troops, 11,000 of them, were rushed to our northern frontier. And as you reported to me more recently, England continues to strengthen the great fort at Kingston, Ontario, with infantry and with the addition of steel Blakely cannons. That was an excellent report, Colonel, how ever did you get those photographs of the fort's interior?"

"By posing, in my role of photographic *artiste*, individual and groups of soldiers in front of installations in which we had an interest, sir."

"Outstanding! From the pictures, and the sketches you made, our engineers have been able to make a blueprint of the entire fortress. You see, Colonel, how much your services are needed. We have no intention of carrying out an unprovoked invasion of Canada, but if the reverse were to occur, we would need to take that fort in self-defense. Your report has already resulted in the reinforcement of our garrison at Fort Ontario near Oswego. That troop movement was carried out under the guise of interdicting the Fenian supply line on our side of the border."

"So," said Seamus, "the Fenian raid has served a number of our purposes."

The Secretary made no comment. He puffed his cigar, and looked away. In a few moments he spoke again.

"I have nothing against England. My own antecedents and those of many here in America are English. But this is my country now, just as it is yours, and though England may be my motherland, I will not allow her to build her empire at the expense of the Republic as long as it is in my power to prevent that outcome. Not the English people, nor the Canadian people, but Canada itself, British America is a weapon aimed at the heart of this nation. So it was during the war with cross-border raids and intrigues, and so it continues to be yet, with the harboring of rebel fugitives and those who still operate secretly against us.

"And that is another reason I need your help, Colonel. The investigation into the President's assassination continues. I must very soon dispatch Mr. Thorne to England in order to get to the bottom of the question of the involvement in the murder of Mr. Lincoln of certain former rebel government ministers who have fled there, and to Canada. In his absence, in addition to the other duties I have outlined, I will need you to be my personal bodyguard."

Seamus sat up straighter in his chair. The Secretary had played the card which could not be trumped; his own safety. Both men knew that Seamus could not deny the request.

"However, Colonel, it is not the security of my humble person which is of concern, but rather the security of the country and of justice which must be served.

"The loss of Mr. Lincoln has been devastating to this nation; far more so than most know. And that was the purpose of the operation which resulted in the murder of the President. It was not just Booth's hatred, nor rebel revenge, nor the desperate act of a rebel government which had not yet admitted defeat. There are powers in the world who did not wish to see America led by a man of Mr. Lincoln's brilliance, character and sagacity. It better suits those powers to see the Republic under the leadership of . . . politicians of. . . . less . . . ability."

The Secretary spoke slowly, choosing his words.

"Mark you, Colonel, I will not speak ill of Mr. Johnson. Lord knows enough are doing so without my adding to the chorus; . . . but, our President is now in a most difficult position. The Radical Republicans despise him because he now wishes to take the path of reconciliation with the South. They would rather have the South treated as a conquered country, both for reasons of vengeance and, for some of them, for more mercenary reasons. Indeed, it is becoming questionable whether or not the more conciliatory plan shared by Mr. Johnson and President Lincoln is still appropriate as the old powers at the South seem bent on returning the African population to *de facto* slavery by lately passing repressive vagrancy and apprentice laws. The Democrats and the border state men see Mr. Johnson as a native Tennessean who was a traitor to the South. In this conundrum, the President tries to please all sides, opposing suffrage for the Freedmen and perhaps soon to receive Mrs. Jefferson Davis at the White House to plead on behalf of her incarcerated husband on the one hand, and on the other, enforcing Reconstruction at the point of the bayonet. I fear he will fall between two chairs, or among a multitude of chairs, and in the end make enemies of all factions and friends of none, to his own detriment and that of the country.

"At present, he is touring the nation, making ill-advised speeches which serve no purpose but to leave fresh bands of antagonists in his wake. And this at a time when we need most to take decisive action for our strategic security.

"Believe me, Colonel, I would love noting better at this, the end of my life, than to go home to Auburn tomorrow and never return; to retire from public service and finish what few days remain to me there, or at my son's house by the shore of the lake. But, that cannot be. I have one more great action to take and that is to flank British America."

"Flank, sir?" Seamus wondered for an instant if the strain of the last year and of the more recent days had not gotten to Mr. Seward. He was going to flank all of Canada?

"Yes, Colonel, flank Canada through the purchase from Russia of her colony of Alaska."

Seamus had heard talk of the purchase, but had dismissed it. The place was impossibly remote. Where would be the profit?

"We cannot make Britain go away," the Secretary was saying, "as we will make France go away from Mexico, and we have no interest in annexing Canada, despite what in the past the scribblers claimed was my intention. For our protection we may purchase Alaska and, if need be, fortify its border with Canada. Never again will England be able to threaten us through her bridgehead in Canada. From that time onwards, we will always be at Britain's rear in Alaska; always able to assault Canada on two fronts at once. The threat to the Republic from that quarter will become a nullity; rendered nugatory. America will benefit as will the Canadians; England will have to grant them a greater measure of autonomy in order to keep their loyalty. For once and for all, our country will be strategically secure.

"Those are the stakes for which we are playing, Colonel. That is the business which I must conduct to the north this month. That is the very reason why Lejeune and his cohorts were here at the Mountain House; to stop me in my confidential negotiations to effect the flanking of England in North America. And that, sir, is the ultimate reason why you cannot refuse my request to remain in our nation's service. Our work is not yet done. This field of endeavor will in some ways be new to you, but it is one for which you are eminently well suited and one which you must not refuse to enter."

The Secretary held Seamus' gaze with his own, adamant and piercing.

After a time Seamus answered.

"Yes, sir, you are, of course, right. Might I have some time to think before I give my final answer?"

Mr. Seward smiled, warm, kindly. He puffed his cigar.

"To be sure, to be sure, Colonel. We will talk again this afternoon. Take your time, but remember; my request to you remains an urgent one."

Seamus rose.

"Until this afternoon, sir," he said. He turned and walked to the staircase at the front of the piazza.

He rested his hand on the banister just where Emily had rested hers at the moment when he had first seen her. He looked out over the valley and then down to the left. A movement caught his eye; a plume of dust followed a bright red coach with tiny turning yellow wheels. It was just emerging from the woods at the base of the mountain.

He looked at his watch and assured himself by the passage of time that it was certainly Emily's coach.

It sped along the terra-cotta road between the open fields, disappeared into a hollow of trees and reappeared, now smaller than before.

Here I am Emily, he said within himself. I see you, do you see me?

Is she looking back? he wondered.

"She is," he said aloud to no one.

And so she goes out of my life, he thought, maybe for a time, maybe forever. Will my life now be this soldier's life . . . or what? . . . this detective's life then?

He descended the stairs, faced right and walked along the cliff where the heat of the day was again coming to the mountain top. He entered the woods on the south side of the hotel and followed the trail just as he had on the day he had found Emily on top of Boulder Rock ready to step into eternity. The shade of the tall pines gave him a shiver. He went on with the scent of evergreen filling his nostrils. The path climbed to the block of pudding stone upon which he had slipped on that day when he had raced to find her. Today he traversed it slowly and easily.

The Secretary's words came to him as he walked the path. The arguments as to why Seamus must join the Department's detective force laid out in Mr. Seward's lawyerly style, building to an incontrovertible conclusion.

He needn't have bothered, thought Seamus. From the moment Emily had declined his proposal of marriage, although he had been slow to accept the truth, there was no other course for him but to accept the position offered. If he could not be Emily's husband, he asked himself, what other life was there for him?

None, he answered with a bitter numbness.

A mob of ravens muttered among themselves, out of sight in the pine tops. They seemed to Seamus to be commenting to one another about him as he threaded the trail below their perch.

No other life, he thought, no other life than this soldier's, or policeman's or detective's life. He thought about the English soldier who had saved him from the Famine, or rather, Aunt Mollie's story about him. A good soldier who used his strength and authority to humbly do good, like the Good Centurion in the Gospel, who begged Christ for the life of his servant.

Is that what I was fashioned for? Is that what I have been spared for, time and again?

He walked slowly amid the blooming laurel and a cool breeze rolled down the ridge of the mountain. It carried the perfume of the pines and the hemlocks, while above the ravens gossiped and croaked.

He came at last to the glade where stood the Eagle Rock and remembered the thing in Ireland which the massive stone resembled. It looked like a druid's altar; a dolmen slanted within the sanctuary of the lofty trees.

The breeze stopped abruptly.

He ran his hand over the rock and over the words someone had carved years before; 'J.W., his lady and daughter, Phila. 1856".

How I would love to carve, he thought; 'Emily, lady of Seamus', and perhaps, 'daughter and son'.

That was not to be, he knew, not now.

He pulled McCain's revolver from his holster and held it before his eyes. He looked at the fine blued steel of its flanks and cylinder and at the gold-filled engraving.

The weapon showed not a sign of rust from its emersion in the creek above the Falls.

Excellent European craftsmanship, he thought. What chance that any of the cartridges would discharge after so prolonged a bath in the cold waters of the stream.

Little chance, he thought.

"We shall see," he said aloud.

The ravens cackled above.

He knew that the cartridge in the next chamber would not ignite. That was the one that had failed when McCain had tried to shoot him.

Still holding the pistol crossways in front of his face, Seamus cocked it. With the failed round now under the hammer, he took aim at the shattered stump of the lightening- destroyed tree beyond in the woods.

He squeezed the trigger.

BOOM! The revolver jumped in his hand, a cloud of smoke blossomed out and a fist-sized chunk exploded from the stump.

The ravens screamed and scattered among the treetops. Off they scrambled to the south and to the west, flying in confusion, cawing and croaking as they went.

Seamus, eyes wide in shock, fired again and again into the destroyed trunk.

BOOM! ...BOOM! ...BOOM!...

Every round discharged without hesitation. The revolver empty, clicking on expended shells; he stopped finally and fell to his knees beside the Eagle rock. He clutched the edge of the ancient stone, his head hung down. At length he raised his face to heaven.

"Thank You," he said.

Another miracle had saved his life. Why had the cartridge misfired when McCain had sought to kill him? It had fired eagerly just now, and after a soaking in the creek.

He lowered his eyes again and shook his head.

No point whatever in asking why, he knew. The plan of the Almighty needed no questions from Seamus Delaney. Just acceptance of the miracles as they came and a willingness to follow the course as it had been laid out before all that is was formed.

He stood up in the midst of the gun smoke and breathed deeply of the familiar scent of battle. The smoke rose up in the calm air, up into the trees. It shown golden in the shafts of light among the green bows.

He holstered the pistol.

No more questions, he thought as he strode the trail back

toward the Mountain House, no more fears either. I will meet the Secretary and accept his offer. I may be of the Wild Geese, but am not rootless. I have a home and a country in Ireland *and* in America. Each is my country equally. I will work with the Secretary for this country with no fear that my duties will ever run counter to the interest of the Irish people. England will ever be Ireland's enemy and never America's friend. The powers that be in London covet all the land in the world and no less the 'lost colonies' they once owned in America. Indeed, someday perhaps America will help Ireland gain her freedom. When that day comes I will be the man to lead the vanguard and serve both my homelands. And too, he thought with a thrilling bitterness, in this service I will be in the best position to continue my own hunt for Booth. From this day onward I will strive to thwart his evil machinations and to make him pay for his crimes.

Presently, he came to the clearing where stood in the full bright of the midday sun the majestic great House. He crossed to the cliff edge and walked the pavement of bedrock. He stood for a moment by the newly carved memento of Smith's Coronet Band, the engraving deep and fresh in the ages-old stone. He moved on to the north and stopped before the stairs where he was standing when he had looked up on the day of his arrival and seen Emily for the first time. He pictured her in her blue and gray plaid dress, her little straw hat resting saucily on her lovely brow.

From the shaded recesses of the piazza above, puffs of cigar smoke betrayed the presence of the Secretary, now sitting further back from where Seamus had left him.

Seamus turned and looked out over the Valley. He recalled his thoughts of that first morning here on the ledge, how he had assumed that the country was at last at peace. Now he knew that the fierce contest continued. He thought how the Secretary had said that he had been dispatched here to learn how to be at peace. Seamus felt he *was* now at peace; at peace in his mind and in his spirit and ready to resume the fight.

From the north there suddenly came a dark shadow; an American eagle sailed by level with the cliff. So close, Seamus thought he could reach out a hand and brush the passing wing. The sun glinted in its golden eye, it flexed and soared up over the crest of the mountain and disappeared traveling to the south and west.

From below on the river arose the strains of a jaunty tune. A steamer plied the waters and the sound of her calliope identified her to Seamus as the *Armenia.*

He listened awhile and now could tell the melody of *Dixie.*

He could now clearly see the steamer but, even with the small spy glass he had given to Emily, he would not have been able to see the figure of the man who stood on the foredeck of the boat, with eyes fixed intently on the brilliant white palace on the mountain. Even if Seamus could have seen the man, who had just come down the stairs by the wheel house, who had just requested the musician at the calliope to play *Dixie*, and after that *The Bonnie Blue Flag*, and after that *Maryland, My Maryland*, Seamus would not at first have recognized the freckle-faced man.

The sandy red hair curling out from under the man's short, black felt hat and the clean shaven lip would have, at first, misled Seamus. But in time, the hunter's eye would tell. Seamus, given the opportunity for a nearer observation, would have noted the man's flattened right thumb, the deep red of the eyebrows. Perhaps he would have seen through the dye to discern the scar above the eye. Certainly, had the new State Department detective time to closely examine the man on the foredeck, he would have discovered the remnant of a burn on the back of the right hand. The hand which now rested in the man's pocket fingering a .41 caliber Derringer, the mate to one which had served the man well in the past but which had been discarded in a theater in Washington. A breeze crossed the deck and ruffled the curls at the nape of his neck. A tumor scar was revealed for an instant.

The eyebrows could be dyed, but the dark burning eyes themselves could not be disguised. Now they were aimed, unblinking in the glare of the river, at the Mountain House. If the man's brutal gaze alone could have destroyed the grand hotel and everyone in it, he would have willed it so. If he could go back there at the very moment and finish his business undetected, he would have done so. But, he knew that he could finish the business he had started at the Mountain House later, to the north. He was going there now and there *would* be another day when retribution would come. He had time, an eternity of time, and hatred to last.